Tango's Edge

CAROLE BELLACERA

CAROLE BELLACERA

ISBN:
ISBN-13: 978-0615532011

(Beautiful Evening Books

REVIEWS FOR TANGO'S EDGE

TANGO'S EDGE is one thrilling ride. It kept this reader entertained and on the edge-of-the-seat with twists and turns I never expected. I love the chemistry of Kerry and Mikhail, not to mention the danger that draws them closer. The intrigue with Elena and Adam really adds a great addition to the storyline. There is never a dull moment with the characters in this story and the adventure of Kerry and Mikhail excites in this page-turner. Carole Bellacera allows her players to lift off the pages in this fast-moving read. The touch of mystery she instills with Kerry and Mikhail is wonderfully done. The plot is great; the dialogue and writing are superb. Each time the dance skaters were on the ice, I could get a feel of the whole setting making this one interesting read.

Linda L., Fallen Angel Reviews

Carole Bellacera's latest novel, TANGO'S EDGE, was such a wonderful palate cleanser. This book was hard to put down because it was a blossoming love story that was pack full of suspense. The plot was never stagnant because the intrigue kept you glued because you really wanted to know who, why, how and what would happen next. The characters were vivid and their personalities tangible. This book definitely gave me the "warm fuzzies" and at times gave me the "cold pricklies"; a perfect suspenseful romance.

Shira, SIMPLY ROMANCE REVIEWS

TANGO'S EDGE is a non-stop action, suspense filled book with surprises, intrigue, and romance included. It will be a shame for you to miss reading it. Exceptionally well-written, this story has characters that you will either love or hate. I could hardly wait to see what was next and stayed up all night in order to finish this book in one sitting. An excellent read to add to your bookshelf.

Matilda *Coffee Time Romance*

TANGO'S EDGE is a thrilling tale from the very talented pen of Carole Bellacera, an author who is highly underrated. With scads of sexual tension and smokin' chemistry between Kerry and Mikhail, it's not long before the two start their own tango of the heart. Mikhail is a man any woman would want. Ms. Bellacera shows a flair for not only characterization, but incorporating Mikhail's heavy Russian accent into dialogue. It's not hard to actually hear the words spoken in your head as you read TANGO'S EDGE. Character development doesn't end with the two main characters, however. Sean and Elena are a nasty duo only out to please themselves. Mikhail didn't have much choice in partnering Elena, and she won't stop until she gets what she wants -- the gold, and hopefully the puppy adoration of Mikhail. She's the kind of woman who loves to have men at her feet, even if she kicks them to the curb when she's done with them. It's not what she can do for them, but what will they do for her?

Karen Find Out About New Books

TANGO'S EDGE hits many notes on the palate for a romantic tale of two lonely people who deserve to find love.

Even if you're not a closet skating fan like me, you'll definitely enjoy Carole Bellacera's newest book. There are not many authors who can make a double axel or a triple toe loop look sexy, but Ms. Bellacera does. Not since Kurt Browning have I had a crush on a male skater, but Mikhail can help me trace my edges any day. Enjoy!
Amy Cunningham, *Romance Reviews Today*

PROLOGUE
Park City, Utah

The applause startled her in the dark arena.

It erupted into the silence after she landed the double axel, then went into her layback. Coming out of the spin, Kerry Niles looked over toward the boards and saw the dark shape of someone watching her. Someone tall and male.

Her brow furrowed in annoyance. Adam, of course. What was he doing here so early? Hadn't last night's argument sunk in at all? She'd made it clear how important this early morning practice time was to her. How she purposely set her alarm at four o'clock so she could get onto the rink before it began filling up with other skaters and coaches.

"Is it six already?" she called out, knowing it wasn't. Her blood began to boil as she skated toward him. After last night's heated exchange, how *dare* he get here early? But as her eyes sharpened on the figure, she realized it wasn't Adam at all. Instead of dark brown hair, she saw the flaxen color, and knew it could only be one person.

Her heart skipped a beat as her blades dug into the ice, bringing her to an abrupt stop a few feet away from the boards. Somehow, she managed to find her voice. "Oh! I thought you were my partner. "

The man didn't speak but just watched her. Mikhail Kozlof, the male half of the Soviet ice dance team of Boiko and Kozlof, stood at the entrance to the ice. Like her, he was dressed completely in black, from his cotton turtleneck sweater to his skates.

Last night during the compulsory dance competition, he'd been wearing white. Kerry's cheeks warmed at the memory of the moment he'd caught her staring at him in the warm-up area. But there had been no way in the world she could've dragged her gaze away from the arresting sight he made as he meditated before taking the ice with Elena.

Eyes closed, he'd crouched near a wall, his back straight, arms spread-eagled at his sides. On another man, his sleek white skating costume might have seemed less than masculine with one arm encased in filmy white gauze and the other bare and off the shoulder. But as he squatted, motionless, in perfect balance, the sinewy biceps of his bare arm flexed, and Kerry had caught her breath at his magnificence.

She wasn't sure how many seconds she'd stood there admiring him before he startled her by genuflecting, and then opening his eyes. Perhaps sensing her gaze, he'd looked straight at her. She'd been mortified, her face growing hot with embarrassment. But still she couldn't look away from him. Then he'd done something that had totally blown her away. He'd smiled. A warm, knowing smile that had sent the blood rushing through her body.

Now, here she was staring at him again. Her cheeks were hot, her heart bumping. She was twenty-eight years old—ancient, almost, by amateur skating standards. But she hadn't felt this young and tongue-tied since she'd fallen in love with Adam at the naive age of fifteen.

The Russian gazed at her with penetrating blue eyes. His cheekbones were high, his nose straight and Germanic. His golden hair was layered expertly away from his face, a bit longer in back. Under his right cheekbone, a faded scar traveled from below his eye almost to his ear. Incredibly, it didn't detract from his good looks, but rather, added character to a face that was almost too classically beautiful.

How had he gotten that scar?

With a start, Kerry realized he was speaking.

"You skate like singles skater," he said in precise, heavily accented English. "Layback and double axel. "

She nodded and somehow found her voice. "I switched to dance when I was fifteen."

A smile flickered about his lips. "You are good at both, yes?"

Kerry shrugged, her fingers worrying at the chiffon hem of her skirt. "Not really. That double axel I landed was a fluke. "

He cocked his head, one brow arched. "This fluke. This is new word for me, but I think is not good. "

Catching the irony lacing his voice, she grinned. "It means I don't land it that way usually. Hardly ever, actually. " There. That sounded like the old self-assured Kerry.

Mikhail nodded. "Will you skate with me? "

Her heart jumped, and just like that, her momentary self-assurance drained away. Before she could reply, he went on, "I have been watching you all week, and I… " He shook his head, struggling with the language. "I don't know right way

8

to say what is…in here. " He tapped a finger against his forehead. "You move like…so lovely. And.." He lifted his shoulder in a shrug. "…I wish to skate with you. "

Kerry wanted more than anything to skate with him. *Had* wanted it since that first morning two weeks ago when she'd seen him here practicing with Elena. But it was crazy! She didn't know his routines. It was insane to think she could simply get on the ice with a complete stranger and move in sync with him.

Mikhail murmured, "I will be right back."

He turned and disappeared through the double doors. Kerry stood there, dumbfounded. He was gone only a moment. As he clomped toward her on his skate guards, music began to play from the PA system, and Kerry recognized the tango selection that all the ice dancers had performed to in the preliminary set pattern dances. Mikhail took off his skate guards and stepped onto the ice. Smiling, he held out his hand. She found her eyes locked on it. His fingers were long, his nails short. A silver ring glinted on his pinkie.

Her heart tripped into overdrive. Somehow, without realizing exactly who touched whom first, she found her hand in his. But when he placed his other hand on her waist and began to guide her away from the boards, she stiffened at the penetrating heat of his touch.

No…I don't…I can't… But the words were spoken only in her mind. She tried to relax and follow his movements, but immediately, her foot tangled with his, and she stumbled to the ice. The cold surface burned into her buttocks, and then her palms as she pushed against the ice to get to her feet. Heat rushed to her face as Mikhail grabbed her arm and pulled her up. How humiliating! Making a fool of herself in front of the best ice dancer she'd ever seen. But his ocean blue eyes were warm as he steadied her with his hands on her upper arms.

"You know this dance. You have done so hundreds of times with partner," he said gently. "Just relax and let yourself feel music. " The warmth of his hand was once again at her waist. "Ready? "

Kerry nodded. He smiled and began to move. She was reminded of last evening when she'd watched him dance with Elena during the competition; she'd fantasized about being in her place. And here she was.

As she relaxed in Mikhail's arms, she realized the routine they were doing was a basic set-pattern dance they'd all done in competition. She knew every step of it, and her mind automatically clicked into the mantra she used during competition. *The tighter the curve, the deeper the edge.* Yet, she was exquisitely aware it wasn't Adam at her side, holding her in his arms so confidently. Mikhail's scent washed over her, a mysterious combination of sandalwood and Eastern spices. This dance, sexual by nature, had never felt so passionate with Adam.

By the second time around the rink, Kerry was dancing with Mikhail as if they'd been doing it forever. Their edges were clean and sharp, their leans elegant. Mohawks, Choctaws, three-turns. Every move they made was fluid, perfect. She found herself praying the music would never end; that she could hold onto this moment forever. She was dancing with a stranger—a foreigner, yet, she felt a sense of security and belonging like she'd never found anywhere before. Not since her childhood in Utah with her father and grandparents.

But the music did end. Slowly, in the middle of the rink, Mikhail drew her to a stop. They stood, facing each other, hands entwined. The angles and planes of his face were shadowed in the dim light, but she felt the intensity of his gaze. An unbearable tension crackled between them, and Kerry knew the heat enveloping her had little to do with the exercise.

For a crazy moment, she thought he was going to kiss her. Crazier still, she *wanted* him to. She knew nothing about this man from the former Soviet Union. Nothing except he was an artist on the ice, and the partner of Russia's new hope for a gold medal, Elena Boiko.

But for the moment, it didn't matter. He was a man, and there was no denying the electricity sizzling between them. And at this moment, she wanted to be kissed by Mikhail Kozlof more than she wanted an Olympic medal.

His eyes, so stark, so earnest, scanned her face, moving over her brows, her cheekbones, and finally, settling on her lips. He leaned toward her, and Kerry lifted her face, offering her mouth.

But he didn't take it. Instead, his hands slid up her arms and tightened on her shoulders. He spoke in a husky undertone, "Kerry Niles, I need your help. Please…"

He took a deep breath, released it and said the words that would change her life forever. "I must defect from my country, and I need your help to do it."

CHAPTER ONE
Park City, Utah – Three Weeks Earlier

Kerry waited until she heard the shower turn on in the room next to hers, then grabbed her gray wool coat and stepped out into the corridor of the hotel. Walking briskly toward the front door, she pulled the coat on over her thick turtleneck sweater and black jeans. Outside, the icy wind hit her like a sledgehammer, sending her long black hair flying. She tugged her white knit cap down over her ears and strode briskly toward the arena.

She stepped into the welcome warmth of the skating rink lobby and breathed a sigh of relief. A smiling young woman looked up from behind the counter. "Hi. Are you one of the skaters?"

Kerry nodded, and dug a badge out of her coat pocket. "You need to see this?"

"Yeah." Her eyes swept over the badge. "Hello, Kerry Niles. Nice to meet you. The rink is that way."

"Thanks." Kerry pulled her hat off, tucked it into her pocket and combed her fingers through her tangled hair to get it into some kind of order. Who knew what important judges might be here, watching the skaters practice? It wouldn't do to walk in looking like Nick Nolte in his famous mug shot.

She heard Handel's "Water Music" coming from the rink, and pushed through the double doors, feeling the cold air

12

wrap around her like an Arctic blanket. Her practice time with Adam wasn't scheduled until the next day, but she wanted to get a first look at the rink they would be using for the next two weeks before the opening ceremony of the Olympics.

A couple glided over the ice, practicing their free dance routine, and Kerry recognized the female immediately. Elena Boiko, the Russian ice dancing star. Why she was a star, Kerry wasn't sure. Yes, she was beautiful. No argument about that. She had that Grace Kelly princess thing going on. But any expert eye could see she lacked a certain grace on the ice. Her movements were often stiff, almost forced. Technically, she was a good skater, but her presentation left a lot to be desired.

Kerry remembered the World Championships in Switzerland two years ago. Even though Elena had tripped on her partner's foot, they'd edged her and Adam out of a medal, and it still rankled.

Under the lights of the rink, Elena's smooth chignon glowed white-blond. She had the tall, lithe body of a ballerina and the elegant neck of a swan. Even from a distance, Kerry could see her eyes were a deep, lapis blue. She was, quite simply, breathtaking, even in her practice attire—a plain gray leotard with a filmy chiffon skirt.

Kerry's gaze moved to Elena's partner, and she caught her breath. She recognized the ice dancer with the intriguing scar across his face. Mikhail Kozlof. Two years ago, he'd been skating with Tanya Novikova. Kerry remembered reading in Skating World Magazine how the director of the Russian skating association had teamed him up with Elena after the death of her partner, Ivan Rostropovich. She also seemed to remember the article had implied that he hadn't been exactly happy with the decision. The partnership had obviously done well for Elena. Kerry had watched their first competition together at Worlds in Cincinnati last March where they'd won the silver. This year, they were favored for the gold.

Kerry smirked. *Good thing you've got Mikhail, Elena, or you wouldn't have a chance in hell.*

Her gaze followed Mikhail as he moved over the ice. There was something so arresting about him, something that went much deeper than his physical good looks. It was in the way he moved on—and off—the ice, the intensity of his expression as he skated. Something about him touched a chord inside her. Made it hard to breathe.

"They are quite magnificent, are they not?" said an accented, feminine voice behind her.

Kerry turned. A pretty woman with dark brown hair and unusual golden brown eyes smiled and extended a slender, elegant hand. "I do not believe we have officially met. I am Tanya Novikova from Russia. And you are one of the American ice dancers, yes?"

Kerry shook her hand, her lips quirking in a bemused smile. "That's right. How did you know?"

"Because I saw you skate last year at Worlds, and was quite impressed by you and your partner. I think you are one of the best dance teams to come out of America in years."

Kerry's smile widened. "Well, thank you. I'm honored, considering that you and Sergey Isavenivic are so wonderful."

Tanya's gaze moved to the couple on the ice. "We are good," she admitted. "But no one will touch those two." One slim shoulder lifted in a very European shrug. "Boiko…how do you say…tied up in a bow the gold medal when she took Mikhail away from me. He was my partner first."

Kerry looked back at the couple on the ice. They were skating a Viennese waltz, their edges deep, lines perfect. Was it her imagination or had Elena's carriage improved since last year? Perhaps skating with Mikhail really had helped her presentation.

"Oh, yes. I heard," Kerry said.

Tanya glared at Elena. "She decided she wanted Mikhail, so she took him away. No matter we had been training for months. She snapped fingers..." Tanya demonstrated. "And just like that, he is gone. And I am looking for new partner."

Kerry's eyes widened. "So, it's true? They made him skate with Elena?"

Tanya gave a sardonic smile. "Things have not changed so much since the old days. There are still people with power, and Elena is one of them. She replaced Mikhail's coach, as well. And Nadya had been with him since he was six."

Kerry glanced at the beautiful blonde on the ice. "I get the feeling you don't like her much."

Tanya's unusual golden brown eyes sparkled with amusement. "That comes through, yes? And I try *so* hard to be good."

Kerry grinned. Here was a kindred spirit—a woman ruled by her emotions, and unashamed by it. She was different from all the other Russian women Kerry had met. Where was that aloof, "don't buddy up with the Americans" attitude most of them adopted? And even if they spoke English, which most did not, they pretended they didn't. That's what she'd heard, anyway. Then again...she reminded herself of the source of that commentary. Adam.

"So, tell me about Mikhail," Kerry encouraged. "What's he like?"

Tanya pursed her lips. "He is something of…mystery. He comes from Estonia. Very independent people, not typical Russian, you understand? I do not know Mikhail well, even though we were partners for a time. Some say he is ladies' man." She smiled. "I do not believe anyone truly knows the real Mikhail Kozlof. Look at him. See expression on his face? There is something very deep and private inside him that is only revealed when he skates."

Kerry understood what she meant. Mikhail's blue eyes were intense, focused upon his partner's face as they moved on the ice.

"Is he involved with Elena?" she asked.

Tanya gave an unladylike snort. "She *wishes*! No, I think he barely tolerates her. But who knows? That may change. Men are ruled by what is between legs, no? And she *is* very beautiful."

The music came to an end at the exact second of the couple's final spin. Entwined, they held their closing position for a moment, and then broke apart. Hands on his hips, his flaxen head bowed, Mikhail moved backward. He appeared to be in deep thought. Elena spoke in Russian, and Mikhail looked up and nodded. They turned and headed toward the boards.

"Would you like me to introduce you, Kerry?" Tanya asked.

Kerry's heart began to drum, but she tried to summon a blasé smile. "Sure. I'd love to meet him…I mean, *them*."

* * * * *

Mikhail saw the young woman as he skated towards the boards. She looked familiar, and he wondered where he'd seen her before. She smiled at something Tanya said to her, and his heart dipped. It had been a long time, if ever, that he'd reacted to a smile like this. His heart rate pumped up a notch, and for a moment, he wasn't sure he could quite catch his breath.

Tanya motioned him over. "Mikhail, come here a moment," she said in English. "I want you to meet someone."

Beside him, Elena expelled a disgusted breath. "Good God! Does she think we have nothing better to do than chit-chat with fans?"

Mikhail glared at her. "Calm down, Elena. It won't kill you to say hello."

But as they skated closer to the twosome, Mikhail realized the attractive girl with Tanya was not a fan. Those blue-green eyes. They weren't easily forgotten. Especially in contrast to that fair skin and ebony hair. He could see that her body was slender and elegant despite the coat and thick Irish sweater she wore over black jeans. Even if he hadn't seen her before, he would've guessed she was a skater.

"Mikhail, this is Kerry Niles," Tanya said. "She is ice dancer with Adam Cutter for America. Kerry, this is Mikhail Kozlof and Elena Boiko."

Kerry held out a slim hand to Mikhail, her face lighting up in a radiant smile. His heart began to race. When he'd first looked through the dossier Immaakin had given him, he'd recognized Kerry's photo as the skater he'd found so attractive two years ago at Worlds. Incredible to know that she might very well be the key to his escape. He took her hand and gave what he hoped was a relaxed smile.

"Hi." Her voice was low and musical. "Nice to meet you, Mikhail."

"Likewise." He was amazed to find his voice sounded normal. "Good luck in competition." A light dusting of freckles across her perfect nose and cheekbones gave her an impish look, made even more so by the sparkling humor in her remarkable eyes.

Her gaze still held his, even though she was tugging at his hand for release so she could greet Elena. Mikhail let go, his face growing hot. He was remembering that moment he'd collided with her backstage at Worlds. She'd seemed distraught, close to tears. Even though she'd been a complete stranger, he'd felt an overwhelming need to take her into his arms and console her. Strange thing, though. He felt the same way now. Not to console her, of course, but to simply take her into his arms. And that was insane! He didn't even know her.

Elena briefly shook Kerry's hand and turned to go. "You coming, Mikos?" she asked in Russian, one perfectly arched eyebrow raise imperiously.

He glanced at her, and spoke in precise English, "We are done for day, no?" It embarrassed him that she was so rude as to speak Russian in front of someone who didn't understand the language.

Annoyance flickered across Elena's haughty face. "Yes, but don't you want to go get some dinner with me?" Russian, again.

The bitch. Mikhail decided to risk alienating her permanently. He could think of nothing more distasteful than sharing dinner with his ice-dancing partner. They'd been together since early morning, and he needed a break.

"Thank you, but no," he said in English. "I am not hungry now. I will see you tomorrow, Elena."

"Fine! But if I were you, I'd watch myself with this American slut. Sergey won't like it if you get yourself involved in an international incident."

Mikhail stiffened. He shot Elena a quelling look. *Sergey can kiss my ass.* He just barely restrained himself from saying it. Instead, he gave Elena a grim smile. "Goodbye, Elena."

With one last murderous glance at the three of them, the tall blonde stepped through the portal, slipped on her skate guards and clopped off down the hall.

Mikhail turned his attention back to Kerry. "I apologize for her rudeness. So, did you just arrive here? I have not seen you on ice."

She nodded. "Just got in this afternoon. The first thing I always do is come and check out the practice surface." Her eyes scanned the rink. "Looks pretty good."

Mikhail shrugged. "Is not bad. A bit small, but you compensate."

A brief silence fell. Mikhail realized he was staring as Kerry's eyes connected again with his. A soft blush spread over her face. He looked away, catching Tanya's amused expression. What did she think was so funny? As if he didn't know. Tanya had never seen him appear to be out of his depth with a woman before. But there was something about this Kerry Niles that made him feel like an awkward schoolboy. He supposed it was partly because she was so pretty—and an American.

But most of all, it was because she could very well be the only person in this country that would help him defect from Mother Russia.

* * * * *

Kerry tried to think of something to say to fill the awkward silence. Tension, thick as smoke, filled the air between the three of them, and she couldn't quite figure out why. For a moment, she'd thought she'd caught a gleam of attraction in Mikhail's clear blue eyes as their gaze had met and held, but now, he was staring at a Coca Cola sign along

19

the boards like it was one of the Seven Wonders of the World.

She shifted her feet uneasily and glanced at Tanya. The Russian girl wore a Mona Lisa smile on her face as if she had a delicious secret she had no intention of sharing. She was so different from the brittle-faced Elena Boiko. The woman had been incredibly rude, speaking Russian in front of her. Little did she know, though, that Kerry was fluent in Russian—thanks to spending seven years in a household where Russian was the dominant language. She'd understood the entire exchange. *How dare Elena!* Calling her a *slut!*

Okay, enough is enough. Kerry decided it was up to her to break the silence. This was so weird, though. She'd never been shy. Why, now, did she feel so tongue-tied?

"Well, I…" Kerry began just as Mikhail spoke at the same time, "You are…"

They both stopped abruptly. Mikhail flushed.

Kerry bit her bottom lip. "I'm sorry. You first."

Mikhail shook his head. "No, please. You were saying?"

Silence. Tanya grinned. "If you two would let me get word in edge-way, I will invite you both to join me for dinner at Olympic Village."

Something like relief crossed Mikhail's face. He smiled and nodded. "Yes. I would like that."

Kerry was just about to say she'd like that, too, when she heard a footstep behind her. "Hey, Kerry?" said a familiar male voice. "Why didn't you tell me you were heading over here? I would've come with you."

Adam. Disappointment flooded through Kerry as she realized there was no way she could accept Tanya's invitation. Catri had made dinner reservations for the three of them at a popular Salt Lake City restaurant for a pre-Olympic pep talk before the start of their grueling practice sessions tomorrow. It was a tradition they'd been sharing for years, and she couldn't believe she'd actually forgotten about it. But then again, she had a feeling that being near Mikhail would make her forget her own name.

Kerry turned to Adam who was gazing at Tanya and Mikhail with wary speculation in his brown eyes. His hair was still damp from the shower. No doubt as soon as he'd realized she was gone, he'd pulled on his clothes and raced right over. Typical behavior.

"Adam, this is Tanya Novikova and Mikhail Kozlof," she said. "They skate for Russia."

Adam shook their hands, his expression only slightly warmer at Tanya's touch than at Mikhail's. Kerry could barely disguise a grimace at his frosty attitude towards the Russians.

It occurred to her that she could do some matchmaking and get Adam and Elena together. They seemed like two peas in a pod, both of them wearing colossal chips on their shoulders. But Adam would never go for it. Brainwashed at a young age by his father's conservative views, he wouldn't be caught dead dating a Russian. Adam maintained an almost pathological distrust of the former Soviet block despite the tearing down of the Berlin Wall.

Which was really weird, considering he'd practically been raised by two former Russians who'd doted on him since he was a junior skater. But when questioned about this contradiction, he'd dismissed it with an offhand, "Oh, you know I'm not talking about Catri and Vladimir. They're special. Besides, they defected."

It was this narrow-minded bigotry that had been one of the reasons Kerry had fallen out of love with Adam so quickly. Once the excitement of first love—and first sex—had diminished, she'd begun to see there were some less attractive qualities to his personality that she could live without. But deep inside, she believed he was a good guy. Misguided, perhaps, and obstinate, but decent—and in need of some intensive personal relations education.

However, at the moment, she could cheerfully strangle him for the jut-jawed way he was eyeing Mikhail like he was an assassin getting ready to bump her off.

"So…studying the competition, are we, Kerry?" Adam asked with a stiff smile.

Mikhail's eyes met hers, and Kerry felt her face grow warm. Damn Adam! Did he have to make it sound like she was involved in an underhanded conspiracy?

"*Admiring* the competition," she said, hoping the edge in her voice would communicate her displeasure.

Tanya smiled at Adam. "We invited Kerry to join us for dinner. We would love you to come, as well."

Adam barely waited for her to finish the sentence. "Sorry. We have plans." His gaze fastened on Kerry. "In fact, you'd better go back to the hotel and get ready. We'll be dealing with rush hour traffic, and we're supposed to meet Catri at seven."

Kerry smiled at Tanya and Mikhail. "Catri is our coach. And Adam's right. I'd better go get ready. Thanks for the invitation, though. Maybe some other time." Adam glowered at her, and she threw him a challenging look. When would he stop treating her like she was his personal property?

She couldn't resist another glance in Mikhail's direction, and felt her heart kick into overdrive. His blue eyes drilled into her, dissecting her in a most pleasurable way. She smiled, and he blinked, then returned the smile with one of his own. Strong, white teeth, Kerry noted with relief. In her experience, more than a few foreign guys had their good looks marred by bad teeth. She was glad Mikhail wasn't one of them.

"It was nice meeting you…" Her eyes moved from Mikhail to Tanya. "…both of you."

As she turned to go, Adam placed a proprietary hand on her elbow to guide her away. She joggled away from him, throwing him a disgruntled look.

"Hey, don't get an attitude with me," he said as soon as they were out of earshot of the Russians.

Kerry gritted her teeth, pushing through the double doors with more force than was necessary. "Well, don't you start acting like you're my father or something. What is *up* with you, anyway? You were downright rude to them."

Adam frowned. "Well, it's not a good idea to get buddy-buddy with the Russians. You know that."

"Oh, jeez, Adam. Why don't you grow up? What do you think they're going to do? Kidnap and torture me until I reveal the deep, dark secret of our free dance technique?" She gave a mock shudder. "Oooooh. The *horror* of it!"

"You just go right ahead and make fun," Adam snapped. "I don't like that guy. Did you see the scar on his face? I'll bet he got it in a knife fight. Hell, for all we know, he's part of the Russian mafia."

Kerry gave him an incredulous look and then laughed. He was *serious*! "You know what, Adam? You should be in Hollywood writing James Bond movies. I'll bet you could make a killing."

He gave her a sulky look and held the front door open for her. The icy wind assaulted them as they stepped outside. Kerry pulled her cap out of her pocket and tugged it down over her ears. "Hey, I'm just looking out for you," he added as they headed down the street toward the hotel.

Kerry bent her head, shielding her face from the frigid wind. "Who asked you to?" she muttered, glaring at her boots.

He didn't answer, but she could feel the anger vibrating from his pores. Jeez, if he got this bent out of shape over her hanging out with a few Russians, she hated to think how he was going to react when she broke the news to him. That after the Olympics were over, she planned to retire from amateur skating.

* * * * *

Mikhail watched Kerry and Adam walk down the corridor and disappear into the lobby. Were they a couple? The man certainly acted like she belonged to him. And that, for some unaccountable reason, annoyed him.

"Hey!" Beside him, Tanya snapped her fingers in front of his eyes. "Hello, Mikhail? Remember me?" When he turned and looked at her, she smiled. "Ah, you like her, no? You can't take your eyes off her."

He felt his face grow hot. "Don't be absurd. She's a pretty girl. "He lifted a shoulder in an offhand shrug. "So, what? I like pretty girls."

"Yes, I know that." Tanya gave him a speculative once-over. "But why do I get the feeling there's more to it than that?"

Mikhail's stomach plunged. He gave her a close look. How could she possibly know? But her eyes were teasing, her smile innocent. His stomach settled. He placed an arm around her shoulders and nudged her toward the lobby. "Did you not say something about dinner? Come on. Elena has worked my ass off today, and I am famished."

Tanya leaned back and peered at his rear end. "Really? Looks like it is there to me, and..." She grinned. "...it's looking quite good, I must say."

He gave her an askance grimace. "Hey, don't start that with me. You had your chance a long time ago, and wanted nothing to do with me, remember?"

"I remember. I was waiting for you to give up your playboy ways and decide you're a one woman man."

He laughed. "And you have finally decided to give up, yes? Because it will never happen?"

She shook her head and gave him an appraising look as he held the door open for her. "No. I've decided that you just have not met that one woman yet." Then, to his disconcertment, she added slyly, "But perhaps you just did."

CHAPTER TWO

Sean O'Malley took a healthy gulp of cold Guinness and eased back into the bubbling hot tub with a satisfied sigh. Who would've thought a town like Park City, and a hotel like this one, could provide a good pint? But then, money could get you pretty much anything you wanted these days. A slow grin spread across his face. He glanced over at the sleeping Rottweiler lying on the floor next to the tub. "Life is good, isn't it, old boy?" Beowulf ignored him, lost in dreamland.

Sean was still thinking about just *how* good life had been lately when through the opened bathroom door, he heard the door to the suite slam, followed by the thump of angry footsteps. His grin faded. Well, money could buy *almost* anything. One of the things he wanted had just come into the suite, and no amount of money was going to buy her.

"Hey, love, is that you?" he called out, sitting up in the tub and reaching for his Guinness. Beowulf woke from his sleep and lifted his massive head, his ears twitching as Elena appeared at the bathroom door. The dog lowered his head and closed his eyes.

Elena's gaze flicked over Sean with cool disdain. "Enjoying your holiday, I see," she said in Russian.

"Damn right, love." He tossed her an engaging smile, one that usually mellowed her out. But not this time, apparently. Her expression remained like stone, as if a sculptor had carved it from exquisite rose marble. "Hey, I was in great need of a holiday, love. Ya know how hard I've been workin'." He purposely thickened his Belfast accent as he replied in English, knowing how it turned her on.

It didn't work this time, though. He could tell that by the wintry look in her big baby blues. Hell! What had happened at the rink? Lately, it took so little to piss her off, and once she fell into one of these foul moods, good Christ! He had to work like the devil to pull her out.

"What would you know about hard work, Sean?" Her voluptuous bottom lip took on that peculiar pouting shape that drove him crazy, and beneath the swirling water, his penis hardened. Not a good time, he reminded himself. When Elena was in one of her moods, there would be no lovin'. Not unless he could find a way to make her forget about whatever hair had crawled up her ass this time.

"Ah, love…" With a sigh, Sean stood up in the bubbling hot tub and reached for the thick, white towel on the ledge. He switched to Russian. "What's wrong, darling?" He purposely moved slowly, allowing Elena to drink her fill of his nude body. Perhaps he could still cajole her out of her nasty disposition. He rubbed the towel over the black mat of glistening hair on his chest, feeling her gaze riveted on him, but the anger still hadn't drained from her eyes. He took his time rubbing the towel over his flat stomach and down his muscular thighs. His penis was still semi-hard, and there was no doubt in his mind that Elena knew it. His body was golden from frequent visits to a tanning salon, and toned from the health club he frequented three times a week. Usually Elena showed her appreciation of the way he kept in shape for her. In fact, any ordinary time, they'd be screwing like bunnies by now. He stepped out of the tub and sighed, knowing that wasn't going to happen.

"Mikhail is what's wrong," she snarled, and whirled away as he draped the damp towel over his lean hips.

He followed her out of the bathroom, his brow furrowed with irritation. Mikhail, again. Christ, he was getting bloody sick of hearing that man's name. Elena had opened the door of the stocked mini-bar, and was peering in as if it contained the answer to all her troubles. She grabbed a small bottle of vodka, twisted off the cap and took a healthy swallow.

Sean watched her, feeling a vague twinge of alarm. "You know you're not supposed to do that, love," he said, consciously keeping his tone mild, non-accusing. "It's not good to mix that with the asthma medication."

"Fuck the asthma medication!" Her eyes blazed into him defiantly. "What does it matter, anyway? Oh, God! Why is everything so difficult for me? You know how hard I work, Sean. Every day for the last nineteen years I've trained on the ice, working for an Olympic gold medal. And now that it's finally in reach, you would think everything would be lovely, wouldn't you? But no!" She lifted the bottle of vodka to her mouth again.

Sean crossed the room and grabbed it just before it reached her lips.

"No, you bastard!" she shrieked, reaching for the bottle of liquor, her eyes shooting blue fire.

He grabbed her hand and held it in an iron grip. "I'm not going to let you kill yourself, Elena," he said quietly. "You know what Anton said. No liquor while you're taking TNG."

"I don't care what he says," Elena cried. "He's a cautious old fool! And I need a drink after the day I've had."

"No."

The battle of wills stretched out for an endless moment, their eyes locked. And finally, Sean saw the resignation cross Elena's face.

"Okay," she murmured. "You are right, darling."

And to his shock, her eyes filled with tears. It had been a long time since he'd seen Elena cry—not since her father died of a massive heart attack over two years ago.

His hand gently cupped her jaw. "What is it, love? Talk to me."

She shook her head, biting her lower lip. "It is Mikhail. Why does he hate me so? I try so hard to be kind to him, and he snubs me at every turn."

Sean's jaw tensed. Again, this Estonian. He was getting bloody sick and tired of hearing the man's name. It seemed with every passing day Elena was getting more and more obsessed with him. At first, Sean hadn't been concerned. He'd figured it was just her fanatic desire to attain that fucking gold medal, and he'd humored her, and yes, supported her in reaching her goal. Christ, if not for him, she'd still be skating with that party boy, Ivan Rostropovich. When she'd bitched and moaned about how she wanted to dump him, and replace him with Mikhail, he'd taken care of the problem, hadn't he? It had been child's play to tamper with the brakes on Rostropovich's Mercedes, and then have one of his employees make sure the man spent the evening tanking up in a Kiev bar before attempting to drive himself to his mama's house.

Now, Sean was beginning to regret that little endeavor. At the time, it seemed like the perfect way to kill two birds with one stone. Elena wanted to discard her partner, and Sean wanted to discard her ex-lover. Now, though, it seemed that her new partner might be even more of a problem. Sean knew Elena, probably better than she knew herself. And there was no doubt in his mind that she wanted Mikhail sexually. It was only a matter of time before the Estonian succumbed. Good Christ, look at her! What man could resist her? But once he did give in to her, he'd have to die.

Because Elena belonged to Sean. And he wouldn't share her. He couldn't.

"What has he done now?" he asked quietly, his thumb tracing a line over Elena's porcelain cheekbone.

She drew away from his caress, a frown marring her pristine golden-brown brow. "Well, for one thing, he can't keep his mind on the training." She sauntered over to the window and pulled back the drapes to gaze out over the village.

Sean's gaze moved down her ballerina-trim figure clad in a gray leotard and a short wisp of a skirt. He imagined stripping it off and peeling down the leotard, kissing her luscious skin as he removed it. But that wasn't going to happen. Not until he coaxed her out of this frightful mood.

She whirled around and glared at him. "You should have seen him. Flirting with this...*American girl!*" She spat the words as if they tasted filthy in her mouth. "It was disgusting the way he was fawning over her. Yet, he barely looks at me when he speaks. I deserve more respect than that, do I not? I am his partner. I am the reason he is here in Salt Lake City."

Sean could no longer hold onto his temper. "Bullshit, Elena," he said shortly. "*He* is the reason why *you're* here. Remember who you're talking to. The guy who knows all your secrets, remember? Lie to yourself if you want, but at least have the decency to be straight with me. You know damn well if it weren't for Mikhail Kozlof, you wouldn't be the favorite for a gold medal!"

Hot color flooded her face. "Bastard!" she hissed. "That is not true!"

Sean shrugged. "Hey, if you need to believe that, go ahead. But you know what, love? I'm thinking there's a whole other reason why Kozlof has got you so hot under the collar. You want to fuck him, don't you? You're not happy unless you have every man around panting after you. Why am I not enough for you, Elena?"

Her lips tightened. "Oh, please! Let's not start that old argument again. And you are wrong, by the way. I don't want to fuck Mikhail Kozlof. I just want him to treat me with the respect I deserve." She began to pace back and forth in front of the window. "Who does he think he is, anyway? He is nothing but an Estonian peasant boy. He is lucky *cesska* allows him to skate. I—" She stopped abruptly, the color fading from her face. Her hand clutched at her chest as a horrible wheezing constricted her throat.

Sean's stomach contracted as he realized what was happening. "Where's your inhaler?"

But even as he snarled the question, he was lunging for the bag on the floor that contained her skates and all the other odds and ends she took to her training. He found the inhaler in the side pocket, and rushed to her side.

Still struggling to draw in a strangled breath, she grabbed the inhaler and stuck it in her mouth, injecting the spray of medicine into her lungs. As soon as she began to breathe easier, Sean took her into his arms, cradling her, his mouth crushed against the silk of her hair.

"Oh, Christ, it scares me so bad when that happens," he murmured.

He knew that Elena's older brother had died of an asthma attack when she was only ten. One night old man Boiko had described the harrowing incident to him while in one of his "talkative" moods, thanks to the fifth of vodka he'd consumed. He'd been with the seventeen-year-old Yuri during the attack, and nothing, not even an inhaler, had been able to save him. Sean lived in fear that one day the inhaler wouldn't save his precious Elena either.

But this time, it had. She drew the inhaler out of her mouth and leaned into him, still somewhat breathless. But the horrible wheezing had stopped.

"Thank you," she said softly, her face nestled against his neck.

His hand caressed a slow circle over her back. "This is madness," he said, knowing his words would do no good, but unable to hold them back. "The skating, the drugs. You're killing yourself. You know that, don't you?"

She didn't respond, but just clung to him.

"Is the gold medal really that important?" His voice was soft, coaxing. "You and I...we could have a good life together. With all the money I've made with the pub in Tallinn and...my other enterprises...we could buy our own island in the South Pacific. Or buy a villa in Rio overlooking the ocean. Staff it with servants who'll answer to our every whim. We could have a houseful of children, Elena. A little girl who looks just like you. A son to carry on the O'Malley name. It would be a grand life, love. All you have to do is give this up, and come away with me."

She didn't answer right away, and for a moment, a brief second, he felt hope fill his heart. Perhaps this time...

Then she drew away, just far enough to place a lingering kiss on the hollow of his throat, and he felt that glimmer of hope drain away.

"We will have that, Sean," she said. "But not until I have my gold medal. I'm so close now. I would be a fool to give up my dream."

Sean bristled, his arms tightening around her. "Even if it kills you? You don't know what TNG is doing to your organs. Especially since you choose to ignore your uncle's warnings, and you continue to drink on the sly. Yes, I know all about the bottles of liquor you hide where you think I can't find them. Not to mention the asthma medication. For all any of us know, the combination of the three could be lethal, yet, you continue to play with fire."

Elena drew away from him with a sigh. "You were the one who first suggested reviving the TNG project. Why were you not so concerned with my health then?"

He stared at her. "That was before I fell in love with you. But I have changed my mind. I'm scared at what TNG may be doing to you."

Her expression softened. "It is doing nothing to me except making me stronger." A smile flickered about her lovely lips, and Sean recognized what it meant. She was putting her bad mood behind her.

Her gaze roved up and down his body, and her smile widened. "Have I told you, Sean O'Malley, how scrumptious you look in that skimpy towel? Maybe now would be a good time to practice on creating those brats you want."

Her words had an instant effect upon his body. Beneath the damp towel, his cock hardened into a brick. "Only practice?" he said, his voice husky with desire. "I'm thirty-seven. Almost an old man for a father."

She moved against him, and casually reached down to wrap her cool, slim hand around his erection. He closed his eyes as a wave of pleasure encased him. With her other hand entangled in his hair, she brought her mouth to his, nibbling and tugging at his lower lip before finally allowing him in for a deep, searching kiss.

His senses swam, and as he had so many times in the past, he gave himself up to her exquisite touch, knowing he'd lost the battle yet again. But at the moment, it just didn't matter.

* * * * *

Mikhail opened the folder the Estonian lawyer had sent him after his arrival in Utah. It was postmarked from Denver with a return address of a ski equipment manufacturer, something that wouldn't raise any eyebrows with the Soviet skating authorities if they were inclined to check incoming mail. But with the brochures of ski equipment was a slender folder containing the names and photos of several Americans who, in Immaakin's opinion, might be of help to Mikhail in his attempt to defect.

He'd met two of them this afternoon. Kerry Niles and Adam Cutter—the American ice dancers. And of the two, Kerry had definitely been the more approachable. He'd felt a distinct wave of hostility emanating from Cutter. But maybe that was simply because he'd felt threatened, thinking that Mikhail was moving in on his woman.

Still…

His thoughts turned to that woman. Kerry. There was something about her. Those unique blue-green eyes, her open, friendly expression that proclaimed she didn't take herself too seriously. And her smile. Just thinking about her smile made Mikhail feel warm all over. It was dazzling, and it made his heart…well…*ache.* As corny as that sounded.

He shook his head and frowned. His mind was going down the wrong road. He had to get it back on track. He flipped to another page in the folder and stared at the black and white photo of a stranger's face.

A sober-looking man with dark hair and grim eyes. Roger Ellery, Special Forces Officer with the CIA in Northern Virginia. Kerry Niles's stepbrother. That's what made Kerry so important. If he could convince her to help him get to America, they could go her stepbrother, and once with him, he would be safe.

Adam had been a possibility as well because his father was a powerful congressman in Washington DC. But as soon as Mikhail had looked into his cold brown eyes, he'd dismissed that avenue.

It would have to be Kerry.

He tunneled his hands through his hair and stared bleakly at the TV. Earlier, he'd started watching this thriller called "Fatal Attraction" about a curly-haired blonde who was trying to get a married guy to resume an affair with her by boiling his kid's pet rabbit.

And he thought *he* had problems. He groaned and turned away from the TV.

How could he approach Kerry? How on earth was he going to be able to get her alone long enough to convince her to help him?

He didn't know. All he knew for sure was that he had to find a way. He couldn't turn back now. He had to avenge his mother's murder. Defection was the only answer.

* * * * *

The exotic strains of a tango filled the Olympic arena as Kerry Niles and Adam Cutter performed the required elements of the Tango Romantica on the ice. The ebony-haired beauty wore flowing ice-pink chiffon, and her partner was in a black tux. Mikhail stood near the boards, watching them with a critical eye. Niles and Cutter were good, but not quite at a top championship level yet. Their timing was just a bit off, their overall skating somewhat wooden. But only a champion, a coach or a judge would see that. To someone who simply enjoyed watching ice dancing, they would look perfect, and the audience was showing their appreciation of the popular American couple. As they rounded the turn close to Mikhail, he found himself watching Kerry's face. She was smiling, but her eyes seemed strained. She knew they weren't skating their best.

Mikhail wished *he* were skating with her. He'd love to see that strained look disappear and be replaced by the sheer joy of moving effortlessly over the ice. It wasn't conceit that made him think he could make that happen. It was a certainty. Somehow, he knew he and Kerry would skate perfectly together.

His eyes narrowed as the couple rounded the next turn, their feet turning, gliding, moving constantly. She didn't like his touch. He didn't know how he knew that, but knew it, he did. He frowned. Again, his thoughts were taking him away from the matter at hand. Like how he was going to find the right moment to approach her.

She was never alone in the Olympic Village. That Cutter guy hovered over her like an overprotective papa. And if he happened to take a bathroom break, her coach, a woman with flaming hair and a thick Russian accent, was at Kerry's side. He hoped that wouldn't be a problem. The three of them seemed to have a good relationship. Just yesterday, he'd noticed Kerry giving her coach an enthusiastic hug. Would she be so loyal to the woman that she would refuse to help him? But then, she might refuse, anyway. Face it, he would be asking a lot of her. It wasn't like he was requesting a ride back to the hotel or borrowing a cigarette or something. He was asking her to take him to Washington DC. To get involved in an international incident that could very well destroy her skating career. And if they were caught, who knew what kind of laws she'd be accused of breaking?

The enormity of it all hit him, and he caught his breath. How could he do this? How could he expect this lovely young woman to drop everything—her career, her very *life*—and help him with something that didn't even concern her? It was insane! Immaakin was insane for even suggesting it.

But then, this whole situation was insane. It was insane that his father had died along with an entire village, and those deaths had been passed off as an influenza attack. And it was insane that that same drug might be poisoning the bloodstreams of Russian athletes even now. For all he knew, *he'd* been injected with the stuff in place of the routine vitamin shots he'd been getting every week.

That's why he had to ask for her help. That's why he had to convince her to do it. With a start, he realized the music had ended, and Kerry and Adam were skating towards the portal.

"Damn," he muttered. There were only two couples between Niles and Cutter and he and Elena. His partner would be wondering why he wasn't backstage limbering up.

Wearing his skate guards, he strode back to the tunnel just as Kerry and Adam entered "Kiss and Cry" to wait for their scores. A moment later, the crowd made known their displeasure with hisses and boos. A low score, apparently. Mikhail wasn't surprised. The judges had most likely seen what he'd noticed. That the couple lacked that intangible chemistry that told the judges they were in sync, a partnership. And that was something no one could learn. It was either there or it wasn't. Odd, then, that he and Elena were favored to win the gold medal. God knows there wasn't an iota of chemistry between them. Maybe they were just good at faking it. Or, more likely, the dislike that simmered between them was mistaken for sexual tension. He shuddered at the thought. *As if.*

He strode through the tunnel crowded with skaters waiting their turn on the ice. A babble of voices in different languages echoed in the cavernous corridor. His eyes swept the area, and he saw a sleek, blond head above the crowd. He headed toward it. It disappeared as Elena did a sideways bend, stretching her torso, and then appeared again. As if sensing him, she turned, and her smoky blue eyes drilled into him. Surprise, surprise. She was angry. Wondering where he'd gotten off to, he supposed. Christ, why didn't she just put one of those dog leashes on him, like the one they'd seen on a toddler at the mall in Salt Lake City the other day. That way, she'd always know where he was. He could be at her beck and call every single moment.

He gritted his teeth. Just a few more days, and he'd be done with her forever.

"Where were you?" she snapped when he reached her. "We skate soon, you know."

From the ice, the tango music began to play again.

"I know that, Elena," he said quietly, trying to hold onto his temper. "I was just checking out the competition."

"Why?" The anger faded a bit, and her full, sensuous lips quirked in something resembling a smile. "We have nothing to worry about. You know that."

He shrugged. "Maybe not this year. But there is always the future."

"Silly boy." Raising a slender arm over her head, Elena did another side bend. "You'd better start stretching. We don't have much time."

Mikhail didn't respond. He just turned his back on her, closed his eyes and began to stretch. Sometimes, the simplest thing to do was to just tune her out.

CHAPTER THREE

Mikhail and Elena skated their final required dance element and left "Kiss and Cry" with scores that had them leading the competition. Backstage, Mikhail turned away from her, disgusted by the smug look on her face. Couldn't she at least *pretend* to be modest?

He left her and started to round the corner leading to the men's dressing room, but paused when he heard an angry female voice speaking in English. Peering around the corner, he saw Kerry and Adam outside the men's dressing room, engaged in a heated conversation. Mikhail eased back out of sight, and on the pretense of adjusting the laces of his skate, he listened. Thank God Nadya had forced English lessons down his throat from the age of seven.

"I told you, Adam. It's precious to me. It's my *private time*. I need it."

Adam's voice was equally grim. "And I'm telling you it's not safe to be alone in that rink at four in the morning. Who knows what kind of lunatics could be hanging around?"

Kerry's breath exploded in a frustrated groan. "That's what the badges are for, Adam! That's why they have desk personnel there all night, so we can get in practice time whenever we need it. I hardly think one of the Olympic skaters is skulking around the rink waiting for the opportunity to slit my throat."

"Oh, yeah?" Cutter's voice was heavy with sarcasm. "You ever heard of Nancy Kerrigan?"

"Oh, for God's sake!" Another exasperated breath. "Adam, I'm serious! You are driving me crazy. I can't take two steps without you breathing down my neck. Hey, if I wanted a bodyguard, I'd hire one." A moment of silence, then, "Ah, jeez, Adam…don't give me that hang-dog expression." Her voice softened, turned pleading. "Try and understand, for God's sake. Those hours from four to six are like church to me. It's my meditation time. Can't you respect that?"

Mikhail's heartbeat tripled. Here was the answer to his problem. She had to be talking about the practice rink in Park City. That's where he would find her alone.

But Adam wasn't ready to give up. "At least let me walk you over there. It's not safe to be out on the streets at that time of morning."

"*No, Adam!*"

Exasperation rang in her voice. In the short silence that followed, Mikhail imagined the couple face to face, eyes locked in battle. "I have pepper spray," she said finally. "I'll be okay."

Another strained silence followed, and then Adam said, "I just want to take care of you."

"I know." Kerry's voice bled sadness. "That's the problem. I haven't needed anyone to take care of me since I was twelve years old. I'm a big girl. I take care of myself." Another pause, then, "I'll see you tomorrow morning, all right? Six o'clock. *No earlier.*"

Her footsteps rang in the corridor, heading toward Mikhail. He quickly untied his lace and began to loosen it. As she rounded the corner, he looked up and smiled. "I cannot bear it another second," he said. Then added, "New skates. Do you not hate breaking them in?"

She looked momentarily startled, and then smiled. As usual, he felt that odd tug in his heart. Dear God, did she know the power of her smile? She looked prettier than ever in her street clothes—faded blue jeans, cowboy boots and a fuzzy-looking lemon-colored sweater that made her black hair, flowing freely down to her shoulders, look almost blue.

"Yeah, by the time they start feeling good, it's time for new ones." She paused in front of him as he loosened his other skate lace and straightened to a standing position. "Congratulations. You and Elena were wonderful tonight. She's like a different skater with you. Oh, damn…" A soft blush crept over her cheekbones. "That was a horrible thing to say. I'm sorry. I just meant…"

Mikhail held back a laugh. He knew exactly what she'd meant, and he agreed with her. "You looked very good on the ice, as well." He wasn't lying. She *had* looked good. She had the potential to be a skating star someday.

Her brows furrowed in a slight frown. "We suck," she said grimly.

"Not true," Mikhail said quickly. "You are in Olympics, yes?"

An abashed smile chased away her frown. "Well, relatively speaking. It's obvious Adam and I have a ways to go before we're competing at your level. I know it. I just wish *he* did. He actually believes we can medal this year. I'm afraid he's setting himself up for a crushing disappointment."

Mikhail decided this was a woman who wouldn't appreciate platitudes. "And you? Will you not be disappointed, as well?"

She looked him in the eyes, hesitated and then said, "Don't get me wrong. I'd love to win a medal. But I'm not going to jump off a bridge if it's not in the cards for me. I'm just happy to be able to do something I love. And going out there and skating my best…giving it my all…is what's important to me." She gave a slight shrug. "I guess the fire of competition has burned out. And when that happens, that means it's time to…" She stopped, and her cheeks filled with color. "I *do* talk too much, don't I?"

He started to protest, thinking that now might be the time to ask her for her help, but then he heard voices coming from behind them. More skaters on their way to the dressing rooms. No chance to ask her now. It would have to wait until tomorrow. At least now, he knew where and when he'd find her.

"I'd better go," he said.

She nodded, but he thought he saw something like disappointment in those incredible eyes of hers. Their blue-green color reminded him of a tropical cove off the windward side of Oahu where he'd spent a few days during last summer's exhibition tour.

She flashed him her heart-melting smile and gave a little wave. "See ya."

He couldn't help but watch her stride off down the corridor, her long, straight hair swinging below her shoulders. She was as graceful in cowboy boots as she was in her skates.

A wave of stark fear washed over him. *What if she refuses to help me?*

He would have to find a way to convince her.

After Kerry disappeared around the corner, he stepped into the men's dressing room and saw Adam Cutter at the sink, staring into the mirror. His brown eyes met Mikhail's in the reflection of the mirror, and then quickly looked away.

But in that one moment, Mikhail recognized the torment on the American's face. And he knew the truth.

Adam Cutter was in love with his partner. And that was sure to make things more complicated for Mikhail.

* * * * *

He stood in the shadows and watched Kerry's trim figure on the ice. On her forward outside edge, she lifted herself into the air and gracefully rotated two and a half times, landing gently on the back outside edge of her opposite foot. A picture-perfect double axel. Mikhail caught his breath as she immediately went into one of the most beautiful layback spins he'd ever seen, her slender arms extended over her head, lovely hands in mesmerizing motion, reminding him of a hula dancer he'd seen in Hawaii. Her long, black ponytail whipped around as her speed picked up, becoming a black blur. Finally, the spin slowed, and she stopped, breathing heavily.

Mikhail applauded. He couldn't help it. He was so blown away by what he had seen. Startled, she stiffened, staring in his direction. Then she began to skate toward him in long, furious strokes, like a hockey player coming after the puck. As she grew closer, he saw two blooms of red on her cheekbones. His pulse jolted at the glitter of rage in her eyes.

"Is it six already?" she said, her voice cold as the ice beneath her skates.

She thought he was Cutter, he realized. He opened his mouth to correct that impression, but before he could speak, her eyes widened and she arced to a stop in front of him, spraying ice.

"Oh! I thought you were my partner."

He stared at her, momentarily unable to think of a thing to say. She was so lovely with her face flushed from exertion, her long ponytail a bit tangled from the spin. Beads of sweat dotted her upper lip, and for a crazy moment Mikhail imagined removing them with his tongue. They would taste sweet, just like her lips. Bad time to be thinking about her lips, he reminded himself.

"You skate like singles skater," he said. "With layback and double axel."

The color on her face deepened, and Mikhail was quite sure it had nothing to do with her workout on the ice. Could it be that she found him as attractive as he found her?

She nodded. "I switched to dance when I was fourteen."

Now that he was facing her, he had no idea how to broach the subject that had to be broached. He tried to smile, hoping it wasn't too strained. "You are good at both, yes?"

She shrugged, her fingers plucking at the chiffon of her skirt. "Not really. That double axel I landed was a fluke."

Fluke. He'd never heard that term before. "This fluke. This is new word for me. I am not sure what you mean, but I think is not good."

She smiled, and some of her nervousness seemed to drain away. "It means I don't land it that way usually. Hardly ever, as a matter-of-fact."

He felt himself begin to relax. He still wasn't sure how he was going to convince her to help him, but for the moment he would put that at the back of his mind and follow through with what he'd wanted to do since he first saw her on the ice three weeks ago.

"Will you skate with me? Now, I mean. Right here."

Her eyes widened, and her lips parted in a silent "o." Before she could refuse—because he knew that was what she was about to do—he went on. "I have been watching you all week and I…" His English faltered, as it often did when he so desperately wanted to be understood. He shook his head, exasperated. "I do not know right way to say what is in here." He tapped his forehead with an impatient finger. "You move like…so lovely. And…" He shrugged, giving up trying to explain further. "I wish to skate with you."

Still, Kerry didn't speak. But something in her eyes told him she wanted to accept his invitation. Yet, he saw apprehension there, too. But that, he would ignore. "Excuse me. I will be right back."

He turned without waiting for her response, and hurried through the double doors and over to the desk. A young man with sleepy eyes looked up from an issue of Rolling **Stone** with Britney Spears on the cover.

"Can you please play Tango Romantica?" Mikhail asked, slipping him a Canadian twenty.

The kid looked surprised, his face losing its sleepy look. "No problem."

By the time Mikhail reached the rink again, the music had started to play. Kerry stood where he'd left her, looking bemused. He removed his skate guards and stepped onto the ice, then turned to her, his hand outstretched.

Seconds passed as she stared at him, and then her cool, slender hand was entwined with his. He wasn't sure, but he thought he felt it trembling. He placed a hand on her waist, and felt the tension emanating from her slender body. They stood still, waiting for the music to loop to the opening movement, and then began to move across the ice. She felt stiff, wooden in his arms. And then her foot tangled with his, and she was sitting on the ice. Hot color flooded her face as she scrambled to her feet.

He reached out and steadied her. "You know this dance. You have done it hundreds of times with your partner." His gaze held hers. "Just relax and let yourself feel music." Again, he placed his hand on her waist. "Ready?"

She nodded. He smiled at her, and as one, they began to move on the ice. Gradually, he felt the tension seep out of her body as their feet moved in perfect synchronization. She'd realized this was the compulsory dance she'd done last night with Cutter. She knew every movement, every step of it by heart. She was light in his arms, performing the elements with grace and confidence.

Mikhail danced over the ice with Kerry, his heart soaring. How could this be? He was dancing with a complete stranger, yet, he felt as if his edges had never been deeper, his curves never tighter. It was as if they'd been ice dancing together for years.

Kerry turned in his arms, and for a moment, they faced each other. She smiled up at him, her face radiant, eyes sparkling. He grinned back. Then he spun her around, and the scent of a fruity shampoo from her hair wafted over him. Then she was at his side again.

The music ended. Too soon. Much too soon. They stopped skating, but he didn't release her. She stared up at him, eyes wide, mouth slightly parted, her breathing shallow. Mikhail gazed at her, struggling with an overwhelming desire to kiss her. He saw in her eyes that she wanted it, too. How easy it would be to go with the moment. To give into the attraction crackling between them.

But no. It would complicate things. He needed her help, but he wouldn't seduce her to get it. She tilted her head, offering her lips. Inviting him. His hands moved up her arms, fastened on her shoulders and tightened.

"Kerry Niles," he said softly. "I need your help. Please…"

Confusion crept across her face. Before she could say a word, he plowed ahead, knowing it was now or never. "I must defect from my country, and I need your help to do it."

* * * * *

"Defect? I don't get it. There is no more Soviet Union. What's there to defect from? Can't you just leave if you want to?" Kerry paced her small hotel room, one finger mindlessly twirling a strand of hair from her ponytail.

He sat on a chair at her writing desk, watching her silently. His second cup of black coffee sat at his elbow, fragrant and still steaming. Kerry turned and glared at him.

"Is clear you do not understand situation in my country. Yes, Communism is thing of past, but if Russian citizen is valuable athlete, is not so easy to leave. Especially if those who want you to stay have connection to Russian mob."

"Jesus!" Kerry exploded. She whirled around and resumed her pacing. "Do you know how crazy this is? I mean, seriously. And why me? Why do you think I would help you?"

Mikhail stared at her soberly. "I do not know. I only hope you will. And yes, it is crazy." He gave a slight shrug. "But nonetheless, it is what I must do."

"But why? You still haven't told me why."

"I cannot give you details. Like I said before, there is information I need to get to the American government. That is why I was told to contact you. Because your brother works for CIA."

"He's not my brother," she snapped. "He's my stepbrother, and I hardly know him."

She tugged the elastic band from her ponytail and her hair tumbled about her shoulders. Mikhail swallowed hard as a wave of desire coursed through him. Focus, he told himself. She began to pace again, tunneling her hands through her glossy black hair.

He'd gotten this far. She'd even brought him back to her room so they could talk without being interrupted by early rising skaters. That was encouraging. She hadn't told him he was a lunatic and stalked off the ice like he'd half expected. She'd listened to the brief explanation he'd rehearsed in his room—that after the death of his mother, he'd discovered some disturbing information in her papers that had to be brought to the attention of the West. And then he'd waited for her to flat out refuse. She hadn't done that. Yet.

"I just don't know," she said now, her fingers pushing at her temples. "I don't know if Roger can help or not. He's an odd fish."

Mikhail took a sip of coffee and watched her move about the room. "If you can get me to him, I can convince him. I know I can. You have car, right? I understand your grandparents live nearby."

Kerry stopped pacing and stared at him. "How do you know so much about me?"

Mikhail glanced at the floor. "There are some people in my country who make it their business to get information. Luckily, they are the good guys." He looked up and fastened his gaze upon her. "So, you do have car, yes?"

She nodded.

"Good. So, will you help me? Take me to your step-brother?"

She stared at him, her face a mask of perplexity. "Let me get this straight. You want me to drive you all the way to Virginia so you can turn yourself in to the Americans? Why the hell can't you just go to the nearest INS?"

Mikhail suppressed a sigh. How to make her understand? "I must go to Virginia. My contact in Tallinn has given me two names. Yours and your brother...stepbrother," he amended. "I am not willing to trust anyone else. I have heard stories about others who have trusted INS, and they were turned away. I cannot risk that."

Kerry stared at him. "What makes you so sure you can trust *me*?"

He looked at her closely. "Can't I?"

She glanced away from him, a soft rose blush tinting her face. "Don't be so sure. I *am* the Bad Girl of skating, you know. You get newspapers in Russia now, don't you? I'm sure you read all about the big scandal that almost got me kicked out of skating."

Something clicked in Mikhail's brain. He remembered a scandal that had rocked the skating world three or four years ago. It had to do with a professional hockey player from Canada and an American figure skater. And it involved drug trafficking.

"You're *that* American skater?"

Her jaw tightened, but she steadfastly met his gaze. "Yeah. But I was innocent. And finally, cleared."

Mikhail nodded. "If you were guilty, you would not be here to have this conversation."

"Right! The only thing I was guilty of was being stupid enough to trust a double-dealing, lying son-of-a-bitch jerk that…oh, let's not go there!" Kerry plopped herself down on the foot of the bed and dropped her face into her hands.

Mikhail watched her, feeling hope rise in his chest. Was she thinking about it?

She dropped her hands to her knees and looked at him. "When were you planning on doing it?"

This time Mikhail had to look away. *Here comes the tough part.* "On Friday."

Her brows furrowed. "Friday? Hey, wait a minute." Her jaw tightened ominously. "Are you out of your freaking *mind*? That's the night before the free dance. You're going to defect on the night before you're due to skate for a gold medal for Russia?"

Mikhail forced himself to meet her eyes. "It must be that night. Once we win gold medal, the media of every country will be all over us. It will be impossible to slip away once we win medal."

Kerry was staring at him as if he'd suddenly sprouted devil horns and cloven hooves. "Oh, my God," she said softly. "I can't believe this. You're asking me to drive you to my stepbrother in Virginia, and if that's not bad enough, you're asking me to give up my Olympic dream to do it?" Her eyes glittered with anger. "Who the hell do you think you are?"

Mikhail swallowed hard, taken aback by her sudden fury. She jumped up from the bed and took a step toward him, fists clenched. "You're very self-centered, aren't you? You think the world revolves around you and what you want? Hey, I told you that getting out there on the ice and skating my best was more important to me than winning medals, but that doesn't mean I'll give up my chance to win one. And yeah, you're right. We probably *won't* win a medal. God knows it would be a miracle if we did…especially with these biased judges we have to put up with…but damn it, Mikhail, I want my chance to go for it. And I would *never* do that to Adam. Do you know how much this means to him? Do you have any *idea*? And you expect me to throw all that away just to help you get to Virginia? You *are* out of your freakin' mind!"

That's when it hit him. She was right. What had he been thinking? How had he expected her to agree to such a thing? Maybe he *was* nuts. But now, the question was, what was he going to do? He hadn't lied to Kerry about the reason why they had to make their escape the night before the free dance. Once their competition was over, and they'd won the gold medal, there would be no peace. No chance to slip away.

He got to his feet. "You are right, Kerry. I should never have asked this of you. Is too much."

The anger had faded from her face, and she was staring at him, eyes wide, lips slightly parted. He turned and swiftly crossed the room to the door.

"Mikhail, I would help you if I could," she said. "But the timing sucks. I just can't do that to Adam."

He reached the door and looked back at her. "I know. Do not worry. I will think of something. Goodnight, Kerry."

He stepped out into the corridor and closed her door. Then he took a deep breath and released it, trying to calm his racing heart.

Now, what? he thought. For a moment there, he'd started to believe she would help him. But her loyalty to her skating partner had been the deal-breaker. Mikhail couldn't help but admire her for that. In fact, if she'd agreed to help him at the expense of Adam's dashed dreams, it would've been hard to respect her.

Still, if not for Adam…

Deep in thought, Mikhail headed for the elevator. If only there was a way to take Adam out of the equation…

CHAPTER FOUR

Kerry sat across the table from her best friend and fellow skater, Brandi Vanderkleef, and watched as she scooped up a huge spoonful of vanilla ice cream dripping with hot fudge.

She slipped it into her generous mouth.
"Mmmmm…heaven," she mumbled, closing her eyes in ecstasy. "Pure heaven."

Kerry narrowed her eyes and stabbed a fork into her salad, dressed with a low-cal vinaigrette. If she didn't love her friend so much, she'd hate her for being able to eat anything she wanted and not gain an ounce. "Mmmm. Bet mine tastes better than yours," she said with as much sarcasm as she could muster.

They were sitting at a table in the Olympic Village cafeteria, having a late afternoon snack. Kerry didn't dare eat more than a salad because of the original dance competition that evening. Lucky Brandi, being a singles skater, had more than a week before her competition began.

At the thought of the competition, Kerry's heart missed a beat. Not really because of the competition, but because of what would happen after it— when she broke the news to Adam and Catri that she was retiring from competitive skating.

She thought she knew how Catri would react. Disappointment, at first, followed by acceptance. A kind-hearted woman, Catri would want the best for her, and if that meant giving up competition, then so be it. Adam, though, would react in a completely different manner. He'd freak. Totally, and without restraint. It would come as a complete shock to him despite the many hints she'd dropped in the last year. Because that was Adam. He heard only what he wanted to hear.

Hard to believe that in just a few short weeks, she'd be out on her own. For the first time, really, and at the ancient age of twenty-eight. She'd been only twelve when her father died in an avalanche in British Columbia. His death had been the first loss of her young life, and another had quickly followed when her mother wrenched her away from her grandparents and moved her to San Diego.

Kerry had never forgiven Jana for that. Her mother had never really wanted her; she just hadn't wanted her grandparents to have her. That fact had been proven quite dramatically to Kerry when, a year later, Jana married Erich Ellery, and packed Kerry off to live with the Petenka's. Although that had quite suited Kerry, because living with Jana and Erich in his La Jolla mansion would've been hell on earth, it still hurt that her mother thought so little of her that she'd allow her to grow up with strangers.

But thankfully, the Petenka's hadn't been strangers for long. They'd become her surrogate parents, and Vladimir had almost made up for the loss of her beloved father.

What am I going to do now? Kerry wondered as she took a sip of iced tea. Get a job in an ice show? Coach? Or…maybe just take some time off and travel. At the age of twenty-one, she'd inherited the trust fund her father had set up for her. It was a considerable amount of money, and she hadn't touched it. Hadn't needed to. Maybe she'd just take some time off and see the world. Really see it. Not just the airports and the skating rinks and hotel rooms. She'd been all around the world, and hadn't really seen a thing.

"So, where's your shadow?" Brandi asked, interrupting her train of thought. Her velvet brown eyes swept the room as she devoured her sundae. "I'm surprised Adam allowed you to have lunch with me without tagging along."

Kerry groaned. "My shadow…as you call him…is starting to learn he's not surgically attached to my side. I've had to point that out to him…quite emphatically, in fact."

Brandi finished her sundae and dropped her spoon into her dish with a contented sigh. "Why is it guys always want the girls they can't have, and the ones who want them might as well be invisible?"

"Because guys are idiots, that's why."

Poor Brandi. She'd had a crush on Adam as long as…well…as long as Kerry first got *her* crush on him. She remembered how the two of them would stay up all night at sleepovers, giggling about how Adam looked *exactly* like JFK, Jr. But Kerry had outgrown her crush years ago. Brandi never had.

Kerry glanced at her wristwatch then looked at her friend. The pretty strawberry blonde was sipping a glass of ice water and glancing about the room at the other athletes. Checking out the prospects. It was one of their favorite off-ice activities, admiring the male athletes. And why not? Lord knows the cafeteria abounded with lots of "eye candy" today. Sitting at a table in the corner were a bunch of Norwegian skiers, all of them with hair of various shades of blond. Not an ugly guy in the bunch.

Must be something in the Norwegian water, Kerry thought.

The Nordic skiers were pretending not to notice the admiring glances of the female athletes in the room, but

Kerry was damn sure they were well aware of their impact. Brandi had been flirting with one of them since they'd sat down—a hunk with sapphire eyes and shoulder-length wheat-colored curls. She was a sucker for a guy with long hair and an accent.

"So, what's wrong with you, anyway?"

Brandi had finally looked away from her Norwegian and was now spearing her with a sharp gaze, a gleam of curiosity in her eyes. Kerry's heartbeat faltered, but she tried to keep her expression neutral. "Nothing. Why?"

"Oh, come on. Is it because I blabbed to that reporter you were thinking about quitting? I said I was sorry. You know how I get when I'm nervous. I talk too much."

Kerry took a deep breath. "No, it's not that, but you *do* realize now I'm going to have to tell Catri and Adam before they read it in the morning papers? Thank you very much."

Brandi blushed and looked down into her empty ice cream bowl. "Sorry," she said miserably.

"Oh, forget it. It's something else, anyway." Kerry hesitated a moment, then went on. "Something strange happened last night…" She felt an odd sensation and looked up toward the entrance, and her throat went dry.

Brandi stared at her, alarmed. "Kerry! What's wrong?"

"N…nothing."

Mikhail stood just inside the entrance to the cafeteria, his eyes fixed upon her. Kerry tried to look away, but it was impossible. Brandi followed her gaze. She caught her breath, then looked back at her. "Hey, have you been holding out on me? Is there something going on with you and that Russian?"

Kerry felt her face grow hot. "Of course not," she said quickly, and only then did she manage to draw her gaze away from Mikhail. "I don't even know him."

"Well, he sure looks like he knows *you*. Or *wants* to get to know you, anyway." Brandi gave a sly grin. "He *is* good looking, isn't he? Except for that scar on his face. It makes him look kind of dangerous."

Kerry glanced over at Mikhail, and was relieved to see he'd turned away and was heading to a table occupied by his countrymen. Was he still planning to defect? She felt a strange emotion wash through her, and for a moment, she couldn't identify what it was, and when she did, she shook her head in denial. Impossible! It wasn't regret. No one in her right mind would want to get involved in something like this. It would be crazy—and undoubtedly dangerous. But still…she couldn't quite banish the thought from her mind—she and Mikhail traveling together, making that long drive to Virginia. All that time…just the two of them. There would be plenty of time to get to know each other.

"But maybe 'dangerous' is too strong of a word," Brandi chattered on. "It's more like mysterious. Like he's got a secret or something. You think that's it, Kerry? He's hiding something?"

If only you knew. Kerry attempted a smile. "You have quite an imagination, you know. You and Adam are perfect for each other."

Brandi rolled her eyes, blushing. "Hey, I know what I saw. He walked into the room, and your face went white. There was enough electricity generated between you two to keep the lifts running all night. So, you're not going to tell me what's going on?"

Kerry pushed away her salad plate and stood. "There's nothing going on. Anyway, I have to go and work up the nerve to break the bad news to Adam and Catri at dinner tonight. Maybe if I do it in a restaurant, there won't be a scene."

Brandi chewed her bottom lip. "Sorry," she mumbled again.

Kerry couldn't stand the guilt on her friend's face. She reached down and hugged her. "No big deal. It's probably better I get it over with, anyway. Wish me luck."

Kerry headed for the door. Her heart skipped a beat when she saw Mikhail's gaze following her.

It was a good thing Mikhail was adamant about leaving on the night before the free dance. Because Kerry was very much afraid that if it weren't for Adam and Catri, and their hopes for an Olympic medal, she might very well be tempted to help him. *And that, Kerry Niles, would make you a crazy woman.*

* * * * *

"*Jesus Christ!*" Adam snarled, his eyes shooting daggers at Kerry from across the table in the elegant French restaurant. *So much for not making a scene in public.* Apparently, she'd been way too optimistic. "I don't believe this! You're quitting? Just when we're hitting our peak?"

Catri raised a hand, halting Adam in mid-tirade. She looked at Kerry. "You've given this a lot of thought, Kerrelyn?"

Kerry ignored Adam and fixed her eyes on her coach. His reaction to her announcement about retiring had been as expected. Over-the-top furious. "Catri, don't tell me you're surprised at my decision," Kerry said. "I'm twenty-eight. Surely you've been prepared for this."

"Prepared?" Adam cut in. "How did you expect her to be prepared? I'm your partner and *I'm* not prepared. This is the first I've heard you mention retirement." He glowered at her. "How can you do this to me, Kerry? We've worked so hard, and now you're quitting on me? What am I supposed to do now?"

Anger sheared through her like a California wildfire. She'd hoped they could keep this discussion civil, but this was just too much. "Why is everything about *you*, Adam? I made a decision regarding *my* life. I've been competing since I was thirteen. I've had enough. *Deal* with it, why don't you?"

"It's my life, too." His eyes sparkled with anger. "We're partners! Do you even know the meaning of that?"

"Oh, yes, I know *exactly* what it means." Kerry stared him down and spoke in a clipped voice, "With you, it means having a father figure hovering over me twenty-four-seven, telling me what to do, *when* to do it and who to do it with. In case you haven't noticed, I'm an adult, and I'm sick to death of you treating me like a half-witted child."

Adam's mouth dropped open. He looked as if a two-ton brick had hit him upside the head. "That's what you really think? I'm just trying to look out for you!"

Kerry clenched her fists and tried not to scream. "What's it going to take to get it through your thick skull that *I don't need you to look after me?*"

His brows lowered. "Obviously, you do."

"*Enough!*" Catri's thick Russian accent cut through their argument.

Kerry and Adam stared at her. It was unusual for their coach to raise her voice, but when she did, she meant business. Her expression was stern as she gazed from one to the other, but Kerry saw something else in her eyes—sadness. She felt a pang of remorse. It wasn't her intention to hurt her coach. She loved her like a mother.

The older woman's gaze returned to Adam, her eyes owl-like behind magnified round glasses. "Please excuse us, Adam. We will meet you in the foyer."

His jaw tightened and his entire body stiffened in protest. "But…"

"Please." Her tone brooked no argument.

He scowled at Kerry, then without another word, stalked out of the dining room.

Kerry stared after him dejectedly. Why was it he always managed to make her feel like pond scum? She had a right to a life, didn't she? She'd given him fourteen years of hers. It was time to move on. Why couldn't he see that?

Catri reached across the table and placed her hand on Kerry's. "*Gollupchic*, look at me."

Kerry met her gaze, and immediately her throat tightened at the tenderness on her coach's lined face. "Is this what you truly want, Kerrelyn?" Catri asked. "To give it all up?"

Kerry nodded. "I'm almost thirty. I've known for a long time that an Olympic medal isn't in the cards for us. Adam can't accept that, but I can. It's time to move on."

Catri stared at her for a long moment without speaking. Finally, she nodded. "Okay, then. What are your plans?"

Kerry thought of Mikhail and of what she wanted to do. Her cheeks grew hot. What if she told Catri the truth? *Well, Catri, I want to run off with a Russian defector and get myself into a whole shitload of trouble.* Oh, God! What was *wrong* with her? Was she going insane?

"Um…well…I haven't thought it all through yet. I'll probably just take some time off…maybe spend a few months here in Utah with my grandparents."

Catri nodded and with a final pat on her hand, she stood, signaling that their meeting was over. Kerry got to her feet, too, her gaze anxiously searching her coach's face. The older woman looked as if she were holding back tears.

"Cattie?"

When the woman paused, Kerry moved to her and gave her a hug. "Thanks for understanding."

Catri's arms tightened about her, holding her close. Kerry breathed in her familiar scent of lavender and Scope mouthwash, wanting to preserve this moment of closeness.

"I knew you wouldn't be around forever," Catri murmured. "I'm happy I had you as long as I have. But I admit it will be hard to let you go. You're like the daughter I never had, Kerrelyn."

Kerry smiled, blinking back tears. "You know I feel the same. As far as I'm concerned, you *are* my mother, Cattie, and that's not going to change."

They clung to each other for a long moment, and then Catri drew back, her eyes misty. "Perhaps you will decide to coach with me, yes? You and I would make a good team."

"Maybe. But give me a few months, okay? I just need some down time."

Catri nodded, then brushed a kiss onto her forehead. "I do not know what I would've done without you after Vladimir died. You and Adam were my salvation during those black days." A gentle smile brightened her face. "He would've been very proud of you, you know. It would've been the greatest thrill of his life to see you two skate in the Olympics. I will always be sorry that he did not."

Kerry gave a wry grin. "Even if we don't medal?"

"Just skate your best. That is all I ask." Catri sniffed. "Now, go. You have made me cry and my make-up is ruined. I will have to go to the ladies' room and repair it."

Kerry gave Catri a kiss on her artificially blushed cheek. "I love you."

"Yes, yes, of course you do. Now, go!" Blinking back tears, Catri gave her a gentle nudge toward the door. "I will be with you in a moment." She started to move away, then paused and turned back. "Is it safe to leave you and Adam alone out there?"

Kerry grinned back at her. "Don't worry. I've got my pepper spray."

"You have my permission to use it on him if he does not behave," she said, a mock scowl on her face.

Kerry breathed a sigh of relief as Catri walked away. She was so glad to have this burden off her shoulders. It had been weighing her down for months.

Soon, her new life would begin.

* * * * *

Sean watched the original dance from the stands, applauding wildly when Elena and Kozlof finished their flawless performance. The predominantly American crowd could be a little more enthusiastic, he thought. But then, that was typical of Westerners. They hated the Russians. Always had, always would.

Sean slipped a thumb and his forefinger between his lips and let loose a shrill whistle. As the couple skated toward 'Kiss and Cry,' Elena glanced up in his direction, but of course, she couldn't see him. He was too damn far up in the stands. His eyes narrowed as she flattened a slim, white hand against the pale blue bodice of her skating dress. Was it his imagination or was she more out of breath than she should've been after that short dance? Christ! He wished he could convince her to stop taking TNG.

Even her daffy uncle had warned her about the possible long-term effects the drug might have on her health, especially since she was mixing it with her asthma medication. Jesus Christ, if that bloody formula did something to her female parts to prevent her from having children, he'd personally slit Anton Boiko's scrawny throat. He wished he'd never told Elena about that fucking formula. From the moment she'd heard the words "performance enhancement" she'd never let up on him until he'd convinced Boiko to revive the project. At the time, he, too, had thought it was a good idea. But now that he was seeing the effects on her—the more frequent asthma attacks, the growing pallor of her luminous skin, the weight loss—the more he was convinced it was a horrible mistake.

Let Big Dan Sullivan have the fucking formula. Sean didn't give a shit if he injected every one of his IRA cronies with the stuff, and turned them into Celtic Supermen. Not as long as Elena stopped taking it, and they could take the millions Big Dan would pay for the formula, and live out their lives in Rio. He didn't care if the entire world, including Northern Fucking Ireland, went to hell. There was a time when fighting for a united Ireland meant everything to him. But as he grew older, his convictions had weakened as he'd realized there were more important things in life than politics. Now, working for the IRA meant pretty much one thing to him—cold, hard cash.

When Kozlof and Elena reached the portal, Mikhail placed a hand on her waist as if to help her as she stepped off the ice, and Sean felt a blaze of pure fury rip through him. It was bad enough that he had to sit and watch that bastard place his filthy hands all over her body during their performances, but did he have to touch her off the ice as well?

His jaw rigid, Sean moved out of the row to the aisle, and started down the steps. The thing that really pissed him off, though, was knowing that Elena enjoyed Kozlof's touch. Wanted and craved it. And of course, he wanted *her*, too. What red-blooded male *wouldn't* want Elena? There was only one reason he hadn't fucked her yet. Sean knew all about these crazy athletes and how they refused to engage in sexual activities before an important competition. Kozlof was just waiting until they got their gold medal, and then he'd be all over her.

Sean smiled grimly. But that wasn't going to happen. Mikhail Kozlof would die before he touched Elena. Sean was going to make sure of that.

A warm applause went up from the audience, and Sean glanced at the scoreboard. 5.8s and 5.9s. No surprise there. Boiko and Kozlof were on their way to the gold. The presentation marks flashed up, and they were just as good. Not much room there for any of the other skaters to move up. Good, thought Sean. *She'll get her gold, and then I'll get her. In a year…two, at the most*, he'd have enough money saved to buy that villa in Rio, and he and Elena would settle down, have a couple of wee bairns and live the good life. And if the deal with Sullivan came through, it would happen even sooner. Of course, he had to get his hands on the formula for TNG. But that was only a matter of time. Anton Boiko was a cagey old bastard, but sooner or later, Sean would find a way to get it.

He reached the ground floor and headed toward the tunnel. A security guard stopped him, and then waved him through when Sean showed his badge. There was some kind of commotion going on in the tunnel, and it wasn't until he got closer that he realized what it was.

"*Somebody get a doctor!*" shouted a frantic voice.

Sean elbowed his way through the crowd, his heart hammering. A sixth sense told him Elena was at the center of the commotion.

And then he saw her. She was in Mikhail's arms, clutching her chest and gasping for breath. Fear and rage engulfed Sean, but he fought it back, knowing it wasn't the time to allow his emotions free range.

"Where's her inhaler?" Sean shouted to Mikhail. "She's supposed to have it with her all the time."

"Here! Here it is."

For the first time, Sean noticed Sergey Fadeyuska, an effeminate-looking middle-aged man fluttering about. Elena and Kozlof's coach. About as useful as a paraplegic at a walk-a-thon.

Sean grabbed the inhaler from the coach's trembling hand, his eyes flitting over the man in disgust. "For Christ's sake, what were you waiting for?"

He dropped to his knees beside Elena and inserted the inhaler in her mouth. She clutched at it, eyes frantic.

"Breathe in, love, nice and slow." Sean tried to keep the panic out of his voice. His gaze darted to Mikhail. "How long has she been like this?"

"Just a minute," he said tersely. "She collapsed right after we left Kiss and Cry."

Elena's hands clawed at him, and Sean realized the inhaler wasn't working. He felt a thrill of panic race through him. "We need an ambulance here!" he yelled. Christ! They were all staring like cows in a field chewing their cud. "We need a fucking ambulance!"

"It's on the way," someone responded.

Sean stared down at Elena. The horrible gasping sounds coming from her throat raised goosebumps on his skin. He realized that Mikhail had relinquished his hold on her, so Sean could take over. He gathered her up in his arms and cradled her. His eyes held hers as he spoke in a calm, reassuring voice that was in direct odds to how he felt. "Relax, love, and let the inhaler do its job. You're going to be fine."

But either she was too panicked to listen, or the medication just wasn't working this time. Eyes wild, she clawed at Sean's shirt, still making that desperate strangling sound. Her lips were blue, and purple shadows smudged the pads beneath her eyes. Jesus Christ! She was dying right in front of him. "*Bloody Christ! Where is the fucking ambulance?*"

Suddenly Mikhail jumped up and headed through the crowd. "We need a doctor here now!" he shouted. "There's got to be a team doctor around somewhere. Somebody find one!"

Christ! I should've thought of that, thought Sean. Of course there would be a sports doctor somewhere in the vicinity. Moments later, an athletic-looking man appeared with a medical kit. Sean and Mikhail watched as the doctor got down on his knees and gave Elena an injection. Within seconds, her breathing began to ease. Sean closed his eyes, releasing a sigh of relief. Oh, thank the good Lord.

"You'll be all right now," the doctor said to her. His gaze went from Sean to Mikhail, as if he were uncertain which one to address his remarks to. "She needs to get some rest. I don't think I've ever seen an asthma attack this bad before. It would probably be a good idea to have her undergo a complete physical."

"No!" Elena gasped. "I am fine now. There is no need."

Sean gazed down at her tenderly. To his horror, he felt absurdly close to tears. He had really thought he was going to lose her. Brushing a finger over her cheek, he smiled and spoke in English, "Ya took ten years off my life, ya did, girl."

He felt the curious gazes of the crowd around them, and realized he wasn't playing the part of a bodyguard, but of a lover. He didn't care. He was tired of pretending he was just her employee.

Elena smiled up at him, her eyes drowsy from the drug. Then Sean saw her gaze shift, and her smile widen.

"Mikhail," she said softly in Russian. "Thank you for getting the doctor."

Mikhail leaned down and patted her shoulder. He answered in their native language. "I'm just glad you're okay."

Sean had lived in Estonia for almost eleven years, and he spoke Russian and Estonian fluently. He felt an icy rage sweep through him at their exchange. Mikhail. Always fucking Mikhail. *Look at the way he's gazing down at her. Like she's his personal property or something.*

Sean stared at him, and allowed the hatred to grow and boil inside him. That fucking scar. How he'd love to give him a matching one on the other side of that pretty-boy face. Maybe he would. Maybe he'd do exactly that. And maybe he wouldn't stop with the face.

Fuck the gold medal. Elena didn't need to be skating anyway, not in her frail condition. It would be better all around if she had to withdraw from the competition.

And what better excuse to have to withdraw? When your ice-dancing partner ends up dead. Sean smiled. Funny, wasn't it? How people seemed to end up dead when they got in his way. Like Liisa. For a moment, he saw her luminous blue eyes, awash with tears as she told him, yet again, that another month had passed, and she still wasn't pregnant. But even then, despite her failure to conceive his child, he would've let her live if she hadn't demanded he give up Elena. By that time, Elena was in his blood. The accident had been unfortunate, but necessary.

And now, perhaps, it was time for another one. Mikhail Kozlof, dead. That had a really nice ring to it. He'd planned to do it anyway. Why not move up the timetable by a week or two?

CHAPTER FIVE

"Guess what? Elena Boiko just collapsed backstage." Brandi's eyes were wide as she relayed the news to Kerry and Adam.

They'd just stepped out of "Kiss and Cry" after getting decidedly mediocre scores from the judges for their original dance. Adam was still sulking, but at Brandi's words, his eyes lit up with hope. "You think she might withdraw from the competition?"

"Adam!" Kerry slanted him a disgusted look. "Don't be mean."

"Hey, it's a reasonable question."

"No." Kerry said slowly. "A reasonable question would be…is she okay, Brandi?"

Brandi nodded. "Yeah. They say it was an asthma attack. A pretty bad one, but she's going to be fine."

"Figures," Adam muttered. He loped off down the corridor.

Kerry shook her head, gazing after him. "Can you say…*poor loser*?"

As always, Brandi jumped to Adam's defense. "Give him a break, Kerry. He's still smarting over losing you. As a partner, I mean. You know…I was wondering. Do you think Catri would let me train as an ice dancer?"

Kerry looked at her friend in surprise. "You'd give up singles for Adam?"

A rosy blush flooded her face. "I've been thinking about it for a while. Ever since you told me you were, you know, retiring. It's stupid, isn't it?"

"Of course it's not stupid. Actually, I think it's a great idea. You and Adam would be perfect for each other." She reached out and impulsively grasped Brandi's hand. "I mean it, Bran. I think you'd be good for him. You're stable and good-hearted. And patient. That's something I'm in short supply of. And I think you'd skate beautifully together."

Brandi grinned. "You think so?"

"I know so. I'll mention the idea to Catri. I'll bet she'll love it."

"Thanks. So…did you see our favorite Russian couple skate? They look pretty hard to beat, don't they?"

Kerry sighed. "They sure do. I don't know what Elena Boiko has done in the past year, but she's like a completely different person on the ice. Skating with Mikhail has really improved her performance."

Brandi grinned, a dimple flickering near the corner of her mouth. "Oh, it's Mikhail now, is it? You know what I think? I think you have a case of the hots for him."

Kerry felt her cheeks grow warm. She was very much afraid that Brandi had hit the proverbial nail square on the head. A case of the hots. That would explain why her temperature rose a degree or two whenever Mikhail was nearby. Even the hairs on her arms seemed to crackle and stand at attention. It was lust, pure and simple. Yep, good old-fashioned lust. Because what else could it be? She didn't even know the guy.

But she wanted to. Wanted to very badly.

Tonight, as she'd watched them skate, all she could think about was what it had felt like to dance in his arms, gliding over the ice with abandon, her heart singing at his touch. His scar had stood out starkly under the bright lights of the rink, and Kerry found herself wanting to trace the mark with a finger, then slide her hands down the smooth cords of his neck, skimming down to his muscled biceps and...

She'd had to give herself a mental cold shower, and she'd done that by looking at Elena, the human icicle. How cool and detached the Russian woman appeared as she danced with Mikhail, wearing a sequined dress of ice blue. Not an iota of emotion in those frosty blue eyes. Her Nordic blond head was just a few inches shorter than Mikhail's. Damn! They looked good together. A great looking couple. And by the way, *were* they a couple?

She and Adam had been waiting to be announced when Mikhail and Elena left "Kiss & Cry." Mikhail's gaze had met hers for a few seconds, and she'd felt as if she'd jumped out of an airplane and was plummeting to earth in a free-fall. What had he decided to do? Would he try to defect on his own? She caught her breath. What if he did and something horrible happened to him? Wouldn't she feel responsible for refusing to help him?

She'd had to force the thought from her mind as she skated out to center ice to take her position before the original dance. And somehow, when the music started, she pushed away all thoughts of Mikhail and concentrated on their performance.

Now, back in her hotel room, she undressed and drew on a long fleece robe, then headed for the bathroom to fill the tub. A long soak in hot bubbles would be just the thing to help her relax.

She was so glad the original dance was over. The free dance would be held in two nights, and because this was the dance where they had free rein with the music and choreography, it was always her favorite part of competition. They'd put together a compilation of different movements from Mozart's Eine Kleine Nachtmusik, and Kerry was fairly confident that she and Adam would put on a solid performance. But what she was really looking forward to was the exhibition skate on the night of the closing ceremonies. They were skating to Ray Charles's "It Had to Be You," a slow, sexy dance that incorporated many unusual twists, turns and lifts—some which were illegal in competition, but always wowed the fans. She wished the World Figure Skating Association would allow skaters to use music with lyrics for competition, but although there had been talk of it for years, it didn't seem like it would ever happen. Too bad because it would open up a lot of creative doors in the sport.

Kerry turned on the faucets to fill the tub. Just as she was securing her hair in an elastic band, she thought she heard something from the bedroom. A knock at the door? She turned off the faucet and listened. It came again, louder this time. Her heart began to pound. Definitely a knock.

Mikhail! But why would it be him? She'd given him her answer, and he'd accepted it.

The knock came again, more demanding this time. She tightened the belt of her robe, moved to the door and peered through the peephole. Then sighed. Adam!

She cracked the door. "It's late, Adam," she said, hoping he'd take the hint and go away. But he wasn't having it.

"Isss importan…" He pushed his way inside, and stood there, swaying, his eyes bloodshot, jaw slack.

He was drunk, which was unusual. Adam wasn't much of a drinker. He didn't do it often, but when he did, he couldn't handle more than a couple of beers before he was juiced. Even before that crazy year with Josh when Kerry had taken binge drinking to a new high, she'd been able to drink Adam under the table and still be able to shoot a clay pigeon from twenty-five yards away. She knew that because she'd once done it on a dare at the tender age of sixteen. Adam hadn't believed her when she'd told him her father had been an Olympic biathlon, and had taught her to shoot.

Kerry sighed and closed the door behind him. "Couldn't you at least have waited until after the competition is over before getting wasted?"

"It's over. Or as good as," he mumbled, his reddened eyes peering at her like a pitifully abused dog. "Sorry I'm such a fuck-up. Such a loser. If it weren't for me, you'd probably win a medal."

Oh, God. He'd gone from "the judges wouldn't know good skating if it came up and bit them in the ass" to "nothing ever works out for me." She knew these stages well because she'd been there before. Like last year after the World Championships. And the year before after Skate America. And...she could go on and on. Jeez, it was like being with Dr. Jekyll and Mr. Hyde, only both personalities were just as bad.

Okay, so she'd play along. "You're not a loser, Adam." She kept her voice low and soothing, quelling any irritation. Which was not easy. "You just need to go to bed and sleep it off. It'll be better in the morning."

"Yeah, I *am* a loser," he moaned. "I lost you, didn't I?"

Oh, no. Not that, again. She tried to hold onto her patience, even though this particular subject was getting incredibly long in the tooth. It had been twelve years since they'd been a couple. A lifetime ago. *Get over it, already!*

Still, she managed to speak calmly, "We were too young to get so serious. The timing was wrong, that's all." God, how she hated lying. She'd fallen out of puppy love with Adam as quickly as she'd fallen into it. But it seemed kinder to make him think it was really only their youth that had caused the break-up.

Or maybe not.

Something in his eyes changed, grew softer, and Kerry realized she'd made a tactical error. Damned if he wasn't taking that remark as encouragement. Before she could move or say another word, he grabbed her, pressing his body against hers.

"Adam, wha…?"

"Mebbe the timing's right now," he garbled just before his mouth slammed down on hers, his tongue thrusting. Kerry's stomach spasmed at the gross taste of stale beer masked by a breath mint.

Damn him! He'd planned this! Apparently, he wasn't as drunk as he wanted her to think. She struggled out of his grip and gave him a hard shove. "Have you lost your mind? *God*!" She wiped the sleeve of her robe over her mouth in disgust.

The slack look had disappeared from his face, replaced by brooding anger. "You didn't used to be repulsed by my kisses."

She stared at him in amazement. "What's *wrong* with you? I was *sixteen*!"

Adam ran his hands through his rumpled dark brown hair and sank onto the foot of the bed. Groaning, he dropped his head into his hands, and then looked up again, eyes wounded. "But we were so good together. Why can't you see that?"

Kerry fought against the wave of pity she felt for him, and lost. She sat down next to him, placing a consoling arm around his shoulders. "We were kids," she said softly. "Each other's first loves. It was special, Adam, but first love doesn't usually last."

He looked at her. "It did for me."

Kerry stared back, at a total loss for words. What was it going to take to convince him to move on?

A tap came at the door, and she started. *Oh, God. Now, what?*

Adam looked at her. "You expecting someone?"

Kerry didn't bothering answering. She got up and strode to the door to look through the peephole. Her heart jolted. It was Mikhail. And like a lightning bolt, the idea came to her. It was outrageous, and totally daring, but it just might work. She took a deep breath and placed a hand over her racing heart. Oh, God, was she really going to do this? If so, it was now or never.

She opened the door and gave Mikhail a big smile. "Well! It's about time. Come in."

One eyebrow arched in question, but he did as requested. *Okay. Here goes.* After he stepped inside, Kerry fastened her hands on each side of his face and said under her breath, "Play along."

His blue eyes widened in surprise. He opened his mouth to say something, but she didn't give him the chance. She reached up and pressed her lips against his in a full-bodied kiss.

For a moment, he stood stiff with shock but then she felt the change come over him. His hands slid up her back as his warm mouth became eager and pliant on hers. Kerry's head began to spin, and the blood in her veins turned to the consistency of rich, hot syrup as she tasted Mikhail's flirting tongue.

Oh, God. Maybe this wasn't such a great idea, after all.

"What the hell is going on here?" Adam snarled, jumping to his feet.

Kerry tried to break the kiss and pull away, but Mikhail had different ideas. His hands tightened on her back, and his mouth nibbled at hers, playful and incredibly erotic at the same time. Her knees began to tremble. She felt close to fainting. *Oh, wow!* Not since Josh had she felt this kind of physical attraction.

"For God's sake, Kerry!" Adam's voice was growing angrier. "Do you know who this guy is?"

This time when Kerry tried to break the kiss, Mikhail released her. She drew away, her breathing erratic, eyes locked on his. He looked mildly amused, his full, sensuous lips quirked in an ironic smile. It made Kerry want to kiss him all over again.

Mikhail's gaze left hers and moved to Adam who was glaring at them with a belligerent scowl.

"Does Kerry *usually* kiss complete stranger?" Mikhail asked in a mocking tone.

Well, not usually. But after this, she might do it more often.

She moved closer to Mikhail, placing a proprietary hand on his muscular bicep—rock hard, she couldn't help but notice—and met Adam's indignant gaze. "We've been seeing each other for…" Her mind went blank.

"Several weeks," Mikhail put in.

"Yes, several weeks."

The color had ebbed from Adam's face. His hands were clenched in angry fists at his side. "But how? When have you had time?"

Mikhail's blue eyes roved over her, sending her body temperature up another notch. "We have *made* time, have we not, *angel moy*?"

She smiled, almost swooning from the sexy come hither look in his eyes and the throaty Russian endearment that had rolled off his tongue. "That's right, Adam. I didn't want to tell you before the competition because I knew it would just upset you."

"Damn *right* it would upset me!" Adam's pale color had disappeared, replaced by a red tide of rage. "Are you nuts, Kerry? Getting involved with a…a…"

Mikhail looked at him, waiting for him to complete his sentence.

Adam's bravado faded. "Getting involved with someone in the middle of an Olympic year?"

Mikhail's hand moved up and down her arm, raising goose bumps under the fleece fabric of her robe. She could only imagine what her reaction would be if he actually touched skin.

"Love does not follow time table, is that not true, *milaya moya*?"

Love? Well, she'd been thinking more on the lines of lust, but hey, if it worked to get Adam off her back, she was all for it.

She smiled up at Mikhail, and he gave her a wink that made her heart spasm. "That's right. So…if you don't mind, Adam, Mikhail and I would like to…you know…have a little privacy."

Adam stared at them. "I just can't believe this! Kerry, didn't you learn your lesson with Josh Mullins? You almost destroyed your career running around with that low-life hockey player!"

Kerry's mouth tightened. She opened the door. "I think you'd better go now."

He didn't move, just stared at them.

"The lady wishes you to go," Mikhail said quietly.

The two men eyed each other for a long, tense moment. The elevator dinged in the corridor outside and laughter erupted as some late night revelers headed to their rooms.

Adam wilted. "Okay," he said, moving toward the door. "Ruin your life, Kerry. Because that's what you're doing, you know. And I won't always be around to rescue you."

Kerry grimaced. "Please, Adam, don't get my hopes up by saying things like that."

"Go ahead and joke." Adam paused at the door and glared at her. "But I bet you won't be laughing when Catri finds out about this." He stepped out into the hallway, and Kerry closed the door behind him.

She turned and met Mikhail's gaze. "Tattle-tailer," she muttered.

His lips quirked. "I do not know what that means, but I think is not good."

She grinned. "You're right. It's not." Her smile widened. "So, we're an item, are we?"

"Item?" A questioning eyebrow rose. "What is this 'item'?"

"You know..." She felt the color rise on her cheeks as she gestured from him to herself. "You and me."

"Oh!" He grinned, his face transforming from dangerous to delightful. "Ah, yes, seems we are." He looked at her closely, his expression suddenly watchful. "I have question to ask you, Kerry. If I can slip away after competition, will you then help me get to Virginia?"

Seconds passed as he waited for her answer. Kerry gazed at him, her heart bumping. It was the moment of truth. Just this afternoon, sitting with Brandi in the dining room, she'd been wishing she could find a way to help Mikhail. Now, he was giving her a second opportunity to do so. And she didn't know what to do.

Then she did what she'd often done in the past fourteen years. She asked herself one simple question. What would Dad do? He'd always been a man of integrity—a gold medalist who'd turned down lucrative endorsement contracts, and instead, joined Greenpeace because he believed so strongly in ecology preservation and the protection of wildlife. Kerry knew her father would tell her to search her heart, and the right choice would be revealed. She'd already done that, and now, she just had to commit herself.

She took a deep breath, released it, and with a confidence she in no way felt, she looked Mikhail in the eye and said, "I must be nuts, but yeah, I'll help you. So…what's the plan?"

* * * * *

The man sat in a late-model dark sedan, watching the entrance to the small hotel. The motor was running, the lights off. Ten minutes ago, he'd watched the Russian figure skater enter the building.

He'd wanted to take a go at him then, but there'd been too many people around. The bar on the corner had a healthy number of people spilling out onto the street, and with the Winter Olympics going on, the village of Park City was bustling with activity, even in the early hours of the morning.

Bad news for the business at hand. But no matter. He was a patient man. The right time would come. He took a draw on his fag and released it. Smoke curled in the air around him. Yep, if he had his druthers, he'd just as soon use his Makarov. But Boss wanted it to look like an accident.

So, it would look like an accident.

He tensed, his eyes fastening on a dark figure stepping out of the hotel. It was Kozlof. Clenching his teeth around the cigarette butt in a snarl, he thrust the gearshift into first and pressed on the accelerator. The Mercedes' wheels shrieked in protest as the car bolted forward.

His hands tightened on the steering wheel. The headlights caught the startled face of the man, the dark eyes widening in horror as the car plowed into him. The driver cackled.

Poor old sot never knew what hit him.

CHAPTER SIX

The phone call jarred Kerry awake. Her gaze darted to the illuminated clock on the bedside. Three o'clock. Who on earth would be calling at such an ungodly hour?

It was Brandi's voice on the other end, and it was almost unrecognizable with panic. "It's Adam," she said, her throat choked with tears. "He was hit by a car outside the hotel."

Kerry's heart froze. "What?"

She and Mikhail had heard sirens just as he was about to leave. They'd watched the ambulance arrive, its lights flashing red on the street below. They'd commented on it, wondering what had happened. It hadn't, for a moment, occurred to her that someone she knew might be involved. Fear clawed up her throat. Oh, God. She'd been exasperated with Adam, but she'd never ever wanted to see him hurt.

"Is he okay," she asked, unaware that she was holding her breath as she waited for Brandi's response.

"He will be. Oh, Kerry!" Brandi burst into sobs. "I was so scared when I heard. I thought he'd...he'd...oh, I love him so much, and I don't care if he never loves me. I just want him to be okay."

"You said he was going to be okay. You said that, right? How badly is he injured?"

"He's in surgery. His leg...his femur I think they said...is broken in three places. They have to put it back together with pins. He's going to be in the hospital for probably a couple of months, but it'll be at least a year before he can get back on the ice. He was lucky, the doctor said. Kerry…" she paused. "It was a hit and run. Can you believe it? How could someone be that cruel? To hit him and just leave him lying there."

Kerry closed her eyes. "Oh, God. It's unbelievable." Her hand tightened on the receiver. "Does Catri know? She's going to be frantic. She can't lose Adam, too. Not after…"

"She knows. She's right here. They called her first. She says Adam's parents are in town for the Olympics, and they're trying to find them. Catri couldn't remember where they're staying."

"The Marriott," Kerry said woodenly. "I have my car. I'll go pick them up and bring them over. Which hospital is it?"

Brandi told her, and then added, "Tell them he's going to be okay. He's going to be fine."

It wasn't until Kerry hung up that she realized why Brandi's closing remark made her feel so uncomfortable. It was almost as if she were trying to convince herself it was so.

* * * * *

"Well…is he dead, then?"

Sean took a drag of his cigarette and stared at the man across the room. His name was Fagan Reilly, and he'd been working in Sean's employ since the good old days in Belfast. They still worked for the Cause, but there were times, like now, for instance, when Fagan did an extra job or two for him that had nothing to do with Ireland and the situation back home. Bloody old Fagan. Revolting man, really. The kind of man that the Prods pointed to when they talked about the filthy drunken Catholics, and how their kind stank up the city. Catholic to the core, even Sean saw they had a point. But then, Fagan served a purpose. Despite a wee bit dim in the light bulb department, he was quite adept at the wet work.

Sean grimaced as the memory of poor, plain-faced Liisa flooded over him. She hadn't been the typical Finnish beauty, that was for sure, but she'd had a good heart. He didn't like thinking about her, about how she'd died, so as always, he brushed the thought of her away. Instead, he remembered how Fagan had handled that little Ivan problem a couple of years ago. And of course, back in December, when Kozlof's mum had flapped her lips a wee bit too much, and stuck her big fat Estonian nose where it didn't belong, Fagan had taken care of her, too. Good thing Sean had an informant working at that newspaper office who'd discovered what the old bat was up to. Question was, had she managed to get any of that information about the massacre to her son? Another reason he wanted to see that bastard dead.

If Fagan was here to give him the good news, well, then, that was fine and dandy. If good old boyo Fagan here, for ten thousand dollars, gave the correct answer, everything would be coming up smelling sweet as fucking roses.

"Don't know, boss."

Sean's mouth tightened. Wrong answer. Fagan shifted uncomfortably under his piercing stare. "I hit him, Sean. Square on. He went splat on the sidewalk, and I would've finished the bugger off except that a great crowd of people came out of the bar just then. I figured it was better that I make a run for it." His thick Dublin accent rose to a whine, and Sean frowned.

"Quiet, you moron. Elena is sleeping in the next room." He took another drag from his cigarette, thinking. "You're sure you hit him? You heard Kozlof go crunch?"

Fagan grinned, revealing a mouthful of half rotted teeth. "He went crunch like a stinkbug under the heel of me boot."

Sean grimaced. Not at his words, but at the ugly mug grinning at him like a fucking Jack O' Lantern on All Hallow's Eve. Christ! You'd think a man would have more pride in himself than to go to the dogs like that. Had Fagan never heard of a bloody dentist? Or a toothbrush, for that matter. Sean shook his head. Thank the good Lord he'd been raised differently. Not like that Dublin gutter rat who didn't give a shit if his teeth were rotten or that he stank of stale Guinness and cheap fags. Ah, well. To each his own, he supposed.

"Okay, then." He reached for his money clip and peeled off twenty one hundred dollar bills. "Here."

Fagan reached out and took the bills, riffling through them quickly. He looked up, his brown eyes confused. "Uh…boss. This is only two thousand. You said ten."

Sean stared back at his employee, his lips twisting in a grim smile. "You're right, I did. I said ten thousand to kill him," he paused, his eyes drilling into Fagan Reilly. "You'll get the rest when I find out Mikhail Kozlof is dead."

* * * * *

Every surface in the hospital room was covered with greeting cards—from fans, judges, coaches and other skaters. A bouquet of brightly colored balloons swayed in the air currents at the head of Adam's bed, one with Bart Simpson's grinning face that read "Get Well Soon, Butthead." When Kerry stepped into the room, wearing her own smiley face, Adam was staring out the window at the snow-capped mountains. He wasn't aware of her presence yet, and wore a curiously vulnerable expression, one that reminded Kerry of a younger, less arrogant, Adam. It brought a pang to her heart. *Oh, Adam, why did things have to get so complicated between us?*

Kerry cleared her throat, and when Adam turned his head, she smiled brighter. "Hey."

Surprise flashed across his face, immediately followed by a sullen expression. "You didn't have to come. I'm surprised you bothered."

Kerry sighed. "Oh, Adam. Don't be like this. Of course I'm here. You're my friend. I care about you."

His jaw tightened, and he turned back to the window. "Yeah, right. You care about me." His voice was heavy with sarcasm. "So, did you bring your Russian lover along?"

She approached his bed, biting her lower lip. How could she get past his anger? It would be so easy to just tell him the truth—tell him there wasn't anything between her and Mikhail. But wouldn't that just give him false hope that there could ever be more than friendship between them?

She stopped at his bedside, staring at his handsome profile. He still looked like JFK, Jr. If only he'd work on his personality a little bit, he'd be a real prize for some lucky girl. A girl like Brandi.

"You're a fool, you know that, Adam?" she said. "You spend so much energy pining after me when there's a girl waiting on the sidelines just hoping and praying for something as simple as a smile from you."

He looked at her. "And who would that be?"

Kerry shook her head in amazement. "Men are *so* clueless." She stared at him. He really didn't know. God, Brandi was going to kill her for this, but tough. "Brandi came as soon as she heard the news. She was here all night while you were in surgery. And even when she knew you were okay, she wouldn't go back to the hotel. Catri had to force her to go back and rest. Adam, you idiot, Brandi

Vanderkleef has been in love with you since we were sixteen years old. And I don't see any sign of her ever getting over it."

Adam stared at her in utter shock. Damn, she'd been right when she called him clueless.

"Do what you want with the information," Kerry said. "But if you break her heart, Adam, so help me, I'll find a way to make you regret you were ever born."

Silence ticked by. Two high spots of color enflamed Adam's cheekbones. He glanced away from her, at a complete loss for words.

"So…where are your parents?" Kerry asked finally.

Adam shrugged, still not looking at her. "I think they went down to the cafeteria to get something to eat."

Kerry glanced at his left leg encased in a cast and suspended by pulleys attached to traction. Poor guy. Here he was laid up in the hospital, and she was berating him for not noticing a girl was in love with him. God, she was such a bitch! Why he was so crazy about her, she'd never be able to fathom.

She placed a hand on his arm. "Are you in much pain?"

He turned back to her, and gave another slight shrug. "They're keeping me well medicated."

"Do you remember anything about the accident?"

His black brows furrowed. "Just the lights of a car bearing down on me. I remember thinking about the competition. About how we wouldn't get a medal now."

Kerry nodded, trying not to allow her thoughts to show on her face. Poor Adam. Had he really believed they could medal? "I'm sorry, Adam."

He looked away, his throat working. *Oh, God, please don't cry. I can't deal with that.* But when he spoke, his voice was under control. "We could've done it, Kerry. I know we could've done it."

Kerry patted his arm. "Sure, we could've. Anything is possible." *Yeah, and Pam Andersen is a virgin.*

He looked at her, his eyes glimmering with hope. "Won't you reconsider, Kerry? Just four more years. One more try at the Olympics. You and me in Turin."

Kerry tried to remember that he was in traction in a hospital bed. It wouldn't be a good idea to grab him by the shoulders and shake him until his teeth rattled. Instead, she contented herself with a baleful glare and spoke between gritted teeth, "In 2006, I'll be thirty-two years old, and I can guaran-fucking-tee you that if I'm on an ice rink, it will be in the capacity of a coach...or a performer in the Ice Capades. And Adam, don't take this the wrong way...I love you...I really do. As a friend. But I don't care if every bone in your body is fractured. I don't care if you're hanging on by a thread. That doesn't give you the right to try and put pressure on me about my life and my choices. Don't ask me to reconsider again. I'm quitting. I won't change my mind. *Got* it?"

His jaw tightened mutinously. "Yeah, sure," he said. "I forgot. It's all about you, isn't it?"

An outraged cry of frustration burst from her throat. Her hands curled into claws, and it was all she could do to stop herself from jumping on him and strangling him until he yelled for mercy.

The door opened behind her, and Catri stuck her red head inside, her mouth stretched in a bright smile. "Oh, hi, Kerrelyn. How's our patient doing?"

Well, Catri, funny you should ask. He's nano-seconds away from being murdered. She gave her coach a bright smile, absolutely certain it looked as false as it felt. "Oh, he's getting back to normal, I'd say."

"Good." Her blue eyes moved to Adam who was still glowering at Kerry. "I have a little surprise for you, *milaya moya*." She opened the door wider, and a stream of skaters filed into the room.

Kerry grinned. They were from various countries, and they carried all sorts of things—cards and flowers and balloons, magazines and games, anything they thought would help Adam to pass the time in the hospital. Brandi was one of the first to enter, and she handed Adam a book about mountain climbing and a package of bakery-fresh chocolate chip cookies. Kerry watched Adam's expression as he accepted her gifts. Was it just wishful thinking that he seemed to be looking at the strawberry blonde differently than he had a few days before?

There was a tap at the door, and Kerry's heart jolted at the couple that entered. Mikhail and Tanya. A dignified silver-haired man and an attractive blue-eyed brunette—Adam's parents, followed them. Mikhail's eyes swept the room and found Kerry. She caught her breath at the question mirrored there. And for the first time since she'd heard of Adam's accident, she realized that now there really was no reason to wait. She'd already told Mikhail she'd help him—as crazy as that decision was. But now that she and Adam wouldn't be skating tomorrow night that meant...

If I'm going to do it, it has to be before the free dance. We'll be under constant watch after we win the medal.

Mikhail finally looked away, his gaze settling on Adam. Tanya smiled and approached the bed, holding out a festively wrapped package. "This is for you, Adam. From Russian skating team. Mikhail picked it out."

The Russian skating team, hmmm? Kerry thought. And where would be the queen of the Russian Skating Team? Her Royal Highness, Elena the Great?

"Thanks," Adam said tightly.

Kerry glanced at Adam's parents who were watching the proceedings. Adam's mother, Barbara, had a fixed smile on her pretty face while his congressman father, Oliver, stared, lock-jawed, at the Russians with barely concealed suspicion.

Like father, like son, Kerry thought.

Adam began unwrapping the box, moving gingerly as if fearful it contained a nuclear device or something equally lethal. He glanced up at the Russians before taking off the lid, his hesitation clearly obvious. At least, it was to Kerry. Again, she felt an overwhelming desire to shake some sense into him. Couldn't he, for once in his life, be cordial to citizens of a former Communist country?

Mikhail nodded, an ironic smile flickering about his lips. "Go ahead. Is not bomb."

Kerry held back a laugh at the startled look in Adam's eyes. He removed the lid and gazed into the box.

"Is brain teaser," Mikhail said. "I found at department store in Salt Lake."

Adam picked up the water-filled globe housing a tee and a golf ball, the objective of which, Kerry assumed, was to get the ball on the tee. He turned it over in his hands, examining it while his parents looked only slightly relieved that they hadn't been blown to smithereens.

"Is popular here in West, no?" Mikhail added.

Adam glanced at him warily. "Golf or *this* thing?"

Mikhail looked confused at his question. "Is hard, I think." His eyes flicked over the traction. "But you, no doubt, have plenty time to devote to game."

"No shit," Adam muttered darkly, glaring down at the globe.

Kerry rolled her eyes and moved closer to the bed, pasting a smile on her lips. "Uh...Adam? Don't you have something to say to Mikhail and Tanya for being so thoughtful?"

How old was he, anyway? Five? And why did *she* have to play mother when his *real* mother was standing right here in the room?

Adam had the grace to flush. "Yeah...thanks," he mumbled. "It's a cool gift," he added grudgingly.

Mikhail's eyes met Kerry's. He smiled, and she felt her heartbeat pick up. Talk about lethal, she thought. Mikhail's smile should be licensed as a dangerous weapon.

The skaters gathered around Adam's bed and chatted for a few minutes until finally, Barbara Cutter suggested that Adam needed his rest, and one by one, they began to leave the room. Tanya and Mikhail were the first to depart.

"Yeah, I've got to get going, too," Kerry said. "I'll stop in and see how you're doing tomorrow, Adam."

And to say goodbye, she thought.

Adam gave her a brief nod and turned to Brandi who still hovered at his bedside. In addition to the book and cookies, she'd brought him an Olympic teddy bear wearing skates and it was now propped up on the pillow next to him.

"You want to stay a while, Brandi?" he asked, and then looked at his parents. "Mom and Dad have to be going, right? Maybe you can hang around and keep me company."

Her freckled face blushed scarlet as her brown eyes widened in amazement, darting from Adam to his parents. "Me?" she asked in a small voice.

"Yeah, you," Adam said gruffly. "Anybody else here named Brandi?"

Kerry grinned. Maybe Adam's head wasn't as thick as she'd supposed.

"Yeah, sure," Brandi said, eyes glowing.

Kerry gave them a wave. "Later!"

* * * * *

"Say that again," Sean spoke into the phone between gritted teeth. "And slower this time. I know I must have heard you wrong."

Fagan's Dublin accent traveled over the telephone line, and the quaver in it had nothing to do with bad reception. "I said I hit the wrong guy." He waited for a response, and when he didn't get one, his tone raised a notch. "I'm sorry, Boss. I saw him go in, and then, it looked like the same guy coming out. I just assumed…"

"You…bloody…*fuck-up*!" Sean kept his voice low. He glanced towards the closed bathroom door. The sound of the shower told him Elena was still in there, soaping her luscious body.

He'd just enjoyed a taste of it minutes before, and his own body was still tingling from the climax she'd brought him to up against the shower wall. Now, though, at the news on the other end of the line, he felt the pleasure seeping out of him, replaced by an icy rage.

"Okay, so who did you hit?"

Fagan's rusty sigh came across the line. "Some American skater. Christ, I don't know his bloody name. But not to worry, he's not dead."

Sean grimaced. "Christ! That's great. Just great, Fagan. You can't even do that right. You left him alive so he can identify you? What are you, a flamin' idiot? Well, if they catch you, Fagan, you're on your own. Got that? I don't know you."

There was a moment's hesitation, and then Fagan said, "What do you want me to do about Kozlof?"

Sean shook his head in amazement. "Do I have to spell it out for you, you imbecile? I want you to take him out! I want Mikhail Kozlof *dead* before the free dance tomorrow night, you understand?"

Sean slammed down the phone. He'd been so involved in his conversation that he hadn't realized the shower had stopped. Elena stepped out of the bathroom, clad in a thick, white terry robe. Her eyes fastened on his face in overt curiosity. "What's wrong, Sean? You're all flushed."

He managed to summon a smile. "Not a thing, love. I'm flushed because I'm still hot for you."

"Who was that on the phone?"

"Just a business associate." He crossed the room to her. Gazing down into her eyes, he worked the knot from her robe and slipped his hands inside the opening to cup the firm globes of her breasts. "Just a little problem that's being taken care of as we speak. Mmmmmm…I want you again already. Why is it I can't get enough of you, girl?"

She smiled up at him, eyes sultry. Her hands crept around his neck, playing with the hair that curled at his nape. "Good thing I don't believe in the philosophy of abstaining from sex while in training." She licked her lips, her gaze on his.

His penis had turned to granite. "Good thing for me," he murmured. "I'd go bloody mad if I couldn't have you." His mouth captured hers in a brutal kiss. She gave back as good as she got, finally breaking away to catch a breath.

Her eyes danced with excitement. "Can you believe it, Sean? One more day. Tomorrow night, I'll be wearing that gold medal around my neck. That's all I'll wear, too. Just me and my gold medal."

Even that enticing image wasn't enough to stop him from stiffening with an unreasonable anger. His hands tightened on her shoulders, but he forced himself to smile down at her.

"You know what? Why don't we just put that gold medal on the backburner for now? I've got something else in mind to occupy your thoughts."

He swept her up in his arms and strode to the bedroom. Placing her on the rumpled sheets, he grinned down into her lust-clouded eyes.

There's no gold medal in your future, love, he thought. *You're just going to have to be happy with me.*

* * * * *

Kerry was walking past the fourth floor waiting room on the way to the elevators when she heard her name called out by a masculine Russian voice. Her heart began to beat a tattoo in her ribcage. She turned to see Mikhail getting up from a chair.

"I was waiting for you," he said. "Do you have moment to talk?"

Kerry took a deep breath, trying not to think about how gorgeous he looked in his red Norwegian sweater and black slacks. He was especially Nordic looking today. She could imagine him posing in a calendar of Norwegian sports stars, half-naked, and bronzed from the sun, his hair golden and wind-ruffled. Oh, God. That image was definitely a mistake. Now, she'd never be able to get it out of her mind. He was standing in front of her, fully clothed, and she had him undressed down to his Jockeys. Did Russians wear Jockeys? Or nothing at all?

Her face flamed. *Don't go there, dummy.* She gave a furtive glance around and stepped over to him. "Yeah, but not here. There might be too many skaters lurking around."

Mikhail nodded. "There is small park across street. You feel like taking walk?"

"Sure."

They were silent in the elevator as it descended to the lobby floor. Kerry was exquisitely aware of Mikhail standing next to her. He was so close, she could smell the intoxicating scent of his cologne, a mix of exotic Eastern spices and sandalwood. She remembered it from the other night when they'd skated together. It reminded her of faraway lands and romantic, moonlit nights under swaying palms.

"Tough break for Adam," he said finally as the elevator reached the ground floor. "I'm sorry you will not get chance to compete tomorrow night."

Kerry shrugged, stepping through the elevator door into the lobby of the hospital. "Yeah, it's a disappointment, but hey, that's life. I'm just glad Adam wasn't hurt worse than he was."

Mikhail followed behind as she headed for the front doors. "Did they catch driver who hit him?"

"Not that I know of. But when they do, I hope to hell they lock him up and throw away the freakin' key. What a slime ball."

Mikhail gave a short laugh. "You do not mince words, do you, Kerry Niles? I like that. You say what you think."

Kerry slanted him an amused look as they stepped outside into a sunny, but cold afternoon. "Yeah, and believe me, I get into a lot of trouble for it."

She tugged down the edges of her knit cap and pulled up the fake fur around her collar as she waited for the light to change to cross the street.

They didn't speak again until they reached the small park across from the hospital. Mikhail tucked his gloved hands into the pockets of his heavy tweed coat, and stared out at a frozen pond glittering in the sunlight a few yards away. He'd pulled on a traditional Russian fur hat as they'd left the hospital, and it had transformed him into a mysterious stranger, reminding Kerry that she really knew nothing about this man. Yet, she'd agreed to help him defect from his country. Was she out of her freakin' mind?

"I grew up skating on pond like that," he said suddenly, nodding his head toward the ice. "Nadya, my former coach, discovered me when I was six years old. I was doing figure eights on pond outside my home town of Tallinn." His eyes wore a faraway look as if he were picturing it in his mind. He gave a soft chuckle. "Oh, how Nadya frightened me the first time I met her. She came to my parents' flat to take me away to Moscow to train for competitive skating."

Kerry stared at him in surprise. "At *six*?"

He nodded. "In Russia, training starts early for talented athletes."

"But you were just a baby! She took you away from your home, your parents?"

He looked at her, a slight smile in his eyes. "Yes. That is not unusual in my country. It was frightening, I admit. But Nadya is good woman. She had no children of her own, and she treated me like a son." He sighed, gazing off at the pond again. "I still miss her."

Kerry's heart plunged. "I'm sorry. Did she...did you lose her recently?"

"Almost two years ago." He turned back to her, saw the look of sympathy in her eyes, and smiled. "No, she is alive and well. But when Elena became my partner, she was replaced by Elena's coach. Against my will, but..." He shrugged. "...orders from Russian Figure Skating Federation cannot be ignored."

"But I thought things were different now. Didn't you have any say in the matter?" Kerry asked.

He gave her a sardonic grin. "Name has changed, but athletes are still under thumb of government. When I first started skating, my goal was to become good enough to be accepted into the Central Red Army Club. *Cesska*, it was known by. Only the best athletes were accepted at *cesska*. For every Soviet skater you saw at world competitions, there were hundreds of others not so gifted, but who yearned to someday gain admittance to *cesska* so they, too, would become Soviet skating stars. It was first goal on journey of Olympic medal."

"And at what age did you make it in?" Kerry asked.

"Ten."

"Wow," she said softly, impressed. At ten, she was skiing black diamonds with her father, but had only skated a few times for fun.

They stood in silence for a few moments, Kerry on his right. She cast a quick glance at him, her eyes sweeping over the scar on his cheekbone.

She almost asked him how he'd gotten it, but just as she opened her mouth, he spoke again. "In light of what has happened to Adam..." He didn't look at her. "Perhaps is callous of me to say such thing, but..." He turned his head, and his eyes met hers. "Do you believe in fate, Kerry?"

She didn't answer, couldn't find her voice. And she couldn't look away from his mesmerizing blue eyes.

His voice lowered to a near whisper. "Our coach is arranging for special dinner for Russian skating team tonight. Everyone will get drunk, and most of them will party into morning hours. It will be perfect time to make my escape. I will have everything ready and out of my room. I will pretend to be drunk, and will stagger out to get taxi back to hotel. That will give me a good twelve hours before anyone will think to check on me. They will just think I'm in my room sleeping off vodka. Instead, if you help me, we can be on our way to Virginia." He paused, holding her gaze. A desperate light gleamed in his eyes. "You said you would help me, Kerry? Can we not move it up now?"

Kerry swallowed hard, and then took a deep, shuddering breath. "Okay," she said. It came out nearly inaudible. She blinked, and then tried again. "Okay, Mikhail." This time her voice rang out clear and confident. "Tonight. Tell me where you want me to pick you up."

CHAPTER SEVEN

Mikhail gazed out the window at the glowing skyline of downtown Salt Lake City, his stomach tight with a mixture of excitement and apprehension. He glanced over at Kerry at the wheel of her monstrous vehicle as they headed around the city on Interstate 84. He hadn't expected a vehicle of this size—a Jeep Cherokee she called it. The automobile somehow didn't fit the feminine beauty of the woman at the wheel, but then, he had a feeling there would be plenty more surprises from her before this was all over. The very first one had been that she'd actually agreed to help him. He still couldn't quite believe it, even though they were on their way out of the city.

"Take a last look at the Olympic flame," Kerry said. "It's probably the last one we'll ever see. Unless it's on TV. Well…me, anyway." She gave him a quick glance. "If you get asylum in America, you'll probably be able to skate for us in the next Olympics."

He shrugged and gazed out at the flame, feeling a deep sadness in his heart. "I will be thirty-three by then. That's quite old for competing in Olympics." He shook his head. "I believe there is no Olympic medal in my future."

"And how do you feel about that?" She looked at him.

He met her gaze. "How do *you* feel about it?"

She thought about it, and then gave an off-hand shrug. "C'est la vie."

He gazed at her for a long moment, trying to figure out if she was serious. Deciding she was, he said, "You are amazing woman, Kerry Niles. When I think of how Elena will react when she discovers I am gone…well…" He gave a mock shudder. "She will not be so complacent. She will go…" He struggled for the right English word.

"Ape-shit?" Kerry offered, her dimple flickering.

"Ape-shit?" He tested the word on his tongue, and then nodded. "Yes, that is good word."

She laughed and looked back at the road. Mikhail turned his head to catch one last glimpse at the Olympic flame glowing orange against the dark sky. *Would* this be the last Olympics in which he'd ever compete? He felt a stab of fear at the uncertainty of his future. Dear God, what if he was doing the wrong thing by defecting? Although he'd never thought of himself as Russian, preferring to acknowledge Estonia as his homeland, the fact was, he'd spent most of his life in Moscow. It had been a good life, one that ordinary Russian citizens would've felt blessed to have. Living in luxury and training for the Olympics. Now, his future was a question mark, and he'd be a fool not to be apprehensive about it.

Kerry glanced at him. "You okay?"

Christ, was she a mind reader, too? He shrugged and looked out the window at the last of the skyline sliding away. "I am thinking of what I am doing. What I have already done."

Kerry remained silent. The traffic was light on the freeway heading out of the city. The Olympics weren't even half over yet, and Salt Lake City was teeming with people. But the Games were over for him and Kerry.

The escape had been easier than he'd thought possible. Sergey Fadeyuska had reserved a private room at a Salt Lake City restaurant in an upscale hotel to entertain their athletes. Mikhail had immediately ordered one screwdriver from the free bar, and then switched to straight orange juice, pretending to grow inebriated with each one. At eleven, he'd said his goodnights and staggered into the lobby of the hotel, and out the front doors where a doorman hailed him a taxi. Mikhail saw Kerry's monster of a truck waiting at the curb, and when the doorman turned to help another departing couple, he'd slipped inside, and they were off.

Earlier that afternoon, they'd rendezvoused at a quaint bistro in the historic part of the city, and Mikhail had given Kerry his meager belongings—a change of clothing, a few toiletries, and of course, the valuable information Vassily Immaakin had compiled to convince the CIA he was telling the truth—and leaving everything else—his skates, his costumes, his luggage in the hotel room in Park City. It was done, and now…Mikhail looked out the window. The lights of Salt Lake City had disappeared.

"When will we reach state border?" he asked. "I will feel better when we leave Utah."

Kerry's front bumper practically kissed the car in front of her, causing Mikhail to cringe and press his foot onto an imaginary break pedal before she swerved into the left lane and passed the car as if it were parked. Did all Americans drive so crazy?

"Oh, an hour…hour and a half," she said, eyes fixed on the road.

He shifted uneasily and glanced over at her profile. She had the most charming nose—slightly tilted and somehow, mischievous. He'd earlier noticed that dimple flickering near the right corner of her mouth when she smiled or grimaced in a certain way. She wasn't smiling now, but looked rather thoughtful. Was she regretting her decision to help him already? His gaze drifted over her. She was dressed completely in black—black slacks, black turtleneck, black leather coat, even black cowboy boots. And why not? She was playing a spy game, wasn't she? Why not dress for the occasion? Her hair was loose around her shoulders, anchored by a black knit cap pulled low over her ears. All she needed was a pair of dark sunglasses and she'd look like she'd just stepped out of a James Patterson novel. It was endearing, really, except…

A fresh jolt of fear shot through him. Did she have any idea what she might be getting into? Had he made it clear to her about the danger, the possibility that somehow, Elena and her granite-faced bodyguard might know what he was up to, and would stop at nothing—even murder—to prevent him from reaching Washington and Roger Ellery? Because, of course, O'Malley had to be up to his eyeballs in this. Elena did nothing without him knowing about it.

"Is not too late to change your mind, Kerry," Mikhail said slowly. "We can turn around and go back. No one will ever know you were involved."

She looked at him. "Are you nuts? How do you think you can do this without me?"

He shrugged. "I will find way."

"Like *hell*!" She shook her head and sighed. "Look, Mikhail, you're just having what we Americans call a case of the jitters. It's too late to turn back now. I'm in. And I'm going to get you to Occoquan, Virginia, or die trying."

"*Do not say that*!" His voice came out in a harsh croak.

She gave him a strange look. "Hey, I was kidding. It's just an expression."

"An expression that could turn out to be apt, Kerry," he said, his voice softer, insistent. He had to make her realize this wasn't a game. "I try to make you understand that there are dangerous people who, if they discover what I am doing, will do anything to stop me. And because you are with me, your life will be in danger, as well. It does not matter that I have not told you details."

"I realize that, Mikhail. Really, I do. But you have to understand something about me, okay?" She glanced at him again, and then looked back at the road. "For the first time in my life I'm on my own...free. Do you know how good that feels?" She looked at him and grinned, making his heart turn over with the appearance of that sweet dimple. "And so are you. How does it feel, Mikhail? To feel so free?"

He stared at her, knowing he couldn't admit the truth, that he didn't feel free at all, that all he felt was fear and an unwelcome sense of isolation. Their eyes met and held for a moment. Mikhail was the first to look away.

He fixed his gaze on an air freshener in the shape of a cat hanging from her rear view mirror. It smelled like cinnamon, not cat. Thank God! He loathed cats. Ever since the day a young female skater brought a cat to the rink, and spooked by the noise of the skates scraping against the ice, it had jumped out of her arms, straight at nine-year-old Mikhail, practically taking his ear off, before slipping and sliding on the ice as it made its maddened escape. He'd hated—and had a phobia—about cats ever since.

"Perhaps when I have asylum I will feel free," he murmured, continuing the conversation.

"Of course you will." Kerry glanced at the illuminated clock on the dashboard. "We should be able to make Denver around first light."

"How do you know area so well?" Mikhail asked. "You are from California, yes?"

"Yeah, but I grew up in Utah with my dad and grandparents. I learned to drive here the summer I turned sixteen." She flashed an impish grin at him. "Grandma Vive said it took ten years off her life."

"I can't imagine why," Mikhail said dryly as she passed another car at such a rate of speed, it looked like it was stalled in the middle of the road. "I did not know I was getting mixed up with crazy driver."

She gave a saucy laugh. "I've had my share of speeding tickets. And of course, there's that little police record thing…"

He glanced at her, unable to hide his curiosity. "What made girl like you get mixed up with Canadian hockey player?"

She shrugged. "Oh, same old story. Impressionable young woman who gets involved with a good looking, but very bad boy. It's not very original, and would probably bore you to death."

Mikhail knew nothing would bore him if it came out of this fascinating woman's mouth. She was an enigma, an unusual combination of coltish girl and sensual woman. He wondered how badly the bad boy had hurt her. And if there had been other love affairs since. He wanted to ask her, but it would be rude to delve into her personal life on such short acquaintance. But he very much hoped that before they reached Washington—or Occoquan, as she insisted on calling it—he would have a chance to get to know her better.

"I would like to hear this story sometime," he said finally, breaking the silence that had fallen between them.

She chuckled. "Okay. Maybe later. But I warn you, Mikhail, once I start talking, you won't be able to shut me up. And you'll be sorry you ever asked."

He nodded, smiling. "I am warned. How long will it take us to get to Wash...I mean, Occoquan? What *is* this odd name, Auk Oh Quan?"

"It's a Dogue Indian name. Means "at the end of the water." It's the cutest little town. Sits right on the Occoquan River. I visited Roger and Sharon there after an exhibition skate at the MCI Center. Sharon took me to this fantastic craft show. They totally closed down the whole town, and blocked off the streets and..." She glanced over, and grinned. "Oh, sorry. I told you once I get started talking, I can't shut up. How long will it take us to get to there?" She shrugged. "Depends on the weather, and how hard we want to push it. Josh and I drove from California to New York that summer, and made it in three days. But he's a speed demon, so..." She gave another shrug.

He stared at her. "And you are not?"

"*No!*" she scoffed. "I just go with the flow of traffic. Seventy-five, eighty...whatever. Do you drive?"

He glanced at the dashboard and shrugged. "I have sports car at home. But this big truck I do not know."

"What kind of sports car? Is it a stick shift?"

He looked puzzled.

"A five-speed?" Kerry said. "You know, like this." She indicated the gearshift between them. "Or is it automatic?"

"It is Mercedes convertible. With shift like this." He shook his head and sighed. "I will miss that car."

"Oh, don't worry, Mikhail." She gave him a sympathetic smile. "Once you turn professional in America, you'll be able to afford several Mercedes. Although, personally, I'd go for a

Porsche. It's sexier. Anyway, since you can drive a stick, you'll have no problem handling Big Bertha here."

He looked at her, confused, and then realized she was talking about her car. Odd thing, naming a car. There was so much he had to learn about Americans and their customs.

"Why don't you try and get some sleep," Kerry said. "After we cross into Wyoming, you can drive for a while. How about a little music?" With her right hand, she pulled a CD from the holder on her sun visor. "You like **Nickelback**?"

He shrugged. "I have not heard such music."

"It's hard rock. You like rock?"

He grinned. "Oh, yes. I play guitar. Maybe I will be rock singer some day. It will be new career."

"No kidding?" Kerry glanced at him. "Yeah, you kind of got that rock star look going on. Maybe someday I can say I knew you when."

She popped in the **Nickelback** CD and tapped the "seek" button to track number two, then began to sing along with the vocalist in a decidedly off-key alto. Mikhail adjusted his seat back and closed his eyes. No way would he sleep. He was too tense. But perhaps he'd just close his eyes for a few minutes. Almost immediately, though, the hum of the tires on the road and the music on the CD player began to work its magic, pushing away his troubled thoughts.

This is nice, he realized, being here in a warm truck driving through the dark winter night. The woman sitting next to him was very much responsible for this momentary sense of well-being. Why he felt so comfortable with her, he didn't know. He liked the way she was so down-to-earth and real. She smelled good, too, like wildflowers and musk. *And listen to her!*

"This is how you remind me," she sang along with the rock group, totally unself-conscious, even though her voice was, to be charitable, more Lucille Ball than Madonna. But even her off-key notes, he found charming. Damn. This was not good. He was becoming entirely too attracted to Kerry Niles. That was a complication that neither one of them could afford right now…not if they wanted to keep their wits about them.

* * * * *

The phone shrilled out on the bedside table in the early morning darkness. Half asleep and cursing, Sean rolled over on his side to grab it before it woke Elena.

"Yeah?" he grunted.

"Fagan, here," said the voice on the other end.

Sean became immediately alert. His voice lowered. "Did you take care of it?"

"Uh…not exactly," came the mumbled reply.

Sean's hand tightened on the phone. *Fuck*! He glanced over at Elena. In the graying light of dawn, he could just make out the black satin mask covering her eyes, her lips parted in slumber. He released a frustrated sigh and found his voice.

"What happened?"

"He didn't come back to the room. I've been waitin' here all the fuckin' night. It's been bloody boring, too."

"I don't give a shit if you're bored out of your fucking mind." In his anger, Sean spoke louder than he intended, and Elena rolled over on her side, mumbling something unintelligible. He closed his eyes, forcing himself to calm down. Then he spoke between clenched teeth, "He left the restaurant just after eleven. Elena said he was sloshed to the bloody gills. And you're telling me he didn't come back to the hotel room?"

"That's what I'm telling ya." Fagan's reply was mildly sarcastic. "I was sitting here, dick in one hand and my Makarov in the other, waiting to send him to Kingdom Come, and the bastard didn't bloody show."

Asshole, thought Sean. Fagan was getting just a little too cocky for his britches. Soon, very soon, he was going to have to put that smelly sod back in his place.

"Hey, Boss," Fagan went on in a more conciliatory tone. Sean supposed his ominous silence had put the fear of God back into him. "Maybe if he was that lit, he got rolled by some enterprising dickhead, and he's floating in the Green River by now."

"You wouldn't be that lucky," Sean retorted. "No. He's probably found a woman, and is sleeping it off in her bed right now. Elena has been bitching that he's been sniffing after that hot American skater with the black hair." He ran a hand through his tangled hair, his brows furrowed in thought. "Look, stay there. He'll have to come back to his room sooner or later, and when he does…" He glanced over at Elena, still on her side facing away from him. "You know what to do."

"Boss, I'm tired and famished," Fagan whined. "If he's in some wee gel's bed, he won't be back for hours. Can I not go get me a wee bit of breakfast?"

"No!" Sean said harshly. "You heard me. Stay there, and take care of the job. Got it, Fagan?"

"Yeh, Boss." His reply was sulky.

Sean hung up the phone, shaking his head in disgust. Jesus Christ! Good help was getting bloody hard to find.

* * * * *

Kerry pulled the Jeep into the brightly-lit gas station and put the gearshift in park. A few errant snowflakes hit the windshield, melting on contact. So much for the good weather holding out. But hey, she was used to driving in snow. No problem-o.

She looked over at Mikhail and grinned. Hadn't he said he was way too wired to sleep? Obviously, he'd been wrong. She wondered if she should wake him up. She had to pee like a racehorse, and if she was going to keep driving for a while, she needed coffee. The cessation of the motor hadn't awakened Mikhail like she'd expected.

Her gaze swept over his face. Oh, how her fingers itched to stroke that strong, stubbled jaw, to run through his silky blond hair. She grimaced. *What was she thinking?* This must be what it felt to be a diabetic longing for a Hostess cupcake, and knowing it would be a huge mistake to sink your teeth into the sweet chocolate. Her gaze moved to his lips, and she remembered the passionate kiss the other night in front of Adam. He had taken her breath away with that kiss. A shiver of excitement zipped through her even now as she relived it.

Stop it, she told herself. That had been a game, a deception. They'd made it out of Utah; there was no reason now to pretend they were anything more than strangers. And it would be stupid—really *really* stupid—to act upon this attraction she felt, even though her intuition told her it was mutual. A woman knew when a guy was interested, and those vibes had been coming from Mikhail from the first moment they'd met. But nothing was going to happen between them. No way. Josh had taught her not to jump impetuously into a relationship. Not that it would *be* a relationship. If anything, it would be a one-night—maybe a two-night—stand. The skating world might have labeled her a "bad girl" but she wasn't into casual sex. And never had been.

She touched his shoulder. "Mikhail! We're at a gas station. I'm going to get some coffee. You want some?"

He opened his eyes. For a moment, he appeared disoriented, and then recognition dawned. His lips quirked mischievously. "Depends." His gaze moved lazily over her lips. "I like mine sweet."

Kerry's cheeks flamed as her heart turned over. She managed what she hoped was a casual smile. "Tanya warned me about you being a flirt. Now, behave yourself. Sugar *and* cream?"

"I will go as well." He opened his door and paused as a frigid wind blew into the Jeep along with a few stray flakes of snow. "I need to stretch legs."

Kerry eyed him as he stretched, not only his legs, but his arms, too. Sinuous as a cat, she thought, then shook her head and got out of the Jeep.

Fifteen minutes later, they were back on the interstate. Mikhail had offered to take over driving but Kerry, wired from the first few sips of coffee, had turned him down.

She glanced into the rearview mirror and wished she hadn't. "Oh, damn," she muttered.

Mikhail looked at her. "What?"

"We've got company." She put on her left turn signal and began to slow.

Mikhail's head whipped around. He muttered a word in Russian that Kerry recognized as an exceptionally foul profanity.

"Don't freak, Mikhail," she said calmly, pulling into the breakdown lane. "It's just the state police."

He looked at her as if she'd just announced she was going to sky-dive off the Washington Monument in pink tights. "They found us already. How did they know?"

The police car pulled up behind her, lights flashing. Kerry reached across the back seat for her purse. "Don't be silly, Mikhail. They're not after us. I might have been speeding."

His jaw dropped. "Might have been? Kerry, your speed has not dropped below eighty since we got on road." He muttered another Russian oath. "Great! Just great. What if I am recognized? What if---"

"Shhhhh!" Kerry hushed him, her eyes on the rearview mirror. "Here he comes. Just stay quiet, Mikhail. Pretend you're asleep."

A uniformed figure appeared at her window, and Kerry pushed the button to lower it. "Hi," she said brightly, giving the cop her most charming smile. "How you doing tonight, officer?"

CHAPTER EIGHT

Kerry gazed up at the granite face of the young Wyoming state policeman. Despite his business-like expression, he looked like he was about seventeen and should be dancing in a nightclub rather than patrolling the interstate in the middle of the night.

A gust of Arctic air blasted into the Jeep, and she shivered. "Cold night, huh?"

He nodded. "Yes, ma'am. Driver's license, please."

"Oh, I'm sorry. I should've had it out already." Kerry dug into her purse for her wallet. "Was I speeding? I was just driving along, singing with the stereo, and I totally didn't realize it if I was."

"Eighty-five in a seventy-five mile zone," he said, then cocked his head toward her. "Is that **Incubus**?"

She looked up and smiled. "Yeah! Aren't they great? This is their new CD, and it's great, but my favorite song is still 'Drive' from the 'Make Yourself' CD." The track that had been playing, "Warning," ended, and she used the break to her advantage. "Whatever tomorrow brings…" she sang out, loud and deliberately off-key. Beside her, Mikhail made a sound that sounded like a cross between a snort and a cough before it became a snore. Ignoring him, she sang a few more bars of the song.

The cop grinned, looking even younger than he had before. "Yeah, they *rock!*"

Kerry smiled, suddenly feeling very good about the situation. They were home free as long as she could keep this cutie's mind on rock music. "Have you heard this CD yet?"

He shook his head. "Nah. But I have 'Fungus Amongus.' It *totally* rocks!"

Dear God! Didn't the poor boy know any other verbs? She'd pulled out her driver's license, ready to hand it over. "Oh, that one *is* good! But wait'll you hear this one. It's *smokin'!*"

Still grinning, the cop glanced at her license. "From California, huh?"

"Uh huh." She smiled brightly.

The patrolman glanced over at Mikhail who had his eyes closed, his mouth open in feigned sleep. "That your husband?"

"No!" Kerry said quickly. "I mean...yeah..." The cop was looking at her suspiciously. "Well, not my *husband*. My...you know...boyfriend." His expression didn't change, and Kerry lowered her voice, casting a furtive glance at Mikhail. "I'm *working* on the marriage thing." Then she summoned her sweetest smile. "Can't you give me a break, officer? I promise I'll keep my speed down." She didn't actually bat her eyelashes at him, but gave him the most earnest look she could come up with. "Please?"

He stared at her a few seconds then gave a grudging nod. "Okay, I'll let you off with a warning this time, but you might want to wake up your boyfriend and let him take over for a while. And by the way, you might think about setting your cruise control." He began to scribble on his pad. "So, where you headed? Back to California?"

"Uh huh." The wind moaned, and another frigid blast of snow-laden air hit her in the face. She pretended not to notice, that the cop was so interesting even bone-clenching cold couldn't stop her from flirting. Her smile widened. "We just came from the Olympics."

Damn, she thought. That wasn't the brightest thing to say!

The cop frowned. "Then why are you in Wyoming? That's an odd way of heading to California from Utah."

Kerry felt her cheeks warm. *Damn!* She could practically feel the tension in Mikhail a few inches away. "Oh, we're heading to Denver to meet his parents before we go back to California. That's what I meant when I said I was *working* on marriage."

Apparently satisfied with her answer, the young cop tore off the slip of yellow paper and handed it to her. "I just don't get the Winter Olympics thing," he said. "Now, the *summer* Olympics are cool. That's where the real athletes are. Not those so-called winter sports. Like ice skating. What's the sport in that? Nothing but a bunch of pretty girls in short skirts and guys in leotards prancing around the ice."

Kerry somehow managed to keep a smile on her face, but she was pretty sure her eyes were shooting daggers. "Oh, yeah?"

He winked at her. "Yeah. You know why the male figure skaters are so light on their feet, don't you?"

"No, why?" Kerry said, knowing what was coming.

"Because they're all *fairies*," he said, and then guffawed.

Next to her, Kerry sensed the steam coming from Mikhail. They had to get out of here before he exploded. "Cute," she said through clenched teeth. They were starting to chatter from the cold. *Hurry up, hurry up, hurry up! You're a cute little bigot, but I'm freezing.*

Still laughing at his crude joke, the cop handed back her license. "Here you go, Ma'am. Remember what I said. Watch your speed. Those Colorado troopers won't be so forgiving."

"You got it," she said brightly. "Thank you, officer."

She pressed a button and her window slid up. She started the engine, and the Jeep lurched forward. Kerry accelerated and merged onto the interstate. She glanced in her rearview mirror as the police car disappeared behind them."Okay, Mikhail. You can wake up now."

Mikhail lifted his head and ran his fingers through his flaxen hair, rumpling it.

Kerry's heart dipped. Oh, God, he was so fine! How was she going to get through the next few days with him without throwing herself at him like a sex-starved nymphomaniac? It had been four years since she'd had an orgasm that wasn't self-initiated. *Stop it!* She frowned. *Think of something un-sexy. Think of...brussel sprouts.*

"Did you hear what that American son-of- bitch said?" Mikhail said, eyes sparking blue fire. "He called me a fairy! I would like to show him what a six and a half stone 'fairy' looks like."

Kerry gave him an amused look. "Remind me not to ever make you mad."

He raked a hand through his hair again and peered at her, the outraged look disappearing from his face. "You are quite smooth operator, Kerry Niles. Cool as cucumber, yes?"

Okay, think of cucumbers. Her cheeks grew heated. *No, not cucumbers, bananas, squash or any other phallic-shaped fruits or vegetables.*

"Where did you pick up that Americanism?" she asked.

He shrugged, looking out the front window. "I like American TV."

"Ah, so that explains it," she laughed.

He nodded, staring at the road. "Yes, you are cool as cucumber. But one thing, Kerry…"

"Yes?"

His amused eyes met hers. "Your singing…it *sucks*."

Kerry's mouth dropped open. He watched her, suppressed laughter in his eyes as he gauged her reaction. She burst out laughing, and he grinned and joined her.

"You are good sport, Kerry Niles. I like you."

Kerry smiled at him, even as her heart began to race. "You know what? I like you, too, Mikhail Kozlof. But I guess that's rather obvious, isn't it? A guy who talks me into dropping my entire life to help him defect…well, I guess he's got some major charisma going for him. Either that, or I need to have my head examined." She thought about that a moment, then added, "But let's not go there."

* * * * *

On the CD player, Stevie Nicks was singing about trouble in Shangri-La, and Kerry was happily accompanying her. It didn't bother her that Mikhail thought her singing sucked. She knew he was just kidding. After all, she *knew* she had a great voice. Hell, if she hadn't concentrated on a skating career for the last fourteen years, she could've given Stevie a run for her money. In fact, Stevie should be counting her lucky stars.

"'I hear there's trouble in Shangri-La…'" she bellowed the chorus, ignoring Mikhail's stare.

"Uh…Kerry," he cut in at the first break. "Have you, by chance, noticed it is snowing?"

Kerry glanced at the thick clumps of snow hitting the windshield. "Um…yeah. Since before we stopped at that gas station. What's your point?"

He looked at the speedometer. "And yet, you drive seventy kilometer per hour. Even though you cannot see very far in distance."

Kerry's lips quirked. "It's *miles* per hour here, not kilometers. And what are you, anyway? A backseat driver?"

He looked confused. "Back seat? I am not in back seat. I do not understand."

Kerry looked back at the road. "What I mean is…are *you* driving or am *I*?"

He had the grace to look embarrassed. "I am sorry. I did not mean to insult you. But when snow comes in Russia…and snow comes often there…I have found that *decreasing* speed is…what is word…prudent?"

Kerry shrugged and nodded. "Works for me."

"*Prudent* thing to do."

"Well, Mikhail, in ordinary circumstances I would agree with you. However, this particular snow isn't sticking to the pavement; therefore, there's no need to slow down. And like I said earlier, I like to keep up with the flow of traffic."

Mikhail looked at the empty road. "Is no traffic. And you almost got ticket."

"*Almost* is the key word." She shot him an amused look. "Is my driving scaring you, Mikhail?"

He folded his arms across his chest in denial and stared straight ahead. "I am not scared."

"Really? Come on, Mikhail. You can be honest with me. Do you think in addition to my singing, that my driving sucks, too?"

"I did not say that," he huffed. "I think simply you drive very fast."

"Yes, I do," she agreed. "And I'll have you know I've never been in an accident." She shrugged. "Just a few speeding tickets is all."

He gave her a look of mock astonishment. "No *shit*?"

She burst out laughing. His oh, so American terminology cloaked in a Russian accent struck her funny bone. "Just *a few* tickets. Hey!" Still grinning, she peered at the clock. "It's almost five. Be light soon. You hungry?"

"Famished. I was too…what is word? Too much nerves…to eat before we left." In fact, he hadn't been able to get more than a bite down at the sumptuous dinner hosted by Sergey Fadeyuska.

"Nervous," Kerry said. "Yeah, I was, too. Want to stop and get something to eat? That sign we just passed said there's a diner up ahead."

Mikhail's eyes lit up. "Diner! I know diners from American films. Yes, let us stop."

Kerry pursed her lips as a thought occurred to her. "You know what, though? Maybe you'd better let me order. Your Russian accent is a dead giveaway, and just in case your evil friends come after you, we might as well not advertise you were here, you know?"

He nodded. "Good thinking. I will be silent. But I want American cheeseburger and French fries."

Kerry gaped at him. "But it's breakfast. I don't know if they will…"

His jaw tightened. He folded his arms across his chest and gazed out at the snow pelting against the windshield. "American cheeseburger and French fries," he said emphatically.

Kerry sighed. "Okay. I'll see what I can do." She looked back at the road and rolled her eyes. High maintenance, she thought. The good-looking ones always were.

* * * * *

The diner, a throwback to the Fifties, appeared to be a renovated railroad car, barely wide enough for a counter and a row of booths lining the front windows. In all other ways, it was a typical roadside truck stop filled with hungry truck drivers and brisk waitresses with frizzy blond hair and slashes of red lipstick who called everyone "hon." The mouth-watering aroma of sizzling bacon hung in the air as a grizzled woman who looked like she'd seen too many early mornings led Kerry and Mikhail to one of the red vinyl booths. On the PA system, Clint Black sang about a gambling venture gone bad.

Kerry waited until the hostess moved away then looked across the Formica table at Mikhail. "If it's Americana you want, Mikhail, you got it here." She grinned. "I feel like we just stepped onto a 1950's movie set."

He glanced around, eyes dancing. *Like a schoolboy on his first field trip to a chocolate factory.* A shiver of pleasure ran through her. She was so glad she'd decided to do this, she realized. It was an adventure, and she had three, maybe four days (if she stretched it out) to enjoy Mikhail's company before turning him over to Roger once they reached Occoquan.

A plump blond waitress with dark roots and a name tag that read 'Sue' poured coffee into their cups, her eyes, alight with curiosity, fixed upon Mikhail. He caught her stare and looked up to smile uncertainly at her. She batted her false eyelashes and gave him what Kerry thought sure she intended to be a coquettish smile. Too bad it was ruined by a missing cusped.

"Hi, there, hon," she said in a thick Colorado drawl. "What can I getcha?"

Mikhail opened his mouth to speak, but then apparently remembered he was supposed to stay quiet. He peered at Kerry. The waitress kept her weary blue eyes on Mikhail.

Hello? Am I invisible? Kerry wanted to ask. She cleared her throat and waited. Finally, the waitress looked at her just as Martina McBride began belting out "Independence Day" on the PA.

Kerry gave her a sweet smile. "My friend has lost his voice. Um…would it be possible for him to get a hamburger and French fries?"

With a bat of her eyelashes and another syrupy smile at Mikhail, Sue the Waitress drawled, "No problem at all, darlin. Anything you want, Big Sue'll getcha."   With a flirtatious wink, she turned to leave.

"Uh…Big Sue?" Kerry called out. The waitress turned and looked at her, apparently startled that she was still sitting there. Kerry pasted on a smile. "I'd like French toast and bacon. Cooked crisp, please. Thank you."

Sue nodded, scribbled something on her pad and waddled off. Kerry shook her head and looked back at Mikhail who was watching her with an amused grin.

"I'm not sure I'm going to like hanging out with you," she said. "I have a feeling I'd better get used to being the Invisible Woman." She glanced around the crowded diner. "Would you look at this? *Everyone* is staring at you. That's not exactly what we need." Her eyes flicked over him, and she shook her head. "You know what it is? You're dressed like a European. That black sweater and tweedy coat. You stand out like a sore thumb."

Mikhail's brow wrinkled. "Sore thumb? How does one get sore thumb?"

Kerry grinned, stirring cream into her coffee. "Never mind. You know what we need to do before we get a room for the day? Or maybe later, after we get a few hours sleep."

"What?"

Kerry took a sip of her hot fragrant coffee and smiled. *Mmmm...wonderful.* Then she met Mikhail's questioning gaze. "We *seriously* need to go shopping."

* * * * *

Elena glanced at her wristwatch, a frown marring her lovely face. "It's almost four-thirty. Why haven't we heard from Mikhail?"

Sean sat at the desk in the living room of their suite, his fingers tapping a dance on the polished cherry wood. He'd been watching Elena pace up and down the room for the past half-hour. She was dressed in her warm-up clothes—red nylons pants and its matching zip-up jacket. Her skating costume for the evening's free dance competition was encased in plastic and draped across the back of a wingback chair. The bag containing her skates rested at the foot of the chair, ready to go. But with each passing minute, Elena was growing more anxious because no one had heard from Mikhail, and the car that was to take them to the arena was due to leave in fifteen minutes.

She whirled around, blue eyes frantic. "I'm going to try his room again. He must be there by now."

Sean grabbed the phone before she could. "I'll try." He dialed the hotel operator and gave her Mikhail's room number. The phone was picked up on the first ring, and Sean heard Fagan's voice. He kept his face blank, his eyes on Elena who was watching him with a hopeful expression.

"Boss, is that you?" Fagan inquired.

"Still no answer," Sean said to Elena.

"No luck, Boss," Fagan said. "Kozlof still hasn't shown up. What should I do?"

Sean kept his eyes on Elena. "I'll go down to the front desk and have them unlock his door. I hate to say this, love, but perhaps he's still sleeping off a hangover." He placed the phone in its cradle and stood.

Elena's brows lowered in fury. Her hands tightened into fists. "I'll *kill* him if that's true." She whirled away and began to stomp around the room. "How could he *do* this to me? He knew better than to get drunk last night."

"Everyone was drunk last night, Elena. Don't think I didn't hear about the two drinks you had. Despite doctor's orders." Sean hadn't been invited to the dinner party, but he'd spent the evening close by in the hotel bar.

Elena's face whitened. "Who told you that? Who is spying for you, Sean O'Malley? I won't have it, you hear me? I'm not your possession, and I won't have you running my life!"

"Things have a way of getting back to me, love. I am paid to watch over you, you know. And I've made it my business to make sure everyone knows you shouldn't be drinking."

"Well, *screw you!*" Elena snarled. "I won't be treated like a child!"

Sean stared at her stonily. "If you persist in acting like a child, you'll be treated like one. Excuse me." He opened the door of the suite and stepped out into the richly carpeted corridor.

As the elevator ascended to the eighth floor, he gazed thoughtfully at the numbers flashing on the panel above the doors. Where the fuck was Kozlof? Could Fagan possibly be right? Had some unfortunate accident happened to him after he'd left the hotel last night? For a moment, his mind entertained the image of Kozlof's robbed and bloodied body floating facedown in the Green River. But somehow, that just seemed too good to be true. Life never worked out like that. There was always some pissing complication that you were never quite prepared for.

He stopped in front of Room 818, glanced up and down the empty hall, and then tapped. The door opened immediately, and Fagan's rabbit-like face peered out at him. With a brusque nod, Sean slipped into the room and closed the door behind him.

"Still no word from him?" he asked, knowing as he spoke what a preposterous question it was.

"Not a flippin' peep." Fagan rubbed his eyes wearily. "And I've just about had it, Boss. Can't keep me bleedin' eyes open."

Sean ignored his whining, his eyes sweeping the immaculate room. "Christ! Where the hell is he?"

The king-sized bed was neatly made, the dresser spotless, the ice bucket and glasses untouched. "Has the maid been in today?"

Fagan slumped into a chair by the window, rubbing his forehead. "She stopped by this morning, and I told her to go away. I thought about putting the 'do not disturb' sign out, but figured Kozlof might think it a wee bit odd if he came back and saw it."

Sean shook his head in amazement. "You figured that out all by yourself, genius?" He strode over to the bathroom and peered in. The counter was clean except for the complimentary shampoos, lotions and soaps displayed in a small wicker basket. Odd. No personal toiletries anywhere. No shaving stuff, no deodorant, not so much as a toothbrush in sight.

His stomach started to churn. This hotel room had been Kozlof's home for the past three weeks, and would be so for another two. Where were all his personal items?

Sean whirled around and strode back into the bedroom suite, his jaw set. Fagan was still sitting as he was before, his hand cradling his forehead, eyes drooped in exhaustion. Sean flung open the closet door, his gaze raking the contents.

Kozlof's skating costumes hung on the rack, covered in plastic. A couple of canvas bags, presumably containing his skates, were on the floor next to a pair of Reebok sneakers and some dress loafers. There were also a couple of pairs of dress slacks and shirts hanging next to the costumes.

"Fuck," Sean muttered.

He moved to the dresser, aware that Fagan had looked up at his profanity, and was now watching him with a mild curiosity. Sean flung open the drawers and saw...nothing. No underwear, no sweaters...nothing but a Bible and a Yellow Pages phone book.

His teeth clenched. "*Son of a fucking bitch*!" He whipped around, skewering a suddenly white-faced Fagan with his gaze. "You...goddamned...*moron*! Didn't it occur to you to check the closets and bathrooms to see if his things were still here? The fucker is gone!"

Fagan seemed to shrink in his chair. "Well, how was I supposed to know that, Boss?" he whined. "I did what you told me! What...what...more could I do?"

"Shut the fuck up!" Sean snarled. "And just get out of here. If I have to look at your ugly mug another second, I swear to God above, I'm going to rip it off and stuff it up your knucklehead ass."

Fagan scrambled up from the chair and made a beeline for the door, still mumbling apologies. After it slammed behind him, Sean took a deep breath and tried to calm himself.

What was done was done. He didn't know what the hell Kozlof was up to, but he had a very bad feeling he wasn't going to like it. For the first time, he seriously considered the possibility that Kozlof knew something about TNG, and the dirty little secret of Kalevalo. If so, what did he intend to do with the information?

Jesus, he should've followed his instincts and had the man killed before they'd ever left Russia. But no, he'd allowed Elena, and her fanatic desire for a gold medal to influence him. He wouldn't make that mistake again. Once he found Mikhail Kozlof, he was as good as dead.

Sean moved back to the closet, his gaze sweeping the interior again to see if there was something he'd missed. He slipped his hands inside the pockets of the two pairs of slacks and found nothing. He squatted in front of the shoes, picked them up and glanced under them. Just as he was about to get up, he saw it. A small rectangular card on the carpet at the back of the closet. He picked it up and turned it over. A name and phone number was printed on it. His heart thumped as he recognized the Tallinn exchange. The name was one he wasn't familiar with. Vassily Immaakin, Solicitor. Why, he wondered, would Mikhail Kozlof, whose life was pretty much run by the skating federation, have need of an attorney in Tallinn?

He stood and tucked the card into the pocket of his slacks. Well, that was something he'd just have to find out. And he knew someone in Tallinn, a very dedicated individual with a talent for collecting all kinds of information, who would be happy to help him out for the right amount.

With a grim smile, Sean went to the desk, picked up the phone and dialed the international operator. "I want to make a call to Tallinn, Estonia, please. Thank you. I'll wait."

CHAPTER NINE

"So! This is Wal-Mart." Mikhail grinned as they walked through the automatic doors of the discount store. "When I was in Colorado Springs, I saw TV advertisements for Wal-Mart. *So* many things for sale."

Kerry nodded and brushed the snow off her parka. "Oh, yeah. You name it, they got it."

It had been snowing fiercely when they awoke a couple of hours ago. After breakfast in the diner, they'd driven for another two hours until full light, and then booked a room with two double beds in a Motel 6 outside a small town in northern Colorado. At that time, it had been snowing lightly, but in the seven hours they'd slept, more than six inches had fallen, and it was still coming down. They'd been in luck, though, because there had been a Wal-Mart just across the highway from the motel. After showering, they'd trudged over to outfit Mikhail in American clothes.

"This way, Mikhail." Kerry unerringly made her way to the men's department. *One thing about Wal-Mart; if you can find your way around one of them, you can find your way around all of them.*

Kerry looked through racks of clothing while Mikhail stood by, silently watching. "Try this." She handed him a couple of T-shirts and a sweatshirt. "What size jeans do you wear?"

He shrugged. "I do not know American sizes."

"Hmmm." Kerry looked him up and down, and for the first time since she'd met him, she had the perfect excuse to look her fill. So why not enjoy it? Even so, she felt her cheeks grow warm. Maybe it had something to do with that devilish glint in his eyes. Like he knew what she was thinking.

"Why don't we try a couple of different sizes? Here, take these." She placed a pile of jeans in his arms. "What else? You'll need a parka. Your coat screams out Moscow. Why don't you go try those on and I'll see what else I can find."

"Uh…Kerry?" Mikhail stood stiffly, his arms full of clothes. "Remember, I told you I have only rubles. How do we pay?"

"We'll work it out later," Kerry said, trolling through the racks for more possibilities. "But you're right. We need to find a bank so we can exchange your money. Now, go try on that stuff."

Mikhail headed toward the dressing room, but paused at a rack of NFL sweatshirts. "Ah, Denver Broncos!" A delighted grin spread across his face. "I watch Denver Broncos play on TV in Colorado. John Elway, yes? He looks like big Viking. You think this sweatshirt is good?" He held out the orange Denver Bronco sweatshirt, his face hopeful like a little boy's on Christmas morning.

Kerry smiled. "Yes, Mikhail. That sweatshirt would be perfect for you. But I think John has long retired. "

Grinning, Mikhail grabbed the sweatshirt and headed toward the dressing room. While he changed, Kerry looked through the coats. A few minutes later, she heard a throat clearing behind her. "Kerry, how do I look?"

She turned, and her eyes widened. "*Wow*! Mikhail! You look so…American!"

And he did. He was dressed in snug jeans and the Denver Bronco sweatshirt. His own hiking boots worked perfectly with the outfit.

Her eyes narrowed. "There's just one thing missing." Her gaze swept the men's department and stopped on a rack of baseball caps. Grinning, she strode over to it. "I don't see any Bronco caps, but what about this one?" She grabbed a cap emblazoned with the "Survivor" motif, and settled it on Mikhail's blond head, turning the bill backward the way the kids wore it. "There. Now, you *really* look like an American."

"Let me see." Mikhail took off the cap and peered at it. He frowned. "I do not like this 'Survivor.' Players are vicious bastards." He looked over the rows of caps, and then grinned. "This one." He handed Kerry the 'Survivor' cap and grabbed another one. "Yes. I like this one."

Kerry looked at it and burst out laughing. "Homer Simpson? How old are you? *Nine?*"

"I will be thirty this August." Unconcerned by her ridicule, Mikhail placed the cap on his head. "And I like Simpsons. Where is mirror?"

Still laughing, Kerry led him to a mirror. He adjusted the cap on his head and grinned. "Yes, this is good. *Now* I look like American."

"Okay, you win. Why don't you go change back into your clothes while I get a cart for this stuff? Then we'll find you a parka. Oh, and some sweatpants. You can't look like an American without lots of sweatpants."

He nodded and headed back to the dressing room. Still grinning, Kerry strode toward the front of the store to grab a cart. But when she returned to the men's department, Mikhail was nowhere in sight. She waited for a few minutes outside the dressing room, and finally stuck her head in.

"Mikhail? You still in there?"

No answer. *Hmmm. Where has he gone?* Kerry pushed the empty cart through the store, her eyes sweeping the aisles for the missing Russian. Humming along with Avril Lavigne playing on the PA, Kerry passed the cosmetics aisle, and caught a glimpse of a big blond guy. She stopped and backed up. When she realized what Mikhail was doing, she wondered why it had taken her so long to find him. The smell alone should've led her right to his side. He saw her and smiled, his eyes lighting up. "Kerry! Come. You tell me if you like this scent?"

Kerry rolled her eyes. "I don't need to come closer to smell it. What have you done? Taken a bath in it?"

He moved to her. "So many different scents. You decide which I buy." He bent down, exposing his neck to her. "This one?"

Kerry caught her breath. She didn't know if the dizziness she felt was because of his closeness or the overwhelming stench of half dozen different colognes. He turned his head and invited her to sniff at the right side. "Or this one."

She flinched away from him. "*Ugh!* That one reeks. Get the first one. Definitely. But it sure smells like you've got more than two on."

He grinned and held out an exposed forearm. "This…I think is Hugo, and this…" He thrust his other forearm under her nose. "…is Old Spice."

Her heart twinged as her father's familiar scent washed over her, bringing back happy memories from her childhood. He'd been wearing Old Spice on that last sunny morning at the lodge just before he'd taken the lift up to ski the backcountry and couloirs of Whistler Mountain. Kerry had planned to go with him, but her changing body had foiled that plan, and ended up saving her life. Earlier that morning she'd awakened on bloody sheets, her stomach cramping worse than on that one unfortunate Christmas Eve when she'd eaten a dozen of Grandma Vive's Finnish butter cookies, and ended up sick through Christmas.

She'd never seen her father alive again. Later that day, he'd died in an avalanche, and Kerry was catapulted into adulthood in more ways than one. A month later, she was living with a stranger in San Diego, torn from her paternal grandparents as cleanly as a surgeon removed a diseased organ from a patient.

"So…?" Mikhail said, interrupting her dark thoughts. "This one, you say?"

Kerry focused on him, and brushed her fingers over the left side of his neck, trying to ignore the tingle she felt at the contact. "I like this one the best."

"Cool Water," Mikhail said, nodding with satisfaction. "Yes, I like this best, as well." He reached for an unopened package, and then gave her a questioning look. "Is okay?"

Kerry smiled. "Sure. I'm keeping a tab for you. Now, what did you do with the clothes you tried on?"

"Here." He turned to a shelf behind them and gathered up the clothing, dumping the whole lot into the cart. "Now what?"

"Your parka. Let's go see what they have."

He nodded, but as they headed back in the direction of the men's department, Mikhail stopped dead in his tracks when he spied the toy section. "Kerry, look! Toys." Like an excited schoolboy, he headed down one of the aisles. Kerry shook her head, grinning. Maybe he *was* nine. She turned the cart and followed him.

He stood at a shelf, staring intently at a bright pink plastic pony with a long mane of silky hair and silver sparkles on its rump. Kerry's smile widened. "Don't tell me? In addition to The Simpson's, you also have a thing for My Little Ponies?"

He glanced at her, one eyebrow raised. "*Your* little ponies?"

"No, silly! That's what they're called. I didn't even know they still *made* them. They were really popular when I used to baby-sit for our neighbor's little girl. She must've had a dozen of them." She shook her head. "I just didn't get it. When I was a kid, I preferred playing with guns and toy soldiers."

"Ah. Tommy boy, no?" he asked with a big smile.

"Tomboy, you mean." She gave a slight shrug. "I suppose so. My father was a real outdoorsman, and my being a girl didn't stop him from including me in the things he enjoyed."

Mikhail brought the My Little Pony to his nose and sniffed. His brow wrinkled in surprise. "Is *perfumed*?"

Kerry laughed. "You probably smell yourself. But yeah, I think it is. Wouldn't surprise me." She was having a blast watching him. He really was like a young boy on Christmas morning. How different he seemed now than the way he had that first time she'd watched him warming up before hitting the ice. He'd been so serious, so aloof. Now, he was anything but. Was she getting a glimpse of the real Mikhail Kozlof? If so, she couldn't wait to learn more.

Mikhail put down the pony and turned to the other side of the aisle. He picked up a globe similar to the one he'd bought Adam. "This might pass time for car trip," he said, and then looked up at her, an amused light in his eyes. "You think Adam likes his?"

Kerry nodded. "He'd probably never admit it, but I'm sure he does. Adam is…complex."

He watched her, tossing the cube back and forth in his hands. "He is in love with you, I think."

Startled, Kerry's eyes met his. "How did you know that?"

He shrugged, but didn't answer.

"Well, he *was* in love with me, but I think he's getting over it. I hope he is."

"And you are not in love with him?"

Her cheeks grew hot. "I'm not in love with anybody. Haven't been for a long time. So, you want to go look at those coats now?" When she saw the reluctance on his face, she added, "Go and ahead and buy it. Like you said, it'll help pass the time during the drive."

He flashed a delighted grin. "Yes! Good idea." He tossed the globe into the cart on top of the clothes.

After deciding on a parka and a few pairs of sweatpants, they found the snack aisle and Kerry began selecting munchies for the trip. "I've been craving chocolate lately. You like Ding Dongs, Mikhail?"

He gazed curiously at the box she held out for his inspection. "I do not know. What is this Ding Dongs?"

"Chocolate cakes with cream filling. Yummy!" She dropped the box into the cart and reached for a can of peanuts. "Okay, that should do it. Oh, let's get some sodas, and maybe we should pick up a little cooler so we can keep them cold for the trip."

Fifteen minutes later, bags in hand, they stepped out of the Wal-Mart into the swirling snow. Kerry looked up at the quarter-sized flakes falling around them and took in a deep breath of the cleansing Colorado air.

"Whoa!" She grinned at Mikhail. "It's really coming down."

Mikhail nodded, smiling. "Looks like Russia."

"Yeah, I'll bet." Kerry glanced over at him. "You know what, Mikhail?"

"What?"

Swinging her bag from her fingers, she hopped across an icy spot on the pavement, and her grin widened. "I think we might have to spend the night right here in our little Motel 6."

* * * * *

Elena practically attacked Sean when he walked into their room. "Well, is he there? What did you find out?"

Sean stared at her, wondering how to break the news. He knew he was experiencing the last moment of relative peace that he would have for God knows how long because the shit was just about ready to hit the bloody fan.

Earlier, he'd been imagining how he'd break the news about Kozlof's unfortunate murder at the hands of a burglar he'd surprised ransacking his room. That, he'd been savoring, imagining how he'd hold a hysterical Elena in his arms, kissing her moist forehead, stroking the golden strands of her hair. Of course, he didn't kid himself that her grief would be at Kozlof's death, but more importantly, at the death of her dream of Olympic gold. Oh, sure, on some level, she'd be sorry he was dead, but Elena was a selfish woman. Sean wasn't blind to that, despite his love for her. Elena's first concern was herself, and always would be.

Looking at her now, at her wide blue eyes and the hopeful expression on her cover-model face, Sean was experiencing the moment right before the tornado touched down—that eerie, electrically charged moment of stillness just before all hell broke loose.

He sighed. Might as well get it over with. He just hoped he'd survive the coming storm. "Kozlof is gone," he said quietly. Her eyes gazed back at him without comprehension. It was as if he'd spoken in an alien language.

"His personal items are missing," he went on when she didn't respond. "His toiletries, sweaters, underwear. They're not in his room."

He watched her face as the message sank in. Her eyes darkened with horror, and a muscle flexed in her jaw. The color ebbed from her face, leaving it a pale porcelain hue. Her hands tightened into fists at her side. And still, she didn't speak.

Sean held her gaze, and said evenly, "My guess is…he has defected."

Elena's face twisted into a grimace of rage as she sunk to her knees on the carpet. Her mouth opened, and a blood-curdling shriek erupted from her lungs. Sean just stood rigid, knowing there was nothing to do but let her scream.

CHAPTER TEN

"Here's the situation, love."

Sean sat on the edge of the bed next to a pale-faced Elena. She lay on her back, the black satin mask hooked securely over her eyes, her full, seductive mouth nearly bloodless.

She'd calmed down a lot since the previous day, once she'd shrieked her fury, thrown a couple of lamps and ripped her skating costumes to ribbons with a pair of cuticle scissors. But then, the team doctor had prescribed a sedative, so that accounted for her momentary calm. Sean had decided it would be a good time to bring her up to speed on what he'd discovered from his contact in Estonia.

Immaakin had been easy to find. He had a law office right in downtown Tallinn. Getting information out of him, though, had been more difficult than anticipated. But in the end, he'd talked. Niko always got them to talk.

"Kozlof has defected," Sean said, stroking Elena's arm. "He has come across information about the TNG formula, and is trying to make his way to Virginia to deliver it to the CIA."

Elena moved her hand, and her nails bit into the skin of his arm. "How could he do this to me?" she said, her voice ragged with anger. "How could he?"

Sean gave a grim smile, knowing she couldn't see his face. In a perverse way, he was enjoying this. And was about to enjoy it even more.

"He has an American girl with him. The ice dancer, Kerry Niles."

Elena bolted up in the bed, and in the same motion, ripped her mask off. Her red-tinged eyes glared at him, wild and enraged like a rabid animal's. "He is with that woman?" she hissed.

"It would seem so," Sean said coolly. "Do not worry, love. They won't get far. I have a couple of men hunting them down. I can guarantee you they won't make it to Virginia."

Elena's nails bit into his arms. "I don't care what you do to that little bitch, but you bring Mikhail Kozlof to me. You understand? You bring him to me *untouched*. I will deal with him, and when I do, he's going to *wish* you killed him."

She flopped back on the bed, and tugged the mask over her eyes again. Sean stepped out into the living room, a satisfied smirk on his face.

Yes, perhaps things were working out for the best. Elena hated Kozlof now, and anyone who knew Elena knew how lethal her hatred could be. He'd do as she asked. He'd bring Kozlof back and let her take care of him.

It might be very entertaining to see exactly how she'd do it.

* * * * *

Kerry stepped out of the bathroom in her warm fleece robe, a towel wrapped around her head. "Okay. Shower's free." She stopped dead in her tracks when she saw Mikhail standing at the window of the motel room, staring out at the falling snow. He was shirtless, wearing only a pair of the jersey sweatpants they'd bought yesterday. She sucked in an admiring breath. The man had an absolutely gorgeous back.

He turned around, and her breath left her body like a balloon releasing its air. *Oh, Lord, save me*, she thought at the sight of his magnificent chest, washboard abs and flat tummy. Could a man *look* better than this? It was obvious from his rippling muscles that he worked out. Of course, being an ice dancer, he *had* to work out. Had to take ballet, too. That accounted for the almost feline way he moved. But even so, she hadn't expected his bare chest and belly to be so…so…*scrumptious!* And this was after eating half that box of Ding Dongs last night. Oh, and it was just the kind of chest she liked, too—not too much hair, just enough to be manly. It was golden-brown, trailing down to a "V" below the waist of his sweatpants. Yes, indeedy, this was a sight for sore eyes…as Grandma Vive often said.

Kerry saw the amused light in his eyes and realized she was staring. She quickly looked away. "Still snowing?" she asked, rubbing the towel vigorously through her wet locks.

"Like a mother," Mikhail said.

Kerry laughed. "You sure pick up on Americanisms fast."

He grinned. "I am quick learner."

He'd learned this latest Americanism from her as they'd walked back from Wal-Mart. And it was still "snowing like a mother" she saw, glancing out the window. Perhaps they'd have to spend another night here. The thought warmed her. It had been fun last night. After a dinner of hearty beef stew at the small restaurant down the road, they'd returned to the motel room, got into their comfortable sweats and watched TV all night, snacking on Ding Dongs for dessert. Mikhail hadn't been kidding when he'd said he loved American TV. He'd laughed his butt off at "Friends" and then later got absorbed in "CSI."

"I will shower now," Mikhail said. "And then we go eat breakfast, yes?"

Kerry glanced at the box of Ding Dongs on the table, and raised an eyebrow. "One Ding Dong left. It seems to me like you've already *had* breakfast."

He shrugged and gave a lopsided smile. "There is something about winter air and snow that gives me big appetite."

"Well, you eat many more of those Ding Dongs, and you're going to lose that nice trim figure of yours."

"Ha!" He scoffed, and pounded his abs with his fists. "I am hard as rock, see?"

"Yeah, I see." Boy, did she ever! "Right now, you are. But I still think after we eat breakfast, we should go walk off some calories. I'll go crazy if we have to sit here in this room and watch TV all day. Once I get you hooked on the soaps, forget it. I'll never get you out of here."

His eyes lit up. "Ah, yes. I have not seen 'Days of Our Lives' since Colorado Springs. Do you know what time it shows?"

Kerry rolled her eyes and chuckled. "Get in the shower, Mikhail! And make it fast. I'm starving."

He headed for the bathroom, and Kerry reached for the last Ding Dong. Might as well go ahead and eat it. If not, the Walking Russian Sweettooth would scarf it down. They'd have to make another pit stop at Wal-Mart and restock. Maybe they'd go for the Ho Ho's this time, or how about those yummy Snowballs covered with marshmallow and pink coconut—or green since St. Patrick's Day would be coming up soon. God, it was so good to be able to eat whatever she wanted without being worried about fitting into a slinky skating dress. Of course, she'd have to be careful not to go overboard. She was pretty sure Mikhail wouldn't be attracted to her if she turned into a moose.

Not that she *wanted* him to be attracted to her, she reminded herself as she unwrapped the Ding Dong.

"*Aha!*"

She jumped and looked around. Mikhail stood at the bathroom door, wrapped only in a towel. Her face flamed at the sight. But of course, he thought she was blushing because she'd been caught unwrapping the Ding Dong.

"I knew I could not leave you alone with last Ding Dong," he said, an eyebrow quirked in jest.

Kerry glanced down at the cake, and finished unwrapping it. "Yeah, you caught me red-handed." She took an enthusiastic bite. "So, what's my punishment?"

He gave her a slow, sexy grin, and she almost choked on the cake. Oh, God. This man was doing things to her libido that she'd never imagined could be done. Maybe a good roll in the snow would help cool her off. With an effort, she turned away from him, and sat down at the small desk, reaching for the newspaper they'd picked up the afternoon before. She took another bite of the Ding Dong, her eyes studiously fixed upon the sports page. Not a word about Mikhail so far. Thank God.

Holding the ends of the towel in one hand, Mikhail crossed over to the dresser and grabbed a plastic bottle. "My new shampoo." He gave her a smile and a wink, and then headed back to the bathroom.

Kerry watched the door close, and then released a breath she hadn't even known she'd been holding. Then she shook her head. "There should be a law about looking like that in a towel," she muttered. She popped the last bite of chocolate cake in her mouth, closed her eyes and chewed slowly.

Chocolate was a *great* substitute for sex.

* * * * *

After breakfast, they trudged through the snow back toward the motel. Kerry estimated that another foot had fallen since last evening, and so far, there had been no sign of any snow equipment clearing the interstate. A few four-wheel drive vehicles had trundled by, so realistically, they could probably get on the road tonight. But…

But she didn't want to.

Why risk driving on snow-packed roads? Would it matter if they delayed here another day? After all, it wasn't as if they had a schedule to keep. Roger had no idea they were coming. What difference would it make if they arrived in Occoquan three days from now? Or even a week from now?

The truth was, she didn't want this time with Mikhail to end. Not yet.

Beside her, he glanced up at the gray sky, blinking to avoid a dive-bombing snowflake. "Still snowing," he said unnecessarily.

But Kerry understood what he meant. "Yeah. It would probably be a good idea if we just stayed put another night." She held her breath, half expecting a protest.

"I like Colorado," he said, turning to smile at her. "Perhaps I make this my new home."

Kerry grinned back as the wind tossed her hair wildly about her head. Her heart suddenly felt lighter. Yes, they would stay another night. Wait until this snowstorm blew itself out, and then head for Virginia. God, it was so beautiful here! She'd never really noticed the wild beauty of this state before. And with the snow, it looked like a scene from a Currier & Ives Christmas card. She glanced around, her eyes lingering on a smooth hill behind the motel, a gentle slope of land covered in drifts of snow like swirling mounds of whipped cream. It was the perfect hill. Just like the one on Grandma and Grandpa's farm where Dad had often taken her sledding.

She stopped in her tracks, a grin spreading across her face. "Mikhail!" She grabbed the sleeve of his parka. "We've got to go back to Wal-Mart. I just figured out what we could do to pass the time."

* * * * *

Fagan sat across the table from a burly Russian with cropped brown hair and a flat nose that looked like it had been broken once too often with a crowbar. He was looking at the menu with incomprehensive brown eyes, and Fagan wondered why he bothered. He could barely speak English. No way could he *read* it.

"Don't worry, mate," Fagan said. "I'll order for us both."

With a shrug, Boris Shlusvaka put down the menu and glanced out the window at the falling snow. Fagan followed his glance.

"Yeh, it's coming down to beat the band, isn't it, now? The road will be impassable soon. Probably be a good idea to find a place to hunker down for a wee bit. Kozlof and the girl won't be getting far in this."

Boris's stone-cold eyes fixed upon him, showing no emotion whatsoever. He didn't speak, but all the same, Fagan picked up on his thoughts, and it was all he could do to control a shudder that wanted to snake up his back.

Fine. Let's hunker down a wee bit, and if the Russian gets away, Boss will have your Irish ass in a sling.

"Christ!" Fagan went on, as if the Russian had said those words aloud. "We couldn't see the bloody road! Why risk our necks? Oh, here comes the waitress." He reached into his coat pocket and drew out two photos, then grinned up at the blowsy blonde in the hot pink uniform. "Hello, me love. How you doing this fine snowy mornin?"

The waitress barely cracked a smile as she waited, pencil poised over a notepad. "I've been better, mister. The durned truck wouldn't start because of the cold, and I had to get a ride from the cook. Should've just stayed home in bed." She glanced out the window with a worried frown. "Probably be here all night now. The way it's coming down. What can I getcha?"

Fagan grinned up at her. She was just the type of woman he liked—blonde, buxom and with some generous meat on her bones. "Well, now, we'll both have the Farmer's Delight breakfast and coffee…the stronger, the better."

The waitress—Sue was the name on her tag—looked over at Boris, and her thick lips twisted in something resembling a grin. "Cat got yer tongue, mister?"

Fagan saw she was missing a tooth, but he supposed that was a fair trade for those beautiful titties thrusting out against the nylon bodice of her uniform.

"Laryngitis," Fagan said.

Sue nodded. "Must be going around. Okay, two Breakfast Delights and coffee. Coming right up."

"Oh! Miss Sue?" Fagan said as she turned to go. "Would you…by any chance…have seen this couple in the last twenty-four hours?"

Sue took the photos of Kozlof and the American girl, Kerry Niles, and peered at them. She nodded and handed them back. "Yep. They was in here before daylight yesterday morning. I remember him, for sure. He's a doll baby. And I'm pretty sure she's the girl he was with. You friends of theirs?"

Fagan nodded and slipped the photos back into his pocket. "Yeh, you could say that. Did they happen to mention where they were headed?"

She shook her dyed-blond head. "Nah. He didn't speak at all." Her eyes slid over to Boris. "Matter of fact, he had the same problem your friend here has. Laryngitis. That's why I said it's going around."

She turned to go again.

"One more thing, love," Fagan called out, and Sue paused. "When did it start getting bad like this? I mean, bad enough to make the roads dangerous?"

She shrugged. "Yesterday afternoon, I guess. Just the four-wheel-drives are getting through."

Fagan's eyes followed Sue's ample figure as she moved back toward the kitchen. He turned to Boris. "Boss said Niles is driving a Jeep Cherokee. It could probably get through some bloody bad stuff. But then…"

Boris watched him, his face expressionless, but Fagan was sure he understood every word.

"My guess is after driving all night, they needed to stop and hole up at a motel off the interstate. And with this blizzard, they'll probably stay put for some time. So, here's what I propose to do…"

Sue appeared at the table with a pot of coffee. Fagan grinned up at her, and then waited until she'd moved on before he finished his sentence. "Let's check into the motel next door, and get a few hours sleep, then as soon as the snow lightens up, we'll head on down the interstate. I'm betting we'll find 'em before dark tonight."

Boris didn't respond. His eyes stayed fixed upon Fagan, and very deliberately, he clenched his beefy hands together and popped his knuckles with a resounding crunch.

Fagan decided to take that as a "yes."

* * * * *

Kerry shrieked, grasping the handles of the plastic sled for dear life as she careened down the hill toward a clump of scrub pine trees. To her right, out of the corner of her eye, she saw Mikhail on another sled, and he was just as much out of control. The hill that had looked so gentle just a short time ago, had definitely taken on a new character once they'd plopped themselves onto the cheap plastic sleds they'd bought at Wal-Mart and pushed off from the top. In fact, Kerry thought, her eyes widening as the pines grew larger through the falling snow, this may not have been the greatest idea she'd ever had. Because…

Her hands tightened on the handles. Oh, Lord! Was that a creek down below, just visible through a break in the trees? Oh, shit. It sure was. And it was getting very, very close. "*Mikhhaaaaaaillllll!*" she screamed, "*The creeeeekkkkkk!*" She closed her eyes and braced for impact with the icy water, praying it wasn't deep. But just then the sled hit a bump, jolting her off. She went flying, landing on the snow on her left side and rolling. She squeezed her eyes closed, expecting to feel frigid water surrounding her at any second. But when she rolled to a stop, she realized she was still on solid ground. Then she heard a panicked shout.

"*Watch ouuuuutttt!*"

A hard body slammed into her, and then they were both rolling down the hill toward the creek. Kerry grabbed Mikhail's parka. His blue eyes stared into hers, wild with laughter mixed with mild panic. Her voice joined his in a whooping shout as they slid toward the creek, so close Kerry could hear the trickle of water. She closed her eyes, holding onto Mikhail as if he were a piece of driftwood in the ocean. If she was going in, damn it, so was he.

But no. Something stopped their progress. Mikhail let out a soft "oomph," and slowly, Kerry opened her eyes. They had slid into a bramble of bushes, laden with snow—the last barrier before the creek. Grasping the nylon of his new parka, Kerry stared into his startled eyes.

He held her in a clumsy embrace, their legs tangled. The thought of what they must look like struck her, and she began to laugh so hard tears blurred her vision. Mikhail grinned. Suddenly a dollop of snow thundered down from the bush that had stopped their slide, landing full on Mikhail's face. Kerry laughed harder. Oh, God! Why hadn't she taken the time to pee before coming out here? Would she never *learn*? Grinning, Mikhail grabbed a handful of snow and shoved it into her face.

"Hey!" she sputtered as the slush slid down her neck. "No fair! I didn't do that to you! The bush did."

"No. But you laugh."

"Because it was hilarious! Come on, help me up."

Mikhail untangled himself from her, and got to his feet. He reached down, grabbed her arms and pulled her up. Kerry looked around and saw they were less than a foot from the creek.

"Oh, that was close. Good thing that bush stopped us, or we'd be hating life right now." She looked up at Mikhail and grinned. "Want to do it again?"

"You are crazy girl," he said, eyes twinkling. He grabbed the collar of her parka and pulled her closer. Before she could take a breath, his mouth covered hers in a warm, searching kiss that jolted her senses. But just as she was starting to enjoy it way too much, he released her so abruptly she almost stumbled. "There. That will teach you lesson." He turned to retrieve his sled, and headed back up the hill.

Kerry stared after him, her gloved fingers touching her tingling lips. "Lessons like that, I could get used to," she muttered.

Mikhail glanced back at her, grinning. "One more time," he called over his shoulder. "Race you."

* * * * *

Okay, this was not working out the way he'd planned, Mikhail thought as he gazed at Kerry over a steaming mug of hot chocolate—one that he really hadn't needed or wanted. Enough heat had been generated between them during the afternoon of sledding that filling their bellies with hot liquid had been totally unnecessary. Mikhail had suggested going over to the restaurant for hot drinks simply to delay returning to the room. Because he knew that once he had Kerry alone in there, it would be almost impossible not to strip off her wet, snow-covered clothes and warm up every inch of her long-limbed body with his tongue.

What insanity had made him kiss her out there by the creek? He took a sip of hot chocolate, his gaze sweeping over her winter-pinked face, her sparkling eyes that looked greener than blue right now, her straight black hair, slightly tangled from the wind. Even with her pert, freckled nose reddened by the cold, she was adorable. And if this table wasn't between them, he'd kiss her again, by God. Just because he couldn't get the taste of her sweet lips out of his mind.

This is crazy, his conscience told him. You can't seduce this American girl, and then leave her a few days down the road. You'll never see her again. It wouldn't be right. But since when had that mattered to him? There had been plenty of other women. Plenty of one-night-stands. Why did this feel different?

She was attracted to him. He'd seen the way she'd looked at him this morning when he'd stood in front of her, clad only in a towel. And what would be wrong with sharing a few nights of love? She wasn't an innocent teenager, and neither was he.

Still, it felt wrong. Making love to her would feel too much like he was using her. Better to keep things on a friendship level. A loaded silence had fallen between them, a silence charged with sexual electricity. It was time to find a safe topic of conversation.

"So, you said earlier you've trained for biathlon," Mikhail said. "What made you change to figure skating?"

Kerry shrugged and took a sip of hot chocolate. "I lost interest after my father died. It just wasn't the same without him. I still cross-country ski occasionally and I can still shoot pretty damn good, but...I don't know. I just couldn't see myself doing biathlon training without Dad to cheer me on. So, I got into skating instead."

"I know what is like to lose parents. My mother and stepfather both died in December," Mikhail said, gazing out the window at the falling snow. His face was etched with pain.

Kerry caught her breath. "I'm so sorry, Mikhail." Then she added, "It's hard, isn't it?"

He nodded, and swallowed. It took him a moment to find his voice. "You still miss father, yes?"

Kerry nodded. "Yeah. It's been sixteen years, and even now, every time I go downhill skiing, I feel like he should be there on the slopes with me. It still hurts that he's not."

"I understand. Is not easy to get over loss of parent. What about your mother? She is still alive, yes?"

"Oh, yeah." Kerry gave a short laugh. "She'll be around forever. She's too mean to die."

"You do not have close relationship?"

"That's putting it mildly." She stared down at the checked tablecloth, tracing its pattern with a forefinger. "Let's just say things are pretty rocky between us. She hasn't been an ideal mother. But to be fair, I'm not a big prize as a daughter, either. I guess I haven't given her much of a chance to be a good mother."

"How so?" He gazed at her intently.

Kerry sighed. "I didn't want to move to California with her after my father died. And I was a real pain in the ass about it. I even ran away once, made it back to my grandparents in Utah by hitchhiking. Jana brought me back, kicking and screaming. I tried to sabotage her romance with my stepfather, but he saw through it." She shook her head and gave a rueful smile. "I guess he really loves her. They've been married now about fourteen years. Anyway, she finally decided I was more trouble than I was worth, and she packed me off to Lake Arrowhead to live with the Petenka's. It's the best thing she ever did for me. They essentially became my parents until I was grown."

A waitress came by and placed the check on the table. Mikhail waited until she'd gone before asking, "And you never see your mother?"

"Hardly ever." Kerry shrugged. "She calls up once in a blue moon and says something about us getting together. I say, 'yeah, okay,' and then blow her off." He supposed he couldn't hide the shocked look in his eyes because she added quickly, "She doesn't really want to see me, Mikhail. She just calls out of a sense of obligation. Birthdays, holidays, you know. I'm just another chore on her long list of things to do." She frowned and glanced out the window at the falling snow. It wasn't coming down as heavily as before. Was the storm finally moving out? "That's okay. I don't need her. I got along just fine without a mother for the first twelve years of my life. I certainly don't need one now."

"What happened with parents?" Mikhail asked. "They were divorced?"

Kerry nodded. "From what I understand, their marriage was a horrible mistake from the very beginning. They met at the 1972 Olympics in Japan. Dad was a biathlon, and Jana, a figure skater. It was one of those lust-at-first-sight things, I guess. But they thought it was love. They got married in secret, and Jana moved to Utah with Dad. She hated it up there, though. See, she grew up in southern California, and she just couldn't adapt to life up there in the north. Well…that was Grandma Vive's take on it, anyway. If you ask me, Jana was a pampered little California girl who was bored to tears by life outside of L.A. Grandma didn't come out and say so, but she was horrified when she found out Jana was pregnant with me. I think she would've aborted me if she'd had half a chance. Instead, she stayed with Dad just long enough to give birth, then she packed up and went back to California, leaving me to be raised by my father and grandparents."

Kerry blinked quickly, embarrassed to find she was close to tears. She stared down at the chocolate remnants in her mug, feeling the heat warming her cheeks. "That would've been fine if Dad hadn't died in that avalanche when I was twelve. I had a wonderful life up there. I had everything I needed…and then Jana came and took it all away from me."

She looked up and defiantly met Mikhail's sympathetic eyes. "She thought after twelve years of neglect, she could suddenly start being a mother to me. Well, I didn't need her then, and I certainly don't need her now."

Mikhail stared at her thoughtfully. "Perhaps not. But do you think *she* might need a daughter?"

Kerry's lips parted in astonishment at his bluntness. Finally, she found her voice, "Jana needs a daughter like she needs another diamond tennis bracelet. Look, Mikhail, you probably had a great relationship with your mother. I know you're still grieving for her. But all mothers aren't the same. Just because one gives birth, doesn't automatically infuse her with maternal feelings. Trust me. Jana could care less about me. The only reason she stays in touch with me at all is to put on this appropriate facade for the outside world. I still don't know why she insisted on taking me away from my grandparents, but one thing is for certain. She wishes she'd never laid eyes on me. And the feeling is mutual." Her jaw tight, Kerry unzipped the front pocket of her parka and pulled out three dollar bills. She placed them on top of the check and looked at Mikhail. "You ready to head back to the motel?"

CHAPTER ELEVEN

"I have upset you." Mikhail stood in the motel room, his hands tucked in the pockets of his sweat pants. He'd just stepped out of the bathroom after showering, and although he was dressed in his Bronco sweatshirt and jeans, his hair was still wet and combed back from his sculptured Nordic face.

Kerry could barely make him out, even though he was only a few feet away. She sat on the middle of her bed, her arms hugging her knees, eyes fixed on the TV screen glimmering in the shadowy room. Her hair, still damp from the shower, hung loose and tucked behind her ears. She wore soft cotton pajamas—a V-neck top and drawstring bottoms ordered from an L.L. Bean catalog years ago. It was the most comfortable article of clothing she owned, and if she never had to put on anything else in her life she'd be perfectly happy. But clothes would be required later for their hike down to the restaurant for dinner.

Too bad there isn't pizza delivery out here. But even if there was, what were the chances they'd deliver in the middle of a snowstorm? Although...last time she'd looked, it had almost stopped snowing. In fact, they probably should go ahead and get on the road tonight. For a moment, she considered suggesting it, but somehow, she just couldn't wrap her tongue around the words.

"I'm not upset," she said now to Mikhail, looking at the TV instead of at him.

She'd got caught up in some woman-in-jeopardy movie on the Lifetime Channel while Mikhail was in the shower. She was pretty sure she'd seen it before, or one very similar.

Mikhail skirted his bed and sat on the edge of it. Kerry felt his eyes on her and turned to look at him. Her pulse gave a kick at the solemn look on his face. "What's wrong?"

"I was thinking about our talk at restaurant. About losing parents." His voice softened. "I never knew my father. Not my real father. He was Sami. Do you know of them? The indigenous people of the North? They are sometimes called Laplanders, but I do not think that is…what is word? Politically correct?"

Kerry nodded. "We read about them in school. They live in the northern section of Scandinavia, right?"

"And in Russia. Two months ago, I did not know I was of Sami blood. It was only upon my mother's death that I learned truth. That she loved another man before the one I thought of as my father."

Kerry gazed at him, now just a shadow in the darkness. "But you had a happy childhood, right? He treated you well?"

Mikhail shrugged. "I did not know him well, since I was taken away from my home so young. For the years I lived with my parents, Stefan was decent man, but he did not know how to show love." He paused, and then added, "If I ever have children, they will *know* they are loved."

Kerry caught her breath at the intensity in his voice. A wave of compassion shot through her. She thought of what it must've been like for him, taken away from the only home he knew at the tender age of six. Poor kid must've been scared to death. "But your mother. She showed her love, didn't she?"

"Yes. And so did Nadya, my coach. She became like second mother." He paused, and when he spoke again, his voice had thickened with emotion. "I lost them both. Once I became Elena's partner, I rarely saw Nadya. And now...who knows if I ever see her again." He stared off into space, eyes bleak.

He's homesick, Kerry thought, feeling a pang go through her. "Oh, Mikhail!"

Without thinking about the consequences, she scrambled off the bed and moved over to sit next to him. In the flickering light of the TV, she could see the sadness on his face, and it broke her heart. There had been so many losses for him lately. His parents, Nadya...his homeland. She lifted a hand to his cheek, feeling the hard ridge of his scar under the pads of her fingertips. How many times had she imagined touching him like this? Freshly showered, he smelled like deodorant soap mixed with the musky oak moss scent of the Cool Water cologne he'd bought.

"You still grieve for your father," Mikhail said softly, turning to her. "Does it ever end? The grieving?"

She cupped his jaw in her hand, tears burning behind her eyelids as she thought of her father's laughing face. "No," she whispered, shaking her head. "It gets easier as time passes, but I don't think you ever stop missing them. Sometimes..." She dropped her hand to her lap as her voice broke. She swallowed convulsively and lowered her head. He placed an arm around her shoulders, drawing her close to him, his chin anchoring on top of her head. "...sometimes," she went on. "I wish it had been Jana who died instead of my dad. Isn't that awful? Doesn't that make me a horrible person? But every time I get out on the ice, and I'm standing there waiting for the music to begin, the same thought goes through my mind. Why can't *he* be in the audience? He would've been so proud to see me skate in the Olympics." A tear trailed down her cheek. "Jana has never seen me skate live. I don't know if she even watches on TV. But you know what? I don't care. I just don't *care*!"

Mikhail leaned away from her, and the next thing she knew, he had her face cupped in his hands, his eyes holding hers. "We are very much alike, Kerry Niles," he said. "We both grieve for lost parents. Even those not of our blood. You have lost two fathers. I have lost two mothers...and two fathers." His thumbs caressed her tear-stained cheeks, sending an inexplicable feeling of longing through her. Her heartbeat accelerated at the soft expression on his face. "But you still have a mother," he added. "Perhaps is not too late to start new relationship with her."

Kerry didn't want to think about Jana right now. She *couldn't* think about her. Her gaze swept over Mikhail's handsome face, lingering on his molded lips, remembering their taste during that blissful moment out by the creek. She knew he wanted to kiss her again. He was weighing the decision right now. All she had to do was give him some sign that she wanted it, too.

Her gaze moved to his scar. Like a magnet, it drew her fingers. She traced it lightly, and saw his eyes darken with desire. But still, he didn't move. Just watched her. Her tongue moistened her bottom lip. "How did you get this?"

His thumb moved slowly over her cheekbone in a tender caress. "Skate blade," he murmured. "I was sixteen, training for pairs. My partner came too close during camel spin."

Kerry's gaze moved from his scar to his eyes. What she saw there caused her to catch her breath. Her heart began to race. "We shouldn't be doing this, should we?" she whispered.

He shook his head, and when he spoke, his voice was husky with longing, "No. Is not good idea."

But neither of them moved. Her finger brushed the ridge of his scar again and then moved down his bristled jaw. Mikhail's hands smoothed her hair back from her temples. Then, cradling her head, he leaned toward her, his lips inches away from hers.

She caught her breath. "We should probably go ahead and leave," she murmured. "It's stopped snowing."

"Yes," he whispered, a smile in his eyes. "That would be wise thing to do."

"If we leave now…" she said breathlessly, "…we could be in St. Louis for breakfast."

"Yes."

His mouth closed over hers in a hot, demanding kiss. Kerry clutched the folds of his sweatshirt in one hand as she opened to him, drinking in the sweetness of his lips. He broke away long enough for each of them to take a gasping breath, then took her mouth again in an increasingly hungry series of slow, burning kisses. Her head swam. Her heart felt as if it were exploding in her rib cage. Under her palm, she could feel his thudding heartbeat. On the TV, a woman screamed and men shouted. There was the sound of gunfire. *Too bad, whoever you are. You're getting shot at, and I'm kissing a hunk. And oh, my, can this hunk kiss.*

Mikhail eased her back onto the bed, his mouth still plundering hers. His hand moved down her neck, teasing at the vee of her top, awakening every nerve, every blood vessel along its trail. Finally, with one last soulful kiss, he dragged his mouth from hers and moved to the hollow of her throat, nibbling and tasting. Kerry gasped, lacing her fingers through his damp hair. She closed her eyes, giving herself up to his touch.

"I have wanted to do this since I first saw you," he murmured, lifting his lips from her neck momentarily. Then he returned to planting kisses along the column of her throat before finally reaching her mouth again, his tongue slipping inside to coax her enthusiastic response.

This is crazy, she thought, eagerly returning his kiss. This is exactly what I've been telling myself I can't do. Get romantically involved with a charismatic Russian on the run. It would just complicate things. It would just...

Still kissing her, his hand moved to the first snap of her top. With a soft pop, it came undone, then the second one. Then the third. He slipped a warm hand inside her top, cupping her bare breast. Her blood went from simmer to boiling. She gave a soft moan, her nails clutching convulsively at his back. In response, his kiss deepened, became urgent. He rolled onto his back, pulling her on top of him, one hand holding her head to maintain contact with her mouth. She could feel the heat of his erection pressing into her belly, and she knew common sense had lost the battle. *Damn celibacy!* She dragged her mouth from his, and straddling him, straightened so she could gaze down into his eyes. He stared back, his breathing labored.

"Let's get this shirt off you," she said finally, her hands going to the bottom of his sweatshirt. She helped him pull it off, and then tossed it to the floor. Flattening her hands on his muscled chest, she skimmed down his flat stomach then moved back up to his nipples. He drew in a staggered breath, watching her. Smiling, she bent down and laved the hollow of his throat with her tongue. Oh, yes. This was all coming back to her. A ragged moan splintered his lips.

She drew back and gave him a wicked grin. "I've wanted to do that since I first saw you."

With a soft growl, his upper half came off the bed, his hands reaching for the opening of her top. With one brisk snap, he wrenched it open, revealing her breasts to his appreciative gaze. "What do they say?" he asked with a delighted grin. "Turn about is fair play?"

Before she could answer, he laughed and rolled her onto her back again. Straddling her, he molded his large hands to her breasts, his eyes dancing. "I am going to drive you crazy, Kerry Niles. I will make love to you all night long. I will make you come over and over."

Kerry gave him a lazy smile, her tongue wetting her bottom lip. "Sounds like a deal I'd be an idiot to pass up."

Twin flames ignited in his eyes as he fastened his gaze on her mouth. "You do know that little trick drives me over edge, yes? You do that on purpose? To drive men wild?"

"Not men," Kerry whispered. "You, Mikhail. To drive *you* wild." Her gaze held his as she pressed her hand against his rigid penis, hot and thick beneath his sweatpants. "Come on, Mikhail. It's your turn. Drive *me* wild."

Fastening his hands at the sides of her head, his mouth took hers in a plunging kiss. With a moan, she arched against him, the aching need between her legs intensifying. His mouth still locked on hers, he moved his hand down to her pajama bottoms, tugging at the drawstring. Kerry pushed at his sweatpants. She wanted to stroke him, to feel the naked power and pulse of him in her hands.

Suddenly his body tensed. He dragged his mouth from hers and stared down at her, alarm flaring in his eyes.

"What?" Kerry asked, her voice ragged. "What's wrong, Mikhail?"

Regret flickered across his face. He rolled off her and sat up, raking his hands through his hair. "We cannot do this."

Oh, hell. **Now,** *he decides we can't do this.* Every cell in her body shrieked in frustration. It was as if she'd been handed a three-pound box of See's Chocolates and told she was forbidden to taste, but could only look and smell.

She rolled over on her side, propped her head on her hand, and eyed him. "Well, let me just say your timing sucks."

He lifted his head and gave her a chagrined look. "Sorry. But..." He shrugged. "I just remembered. I have no protection." An eyebrow rose in question. "Do you?"

"Uh...no." Kerry flopped onto her back and stared up at the ceiling. Her heart was still thudding with excitement, her limbs weak. "Condoms weren't on my shopping list. And I haven't been on the Pill for four years." Not since Josh. But she didn't intend to share the particulars. "I'm shocked *you* don't have any, considering the rumors I've heard about you being such a womanizer."

Mikhail winced. "Rumors greatly exaggerated."

Silence fell between them. Kerry stared up at the ceiling. *Why is it all motel ceilings look alike?* she wondered. *That cheesy-looking stucco stuff and a smoke detector blinking its little green light every few seconds. Damn it, Mikhail Kozlof, you've got my body so wired, I feel like my blood could produce enough energy to light up the entire city of Manhattan. And you had to go and remember you don't have any condoms.*

She gnawed at her bottom lip. Hell, there was virtually no chance she could get pregnant. She'd just had her period the week before. But then, of course, pregnancy wasn't the only thing they had to worry about. There was, oh, just a little thing like...death from AIDs. She supposed she really *should* be grateful to Mikhail for keeping a clear head...although

155

that wasn't exactly a compliment to her seductiveness, was it?

Mikhail lifted his head and stared at the TV. Kerry frowned. Okkkaaay. *So we'll forgo the sex and watch a little TV instead. Hey, what about HBO? We can <u>watch</u> people having sex. Oh, happy day!*

Mikhail was still gazing glassily at the TV, his brows furrowed. Then he grinned. "I just remembered." He turned to her, his eyes sweeping over her face and down to her opened top.

Kerry had never been a particularly shy person, and was certainly comfortable with nudity. She felt Mikhail's gaze on her exposed breasts, but didn't bother to cover up. After all, a few minutes ago, he'd had his hands all over them. No point in playing the shy schoolgirl now.

But apparently, Mikhail felt differently. His lips tightened, and he sat up, reached over and covered her up. Then, methodically, he began to re-snap her top. "You make it hard to think," he said shortly.

Kerry grinned, and rolling over on her side, she allowed her gaze to wander down to his bulging erection. "That's not the *only* thing I made hard, apparently."

Mikhail's lips quirked, and she couldn't tell for sure but she thought he might be blushing. "Kerry Niles," he said slowly, in mock astonishment, "You *are* bad girl."

"I know. I am what I am. So, what is it you remembered?"

He nodded, excitement flaring in his eyes. "Yes! Remember when you checked into motel? I went down hall to use men's room. I think I saw sex machine in there."

Sex machine? Her heart bumped. "You mean a condom machine?" She *hoped* that was what he was talking about. A friggin' *candy* machine just wouldn't cut it right now.

He nodded, and scrambled off the bed, grabbing his sweatshirt from the floor. His head disappeared, and then reappeared through the hole, his hair tousled. "Do not move. I will be right back. Oh!" He stopped and looked at her, hesitation written on his face. "Can I borrow dollar?" he asked. "Remember, we still have not found bank to exchange rubles."

Kerry couldn't help it. She laughed. It just struck her so funny. The horny Russian, desperate for condoms, and with only rubles to buy them. Still snorting with laughter, she moved off the bed and grabbed her purse from the desk, drawing a couple of singles from her wallet. She handed the money to him, giving him a big grin to go with it. "Consider it my contribution to the cause."

He took the bill, placed a hand on the back of her head and gave her a hot, succulent kiss that immediately sent her head spinning. "I will be back."

Kerry's fingertips brushed her burning lips as she watched him race to the door. "Oh, I'm counting on that."

* * * * *

Mikhail hurried through the side entrance of the motel office and down the hall to the men's restroom. From the desk around the corner, he could hear the motel clerk gabbing to someone about the snowy weather. It was the same man who'd checked them in—a long-winded old guy with a shock of white hair. Poor Kerry had stood there for fifteen minutes with the key in her hand, while the garrulous owner talked her ear off about the Olympics and why, in his opinion, the Americans hadn't brought in as many gold medals as they should have. Mikhail hoped whoever it was out front would keep the old guy talking because he sure didn't want to get waylaid by him now. Not with Kerry waiting for him back in the room.

He deposited the money into the vending machine, his heart thudding at the thought of her flushed, sexy face, her beautiful blue-green eyes cloudy with desire. A small voice inside him reminded him that sleeping with her would be a mistake. The double-pack condoms dropped into the tray, and he mentally ordered the voice to be silent. Pocketing the package, he stepped out of the restroom and turned left to head for the exit door.

That's when he heard it. Another male voice coming from the lobby around the corner. Mikhail stopped, listening, and a chill crawled over his skin.

"Have you seen this man? He may be traveling with this young woman."

The accent was unmistakably Irish.

* * * * *

As soon as Mikhail left the room, Kerry hurried into the bathroom and began to brush her teeth with more energy than she'd had in months. After swishing some minty-tasting mouthwash for a few seconds, she grabbed her travel bag and dabbed a few drops of Michael Kors perfume onto her pulse points, then gazed into the mirror. She grabbed a brush and began to run it through her now dry hair, smiling at the flush on her cheekbones and the bright excitement in her eyes. It had been a long time since she'd felt like this. Since she'd *allowed* herself to feel like this. So *what* if it was a mistake? It probably was, but right now, she didn't care. She'd worry about it tomorrow. Right now, she couldn't wait to be back in Mikhail's strong, sexy arms.

A knock came at the door. Kerry put down her brush, smiled into the mirror then flew across the room. "Did you get them?" she asked, flinging open the door. Her smile froze and her heart plunged.

It wasn't Mikhail.

CHAPTER TWELVE

Heart pounding a kettledrum beat in his chest, Mikhail raced back to the motel room. Somehow, O'Malley had tracked them down. How? How had he known? And how had his men found them so quickly? No time for that now. They had to get the hell out of here. Thank Christ he'd gone into the office when he did. The alternative made him weak in the knees. They would've been caught like reindeer in the headlights of a snowmobile.

He unlocked the door of the motel room and burst inside. "Kerry! We must go!"

The room was dark in the late afternoon gloom, but in the light of the TV, he saw a blur of movement, followed by what sounded like a whoosh of air and then a strangled squeak of pain, followed by a Russian profanity.

"*Mikhail!*" Kerry rushed toward him, her face pale-blue in the light of the TV. "*We've got to get out of here!*"

Mikhail moved across the room and looked down at the groaning man folded into a fetal position. He was clutching at his genitals, his face twisted in agony. A stranger. "No shit. And he is not alone. Get your stuff."

It took them only a moment to grab everything they could carry, but after Kerry reached the Jeep, she tossed in her suitcase, and whirled around, still clutching her purse. "Wait!"

Already inside the Jeep, Mikhail watched in horror as she ran toward the office. "What are you doing?" he shouted. Had she lost her mind? He opened the door of the Jeep to run after her.

She was standing in front of a black Mercedes, fumbling around in her purse when he reached her side.

"Kerry! We must go!"

Ignoring him, she pulled out a lethal-looking nail file, and squatting by the front left tire, rammed it into the rubber. A soft hissing sound broke the silence. She grinned and hurried back to the left rear tire. Just as she was standing up, the office door opened and a man stepped out.

"Shit!" Mikhail muttered, grabbing her arm. "Come on!"

They ran. Mikhail heard a shout behind him. He risked a look backward as he jumped into the passenger side of the Jeep, and saw the man's feet slip on the ice. Kerry scrambled into the truck and inserted the key into the ignition.

"*Fuck!*" the man shouted, as he tried to stand, and fell again.

Kerry turned the key, but the engine only grumbled, refusing to turn over."Damn," she muttered as the engine protested. "I should've been coming out and starting her up."

The man was on his feet again and running toward them. Kerry turned the key again, pressing on the accelerator. "Start, you bitch. *Start!*"

The man reached Mikhail's door, and began pounding on the glass. And at that moment, the engine turned over and began to run, albeit, raggedly. Mikhail stared into the man's weasel-like face. His dark hair was cropped short, his forehead low and broad. He grasped at the locked door, cursing, his mouth twisted in a snarl revealing a half-dozen rotted teeth.

Kerry thrust the gearshift into reverse. The Jeep bucked, and for an awful moment, the engine coughed and sputtered. Mikhail's stomach dipped. But as Kerry thrust into first, it recovered. She pulled out of the parking lot, tires skidding on the icy road.

"Do you think he'll come after us?" Kerry asked, glancing into the rear view mirror.

Mikhail looked over his shoulder at the road. No headlights yet. "Not in that car. Thanks to you. Besides, he'll have to wait for his partner to recover from whatever you did to him."

Kerry glanced over and gave him a wry grin. "Let's just say he'll be hitting some high notes for a while."

"How did he get in?" Mikhail asked.

"I thought it was you. That you'd forgotten your key. When I opened the door, he pushed his way in and grabbed me. I was so startled, I froze. Then when I heard you at the door, my instincts kicked in and I did a little maneuver on him, something I learned in self-defense class."

Mikhail looked at her. "You surprise me, Kerry Niles. Over and over. That was smart thinking. To ruin tires." He shook his head. "But very risky."

Kerry shrugged, her eyes fixed on the road. "We had to make sure they don't follow us. As for the other thing, I started taking self-defense classes a few years ago after a good friend of mine was raped. This is the first time I've ever had to put what I've learned to the test."

Mikhail looked out his window into the darkness. "Because of me. I should never have brought you into this."

Kerry didn't speak for a moment. Finally, she looked over at him. "Okay, I know you feel guilty, so let's get it out of your system. Because from here on in, I don't want to hear it. You told me from the beginning it could be dangerous.

You said someone might come after you. I agreed to help you, even with that knowledge. So, let's just do the job and get you to Virginia, okay? So, who do you think it was?"

Mikhail ran a hand through his hair, not surprised to find it was trembling. "Sean O'Malley. Elena's boyfriend. I just do not understand how his men knew where to find us so quickly."

"Unless they've been tailing us from the very beginning," Kerry said.

"But why? How could they know?"

She shook her head, but didn't answer.

He looked at her. "Were you not frightened?"

"Of course. I'd be an idiot not to be."

"Let me see your hand."

She glanced at him, her brow wrinkled. He held out his hand, fingers beckoning. Kerry took her right hand off the steering wheel and placed it in his.

At the touch of her warm skin, a memory of her bare breasts flashed through his mind. He remembered the sweet taste of her lips, the promise of her body pressing against his. And to think, if he'd had a condom, they'd probably be in the hands of the O'Malley right now. And maybe dead.

He dropped her hand as a chill went through him.

"So?" Kerry asked. "What was that all about?"

"You are not trembling. Your face still has color. And you say you were frightened?"

Kerry sighed. "Well, it's a funny thing about me and fear, Mikhail. I don't show it the same way most people do."

"What do you mean?"

"Well, as long as the adrenalin has kicked in, I'm okay. It's only afterward that...oh, damn." She took a hand off the wheel and clutched at her belly.

"What is wrong?"

Kerry slammed on the brakes. The Jeep shuddered as she pulled off the road, coming dangerously close to a mound of snow. She shoved the gearshift into park, and clutching a hand to her mouth, jumped out of the vehicle and slammed the door. She'd parked so close to the snowdrift that Mikhail couldn't open his door. He could only watch helplessly as Kerry slipped and slid her way to the front of the Jeep where she squatted, retching into the snow.

Mikhail opened the center console, and found a packet of travel tissues. He had a handful of them waiting for her when she slipped back into the driver's seat, her eyes tearing, her skin as white as the snow drifts outside.

She gave Mikhail a sheepish look. "That's what happens when I get scared. After it's all over. It's better than it used to be. When I was first competing, I'd have to make a beeline for the bathroom as soon as I left Kiss & Cry. We'd better get out of here." She shifted into first and pulled out onto the empty road. "I think it would be a good idea to stick to the highway instead of the interstate, don't you? So…this Sean O'Malley. That's not a Russian name. What's the deal with him?"

Mikhail stared grimly ahead into the darkness. "He is ruthless man. Worse than KGB ever was. Rumor has it that his pub in Tallinn is front for racketeering and gun-running for IRA."

She slanted him a glance. "How do you know all this?"

"Like I said, is rumor."

Kerry's hands tightened on the steering wheel as the Jeep skidded on an icy patch. "I still don't see how they found us so quickly."

Mikhail braced himself on the console, grimacing as Kerry easily handled the skid and kept going at a pace way too fast for the snow-packed road. Yet, he didn't tell her to slow down. With those goons after them, they needed to put as much distance between them as possible. He glanced at her profile. Her face was tense as she concentrated on the road, yet, not panicked, or even especially frightened. He admired her courage. But perhaps she just didn't realize how dangerous their situation had become.

"So, tell me, what is this little trick you used to overpower that Russian? He looked like big, muscular guy."

She glanced at him and grinned. "It's called 'bite the shit out of his hand and then knee him as hard as you can in the balls.' I also like the 'ram your knuckles up his nose followed by a nut twist with the other hand' move, but it all depends on the position he's got you in."

"Remind me never to piss you off," Mikhail said wryly. Then he sighed. "This changes things, yes? I had hoped we'd be able to get closer to Virginia before they let the dogs go for us."

He sounded so sad that Kerry decided not to joke about his screwed-up colloquialism. She reached over and gave his hand a squeeze. Their eyes met, and she knew he was thinking the same thing she was. That if Sean O'Malley's men hadn't arrived, they'd probably be making love right now.

She looked back at the road. "We'll trade in my Jeep for something more…discreet in the morning. And we'll keep to the back roads. It'll be okay, Mikhail."

He was silent for a long time, and then he said, "I hope I will not be sorry I brought you into this."

"I wanted to do it. I'm still glad I'm doing it." She bit her bottom lip and then went on, "My father started working for Greenpeace after he won his Olympic gold. It used to upset me when he'd go away for long periods of time. I remember once he was going to miss my seventh birthday, and I was really ticked off at him. He was on his way to Newfoundland to save the baby seals instead of staying home and celebrating my birthday, and I just didn't get it. Why was that so important? What about me? Wasn't I important to him, too? You know what he said? 'Sometimes, you have to make sacrifices to do what you know is right.' That's what I'm doing, Mikhail. I don't know why you feel you have to leave your country, but I do know, just for the short time I've known you, that you wouldn't do it for an insignificant reason. That's why I'm helping you, and I don't regret it. I *won't* regret it."

"I hope that will be true." He gazed into the darkness out the passenger window. "I would tell you if I could," he added softly. "But I must not. It could put you in even greater danger."

She nodded. "I understand that." She glanced into the rear view mirror to see if they were being followed, and was relieved to see nothing but darkness behind them. "Why don't you get some sleep? I'll wake you in a couple hours and let you take over."

He nodded, and adjusted his seat back. After a few moments of silence, Kerry reached for a CD. Maybe a Van Morrison would calm her nerves.

"Perhaps it is for best," Mikhail said suddenly.

She glanced at him. "What?"

He didn't look at her. Just stared up at the ceiling of the Jeep. "You and me," he said quietly. "What did not happen back in motel room."

Kerry's heart thudded. She knew he was right. She agreed with him. Absolutely. But God, it hurt to hear him say it. She swallowed hard, and found her voice. "Yes, you're right. It is for the best."

He didn't speak again as they drove on through the darkness toward the Kansas state line.

* * * * *

The road conditions improved the closer they got to Kansas, and by the time they crossed the state line, a weak sun was just beginning to rise.

Kerry yawned, and glanced over at Mikhail who was taking his turn at the wheel. "You okay?"

He nodded. "This Jeep Cherokee, I like. Handles very good."

"Yeah, I like it, too." She frowned. "Too bad…" Then she caught herself.

He looked over at her. In the early morning light, she could just make out the sober expression on his face. "Too bad you must sell?"

"It's okay," she said. "I've been thinking about trading it in, anyway. Get something a little more…you know…feminine."

That made him grin. "I think Jeep Cherokee is perfect for you."

She slanted him a derisive look. "Are you saying I'm not feminine?"

Color flooded his face. "No! You misunderstand. You are…most feminine, but unlike any woman I have ever met."

"Oh, I was just giving you a hard time. *Look*!" Her eyes fastened on a green sign along the roadway. "Norton is less than two hours away. We should get there about the time the used car lots open. Still no sign of our friends?"

Mikhail shook his head. "No. Very little traffic."

"Good. Maybe they still think we took the interstate."

Mikhail stifled a yawn, and then said, "Kerry, I'm famished. We never had dinner last night, remember?"

Oh, did she ever. His words immediately brought to mind those exquisite moments on the bed, the warmth of Mikhail's body, the touch of his hands and his mouth tenderly exploring hers. Heat shot through her, and biting her bottom lip, she reached out to turn the temperature control down a notch.

"I'm hungry, too," she said. "Should we risk stopping for breakfast?"

Mikhail shrugged. "We have to eat."

They found a truck stop, and pulled in, carefully glancing around to make sure no one was watching them before they got out of the Jeep.

Everything seemed normal inside, just the usual mix of truck drivers and families on the road. A waitress led them to a booth overlooking the parking lot, and they ordered eggs, bacon and coffee. As before, Mikhail remained silent, allowing Kerry to do the ordering. This time, though, the waitress barely acknowledged him. Kerry supposed they'd been successful in turning him into just another American guy, albeit, a really *great-looking* American guy.

An hour later, they were back on the two-lane highway heading for Norton. It was eight o'clock when they pulled into a used car lot just off the road. Kerry turned off the ignition, and looked at Mikhail. "You'd better let me handle this. Your accent would really make you hard to forget."

The corner of his lip lifted in a wry smile. "No problem," he said. "I play henpecked husband."

The used car lot was quiet this early, and Kerry didn't see a salesman anywhere. Hands tucked deep in the pockets of her insulated parka, she picked her way through the brown slush, casting a critical eye over the variety of vehicles in the car lot. Mikhail followed behind her silently.

"So, we're going to stick to the northern route," she muttered, thinking aloud. "Because they'll assume we're planning to stick to I-70…the sane route in the dead of winter. That means we need to find something that can handle the snow. But what? I have no idea how much they'll give me for the Jeep."

Mikhail stopped behind her, eyeing a sleek black Camaro. Kerry noticed and gave a short laugh. "No way, Mikhail. Move on."

"Ah, you're breaking his heart, Ma'am. Be a sport."

Kerry whipped around to see a little man with twinkling blue eyes standing a few feet from them, his hands tucked into a black parka etched with **Buddy's Pre-Owned Autos**. He grinned, and Kerry immediately felt a kinship with him. In some weird way, he reminded her of Grandpa Johan. *Used car salesman*, she reminded herself sternly as she automatically returned his smile. *Not to be trusted.*

"Good morning," she said.

"Good morning to *you*, folks. What can I do you for?"

Kerry took a deep breath. "Well, my…er…husband and I want to trade in our Jeep Cherokee for something more…oh, I don't know…practical?"

The salesman's eyes widened, but he recovered from his surprise quickly, thrusting out a gloved hand. "You can call me Buddy." He shook Kerry's hand, and then Mikhail's who nodded and smiled, but didn't speak. "Okay, now…let's see…" The car salesman rubbed his chin thoughtfully. "Something more practical than a Jeep Cherokee. That's a tall order…uh…" He slanted a look over at Mikhail. "Something wrong with the Jeep?"

"Not at all," Kerry said quickly. "It's just that…uh…" With a flash of inspiration, she patted her belly through the thickness of her parka. "We have a little one on the way, and we just want something…you know…sturdier. Safer. Something good in snow, but not too expensive. Something good for a long trip. But not too flashy. In fact, the more boring, the better. You got anything like that?"

Buddy's eyes burned with curiosity as he looked from Kerry to Mikhail. Mikhail grinned and nodded. "Um…well…I'll have to think on that," Buddy said. "Tell you what let's do. Let me take a gander at that vehicle of yours, and then we'll know what ball park we're in. How's that sound?"

"Hunky dory," Kerry said, starting to enjoy the game. "Come, Michael. Let's go show Buddy our car."

A half hour later, they sat in Buddy's office signing the papers for the trade of the Jeep for a 1997 Volvo.

"She's really good in snow," Buddy was saying as he put the paperwork together. "Yes, Ma'am, chocolate on a stick in snow. You're going to really enjoy her. I drove her over from KC during a sumbitch of a blizzard…excuse me, Ma'am…a couple months ago, and didn't have nary a problem with her. Too bad, though, we don't have something in a better color. That charcoal gray is a little drab, but hey, it'll get you where you want to go, and that's what counts, right?"

"I like the color," said Kerry. "And so does Michael. Don't you, Michael? Don't you like the color?"

"Uh huh," Mikhail said slowly, with a smile that looked about as genuine as Pamela Andersen's breasts.

Buddy flashed him an appraising look. "You're the strong, silent type, aren't you, partner?"

Kerry laughed. "Oh, that's Michael, all right. Only speaks when he has something to say. And of course, it's hard to get a word in edgewise with me around." She laughed heartily.

Buddy slid some papers over the desk toward them. "Okay, just need both of your John Hancocks right here, and you'll be on your way with your new car."

"Oh, Michael doesn't have to sign," Kerry said. "The Jeep is in my name, and I'm going to write you a check for the balance...although, I really think you should let that two thousand slide. Seems like a fair trade to me...but...oh, well...we've been through this, haven't we?" She reached for the pen.

Buddy sighed. "This is the very best I can do, Mrs. Niles. You got my word on that. Okay, now, we're all set," he said as Kerry signed the papers. He stood and gave her the keys, then stretched out a hand. "She's all yours. Good luck to you." He turned to Mikhail, hand outstretched. "And you, sir. Come on back when the Missus gives you permission to buy that black Camaro out front." His eyes twinkled with humor, and Kerry could practically read his mind.

You'll get that Camaro, friend, on the day Hell freezes over.

"Okay, then..." Kerry jangled the keys. "You ready to hit the road, Michael? It's a long way to California."

"Uh huh," Mikhail said.

A few minutes later, they slid into their newly acquired Volvo, Kerry, of course, at the wheel. She waved warmly at Buddy as they pulled onto the street.

"No point in shattering Buddy's illusions," she said with a grin, "about who's wearing the pants in *this* marriage."

Mikhail eyed her. "You enjoyed that, did you not?"

Kerry laughed, and a tingle of pleasure raced through him at the joyous sound of it. He was glad she could still laugh after their close call last night.

"Mikhail, you've got me all wrong! Do I look like the type who would enjoy hen-pecking a husband?"

He examined her thoughtfully. "Not hen-peck," he said finally. "But I think you are woman who enjoys having her way. Being in control."

Kerry turned this over in her mind, and then gave a grudging nod. "I suppose that's true. When you've been on your own…figuratively speaking…as many years as I have, I suppose it's hard to give up control." She glanced at him. "Do you find that unattractive in a woman?"

A slow flush crept over his face, and he avoided her eyes, looking out the window at the town of Norton. When he spoke, his voice was barely audible, but she heard it all the same.

"I find *nothing* unattractive about you, Kerry Niles. And that scares hell out of me."

* * * * *

The day passed quickly as they sped toward Missouri, taking turns driving, and stopping only for gas and a quick lunch in St. Joseph. They hoped to make St. Louis by nightfall, but it didn't look good. Darkness came early in the plains in February, and the pregnant gray ceiling of clouds hinted of more snow, and perhaps lots of it. Despite Buddy's promise that the Volvo was "chocolate on a stick" in the snow, Kerry wasn't looking forward to trying it out in a blizzard. Or was she kidding herself? Was she just making excuses to prolong her time with Mikhail? She'd never been nervous about driving in snow before. What was different about now?

There was no doubt in her mind, though, about their fatigue. They'd been driving now for over sixteen hours, with only three breaks. Despite taking turns at the wheel every two hours, they both were exhausted. There'd been no sign of their pursuers, and finally, at four o'clock in the afternoon, Kerry said what Mikhail had been thinking.

"Let's pack it in for the night."

As they approached the small town of Mexico, Kerry saw a quaint L-shaped motel, a throwback to the Sixties, with rooms that opened up directly to the parking lot. Not exactly the safest place to stay, but Kerry knew if they continued on, they would be in more danger from a car accident than being caught by O'Malley's thugs.

She pulled up under the portico of the office where a big neon sign flashed, "Office. Vacancy."

"We might as well keep playing the hen-pecked husband and overbearing wife," she said, opening the driver's side door. "I'll check us in."

There were only a couple of other cars in the parking lot, she noticed. One with Minnesota tags, the other with Nebraska. A white dog sniffed around a garbage can at the side of the office building, looking up at her approach, and giving a half-hearted wag of his tail.

"Hey, Pooch," she greeted him. "What are you doing out here in the cold?"

A stray snowflake drifted down from the dark sky. Her heart lifted. Snow, she pleaded to the heavens. Snow all night, all day tomorrow, for a month. The more the better. *Snow is my new best friend.*

Five minutes later, she stepped out of the office with a key. Mikhail was reclining in his seat, eyes closed in slumber. Kerry regarded him tenderly for a moment. *Poor baby. You didn't know what you were getting yourself into, did you? I guess I didn't either.*

But oddly enough, she didn't regret anything. Despite the danger, the fatigue, the uncertainty of what the next day would bring, she couldn't regret being here with him. For the first time since her father died, she felt fully and joyously alive, and even with the fear of bad people chasing them, she wanted to hold onto this time, this adventure. Hold onto every precious moment with Mikhail.

Oh, God. What is happening to me? She hadn't felt like this since those early days with Josh. When she'd felt like she was walking on air, and every tissue, every blood vessel inside her felt electric and wild and heady with newfound love. But look what that had got her. A broken heart, a police record and a stern dressing down from the USFSA.

She gazed at Mikhail's sleeping face, and despite the warning bells tolling inside her head, she wanted to reach out and touch him. Brush her fingers down his bristled jaw, trace the outline of his full, perfectly molded lips. It took everything she had to turn away from him and start the engine. He awoke, his senses at full alert.

"I've got us a room, Mikhail," she said, her voice husky. "In a minute, we'll be able to crawl into a nice warm bed and sleep. Doesn't that sound wonderful?"

He gave her a warm smile, and its power was such that she felt shattered, as if her defenses were crumbling into a thousand tiny pieces.

* * * * *

They slept in separate double beds through the night, so exhausted that neither of them moved even when the winds whipped up to a howling frenzy, and the snow, mixing with sleet, beat against the small window overlooking the parking lot.

When Kerry finally opened her eyes and stretched out her legs with a long, satisfied groan, she thought it was still the middle of the night. It was unbearably hot in the room and so dark she could barely make out the large bump on the other bed hunched under a blanket and a purple paisley bedspread. Her skin was slick with sweat, her hair damp. She threw off the bed covers, and felt immediate relief. The drawstring pajamas and skimpy camisole top she wore was soggy with perspiration.

She'd turned up the thermostat upon entering, and hadn't bothered to turn it down before crawling thankfully into her bed. She supposed she should get up and turn it down now, but she couldn't seem to make herself move.

Turning on her side, she looked at the alarm clock on the bedside table and saw that the illuminated hands indicated it was six o'clock. Impossible, she thought. She'd had to have slept more than two hours. Gingerly, she swung her legs over the bed, and stood, glancing again at Mikhail's slumbering form.

God, wasn't he steaming under all those covers? She crept across the dark room to the thermostat and turned it down to sixty-five. *There, that should cool it off in here.* Then she moved to the window to peer out and make sure everything looked as it should. She caught her breath.

A glaze of ice covered the window so thickly it was like looking through a frosted shower door. That's when she noticed the wind. She must've been hearing it all the time, but she'd just assumed it was the furnace. But no, it sounded more like the howl of a lonely wolf as it whistled through the eaves and hammered against the fragile walls of the old-fashioned motel.

Kerry tiptoed to the door, and turned the double latch, then cautiously, opened it a crack. The wind whistled in, bringing with it a torrent of whirling snow. A pale, ghostly light told her she'd been wrong. It was six in the morning, not night, but it was definitely not the kind of morning for travel. A drift had piled up knee-high on the threshold, and from the look of things, the snow wouldn't be stopping any time soon. Kerry slammed the door and locked it, her heart pounding.

Oh, thank you, God. Yes, this is exactly what I prayed for.

She turned back to her bed, a pleased smile on her lips. Might as well crawl back under the covers and get some more sleep. They weren't going anywhere today.

Just as she reached her bed and sat down on it, Mikhail moaned and threw off his covers. Kerry's heart jolted at the sight of his bare chest and his long, lean haunches as he stretched out on his back, clad only in a pair of red boxer shorts. A slow-moving tide of heat crept through her, and it had nothing to do with the temperature of the room. Oh, how she wanted to follow her instincts and cross that small space separating his bed from hers, crawl up next to him, and fit her body against the pulsating heat of his.

He was totally vulnerable to her now, still lost in whatever dreams that were playing across his brain. If she wanted to, if she had the nerve, she could slide her hands over the light carpet of hair on his chest, travel up his strong, corded neck, and capture his mouth with hers. He would make slow, sensuous love to her, and not even be fully aware he was doing it. She knew she could make it happen.

If she had the nerve...

CHAPTER THIRTEEN

"Bloody Christ!" Sean slammed down the phone on the desk and strode over to the liquor cabinet. "I've got nothing but bleedin' idiots working for me, and that's the God's truth." He splashed a finger of Johnnie Walker Black Label into a glass and downed it, then stared blackly across the room at Elena.

She reclined on the bed, her blond head propped on a pillow, eyes fixed rigidly on the TV where a male figure skater pranced about on the ice. Sean couldn't understand why she was torturing herself like this, especially watching those faggy male skaters. Everybody knew almost all of them were bloody Nancy boys, preferring the taste of dick rather than pussy. Except, damn the luck, Mikhail Kozlof, of course. It bloody figured that the one straight man in figure skating was—or had been—Elena's partner.

She still hadn't responded to his cry of outrage after he'd got off the phone with dickhead Fagan, and her expression was as remote as the peak of Mount Bloody Everest.

"Jesus Christ, Elena!" He snarled. Beowulf lifted his head from between his paws and looked at him solemnly. Sean glared at the pale blonde. "Are you ever going to quit sulking about that fucking gold medal?"

Slowly, she turned her head, and her sapphire eyes impaled him. Emotionless and distant. She looked delectable in a white crocheted pajama top that hugged her firm breasts, and revealed tantalizing glimpses of flesh. It drove him crazy. The bitch hadn't allowed him to touch her since she'd found out about Kozlof's disappearance, and the nights lying beside her in the king-sized bed had been sheer agony.

After a long moment, Elena turned her icy gaze away from him and back to the TV. Rage washed through him. He'd never been a man to be ignored, and he wasn't about to start now.

He set his glass down on the liquor cabinet and moved to the TV. One stab at the power button, and the screen went blank.

"Why did you do that?" Elena asked, still revealing not an iota of emotion in her expression or her voice.

"Because I'm bloody well sick and tired of being treated like a stick of furniture around here. One you're getting ready to throw out on the garbage heap."

Elena took a deep breath, folded her arms across her luscious chest and looked at him the way a mother looks at an unreasonable child. "All right. Tell me what Fagan said to get you so cranky."

Sean glared at her. "One would think you didn't give a goddamn about what's happening with Kozlof and his little American slut." He gauged her reaction to that, and was pleased to see her eyes darken with fury. Good. He was getting just a wee bit worried about her. Once her rage had run its course, she'd almost seemed to lose interest in everything. Perhaps it was just shock. But it was frightening to see Elena defeated. And he knew he had to find a way to arouse her anger again. He thought he just had. Any mention of the American girl, and her eyes ignited.

"So, what did you find out?" she asked, lips tight.

"Those bloody fools I have tracking them almost got them at a motel in Colorado, but they blew it. Believe this if you can, but the American girl practically realigned Shlusvaka's nuts, and they managed to get away. And then, of course, the blithering idiots lost their trail." Sean shook his head, unable to hide a grin of admiration. "One thing I'll say for Kozlof. He's got good taste in women."

Elena hissed like a cat, and threw the covers back. "Mikhail Kozlof is a moron, throwing his life away for a bitch like that." She swung her long, silky legs over the side of the bed and stood.

Sean caught his breath at the sight of her lush body clad only in the skimpiest of satin panties and her little crocheted top. His penis stirred and swelled. She was well aware of her effect upon him, he knew, and took great pleasure in the power her body held over him. That's why she strutted around provocatively in front of him, and simultaneously withheld sex. It drove him mad, and she knew it.

Keenly aware of Sean's impassioned gaze, Elena sauntered over to the desk where a newspaper was opened to the sports page. His perusal gave her flesh a warm, tingling feeling, and she knew she couldn't hold out on him much longer. She'd been punishing him for Mikhail's betrayal despite the fact that, intellectually, she knew he had nothing to do with it. But *someone* had to be punished. Still, the two days of celibacy was starting to wear on her, as well, and Sean was a hard man to resist. Their sexual appetites were evenly matched, and that's why they'd been together for the past few years. If only he wasn't a traditionalist at heart, wanting marriage and children. So boring!

Her eyes scanned the photo of herself and Mikhail performing the other night's original dance. It was a good photo, especially of Mikhail. He had an expression of passion on his lean, angular face—passion for the sport, of course. But one would think by looking at this picture, that his passion was for her, the gorgeous woman in his arms. She gazed bitterly at the photo. Why couldn't he be like other men, and want her like they all wanted her? What did he see in that skinny freckled-faced Yank? She was nowhere near as beautiful as *she* was.

She wanted him back. She *needed* Mikhail back. If Sean could force him to return, what could she do to keep him skating with her? To keep him happy? With an ordinary man, the answer would be obvious. But Mikhail had made it clear he didn't want her. *Damn the man!*

Pouting, Elena read the headline accompanying the photo. **Russian Athlete Missing at Olympics**. The article didn't contain much information. Just that Mikhail hadn't shown up at his hotel after drinking the night away, and was still missing when he was due to compete in the final of the ice dance competition. Then it went on to give some background on Mikhail, how he'd trained for years with another coach before being assigned—reportedly, against his will—to partner Elena.

Her mouth tightened. It made it sound like he'd been horribly unhappy with her. And that wasn't true. Oh, sure, maybe he wasn't thrilled, but he'd accepted it. Just like he'd accepted that Nadya would be replaced by Sergey.

Nadya. Elena's frown turned to a musing smile. Perhaps she could use his old coach to get him back. She turned to face Sean. He was sitting in one of the Chippendale chairs, holding another glass of scotch between his hands, his brown eyes fixed moodily upon her. She hid a smile, knowing what was going through his head. He was trying to figure out a way to convince her to make love with him.

All in good time, Sean, darling.

She moved seductively toward him, watching with satisfaction as his eyes lit up with hope. She didn't stop until she reached the apex of his parted legs. He grinned wolfishly up at her, knowing the Cold War had ended. Elena knelt between his knees, hands pressing on his muscular thighs. She gazed into his eyes. "Baby," she said softly.

"Yeah?"

Her hands traveled leisurely up his thighs. "Promise me you'll bring him back."

His muscles tensed, and the sparkle of excitement in his eyes turned to anger. Elena's hand closed over his erection. "No, don't get mad," she said, expertly massaging his hard-on. "Just promise me."

"I...already...did," Sean growled through gritted teeth.

Slowly, Elena unzipped his slacks, her eyes still holding his. "Bring him to me, and give me another year with him." She deftly unsnapped his boxer shorts, unleashing his rigid cock from its confinement. She ran her hand down to its base and up again, watching the tortured expression on his face. He groaned and closed his eyes. "Give me a year with him to win a gold medal at Worlds next March, and if you do that..." She leaned toward him, her breath fanning his penis. "I will marry you. I'll go with you to South America, and have your little Irish brats."

He opened his eyes and stared at her, stunned. Her words were so surprising, he forgot about what she was doing to him with her silken hand and the tantalizing promise of her pouty lips.

"You're serious? You'll marry me?"

He'd been pleading with her to marry him for two years. And she'd steadfastly refused.

She smiled, and lowering her head, swirled a hot, hungry tongue over his throbbing tip like it was an ice cream bar she was planning to savor. Sean trembled, and his nails dug into her tender shoulders.

She drew away and peered up at him out of cloudy ocean blue eyes. "Yes, Sean," she murmured. "You give me Mikhail for a year, and I'll marry you."

"Okay," he managed to gasp, as her voracious mouth closed over him. "It's a deal."

* * * * *

Mikhail knew he was dreaming. Because there were just too many things going on that didn't make sense. Like the Zamboni on the ice while he was dancing the Romantica Tango with Kerry. They had to keep avoiding it as they skated the intricate steps. And it was incredibly hot on the ice. Mikhail felt the sweat oozing out of his pores and seeping through his billowing white shirt as he flew across the rink. Over there in the corner, spinning like a child's top, was Ilka Stanislav, the sixteen-year-old skater whose blade had sliced open his face from cheekbone to chin. And there was Nadya, standing just behind the boards, her small height only a couple of feet higher than the wood structure separating the ice from the stands. She was smiling and gazing with approval at Mikhail and Kerry. But what really convinced him it was a dream was the couple he saw in the audience.

His mother was sitting beside a blue-eyed man dressed in the traditional red and blue costume of a Sami tribesman. Even though he knew it was a dream, Mikhail drew to a stop, and releasing Kerry's hand, skated over to the boards to greet the father he'd never met. The Sami tribesman watched his approach, his blue eyes warm with welcome.

"Father," Mikhail said, clutching the boards.

The man's eyes crinkled as his lips widened into a tremulous smile. He stretched out a hand toward Mikhail.

Mikhail reached out to grasp his hand, but before he could touch him, his father's image faded away. But his voice, a voice he'd never heard in life lingered in his mind.

You must go now, my son. The bad men are coming.

Mikhail opened his eyes and blinked into the gloom. He knew now that he'd been dreaming, yet, why did he still hear the roar of the Zamboni?

His hand slid over the slick perspiration coating his chest. He'd kicked the covers off sometime in the night, but even so, he felt uncomfortably warm. He turned over on his side to see if Kerry was awake, and felt a peculiar sinking sensation in his stomach at the sight of her spread out on her stomach, her legs splayed, one of them hanging off the bed. She was sleeping in drawstring pajama bottoms and a little spaghetti-strapped tee shirt that exposed her midriff. Her black hair was tangled and hid the side of her face. His eyes centered on her perfectly shaped bottom, and he felt the temperature in the room soar another degree or two.

Christ! This forced intimacy would be the death of him. They'd both agreed in the car that it would be foolhardy to get physically involved during this trip to Virginia. But these shared motel rooms were dangerous. He'd finally been able to exchange some rubles at a bank in Omaha, but his cash flow wasn't limitless, and it seemed ridiculous to spend money on two motel rooms. Besides, when circumstances warranted it, like at the car dealership in Norton, they were pretending to be married.

Still, for the sake of his sanity, he had to quit thinking such provocative thoughts about Kerry. He had to forget he'd ever sampled the sweet taste of her lips, and felt the welcoming tremble of her body under his touch.

His mind returned to the dream. To his father, and the warning that had come from his lips. "You must go now, my son. The bad men are coming."

Estonian, he might be, but Mikhail was still Russian enough to be superstitious about dreams like this. He believed in an afterlife, and felt very sure that if situations required it, the dead could contact the living with important messages. Crazy as it sounded, and Mikhail would never admit it to anyone, but what *if* the dream had been a warning from the other side?

He got out of bed and moved over to the window, drawing aside the curtain to peer out. A light glaze of ice covered the glass, but it was thin enough to make out the snowplow grinding its way down the highway in front of the motel. So, there was his Zamboni.

The snow had stopped falling, and a watery afternoon light washed the west Iowa landscape a dull, dishwater gray.

An ugly winter afternoon. But…the snow had stopped.

Mikhail turned toward the beds and saw the red illuminated numbers on the radio clock on the bedside table. Nine-twenty. They'd been here over seventeen hours.

It was time to move on.

He moved purposely toward Kerry's bed, reached down and touched her shoulder. "Kerry? Wake up, *gollupchic*. We must get going. It is dangerous to stay here longer."

Kerry moaned, but didn't move. Mikhail stared down at a dark shape on the small of her back just above her drawstring pajama bottoms. It looked like the head of a turtle. A tattoo, he realized. His fingers itched to push down the fabric so he could see the rest of it, but that was dangerous thinking. His jaw tightened. He gave her shoulder another shake. "Kerry, wake up!"

Eyes closed, she turned over and stretched her arms over her head. Mikhail felt his stomach spasm at the sight of her flat tummy and luscious navel exposed by the little nothing of a top. Her taut nipples pressed against the soft knit fabric, inviting his touch. He fought back the almost overpowering urge to bend down and dip his tongue into her navel. He imagined running his hands over the velvet of her belly, slipping up under her top and…

"Wake up, Kerry," he said, more urgently. Eyes closed, she pushed his hand away as if trying to get rid of a pestering fly. He perched on the edge of the bed and shook her shoulder again.

A frown marred her black brows. "No," she murmured. "Just a little longer."

"You've slept over seventeen hours. Is enough."

Finally, Kerry opened her eyes and gazed at him dreamily. Her lips parted in a soft smile. "I was dreaming about you," she murmured. "It was a…really naughty dream." She released a soft sigh, her tongue licking at her bottom lip.

A wildfire rush of heat encased his loins. He made a move to stand, but her hand on his arm stilled him.

"Kiss me, Mikhail," she whispered. "Like you did in my dream…like you did the other night."

"No." He shook his head, his heart thrumming. "We cannot…" Staring down at her sleep-warmed face, her cloudy blue eyes soft with arousal, his protest died on his lips.

"Please," she whispered. "Just one little kiss."

With a soft groan, Mikhail surrendered. His head lowered, and his mouth captured hers in a burning kiss. Her nails dug into his bare biceps as she opened her mouth to his exploring tongue. Their lips finally parted, but it wasn't enough. He nipped at her mouth, tasting and nibbling, suckling and exploring. His urgency to leave was driven out of his mind by Kerry's intoxicating mouth and yielding body. But when he felt her hand molding against the iron rod of his erection, he pulled away as if her touch had been a flaming torch.

"*No! We cannot!*"

He stood abruptly and moved away from the bed, tunneling his hands through his tousled hair. He felt her startled gaze, and turned to face her. Steeling himself against the sight of her flushed face and enticing body, he stared at her, his limbs trembling with need.

"I feel we're in danger here," he said slowly. "I do not know how to explain…but we must go. Now."

Kerry blinked, and then nodded slowly. She sat up and swung her legs over the bed. "Okay," she said, in a tremulous voice. "I'll go get ready."

Mikhail watched as she crossed the room and disappeared into the bathroom, closing the door behind her. Slowly, he clenched his left hand into a fist, and pounded it against the palm of his right.

"Dear God," he whispered through gritted teeth. "Give me the strength to get through the next few days with this woman."

* * * * *

"Okay, Old Man," the rotten-toothed Irishman said through the cigarette between his lips. "You're sure you've seen this couple? Tell me all about it, and I'll make it worth your while."

Buddy stared down at the wad of greenbacks thrust in his direction, and felt a wave of distrust flood through him. English to the core, he didn't have much use for liquid-tongued Irishmen, especially ones with bad breath. He also didn't like the looks of the big, flat-nosed guy with him who hadn't spoken a word, but whose brown eyes were cold as the frigid outside temperature. Buddy wished he could take back his admission of a couple of moments ago, but it was too late now.

"Keep your money, mister," he said with disdain. "The name's Buddy. And I kindly ask you not to refer to me as 'old man,' if you don't mind."

The Irishman grinned, revealing more stubby brown teeth. "No offense meant, Buddy." He tucked the money away into his coat pocket. "So, what can you tell me about this couple?"

"Not much," he said, in a deliberate Kansas drawl. "They drove in here yesterday morning and traded in this Jeep for a...ah...a blue Honda. Yep. One of my favorite cars, it was. Nice young couple. He was sort of quiet, though, but Lord, she made up for it. Just jabbered on and on."

Buddy wasn't sure why he felt inclined to lie to this rabbit-faced man and his Darth Vader companion. Maybe it was because he'd felt a certain kinship with the young couple that'd traded in the Jeep. The girl, maybe because she was the pants-wearer in the family, reminded him of his own granddaughter, Emily, down in Little Rock, Arkansas. A feisty thing, Emily was, ruling the roost with her string of boyfriends, and just about everybody she met. His own wife, Sarah, God rest her soul, had cracked the whip when she had a mind to, and had kept Buddy on his toes for the fifty-one years they'd been married, and he'd loved pretty much every minute of it. Still missed her like crazy even though she'd passed on four years ago.

"Did the man have a Russian accent?" asked the Irishman.

"Wouldn't know." Buddy shrugged. "Barely said a word. The pretty gal did all the talking. What are you, some kind of cop?"

"Private investigator. Did they happen to say where they might be headed?"

Private investigator, my eyetooth, Buddy thought. "How about showing me some identification before I answer any more questions, partner?"

The big guy's face grew even grimmer, and Buddy wondered if he'd screwed up. Darth, there, looked like he'd just as soon beat the crap out of him, and be done with it. But the Irishman only shrugged and drew out his wallet. Buddy eyed the Massachusetts driver's license and the business card that claimed he was a private investigator named Sully Patterson. But the warning bells were still clanging in his head.

He looked the Irishman straight in the eye and said, "She mentioned they was headed for Texas. Fort Worth, she said."

The Irishman and the big guy exchanged a look. Kind of a baffled look. Good. Buddy didn't know what this was all about, but his sixth sense told him these two jokers were not on the up and up. And the young couple? He didn't know what they'd done to get these two scalawags chasing after them, but he'd bet a dollar to a donut that if they were caught, things wouldn't go well for them.

"Are you sure they said Texas, old ma...I mean, Buddy?" asked the Irishman.

Buddy nodded, his gaze unwavering. "Fort Worth, Texas. Driving a bright blue Honda. I'll get you the license tag if you want."

Sully Patterson—if that was really his name—gave him an ingratiating smile that looked all the more revolting with his rotten teeth. "Well, that would be grand, indeed."

Buddy led the two men to his cubicle where he tapped into a computer and brought up the records of a '2000 blue Honda parked in the used lot outside. He scribbled down the number and passed it over. The Irishman thanked him. Buddy watched as they left the showroom and got into a black Mercedes with brand new tires. He grinned as they drove right past the blue Honda and pulled out onto Rt. 283, heading south.

After they were gone, Buddy stood, hitched up his pants and ambled out of the showroom toward the snack bar. It was mighty cold outside, and dreary, to boot. A nice cup of hot, black coffee would surely hit the spot—even that swill they made here. Jesus H. Christ, it was so bad, they could probably use it for motor oil in the service area, and nobody would know the difference.

He passed through the customer waiting room, paying only scant attention to the ever-present drone of the TV set anchored on the wall. It was tuned to CNN, and a pretty blond anchorwoman was talking about some Russian Olympic athlete defecting with the help of an American woman.

Buddy shook his head, and stepped into the snack bar.

Another Olympic scandal. Lordy, Lordy, it was always something.

CHAPTER FOURTEEN

In the bright morning sunlight, Kerry squinted at the road map on her lap, tracing her finger along the route they were traveling. Damn! It was time for an eye exam. She couldn't read worth a darn in her contacts, but she was way too vain to wear glasses while traveling with Mikhail.

He was at the wheel of the Volvo, a pair of dark sunglasses protecting his eyes from the glare of the sun on the vast acres of snow drifts hugging the road. The ice crystals sparkled like thousands of diamonds in the sunlight. Kerry looked up at the endless highway stretching in front of the hood of the car, the mile markers slipping past as they made their dogged way eastward. A sigh escaped her lips. Soon, they'd be in Virginia, and once Roger and the CIA got hold of Mikhail, who knew when she'd see him again?

It was a gorgeous late February morning with cloudless blue skies and calm winds, but bitterly cold with the temperature hovering in the low single digits. Two hours earlier, the car had protested at starting at the motel in Ohio, but had finally rumbled to life. It had made them wary about stopping for breakfast. What if they couldn't get it started again?

Chocolate on a stick, indeed, Mr. Buddy, she thought, as her stomach gave a protesting growl.

Mikhail must've heard it, even over the sound of Mr. Mister, on the CD player singing 'Broken Wings.' "Want Ding Dong?" he asked with a smile.

Kerry groaned. "If I ever see a Ding Dong again, it will be too soon. Let's stop for breakfast, Mikhail. The car has been running for two hours. Surely it'll start again." As if on cue, she saw a familiar sign up ahead. "Look! There's a Shoney's. They have a really good breakfast buffet."

Ten minutes later, Kerry sat in a booth opposite Mikhail, a plate in front of her piled high with biscuits and gravy, scrambled eggs, hash browns, bacon and French toast dripping with maple syrup.

She grinned. "Doesn't this look scrumptious? God! I thought I was going to pass out from hunger."

Mikhail eyed her food ruefully. His plate was just as full, and beside it, there was another one holding two huge pancakes smothered with strawberries and whipped cream.

"You eat like a man," Mikhail said as she took a generous bite of French toast. "How do you keep trim figure eating like that?"

Kerry narrowed her eyes at him. She swallowed and said, "That could be construed as a sexist remark, but I'll let it slide. Since you ask, though, I probably *won't* keep my figure. I haven't eaten like this in years. But now that I'm not skating anymore, I've got to get it out of my system. The freedom is awesome."

His eyes swept over her, and Kerry felt her cheeks grow warm at his perusal. "Few extra...pounds, is it? Will not hurt. You still have beautiful body."

Their eyes met, and an awkward silence fell. Mikhail was the first to look away. A waitress stopped by to refill their coffee mugs, and then moved on. The restaurant was packed with customers, and the hum of their conversation ate up the silence. Utensils clattered, the cash register jingled, and over it all, Pam Tillis wailed "Spilled Perfume" on the sound system.

Kerry fastened her eyes on the view outside the restaurant—nothing but a few snow-laden bushes and grimy, salt-coated cars in the parking lot. Things had been tense between her and Mikhail since they'd left the motel in Missouri. They'd driven until after ten that night before stopping at a nondescript motel in a small town southwest of Cleveland. Exhausted, they'd fallen into bed and slept straight through until early this morning. There had been no repeat of the dangerous behavior they'd…or rather, *she'd*…initiated in the motel in Missouri. God, what had gotten into her? She'd practically demanded that he make love to her. And if he hadn't put on the brakes…

Her cheeks warmed, and to cover it up, she hastily scooped up a forkful of hash browns and popped it into her mouth. She supposed she could blame the whole thing on the fact that she'd awakened just after having an especially steamy dream about being naked in a hot tub with Mikhail. But why lie to herself? She'd known exactly what she was doing when she'd begged him to kiss her. She'd contemplated doing it earlier when she'd seen him stretched out on the bed, covers tossed aside to reveal his lean, bare body clad in red boxer shorts. Only steel resolve had made her crawl into her own bed and force herself to go back to sleep. And she had, only to dream about him—hot, erotic dreams that made her toss and turn in feverish anxiety. Later, when he awakened her, she'd found him sitting on her bed, bare-chested, and still wearing those wicked boxer shorts. Who could blame her? Her id had taken over.

"Let's see if there's anything interesting in the paper." She took a sip of coffee and opened the newspaper to the sports section. She'd grabbed it on the way inside, wondering if there was any word on Mikhail's disappearance. "Uh oh." She glanced up at him. "Looks like we've made the paper. Look at this." She pointed to an item halfway down the front page. **Russian Athlete May Have Defected With Help of American Skater**. Alongside the two-paragraph article were two photos—one of Mikhail, and one of Kerry.

"What does it say?" Mikhail asked.

"Give me a minute." She scanned the article. "Not much. Just that they think we're together, and I'm helping you defect. Well, at least they used good photos of us. But how did they get this information? I mean, seriously! How did they put it together? Just because I disappeared at the same time?"

"Think about it," Mikhail said. "Who do you know that would jump to conclusion?"

Her gaze met his. "Adam, of course. I wouldn't put it past him to tell the authorities you kidnapped me. God! You don't think he'll do that, do you?"

His eyes flared. "If you get hurt because of him…" He muttered something in Russian, and it didn't sound like a compliment.

"They would've figured it out sooner or later, Mikhail," Kerry said. "And Adam is only acting from his concern for me. He probably has no idea—"

"He is *fool*!" Mikhail snapped. "If he truly believes you are involved in helping me defect, he must know that talking to newspaper about it could put you in danger." His hand tightened on his fork. "Is too bad that accident did not put him in coma for few months."

"*Mikhail*!" Kerry stared at him, shocked. "That's an awful thing to say!"

He looked away from her, his face reddening. "I am sorry. You are right. Of course, I do not mean that. But he is very stupid man." He took a sip of his coffee, and looked out the window, his expression distant.

Kerry watched him a moment. There were so many facets to this man. The funny, boyish side. The sexy, magnetic side. And now, this ruthless, cold side he'd just displayed. Which one was the real Mikhail? Or was he all of them?

She pushed away her plate, realizing if she ate another bite, she'd surely explode. The waitress came by with a pot of coffee and refilled their mugs. After she moved off again, Kerry looked at Mikhail and said, "I have an idea."

He looked at her, his brow arched. "Yes?"

"I was looking at the map earlier, and I think if the weather holds out…" She glanced out the window at the sunny skies. "And it looks like it will; we should be able to make Gettysburg by evening."

Mikhail's eyes lit up. "Ah, Gettysburg! I have heard of such place. I saw film about American Civil War. Do you think we might have chance to go to battlefield?"

"Well, that's what I want to talk to you about." Kerry ran a finger around the rim of her coffee mug, almost afraid to go on.

Would he see through this idea as a ploy to keep him with her for an extra day? And what if he did? It was true, wasn't it? Partially, anyway. She *did* want to see Dale. It had been years, and with every Christmas card she'd received from the woman who, if life had been fair, would've become her step-mother, Dale had begged Kerry to come to Mount Carmel for a visit.

"My father's former fiancée lives on a mountain overlooking the battlefield. She runs a bed & breakfast there.

The Mount Carmel Inn." Kerry finally dragged her gaze to Mikhail and found him watching her with interest. "I've always wanted to go visit her, but..." She shrugged. "With my schedule, you know...it just didn't happen. Anyway, we'll be going right by there..."

Mikhail smiled. "I would love to see Gettysburg." He paused, then, "This woman. Were you close to her?"

Kerry's cheeks warmed, and she looked away from him. "We had our ups and downs. They were going to get married that summer, but then we had to get that last ski trip in, so the three of us went to Whistler. Dale really was a sweetheart, but I guess I was too young—and too jealous of her—to realize it. I suppose I thought once she married my dad, he wouldn't have any time for me. If I'd only known our time was running out anyway..." To her horror, tears blurred her eyes. She blinked quickly. This was too stupid! That had all happened so long ago.

Mikhail reached over and took her hand. His eyes held hers, and her heart jolted at the warmth she saw in them. "I would like to meet this Dale. Perhaps a visit for you is overdue."

Kerry nodded, trying to dislodge the lump in her throat. His hand squeezed hers, and she felt closer than ever to tears as a memory washed over her. Dale's concerned blue eyes gazing down at her as she writhed in pain, the cool palm of her hand against Kerry's sweat-dampened brow. It had been the morning of her father's death, and if not for the sudden arrival of her first period, Kerry would've been with him that afternoon when the avalanche thundered down the mountain, burying him under tons of snow.

"You ready to go?" Mikhail asked.

Kerry looked at him, and a flash of blue beyond his left shoulder caught her attention. Her sharp intake of air alerted him.

Alarm flickered in his eyes. "What is it?"

Kerry looked down at her plate, cradling the side of her mouth against her palm. "Police," she said under her breath. "Two of them. They're coming this way."

What if the cops recognized them from the newspaper? And if they'd made the newspaper, their disappearance had probably been covered on the morning news shows, as well. Oh, God. Cops all over the country were probably on the lookout for them.

A hostess was leading the policemen right toward them. Kerry's heart pounded. She grabbed her coffee mug and took a sip of the tepid remains, casually looking out the window. But she felt the gaze of one of the cops as they passed their booth and settled into the one right behind them.

Would it look weird if she and Mikhail got up and left now? Or would it look like they were trying to run?

She met Mikhail's gaze across the table. He was waiting for her cue. Behind her, she could hear the cops ordering coffee from the waitress who'd just appeared. Her heartbeat steadied. Their voices sounded normal.

"And I'll have Adam & Eve on a raft—wreck 'em," one of the cops said in a grating Midwestern twang. "With a side of bacon cooked crisp. Burn it, if you have to, but don't bring me any limp bacon."

Relief coursed through her. The cops were obviously more concerned with feeding their faces than looking for Russian defectors and their accomplices. She smiled at Mikhail. "I'm ready. Oh, let me leave a tip." She drew a couple of dollar bills from her wallet and placed them on the table, then reached for her coat, purse and the newspaper.

She slid out of the booth and turned to follow Mikhail who was heading to the cash register in a casual stride.

"Hey, lady!" A voice boomed from behind her.

Her body stiffened, and she felt the blood drain from her face.

"Yeah, you. In the black leather."

What to do? Run for it? Try to play it cool? Pretend she didn't hear him?

"You dropped your glove," the voice said.

Kerry looked down, and saw her black leather glove lying on the floor. She glanced over at the cop who'd spoken. He was a young guy with a crew cut, a prominent Adams' apple and soft brown eyes. She gave him a sheepish smile. "Thanks," she said, hoping her voice didn't betray her anxiety. "I'm always losing these."

He grinned at her, his eyes scanning her in admiration. "Don't want to do that on a morning like this. It's a day fit only for penguins out there."

"Yes, it sure is cold," she said, trying to keep her voice casual as she snatched up her glove. "Thanks, again."

"No problem, ma'am." The cop beamed at her. "Have a good day."

She smiled and turned away. Mikhail was already at the cash register, paying for their breakfast. She scowled at him as she reached his side.

"Making a run for it?" she asked under her breath.

He smiled at the waitress when she handed back his change, and didn't speak until they stepped outside into the numbing cold.

"He was only flirting with you. This was obvious to me."

"Well, I'm glad it was to *you*. It scared the *crap* out of me!"

196

His eyes danced in amusement. "You have such way with words," he said as they headed for the car.

* * * * *

"Where the *bloody* hell did you say you were?" Sean snarled into the phone. Fury rampaged through his body, and he wished with every sinew that Fagan—the bleedin' idiot—was standing in front of him right now so he could beat the stupid out of him. Sean had heard very well where the man had said he was, but he still couldn't believe it.

Like the moron that he was, Fagan dutifully repeated, "Abilene, Texas."

Sean closed his eyes and took a deep breath, trying to calm himself. He counted slowly to ten before speaking in a deceptively soft voice, "And why are you in Abilene *bloody* Texas?"

"Because that's where that car salesman in Kansas said they were headed, Boss," Fagan said, his tone millimeters away from a defensive whine. "So, I figured we should go ahead and try and track them down here."

"Do I pay you for making decisions on your own, Fagan? Or do I pay you for reporting everything…I mean, *everything*…to me, and then wait for orders?"

Silence.

Sean gritted his teeth. Was the bloody fool thinking over his answer?

"Fuck," Sean muttered. "Fagan, you and Shlusvaka get your asses to Occoquan, Virginia. That's their destination. I don't know when they'll get there, but you're going to be waiting for them. Listen closely. Get Kozlof before he makes contact with Roger Ellery. Got that?"

"Yeh, Boss. Uh…what about the girl?"

"Yeah? What about her?"

"What do you want us to do with her? Kill her?"

Sean thought about it. She was a pretty thing. It would be a shame to kill her. Besides, he wasn't a monster. Just a businessman. Still, if Kozlof had told her anything about TNG, she could be a danger to all of them. But would he be that stupid?

"Bring her to me," Sean said, making up his mind. "I'll find out if she knows anything. And this time, don't fuck up!"

He slammed down the phone and turned to the closed bedroom door. What was Elena doing in there?

Everything had been much better between them since she came out of her funk a couple of days ago. She'd stopped watching the Olympic skating on the bloody telly, so that was a good sign. Even their lack of success in finding Kozlof hadn't seemed to bother her all that much. And since she hadn't been spending any time at the rink, her health appeared to be better than it had been in months.

In fact, there had been no asthma attacks since the one after the original dance. Was that because she hadn't received a TNG injection since leaving Russia? It had been too risky to try to smuggle the drug into North America. And was it his imagination or had Elena's skin lost its pallor, becoming more luminous in the three weeks she'd been off the drug? He really would have to try and talk her into not resuming the shots once they returned to Moscow. Sure, TNG gave her the stamina and strength she needed for competition, but the side effects frightened him. He wasn't a doctor, but even *he* knew that yellowish tinge to her skin meant liver damage, and it was also clear to him that the drug worsened her asthma. But God! The woman was stubborn. And now that she'd decided to train for next year's Worlds...

Sean shook his head. He should never have agreed to her proposal. But she'd dangled the one carrot in front of him he couldn't resist.

Marriage. And children.

He strode to the door, gave an abrupt knock and walked in. He stopped short, his body stiffening. Elena stood at the foot of the bed, packing a suitcase.

"What are you doing?"

She gave him a cool look. "Are you blind? I'm packing. I'm going back to Russia."

He scowled. "Since when?"

"Since about an hour ago. Since I decided I'm bored out of my mind. And I need to start training again. I need my shots."

Christ, Sean thought. He recognized the jut-jawed look of obstinacy on her face, and knew better than to argue with her. So he decided to try a different tactic.

"What about Kozlof? I thought you wanted to wait until we found him."

She gave a European shrug and folded a silk sweater into a small square. "I have no doubt you will bring him back to me. You promised. But I cannot wait here until it happens. You bring him to me in Russia." She closed the suitcase, and then looked up to give him a sultry smile. "And I will give you a sample of how I will repay the favor." She glanced at her slim gold wristwatch. "I have a half-hour before I leave for the airport."

* * * * *

Welcome to Pennsylvania, the Keystone State.

Kerry saw the sign and felt her heart dip. Another state closer to their destination. She chewed her bottom lip and glanced over at Mikhail. His head was tilted at an angle that looked exceedingly uncomfortable as he dozed against the window. It was almost time to wake him up so he could take his turn at driving again. She'd been at the wheel for almost three hours, and it would probably be a good idea if she could get some sleep, especially since they wanted to make it to Gettysburg by nightfall. But her mind was racing, and she knew it would be impossible to sleep.

She'd felt on edge ever since that morning when they'd left the Shoney's in Ohio. And she knew it wasn't because of the cops. It was Mikhail, and what he'd said about Adam.

It is too bad that accident did not put him in coma for few months.

The CD playing, Matchbox Twenty's "Mad Season," came to an end, and Kerry ejected it. She reached for an old favorite, U2's "October," and slipped it into the CD player. As Bono began to sing "Gloria," she glanced over at Mikhail again. The afternoon sunlight streamed over him, turning his flaxen hair bright gold. In sleep, his face held a hint of boyish vulnerability that brought out the protective instinct in her. But when he'd made that comment about Adam, there had been nothing boyish or vulnerable about the expression on his face. His eyes had been icy; his lips thin, almost cruel. Or was that her imagination?

No. She didn't think so. She'd seen a new side to Mikhail in that moment, one she'd never suspected. It was almost as if he were *glad* Adam had been injured—and disappointed that his injuries weren't worse.

"Damn," she whispered as a thought took shape in her mind. It was so preposterous she almost dismissed it immediately. But once it appeared, there was no shaking it.

Could Mikhail have been responsible for Adam's accident?

Her fingers grew cold on the steering wheel as the question reverberated in her head. After all, the timing couldn't have been more perfect. She'd initially refused to help Mikhail because he'd insisted on leaving before the free dance.

I won't do that to Adam, she'd told him.

And what had happened? A hit-and-run driver had taken Adam out of the equation. It hadn't *been* Mikhail, of course. He'd been with her in her hotel room when the accident occurred. But suppose he had connections…someone…who had worked with him to remove the problem of Adam?

She shuddered. This was crazy, yet…it fit. Because of Adam's accident, she had agreed to help Mikhail. Wasn't that just too convenient for him?

"Are you cold? I turn heater up?"

She jumped at the sound of his voice, and then turned to see him watching her with amused eyes. He held the golf globe in his hands. How long had he been awake?

"Sorry," he said. "You were far away with thoughts?"

"Mmmm…yeah, I guess so. What did you say about the heater?"

"You shivered. I wonder if you are cold?"

"No. I mean, yeah, maybe." No, she wasn't cold. She was sick. Her stomach was churning, and had been for the last few minutes. She recognized it for what it was. Fear. Had she made a horrible mistake? Giving up the life she'd known to help a man who, for all she knew, could be a dangerous spy? It wasn't unheard of, was it? Just because the Cold War was over didn't mean that Russia wouldn't use their citizens to conduct clandestine operations. And what better citizen to use than a champion ice skater who traveled freely in the West?

Mikhail had refused to tell her anything about his reasons for defecting. What if it was all a grand ploy to get inside CIA Headquarters? She'd seen plenty of James Bond movies, and sure, they were a little over-the-top, but weren't they somewhat based on reality?

She saw a gas station coming up on the right, and flicked on the turn signal.

"You ready to drive?" She managed to say through the sudden flow of saliva in her mouth. She knew what it meant. She had to find a bathroom—and fast.

"Sure," Mikhail said.

Kerry pressed on the accelerator, fighting the nausea welling inside her. The car spurted into the parking lot of the Exxon station, tires squealing as she swung it into a parking space. Thank God it wasn't busy.

Cupping her hands over her mouth, Kerry jumped out of the car and ran, coatless, to the outside restroom.

Please don't be locked, she prayed, forcing back a gag.

It wasn't. She burst into the restroom and bent over the toilet, expelling the remains of the Wendy's double cheeseburger she'd so enjoyed a couple of hours before.

Wiping her face with a wet paper towel, she stepped out into the frigid sunlight and headed for the passenger side of the car. Mikhail was at the wheel, waiting. His eyes mirrored concern as he watched her slide into the passenger seat.

"Are you okay?" he asked.

She nodded, still dabbing at her forehead with the damp paper towel, avoiding his eyes. "I'll live. I guess that cheeseburger didn't agree with me."

His lips twitched. "Perhaps you should have ordered single."

"What are you, my mother?" She slanted him a disgruntled look. "Let's go, okay? I want to try to get to Gettysburg by tonight."

He looked startled at the curt tone of her voice, and somehow, or so Kerry imagined, hurt. She almost apologized, but then remembered that he might well be a calculating espionage agent who may have put Adam into the hospital, so she remained silent. Let him think what he damn well wanted.

Mikhail didn't speak again until they were back on the highway. On the stereo, Bono was belting out "Stranger in a Strange Land."

Apt, thought Kerry. That was Mikhail, all right. He was a stranger, and this was for damn sure, a strange land to him. That was something she needed to keep in mind. He was a virtual stranger. What did she know about him, really? Maybe it would be best if she backed away. Things had gotten way too friendly between them. And if he *did* have something to do with Adam's accident…

"This land," he said suddenly, making a sweeping gesture toward the snow-covered rolling hills of western Pennsylvania. "…Very beautiful. What is like here in summer?"

She shrugged. "I don't know. I've never been here in summer. But I hear it gets awfully hot and muggy."

He nodded. "I like hot and muggy. Maybe I will live here after I get asylum. Or perhaps Colorado. I like Colorado, too."

"Well, if it's hot and muggy you like, you shouldn't choose Colorado. Now if—" She bit back the words she'd started to say. *Damn!* Why couldn't she keep her mouth shut? Two minutes ago, she'd decided to keep things impersonal between them. But here she was, giving him advice on where to live.

He glanced at her. "Yes? You were saying?"

She shook her head and looked out the window at a raging brook flowing over snow-covered rocks. "Nothing. Never mind."

She felt his puzzled gaze, but refused to look at him.

"What is wrong, Kerry?" Mikhail asked after a moment. "You are acting strange."

The stop at the gas station restroom had alleviated her nausea, but her thoughts were still roiling around in her brain like lava threatening to burst from the mouth of a volcano. It was a weakness in her, she knew, but Kerry had never been able to stop an eruption once it had reached the boiling point.

And the boiling point had been reached.

She turned in her seat and fastened a hard gaze upon Mikhail's bewildered face.

"I want the truth, and I want it right now, Mikhail Kozlof, or I swear, I'll dump your ass out onto the side of the road, and leave you to freeze there. *I swear it!*"

His jaw slackened in shock. "Truth about what?"

Her mouth tightened. "About Adam. Did you arrange his accident?" She stared at him, every muscle in her body vibrating with tension as she waited for his answer.

Slowly, the blood drained from his face as the impact of her words hit him. He looked back at the road, his expression inscrutable. A nerve twitched in his jaw. And still, he didn't answer.

A minute ticked by, keeping time with the savage beat of Larry Mullen's pounding drums in "Is That All?" She felt Mikhail's anger. No, it was fury. It emanated from his body, an electric energy almost as potent as the sexual energy that so captivated her. But this...*fury*...she sensed now, was so alien coming from him, so intimidating, she didn't dare speak. Not until he responded to her accusation.

He flicked on the turn signal and pulled off the road into the parking lot of an old abandoned grain elevator. His jaw set, he put the Volvo in park, and turned to her, his eyes icy.

As if on cue, the U2 song came to an end, and there was a sudden silence in the car.

"Is that what you think?" he asked, his voice barely audible.

Kerry took a deep breath, and defiantly met his gaze. "It doesn't matter what I think. I want the truth." The CD began to play at the beginning again with Bono enthusiastically belting out "Gloria."Kerry reached over to turn down the volume. "Did you have anything to do with Adam's accident? You have to admit it was very convenient. It got you what you wanted—my help. And being able to escape before the free dance. I'd be a fool not to wonder."

"Why did you not wonder before?" He asked tightly. "Why did you not ask me that day at hospital? We took walk outside. If you were suspicious, why did you not ask?"

"I wasn't suspicious then. It never occurred to me you might have...you know...had something to do with it. It wasn't until you...back at the restaurant...when you made that horrible remark about Adam being in a coma. That got me thinking."

Mikhail swore in Russian. He looked away and shook his head. Then with an unexpected violence, he slammed the palms of his hands against the steering wheel. Kerry flinched.

His fingers curled around the steering wheel. Kerry wondered if he was imagining it was her neck he was gripping with such violence. He turned to her, his eyes blazing. "I am *insult!* You know, you are no different from Adam. You pretend you are open-minded, yet, you show true colors now. You think all Russians are evil communists. Maybe spy. You think this, no? Tell me. Is that what you think? I am spy?"

"*No!* I mean, *I don't know!* How am I *supposed* to know?" Kerry shot back, her anger matching his. "We've known each other, what? A couple of weeks? How do I know who you are, at all? You won't tell me why you want to defect! And you still haven't answered my question. Did you, or did you not, have something to do with Adam's accident?"

"*No!*" He turned and grabbed her upper arms, his hands tightening on them with an iron-like grip. His eyes impaled her. "I did not have *anything* to do with accident. *Kerry!*" He stopped, staring at her. His voice softened. "Kerry, you almost made love to me. Do you think you would want the kind of man who would do such a monstrous thing? We may not have known each other long, but I believe you know me better than you think you do."

For a long moment, Kerry stared into his earnest blue eyes. She *did* believe him, she realized. Or else, she *wanted* to believe him so desperately that she was convincing herself his story was true. Why? Because she was so over the moon for him that she refused to believe he could be anything but what he said he was? Could he have mesmerized her that much?

Jiminy Freakin' Cricket! What was she thinking? In love? No, impossible! She'd vowed never to fall in love again. Not after Joshua. Falling in love just led to too much trouble. So, why was she thinking "over the moon" in relation to Mikhail?

His gaze swept over her face, lingering on her lips. The anger had completely disappeared, replaced by molten desire. He was like her, in that way. He could no more hide what he was feeling than Britney Spears could sing and dance without grabbing at her crotch.

"Do you still want me, Kerry?" Mikhail asked huskily. "Because I sure as hell want you."

His hands imprisoned her head, and his mouth claimed hers in a hot, hungry kiss. Kerry sighed against his questing tongue, and gave herself up to it. His fingers threaded through her hair, gathering and releasing as they kissed, breaking for a moment of air, and merging again for more intoxicating sweetness. Over the rapid beat of her heart, she heard the sound of passing traffic on the highway, and on the stereo, Bono, singing about throwing a brick through a window. And Mikhail's staggered breathing. She could feel the thudding of his heart beneath her palm. His scent surrounded her, a combination of rosemary, sage and oak moss from his cologne, and the muskiness of his own unique maleness.

Mikhail's hands slid down her neck, and onto her shoulders as his tongue played with hers, teasingly erotic. He touched her breasts through her cotton sweater, and a furl of heat exploded from her womb. A soft moan escaped her mouth as he released it momentarily to nuzzle at a point on her neck just below her ear. Her hands crept up to tangle in his hair, and she angled his head so that his mouth was once again seeking hers. His fingers latched onto her nipple, stroking, teasing. With a soft moan, she arched her body against his, her knee ramming against the gearshift as she tried to position herself where she needed to be.

"*Cheri!*" Mikhail cursed, breaking the kiss, and shoving his body back in his own seat. He ran trembling hands through his rumpled hair. "I will not fuck you in car like barnyard animal."

Gasping for breath, Kerry stared at him in astonishment. "You…you…*what?*"

He slanted her a chagrined look. "You heard me. This…" He gestured to himself and then her. "This thing between us…is more than down-and-dirty sex. I will not fuck you in car like barnyard animal."

Kerry burst out laughing. Something about the way he said it, the frustrated, yet, embarrassed look on his face, the entire ludicrous situation, struck her as absolutely hilarious. She laughed so hard that tears misted her eyes.

He looked at her, startled. "What is so funny?"

She tried to speak, but couldn't. Every time she tried to get something out, the giggles took over again. He leaned back, folded his arms across his chest and watched her, trying to keep an affronted look on his face. It didn't work. Reluctantly, his lips twitched, and his blue eyes grew amused.

When it seemed like she'd finally regained control, he spoke, "I am happy to be your comic entertainment."

And that set her off again. He shook his head, a bemused grin spreading over his face. "You are crazy woman, Kerry Niles," he said.

"I know." Still snickering, Kerry wiped the tears from her eyes. "It's a bitch, but I've learned to live with it."

"Are you ready to tell me why you find me so amusing?"

"It's not you, exactly," she said, grinning. "It's just the way you said that." She arranged her face in a somber expression and lowered her voice to imitate a macho Russian accent, "'I will not fuck you in car like barnyard animal.'" Another peal of laughter rang out. "First of all, I don't get the analogy. It's not the habit of barnyard animals to fuck in cars. Not to my knowledge, anyway. And also…you just looked so damn cute when you said it."

His brow arched quizzically. "Like I said, I'm happy to be entertainment."

"You idiot!" Kerry reached out and imprisoned his head between her hands. She kissed him, a hard, bruising kiss on the mouth, and released him just as he was getting into it. "But you're right. This is not the place to…uh…continue down this path. We should get going."

Mikhail nodded, and put the gearshift into drive. He glanced over his left shoulder, and pulled out onto the highway. On the stereo, Bono was singing "Fire." Kerry was sure she'd never be able to listen to this CD again without cracking up…or getting exceedingly horny.

For a few moments, Mikhail drove without speaking. Kerry gazed out the window, twirling a lock of hair around her index finger, and trying to quell the waves of pulsating sensations going on down south. *Damn the man!* He was getting really good at bringing her to fever pitch then putting on the brakes.

"Fire" ended, and in the momentary silence between tracks, Mikhail cleared his throat. "Kerry, your friend who runs this bed and breakfast…" He stared straight ahead, seemingly concentrating on the road.

"Yes?"

"Do you think she would have problem with us sharing room?"

Kerry's jaw dropped. She turned to look at him as her heartbeat picked up. He continued to stare at the road as if it were the most interesting thing he'd seen in years. Kerry coughed, and then said, "I don't think she would have a problem with that."

He nodded, and then looked at her. The impact of his smoldering blue eyes took her breath away. "This is good," he said.

Kerry swallowed hard and turned to look out the window. A slow grin crossed her face, and she began to sing along with Bono, "Won't you come back tomorrow?"

CHAPTER FIFTEEN

The weathered stone house nestling in the snow-covered trees at the summit of Mount Carmel looked like a postcard of the ultimate winter getaway. It looked like…

Kerry drew in a sharp breath, braking gently on the snow-packed winding road, as the thought went through her mind. It looked like a honeymooner's paradise. The perfect place for a getaway, a place to while away long, lazy afternoons making slow, sweet love.

Her hand trembled on the steering wheel as she pulled up next to a navy BMW with Maryland tags. There were several other expensive cars in the parking lot, some from as far away as New York. Apparently, Dale was doing well for herself. Kerry glanced at Mikhail, her cheeks still burning from her amorous thoughts.

"Well, this is it. Mount Carmel Inn. What do you think?"

Soft floodlights illuminated the stone house and its protective boundary of snow-powdered trees. The stone walkway leading from the small parking lot to the steps had been cleared and salted. Carriage lights framing the burnished oak door with etched glass sidelights beamed a cheerful wintry welcome as did the flickering candles set in crystal blocks lining the steps to the porch. Frozen luminaries, Kerry recognized. She and Grandma Vive had made similar ice candles in Utah that had lasted all winter long. Dale had certainly used her Finnish heritage to turn this place into a winter wonderland.

"Is very beautiful," Mikhail said quietly, staring at the inn. "Looks like perfect place to…" He turned his head, his eyes finding hers. "…love you."

Kerry gasped, her gaze darting away in confusion. Flustered by his directness, she turned off the ignition and reached for her purse on the back seat. She tried to sound casual, but the catch in her voice gave her away. "I haven't seen Dale in years, and I know she'll have a million things to talk about."

He nodded and reached for the door handle. "I am patient man."

She got out of the car and pulled on her coat for protection against the biting wind. A few flurries drifted through the night air. The radio station they'd picked up in Harrisburg had called for clear weather through the next few days, but maybe up here in the higher altitude, they would get a little snow.

Good, Kerry thought. Getting snowed in up here with Mikhail wouldn't be a devastating problem. Funny, how a few hours ago, she'd half-convinced herself she was traveling with a desperate Russian spy. What had she been smoking?

The front door of the house opened as they made their way up the walk, and a slim woman with a grayish-blond bob called out an excited welcome. Earlier, Kerry had called Dale from a pay phone in Harrisburg, asking if they could stop by. Her father's former fiancée had been thrilled, exclaiming that by incredible good fortune, she'd had a cancellation just that morning, and a suite was available. Apparently, with nearby Ski Liberty doing a brisk business in an especially snowy winter, the Mount Carmel Inn had been packed to capacity all season long.

An omen, Kerry had thought, as she hung up the phone. She was through fighting her attraction to Mikhail. Obviously, whatever was going to happen between them was meant to be. And now, even the fates were giving their approval.

"*Kerry*! It's so good to see you!" Beaming, Dale Tuomas stepped gingerly out onto the front porch. "Careful, now, both of you. It's icy."

Fresh-cut pine boughs carpeted the entrance to the house, a sight familiar to Kerry from her early years in Utah with her father and grandparents—a Finnish tradition that simultaneously welcomed visitors into a home while keeping slush from snowy boots out. Would Dale also have cozy felt boots waiting inside the foyer for guests to change into upon entering? Grandma Vive kept a supply of them handy throughout the winter.

Kerry walked up the steps, past the flickering luminaries, feeling butterflies jumping in her stomach. It was silly, but she couldn't stop thinking about how the pre-teen Kerry had treated this lovely woman. Oh, she hadn't been obnoxious—not the way she'd been with Jana when she'd first moved to San Diego. But she'd never exactly welcomed Dale into their lives. She'd been too threatened by her, and by her father's obvious love for the woman.

"Hi, Dale." Kerry smiled at her, but made no move to touch her. "Thanks for letting us come by."

Dale's gentle blue eyes swept over her. "You're all grown up! Come here." The woman reached out and enveloped Kerry in a warm embrace. "Oh, I'm so glad you're here."

At first, Kerry was startled, but breathing in her familiar scent of lavender and thyme, she relaxed into Dale's hug as a memory washed over her. Another time when she had been the one embracing Dale. The day of her father's funeral.

Kerry had found her sobbing quietly in Grandma Vive's kitchen, and without hesitation, she'd gone to her and wrapped her arms around the woman's willowy waist.

"It's okay," she'd murmured. "We'll get through this together."

And that had been her first real overture to the woman who'd wanted to come into her life and be a mother to her. Too late, Kerry thought now as she hugged the older woman tightly, swallowing a marble-sized lump that had formed in her throat. She'd accepted her too late.

Dale finally released her, laughing softly. She turned to Mikhail who stood just behind Kerry, and extended a slim hand adorned with a glittering sapphire ring. "Hello. I'm Dale Tuomas. Welcome to Mount Carmel Inn."

Kerry cleared her throat. "Dale, this is…my friend, Mikhail. I told you about him on the phone."

Dale's eyes scanned Mikhail, and Kerry immediately realized they would pull nothing over on her. Not that she'd intended to do that. She'd planned to tell Dale everything, but she could see by the appraising look on the woman's face that it wouldn't be necessary.

Mikhail shook Dale's hand, murmuring a greeting.

"Well, come on." Dale smiled. "Let's get in out of the cold. Have you two eaten? I just started a pot of homemade potato soup, and I made fresh bread today."

"Sounds heavenly," Kerry said, following Dale into a spacious pine-floored foyer.

The interior of the inn looked exactly how Kerry would've expected. It spoke of Dale's Finnish heritage with clean, fresh lines, potted plants and personal touches of elegance and comfort throughout. Colors of cobalt blue and pristine white predominated, accented with natural fabrics and soft sheepskin rugs.

"Oh, but first, let's get you situated in your suite." Dale took a key from a pine writing desk on one side of the foyer. "You'll probably want to shower before dinner. But…" Her high cheekbones grew rosy as a thought occurred to her. She looked from Kerry to Mikhail. "I told you on the phone there's only one available suite. Ordinarily, I would have a spare bedroom to put you up in, but they've got this special thing going on at Ski Liberty…"

Kerry met her gaze. "No problem, Dale. We'll make do."

Her smile returned. "Okay, then. Your suite is this way."

Dale led them down an enclosed glass breezeway that led from the back of the house to a separate building. "I had this built on when business picked up a few years ago," she said, her voice humming with pride. "I had people on a six month waiting list to get into the inn. Can you believe that?" She glanced over her shoulder and smiled at them. "Word of mouth really got around. I've had a lot of politicians from Washington and…" She winked. "A few celebrities. And now, I have you two. Anyway, I decided to build on this special suite. It's the most luxurious of all of them. Here we are—the Summit Suite."

She unlocked the door, and stepped aside so Kerry and Mikhail could enter. Kerry stepped into the living room, and caught her breath. A huge stone fireplace immediately drew her gaze, taking up the expanse of one wall, a cheerfully blazing fire in its grate. A cluster of cobalt velour chairs and an L-shaped white sofa were positioned around it for maximum enjoyment. In front of the sofa, a glass coffee table held a beautifully bound book about Gettysburg and a two-pound box of Godiva chocolates. Kerry immediately decided that Mikhail could enjoy the book, and she'd take care of the chocolate. But then remembering his fondness for Ding Dongs, she resigned herself to sharing.

On the other side of the room, a breakfast bar separated the living room from a full-sized kitchen. A basket of fruit and nuts rested on its sea-green marbled counter-top.

"I don't expect you'll be cooking," Dale said, moving into the kitchen and opening cabinets. "But just in case, you'll find the cabinets well stocked with staples. Coffee, hot chocolate, popcorn. Of course, I'll be bringing breakfast to you at whatever time you choose tomorrow morning. Just fill out this little card with what you want, and leave it on the door handle. Now, let me show you the bedrooms." She headed down a hallway, gesturing for them to follow. "There are three bedrooms in this suite. We often get a lot of families who come for a week of skiing."

Kerry glanced back at Mikhail, and saw the amused look on his face. She blushed, reading his mind.

We will only be using one bedroom.

"Oh, this is the bathroom." Dale paused at a door on the left. "We have a Jacuzzi, candles, bath oils, and music is piped in from the stereo in the living room. And we have a separate shower, of course." She smiled. "I imagine you'll be fighting over that in a few minutes. Car trips are so tiring, aren't they?" She turned and headed back down the hall.

Kerry felt Mikhail's hand on her shoulder, and a second later, the warm air of his breath as his mouth dipped toward her ear. "No need to fight," he whispered. "We can always shower together."

A delicious shiver snaked up her back. "Behave yourself," she said under her breath, flashing him an admonishing frown. He gave her a slow, suggestive smile. The smoldering look in his eyes turned her knees to mush. "I *mean* it, Mikhail!"

"The master bedroom," Dale said, standing at the threshold of the room straight ahead.

Kerry stepped inside, her eyes widening. "Oh, Dale! It's *gorgeous!*"

A Scandinavian pine king-sized bed dominated the room, its iron-framed canopy draped with white lace. Beside the bed on a matching nightstand awaited a chilling bottle of wine in a silver ice bucket. A floor-to-ceiling pine armoire held court adjacent to the bed, and on the other side of the spacious room, two soft chairs cuddled around another stone fireplace, a smaller replica of the one in the family room. A fire was burning in this grate, as well.

Dale saw Kerry looking at the fire, and smiled. "I know. I love the smell of wood fire, too, but it's just too inconvenient for guests. I had the fireplaces changed over to gas after the first year of business. It was an easy decision to make after one of the guests practically burned down the whole place." She clapped her hands together and grinned. "Well, that's the two-dollar tour. Tell you what, you two get settled in. Shower, take a nap...whatever. And I'll go finish dinner. Eight o'clock, okay? I don't usually serve dinner to my guests, but then, I don't consider you guests, but family. Will that be enough time for you?"

"Sure, that'll be fine." Kerry didn't have to look at her watch to know it was pretty close to six-thirty. "Thanks, Dale. It's a beautiful place."

"Yes," Mikhail said, giving Dale a warm smile. "Is lovely...just like our hostess."

Dale beamed, and her color heightened. She glanced from Mikhail to Kerry. "I'm beginning to understand how he talked you into helping him."

A startled look crossed Mikhail's face, and Kerry almost burst out laughing. Apparently, he'd had no idea that Dale had figured out who he was. She looked back at the older woman, her lips twitching. "Yeah, if I didn't know better, I'd swear he was Irish, considering how good he is at talking blarney."

Dale shook her head wryly. "Reminds me of someone I used to know." She turned to go, and it wasn't until she'd stepped out of the room that Kerry realized she'd been referring to her father. It had never occurred to her before, but Dad had possessed a charisma very much like Mikhail's. Was that why she felt so close to him?

"See you at eight," Dale called out as she opened the entry door. It closed behind her.

Kerry stood in the hallway, staring after her, and then she sensed Mikhail's approach. A moment later, his arms curled around her waist. He drew her against his hard, muscled body, and she caught her breath at the swell of his erection against the small of her back. His mouth trailed along the length of her neck. "I vote for...*whatever*," he murmured.

Heat pooled deep in her belly at the touch of his tongue against her skin. She closed her eyes and leaned into him. His hands molded against her abdomen, stroking.

"Mmmm...what do you mean...whatever?"

His mouth drew away from her neck momentarily. "Dale's suggestions." He paused to nip at her throat. "Shower." Another soft stroke of his tongue. "Nap." He lapped again. "Whatever." The tip of his tongue curled into the shell-like opening of her ear. "I like *whatever*."

Liquid fire shot through her bloodstream, and Kerry shivered. With an effort, she drew away from him, and turned around to cup his face in her hands. "Stop this *right now!*"

His blue eyes gazed back at her, guileless. "Stop?"

"Yes, stop. We have...uh..." She lifted her hand to peer at her watch. "Exactly...an hour and thirty-five minutes before dinner. We need to bring in our stuff, shower..." She sniffed, and made a disgusted face. "God! I can't believe you want to make love to me when I smell like this. Has it been that long, Mikhail?"

"You smell like fresh daisies," he protested, reaching for her again.

She backed away. "*No*! Later, Mikhail. Trust me, you'll be glad we waited."

He looked doubtful, but then sighed. "If you say so. I will get luggage."

"Good." She smiled at him. "I'll go ahead and jump in the shower. Can you bring my suitcase into the bathroom? And no peeking, okay?"

He gave her an affronted look. "Do I look like kind of man who would resort to *peeking*?"

She laughed, and gave his blond head a ruffle with her fingertips. "Yeah, as a matter-of-fact, you do."

Mikhail's heart dipped as she gave him a saucy smile and disappeared into the bathroom, closing the door behind her. For a long moment, he stared at the closed door, his heart bumping. The realization had come out of nowhere, simultaneous with Kerry's come-hither smile, and it had jagged through him like a lightning bolt.

He was in love with her.

* * * * *

Kerry stepped into Dale's kitchen, wearing her oldest pair of faded jeans and a thick off-white turtleneck sweater. Her hair was still damp from the shower, and because she hadn't wanted to take the time to blow-dry it, she'd French-braided it and secured it with an elastic band. She was anxious to talk to Dale one-on-one. There were so many things she wanted to say.

The kitchen smelled heavenly with the aroma of baking bread, brewing coffee and whatever was cooking on the stove. Potato soup, wasn't it? The slim blond woman stood at the stove, stirring chopped carrots into a cast-iron Dutch oven. She looked good, Kerry thought. Life must've treated her well in the seventeen years since she'd last seen her. She must be, what? Close to fifty now, Kerry guessed, yet her trim, athletic body could pass for a woman of thirty. Oh, how Dad must've loved her. Now that Kerry could look at it without the jealous mind of a twelve-year-old, she realized what a great match Dale had been for her father. Like him, she came from tough Finnish stock, and loved the outdoors, especially when it came to winter and all the snow activities that came with it. She skied, almost as well as Dad had, and like him, loved snow-shoeing and ice fishing. They'd gotten along so well.

A wave of sadness washed over Kerry. Why had she never seen that? Poor Dad. He'd had such a bad marriage with Jana. He'd so deserved a woman like Dale. Why had things turned out the way they had?

Dale looked up and smiled. "Oh, hi. You look nice and fresh." Her brow furrowed. "What's wrong, Kerry? Why such a sad look on your face?"

Kerry shook her head and spoke candidly. "I was just wishing I'd been nicer to you all those years ago."

Dale wiped her hands on a towel hanging on the stove, and then shook her head. "Oh, honey. You were just a kid afraid of changes. I knew that." She closed the distance between them, and took Kerry into her arms. "I had no doubt I'd get you to love me. All I needed was time."

Tears clogged Kerry's throat as she clung to Dale, remembering that horrible evening the two of them had waited in the Whistler Lodge for news of her father. And then, it had come, and their lives had been shattered. "And time was the one thing we didn't have," Kerry said, her voice breaking.

Dale stroked her braid a moment, and then released her. Tears shimmered in her blue eyes. "No. But I've never regretted a moment I spent with Kell. He was the love of my life."

"I know."

Dale turned back to the counter. "I just made a pot of coffee. You want a cup?"

"That would be awesome." She took a deep breath, trying to gain control of her tremulous emotions, and slid onto a stool at the breakfast bar. She watched as Dale took two Dutch blue ceramic mugs from the cabinet. "So, Dale, you never got married in all these years?"

Dale glanced over at her and smiled, the laugh lines around her eyes deepening. "I almost did a few years ago." She poured steaming coffee into the mugs. Its rich, Colombian aroma drifted through the air, causing Kerry's stomach to rumble with anticipation. She was starving! How long had it been since she'd had that Wendy's cheeseburger?

"What happened?" Kerry asked as Dale placed a mug in front of her and pointed out a matching ceramic sugar bowl on a Lazy Susan.

Dale shrugged and took a cream pitcher out of the refrigerator. "Oh, I was dating this guy for a while, and he wanted to get married, but...you want cream?" At Kerry's nod, she placed the creamer on the counter, and went on, "When it came right down to it, I couldn't do it. I had my life, this place, the solitude. And I decided..." She shrugged. "I was happy with the way things were. Why change it?" She gave a sad smile and positioned herself on the stool next to Kerry. "Well, he didn't see things the same way, and eventually, he moved on. I couldn't blame him." She took a sip of coffee, then met Kerry's gaze. "It's just hard, you know. I kept comparing him to Kell, and he came up wanting." Her lips twisted in a wry smile. "I guess a psychiatrist would have a field day with that, huh?"

"Oh, I'm thinking they've probably heard it all before," Kerry said lightly.

Dale set down her coffee mug and turned to her. "So, whatever made you go on the run with your good-looking Russian? It's been all over the news. What are your plans?"

Kerry laughed. "One question at a time. I don't really know why I did it. Let's just say he's very convincing."

Dale's eyes danced. "I'll *bet* he is."

Kerry felt her cheeks warm at the innuendo in Dale's voice. Was it so obvious she was attracted to him? *Well, duh!* Could it be because she was panting after him like a love-starved puppy?

"As for our plans, we're heading to my step-brother's house in Occoquan, Virginia, and then, I guess he'll take Mikhail into CIA Headquarters for…what is it…debriefing? It's been quite an adventure, I'll say that. We almost got caught in Colorado by a Russian goon and his Irish partner, but managed to get away."

Dale's gaze sharpened, a glimmer of worry appearing in her eyes. "Just that one close call? People like that don't usually give up."

Kerry's brow puckered as she stared down into her coffee mug. "I know. I've been thinking about that, too. We haven't seen a sign of anyone tracking us since then. We've been really watchful, too. That *is* weird, isn't it?"

A buzzer went off on the stove, and Dale slid off the stool. She turned it off, and then opened the refrigerator door to pull out a half-gallon of milk. Frowning, she poured some into the cast-iron pot on the stove, stirring. She covered the pot again and placed the wooden spoon on a plate near the burner.

"My guess is…they're waiting for you in Occoquan," she said slowly, looking up and meeting her gaze.

Kerry's heart lurched.

"They've probably figured out where you're headed and they plan to get to you before you can get to your step-brother."

Kerry felt the blood drain from her face. Of course! Dale was right. That was exactly what they were going to do.

"I can't let them get to Mikhail, Dale," she said quietly. "What are we going to do?"

Dale smiled, and turned back to the refrigerator. She brought out a head of lettuce and fixings for salad. "That's easy enough. We'll simply have your stepbrother come to *you*. I'm sure he's been alerted to the situation, and is expecting you. We'll simply call him, and have him drive up here and get you." She rinsed the lettuce under running water and placed it into a spinner. Then she looked up and gave Kerry a radiant smile, her eyes misted with tears. "I'm so glad you found the love of *your* life, Kerry."

* * * * *

"After you, *angel moy*." Mikhail stepped back from the door of their suite and smiled.

Kerry's heart, which was already beating about a thousand times faster than usual, wrenched up a notch. Great, she thought. She'd have a heart attack at the tender age of twenty-eight, and her plans for a sensuous evening featuring sweet, slow love-making with Mikhail would be ruined.

It had been tough getting through dinner, carrying on polite conversation with Dale while feeling Mikhail's burning gaze upon her, and knowing what they planned to do once they were back in their suite. Hard to concentrate, to say the least. And of course, Dale knew exactly what was going on, except that Kerry had a feeling she thought they'd been sleeping together for some time. If their speed at getting through dinner, and then dessert and coffee, was a puzzlement to her, she didn't let it show.

By the time they excused themselves, it was nine-thirty. Much to Mikhail's frustration, which he tried, and mostly succeeded at hiding, Kerry had insisted on helping Dale with the dishes. Finally, after saying goodnight, she'd followed Mikhail back to their room—at a pace faster than she'd ever seen him move.

She stepped past him into the living room of the suite, and the door closed behind her. Pressing a hand over her pounding heart, she took a deep breath and released it slowly. This was so silly! She felt like a timid virgin in a Victorian novel, about to be ravished by a rakish highwayman. One that was gorgeous, and ultimately heroic, of course. But really! She'd been around the block a few times. Her affair with Joshua had stripped her of all innocence years ago. So, why did she feel something uncomfortably close to…?

She swallowed hard, and clutched a hand to her suddenly unsettled tummy.

…*fear*?

No, not fear. Nerves. But sometimes, the two emotions were very close cousins, and damned if they didn't have the same result on her equilibrium.

The skin on her arms tingled as she felt Mikhail's approach behind her. She turned abruptly, and drew in a sharp breath at the smoldering look on his face. His eyes roved over her, bluer than ever, heated to a slow simmer.

He placed his hands on her shoulders and gazed down at her. "Day has been long, yes?"

Kerry tried, but couldn't speak. Her heart was still pounding like a kettledrum, and her stomach felt like it was going to make her the star attraction in a Humiliate Kerry Show. Mikhail's eyes focused on her lips, and as his head lowered for the kiss, she brought her fingers up to cover his mouth.

"Wait!"

He paused, eyes questioning.

"Onions," Kerry said. "Dale had onions in her potato soup." She breathed air onto her palm, sniffed, and then faked a cringe. "Yep. Onions. I've got to go brush my teeth first...and when I'm done, you might want to do it, too." She whirled around and hurried down the hall to the bathroom, slamming the door behind her.

Leaning against it, she took a deep breath and closed her eyes. Idiot, she thought. He probably thinks you're some kind of freak. *And maybe you are.* Cradling her tumultuous stomach, she took another deep, cleansing breath. Non-freaky people didn't get queasy at the thought of making love. But why now? This had never happened before. She liked sex. Always had. But this time, oh, God! This time, it was with Mikhail.

Another deep breath, and the butterflies in her tummy began to dissipate. Good. Maybe it was all in her head. She went to the sink and began to brush her teeth. A memory flitted through her mind. That other time they'd almost made love. She'd been brushing her teeth while he went for condoms. Why was it she hadn't had butterflies that night?

Because you weren't in love with him then.

She gasped and stared into the mirror. Her startled eyes stared back. Oh, God! It *was* true, wasn't it? She'd fallen head over heels for the man. No point in denying it any longer. She spit into the sink, grabbed a glass and rinsed out her mouth, still musing over this revelation.

She'd gone and done it now, hadn't she? Exactly what she'd told herself she couldn't, under any circumstances, do.

What a moron.

Shaking her head, she rinsed off the toothbrush and grabbed a tube of lipstick from her cosmetic bag. Color! That's what she needed. She looked as if she'd spent an afternoon at the blood bank. She smeared the lipstick on, and examined herself in the mirror. Better, but her face still looked only slightly healthier than an anemic albino. Maybe some blush would help.

Fifteen minutes later, she stepped out of the bathroom, her face completely made up—foundation, eye shadow, blush—the works.

"Mikhail?" She glanced around the living room, but it was empty.

"In here," he called out from the bedroom.

Her brow furrowed. His voice sounded odd. There was an undercurrent of…something…in it. Anxiety? Maybe even fear?

Kerry headed down the hallway. She hoped Mikhail wasn't having an attack of nerves, too, or they'd never get this show on the road.

"Mikhail, what—?"

She stepped into the bedroom and stopped short, eyes widening.

"Please…" Mikhail spoke slowly and carefully. "Get…it…off…me?"

Kerry began to laugh. She couldn't help herself. It was the funniest thing she'd ever seen in her life. Mikhail lay in the bed, bare-chested, his body rigid with fear at the tiger-striped cat lying on his stomach. It, on the other hand, looked perfectly at ease, nonchalantly licking its paws.

Mikhail's eyes darted from the cat to Kerry, still standing in the doorway, giggling helplessly at the sight of a grown man terrorized by an adolescent kitten. "I'm sorry," she mumbled. "It's just so...so..."

"Go away, cat," Mikhail said, glaring. "Kerry, *please*! Take cat away."

"Okay, okay." Kerry went to the bed and grabbed the cat, which protested with an annoyed meow. "Ah, it's so cute!" She cradled the animal in her arms, stroking its soft belly. It peered up at her with golden eyes and stretched its mouth in a feline yawn. "How can you be scared of such a sweet little thing?" Kerry asked, scratching the cat's neck. A contented purr rumbled from its throat.

"Long story," Mikhail said grumpily. "Please, take cat out."

"Okay. I'll be right back."

She deposited the cat outside the entry door, and it trotted off toward the main part of the house. She wondered when it had gotten into their suite. Probably when Mikhail had brought in their luggage. Dale had mentioned at dinner that she had a couple of cats, and now that she thought about it, at that very moment, Mikhail had looked as if he'd bit into something hideous. That could be a problem to their budding relationship, Kerry thought, considering that she was most definitely a cat person. She'd grown up with cats at Grandma Vive's, and had planned to get one for herself once she'd established a stable home. Typical. And now, she'd gone and fallen in love with a cat hater.

Oh, well. Too late now. Kerry headed down the hall toward the bedroom. Funny, she didn't feel nervous anymore. Nothing like laughter to drive away the pre-sex butterflies.

As she passed the bathroom, she saw the door was closed, and behind it, she heard the sound of running water. The shower, not the sink. She smiled. Poor Mikhail was trying to shower away cat residue. Somehow, she found that endearing.

In the bedroom, she stripped off her sweater, and then slid her jeans down her hips. She turned to the mirror and gave her body a critical scan. In anticipation of the night, she'd chosen to wear her lacy rose-colored bra and matching panties—attire appropriate for seduction. Reaching up, she released her hair from the French braid, and it tumbled to her shoulders in shining black ripples. She liked the way it gave her a hippie sort of look. But...she frowned...the make-up was all wrong. What had possessed her? She looked like she was auditioning to appear in Christina Aguilera's "Moulin Rouge" video. With a groan of disgust, she reached for a tissue and began to rub off as much make-up as she could without water or make-up removal, which, of course, was in her toiletry bag in the bathroom with Mikhail. Oh, God! Maybe she should go back to the bathroom and wash her face after Mikhail got out. At this rate, Roger would be here before she and Mikhail made love. Except...

She grinned. She hadn't exactly called him yet. Tomorrow, she'd decided. Tonight would be for her and Mikhail, with no thoughts of anything else.

There. Her face looked almost normal now, except for the unnatural red of her lips. Potent dye, that stuff. Probably saturated with cancer-causing agents. She'd have to change brands. Surely one of those environmentally safe cosmetic companies made a shade similar to Wicked Devil Red. Then, again, maybe she should reconsider the shade, she thought, as she scrubbed at her lips with a tissue. This one definitely screamed out *tart*.

"*Laskovaya moya*..."

Kerry whipped around at the sound of the Russian phrase. And her breath left her body.

Mikhail stood in the doorway, totally nude. She stared, her heart tripping into overdrive. Totally unself-conscious, he watched her as she absorbed the beauty of his body—the toned, hair-roughened chest, the muscular biceps, the narrow waist and hips. Legs, strong and corded from years of skating and ballet, carpeted with golden hair. Her cheeks burned hot as her gaze swept over his groin. Natural blond, she saw. And most definitely aroused.

Apparently, that old wives' tale about big feet, big cock, was true.

Her temperature shot up another degree. She quickly averted her eyes, and turned to the mirror to fiddle with her hair.

Like a graceful panther, Mikhail crossed the room and stood behind her, not touching, but so close she could feel his body heat. He gazed over her shoulder into the mirror, his eyes meeting hers.

"You are most beautiful woman I've ever seen," he said softly.

Still holding her gaze in the mirror, he reached out, and his fingertip skimmed over the freckles that dotted her nose and cheekbones. He smiled, and her heart dipped.

"I love your freckles," he said, his Russian accent thicker than ever.

"I hated them as a kid," she spoke breathlessly as his finger traveled down her face to her neck. "But I had a change of heart about them when I got older. I decided they were mine for better or worse, so I might as well accept them."

He bent his head and planted a gentle kiss against her neck. A tremor ran through her. Her legs suddenly felt so weak, she was sure they were about to give out on her. His lips were the only part of his body making contact with hers, but his heat rolled over her, turning her blood to lava. He looked up, again meeting her eyes in the mirror. Then positioning his hands on her shoulders, he drew her bra straps down, and then followed the movement with his lips, kissing one shoulder along its length, then the other. Kerry's legs began to tremble more violently. Reaching both hands around, he unfastened the front closure of her bra, then parted the lacy material. For a moment, his eyes watched her face, and then moved down to her taut brown nipples. He gently drew the bra off her shoulders and let it drop.

Kerry drew in a ragged breath, watching him. His breathing was irregular, too, his eyes bright with desire. For a moment, he didn't move. Then finally, his big hands came around her and cupped her breasts. Her sharp intake of air broke the silence. She watched his hands, mesmerized by his long, artistic fingers. Silver glinted in the firelight—his pinkie ring she'd noticed that morning when he'd asked her to skate with him. He always wore it. Did it have some special significance for him? There was so much she needed to learn about this man who so captivated her.

His eyes met hers in the mirror. "I love your breasts, as well," he murmured, his hands stroking her. "Ever since that night in hotel, I have been dreaming about your lovely breasts."

He nestled against her, still caressing her, and now, she felt his rigid heat against the small of her back. She closed

229

her eyes and arched her body against his. A ragged groan splintered from his throat.

Abruptly, he turned her in his arms, and grabbing a handful of her hair, he angled his mouth over hers. There was nothing subtle about his kiss. Her mouth opened under the onslaught of his tongue, her nails digging into the skin of his back. His erection prodded at her belly, insistent, urgent. Her head swam. She wanted him inside her now. She was frantic for him.

But Mikhail had other ideas. Breaking the kiss, he swept her up in his arms and carried her to the bed. His body covered hers, his hands roaming over her, touching her neck, throat, breasts, and tummy. It was as if he wanted to touch her all over, and all at once. Meanwhile, his mouth traveled its own seductive path. His tongue delved into her navel, and she writhed, her fingers entwined in his hair. He reached the lace edge of her bikini panties, and kissed his way along it—tender, wet kisses on her lower belly. His fingers explored the sensitive spot of tender flesh on her inner thighs.

"So sweet," he murmured, raising his head slightly. "Just like I knew you would be."

Kerry moaned and arched toward him, begging for him to touch her. She ached for him. Somehow reading her thoughts, he brushed his fingers over the damp crotch of her panties, and she flinched and cried out. Hooking his fingers on each side of the elastic, he drew the wisp of material down over her legs, and tossed it to the floor.

"Mikhail, please..." Kerry cried out, thrashing her head back and forth. She needed...she had to have...

He pulled her down on the bed and parted her legs. She felt his breath upon her swollen heat, and then, finally, his hard, wet tongue took her into the stratosphere.

Still quaking from her intense climax, he gathered her into his arms, and held her. After she was finally still, he cradled her face in his hands, and took her mouth in another long, soul-shattering kiss. Afterwards, she gazed into his eyes, her finger tracing the scar on his face from jaw to cheekbone.

"Oh, Mikhail," she whispered. "I never dreamed…"

"It is exactly how I dreamed," he said. He reached over to the bedside table and grabbed a rectangular packet. When had he put the condom there? He deftly opened the foil, and rolled the condom onto his stiff shaft. She caught her breath, her heart hammering. And just like that, her body was at a simmer again.

He moved over her, covering her body with his own, supporting his weight with his hands. His penis pressed against her pubic mound. "I do not want to hurt you," he said softly. "But I am…so much…want…" He shook his head. "I will try to be gentle."

Kerry grabbed a handful of his blond hair and nudged his head down so her mouth could take his in a succulent kiss. "I have…want, too," she said, and smiled. She rotated her hips against him in a saucy invitation. Her smile widened. "Make fuck to me, Mikhail."

"No," he said, eyes solemn. "Not make fuck. Make love."

He slowly entered her, and she gasped, closing her eyes in astonishment at the exquisite sensation that rivered through her. He didn't move for a moment, but just held motionless, allowing her to feel his fullness, his strength.

"Okay?" he asked, watching her.

She chewed her bottom lip, trying to hold back, to hold onto the rightness of the moment. "Yes."

He began to move. He held her gaze, his hands smoothing back her hair as he loved her. Keeping a steady rhythm—sweet and slow—he dipped down to play with her lips, using his mouth and tongue. In between, he watched her, his eyes riveted on hers as he gauged where she was, what she wanted. And always, that slow, exquisite drive in ever increasing intensity.

Kerry was lost in his blue eyes, in the magic of their union, the rhythm and tempo and primal need. At the moment of her climax, Mikhail called out her name in a hoarse voice, and with one final powerful stroke, he shuddered in release. Kerry clung to him, gasping. Finally, he collapsed against her, his breath hot against her neck. She felt his heartbeat pounding, in synch with hers, and the lyrics from a U2 song swept through her mind. "Two hearts beat as one." She smiled.

He lifted his head and gazed down at her. Her heart contracted at the tender look on his face. Cradling the sides of her head in his hands, he traced his thumbs over her brows, and then followed the caress with light kisses, first over her brows, down the bridge of her nose to finally settle with sure mastery on her lips. With a soft moan of surrender, she kissed him back. When their lips parted, Kerry gazed up at him, still intensely aware of him inside her.

"I don't want you to go," she said softly.

His eyes glimmered with sadness. "I do not want to go."

Her words, she knew, held a deeper meaning, but she wasn't sure what it was. Thoughts skated through her mind like passing clouds. He felt so good inside her, she didn't want him to go, but it was more than that. She didn't want him to go to Langley. Some weird sixth sense inside her warned that if she turned him over to Roger, he'd disappear out of her life, and she'd never see him again.

Slowly, Mikhail withdrew from her, and turning on his side, gathered her up against his heated, damp body. Her lips brushed the hollow of his throat, and she breathed in his spicy male scent. He tightened his arms around her, his hand moving sensuously down the small of her back. His lips brushed over her forehead in a delicate feather-touch. For a long moment, there was silence in the room with only the hiss of the gas fire, and the sound of their soft, mingled breathing.

We're so in tune, Kerry thought.

It was like nothing she'd ever felt before, this feeling of rightness, lying here in Mikhail's arms. She thought back to that first moment in Geneva when she'd watched him doing his stretches before taking to the ice. Even then, he'd captivated her. And now, she'd done what she'd been warning herself not to do from the moment he'd taken her hand and led her into a dance on the ice. She'd fallen in love with him—and even more foolhardy, had made love to him. But God, she didn't regret it! What, now, though? Where would they go from here?

A sigh rumbled from Mikhail's throat, and Kerry's heartbeat faltered. Was he regretting it already?

"My mother was murdered," he said quietly.

Her pulse jumped. She searched for something to say, but before she could think of anything, he went on. "She was working for an Estonian newspaper, and she discovered that the KGB conducted drug experimentation on a Sami village in the early Seventies." As he spoke, his voice grew progressively quieter. Kerry lay still in his arms, barely breathing. "Entire village died. My real father was one of victims. This, I found out just few months ago. At first, I wish to ignore this. Go on with my good life as privileged Russian athlete. I say to myself it is old history. That nothing will bring my parents back to life. But then, I realize that if I turn my back on what happened, my parents will have died for nothing, and I am then, no better than their killers. This is why I asked you to help me."

He rolled her over so he could peer down into her eyes. His face wore a solemnity Kerry had never seen before. "I do not know what will happen tomorrow," he said. "Your step-brother will probably take me away to safe house. I do not know when I will see you again."

Kerry's fingertips touched his lips. "It won't be long," she said quickly. "Once you tell your story to the CIA, they'll put you in protective custody, and yeah, you might have to stay in hiding for a while, but I'm sure Roger will let me visit you. As soon as the danger is over, you'll be free to go anywhere you want." She almost added, "with me," but bit back the words at the last second. She didn't want him to think she was putting pressure on him just because they'd slept together.

The somber look remained on Mikhail's face. "Kerry…" He traced the line of her eyebrow with his thumb. She trembled at the gentle caress. "They may send me back to Russia," he said slowly. "The information I have may not be strong enough to allow me to stay."

Her heart lurched. She fastened her hands on his jaws and forced him to meet her eyes. "*No!* I refuse to believe that. Roger won't let you down, Mikhail. I won't let him."

He stared at her a long moment, then said, "He may not have choice. I want to believe you are right. But I am very much afraid now." His fingers brushed back the hair from her forehead, and then moved over her cheekbone to gently cup her jaw. His eyes held hers, so tender it made her heart ache. "Especially now. I cannot imagine a life without you."

Kerry smiled through sudden tears. Her hand curled around his, and she brought it to her lips, brushing his knuckles. His silver pinkie ring glinted in the moonlight streaming through the skylight. "You always wear this. Does it have special meaning?"

He smiled. "Nadya gave to me when I won first medal at fifteen." He turned his hand in hers to peer at the ring. "It fit ring finger for two years, then I had to move to little finger because of growth spurt. Later, I show you inscription. It says 'To Mikhail, Son of my Heart.' Nadya has always treated me as son."

Kerry saw the wistful look on his face, and her fingers tightened on his. "You really miss her, don't you?"

He nodded. "I wish I could bring her here. She loves America."

"Maybe you'll find a way to do that someday. Maybe I can help."

He drew her close, his lips brushing her forehead. "I can do nothing for Nadya until I know what future holds for me here."

Kerry drew away just far enough to place her fingers on his lips. "Let's not think about tomorrow," she said softly. "Let's just make tonight last."

She drew his head down for a kiss, and as soon as his mouth met hers, she stopped thinking.

CHAPTER SIXTEEN

Kerry awoke to the sensation of Mikhail's lips on the small of her back. Still half-asleep, she smiled. Even in this hazy twilight between sleep and wakefulness, she knew he was kissing her turtle. The sensation of his warm lips on her skin sent a flooding heat through her lower half, and she released a soft, breathless sigh. A low chuckle came from Mikhail's throat, and his hand tightened possessively on the curve of her naked hip. His tongue traced another wet, leisurely path over her skin, and an involuntary cry escaped Kerry's lips.

His mouth lifted. "When did you get tattoo?" he asked, fingers skipping playfully down her thigh, sending goose bumps erupting in his wake.

"During my rebellious stage," Kerry murmured through clenched teeth.

Mikhail laughed. "When was that?"

"Oh...from about..." she spoke haltingly, trying not to think about the sensations his tongue was arousing in her. "Thirteen to...twenty-three...but I got the tattoo...when I was sixteen. Catri had...a fit."

His fingertips trailed over her turtle tattoo in a soft caress. Kerry gasped as liquid fire arrowed through her womb. How many times had they made love last night?

Three...four? Whatever, it apparently hadn't been enough because she wanted him again.

But apparently, Mikhail was more interested in talking. "You said in car you would tell me long story about boyfriend. Joshua, yes?" His hand continued to stroke her skin, but he'd rolled over on his side, propping his head on his hand.

"It's not really a long story," Kerry said. "He was a bad-boy hockey player, and I found him irresistible. I guess you could say I was blinded by lust. Our relationship lasted for a couple of years."

"Until scandal?"

Kerry nodded. "That was my wake-up call. That drug possession arrest nearly got me kicked out of skating. Even though I wasn't the one who had the marijuana. But I was with him, so I was charged, too."

"But charges were dropped, yes?"

"Yeah. Josh served sixty days and had to go through a drug rehabilitation program. He's still playing hockey, and from what I hear, is as wild as ever. The whole thing scared the crap out of me, but even then I thought I still loved him. I'm ashamed to say I stuck with him for a few more months until he decided a stripper at a Hollywood club was more to his taste."

"Stupid man," Mikhail murmured, his hand moving down the curve of her hip. He leaned toward her, his breath warm on her skin. "But I am happy. I do not wish to compete with bad-boy hockey player."

"No competition," Kerry murmured.

She caught her breath as Mikhail's mouth returned to her turtle. Her hand grasped a corner of the sheet and squeezed. She closed her eyes, murmuring, "You're driving me out of my mind, Mikhail."

His lips moved away, and she could hear the smile in his voice as he said, "Turtles have just become my favorite reptile." His finger traced over the design, then trailed up the middle of her back. He flattened his hand against her skin and moved down in a slow, seductive journey. His head lowered again. Kerry stiffened at the heat of his tongue, and the wet contact it made as it traced the turtle at the small of her back.

That's it, she thought. *Can't take it anymore.* She turned over abruptly, and slid her body up against Mikhail's hair-roughened chest. He caught his breath as her hand wrapped around his healthy erection.

"Did you hear me?" she said, meeting his gaze defiantly. "You're driving me crazy, Russian boy." She stroked him, once, twice.

He groaned. "Estonian," he said through clenched teeth. Two hot spots of color circled his cheekbones.

Kerry grabbed a handful of his blond hair as she continued the repetitive motion with her other hand. "I apologize. Here, let me make it up to you." She kissed him, and his mouth opened to hers obligingly.

For the next twenty minutes, they took their time, savoring, learning the map of each other's bodies. This time, their lovemaking was even better than all the times before. It was slower, yet, more intense, almost desperate. Later, Kerry would look back and wonder why there had been that urgent sense of desperation. And she would wonder if it had been a premonition. That somehow, deep inside the core of their souls, they'd known it would be the last time.

* * * * *

Feathery flakes of snow fell from an overcast sky as Kerry walked hand-in-hand with Mikhail through Gettysburg's Evergreen Cemetery. Although he didn't know a great deal about America's Civil War, he'd been enthusiastic about visiting the famous battlefield. Kerry, who'd never been particularly excited about history, was just happy to accompany him as he went from monument to marker, reading about the devastating three days of battle. And she was especially happy that it was snowing. Maybe the weather would delay Roger's arrival.

She'd called him from Dale's phone just after they'd finished the huge country breakfast the older woman had prepared for them. As Dale had suggested, Roger hadn't seemed surprised by her call. A man of few words, he'd listened to her brief explanation about Mikhail and had tersely told her to stay put, that he'd be up to get them right away. She'd had to bite her lip to stop herself from saying, "Don't hurry." But even if he left right away—or sent someone right away—it was still a good two, maybe three hour drive from Occoquan, depending on traffic. And now, with the snow…who knew?

As Mikhail peered at an aged headstone, Kerry glanced beyond the fence at the white snow-covered landscape. Her heart lightened. Another night, she thought. *Just one more night with Mikhail before we have to go back to the real world.*

Surely if it were snowing like this down in Virginia, Roger would postpone the trip. Oh, God! *Why* had she gone ahead and called him this morning? She hadn't wanted to. Picking up the phone and dialing his number had been harder than she'd ever expected it to be. Especially when her brain was shrieking "give us another week together, just one more week." But common sense reminded her that Mikhail would be safer with Roger. She couldn't sacrifice his safety for her own selfish desires.

She felt his gloved hand squeeze hers, and turned to look at him. Her heart contracted at the softness in his eyes.

"Do not look so sad, Kerry," he said. "It will all work out." But his face was somber, too, and she knew his words were as much to convince himself as to reassure her.

A shiver ran through her, and she knew it wasn't the cold of the winter afternoon that caused it. A knot formed in her throat. "How do you know?" she whispered. Her chin quivered as she tried to hold back tears. Funny, how this time *she* was the one feeling as if the ax was about to fall.

Mikhail turned to her, placing his hands on the shoulders of her parka, and peered into her eyes. "Because...I have reason now...more than ever...to make life in America. It will work out. Believe this, Kerry." His hands tightened on her. "I do. I *must*."

He bent his head, his mouth claiming hers in a warm, head-rushing kiss. Kerry closed her eyes, drinking in his heat, the intoxicating scent of him as she returned his kiss, allowing it to drive out the demons of uncertainty from her chaotic mind. When she found the strength to draw away from him, she was trembling. Despite the frigid, wood smoke-scented air and the pelt of wet snowflakes on her face, her skin felt flushed as if she'd just stepped out of a sauna.

"Let's go back to the inn," she said breathlessly, noting the heightened color on Mikhail's high cheekbones. "Maybe there's time before..."

Her words were drowned out by the beat of helicopter blades in the overcast sky above them. Alarm flickered in Mikhail's eyes as he looked up. Kerry knew what he was thinking because she was thinking it, too.

"No," she whispered, shaking her head in denial. "He wouldn't…"

But she knew he would. *Of course*, he would. Roger never did anything by halves.

Two helicopters emerged from the gray-white sky, flying in close formation over the snow-laden trees of the battlefield. Kerry and Mikhail watched as they disappeared from sight toward the northeast. Gradually, the whomp-whomp of their blades faded into silence.

Kerry looked back at Mikhail, her heart in her throat. "Maybe it's not…" she whispered through dry lips.

Mikhail didn't respond, but only gazed back at her with desolate eyes.

* * * * *

The helicopters were parked on a relatively flat knoll near the parking lot of the Mount Carmel Inn. Kerry's hands, despite the warm leather gloves she wore, were ice cold as she parked the Volvo. She didn't know anything about flying helicopters, but she bet it took a great deal of skill to land two of them on the top of a mountain in a snowstorm. Not that it had turned out to be much of a snowstorm, she thought, as she turned off the ignition. Even the weather had turned against them. The snow had stopped shortly after the helicopters had flown over.

She felt Mikhail's eyes upon her, but as she turned to look at him, his gaze shifted to the inn. She followed it, stiffening at the sight of four men standing on the front porch. One of them she recognized as her dour-faced stepbrother, Roger Ellery. She hadn't seen him in years, but she knew it was him all the same. He stood in a peculiar, hunched-shouldered stance, and even from a distance, she could feel his sharp, eagle-like eyes piercing into her.

For a moment, she sat still, her hands grasping the steering wheel, unable to move a muscle to open the door. Everything was about to change for them; she knew that with a certainty that left her paralyzed. Mikhail's stark face told her he knew it, too. She looked at him, knowing the desperation she felt must be showing on her face. There were so many things she wanted to say to him, but their time had run out. The men were making their way down the steps and heading toward them.

"Mikhail!" She grabbed his hand.

He clutched it, squeezing. "Be strong, *angel moy*." Urgency threaded his voice. "We will get through this." He glanced through the window and saw the advancing men. Turning back to Kerry, he clasped her head between his hands and gave her a hard, earnest kiss.

Tears burned behind his lids as he felt her body respond. Finally, he broke the kiss and drew away, his eyes holding hers. "Remember," he said, just as the men reached the car, two on her side, two on his.

"What?" Kerry asked, eyes wide.

Mikhail ignored the men standing silently outside the Volvo, his hands tight on her shoulders. "Remember," he said slowly. "This Estonian loves you."

Kerry stared back at him, and something like panic flared in her eyes. Say it, he silently urged her. *Tell me you feel the same way. I know you do, but I need to hear it.*

One of the men knocked on the window on Kerry's side. His face was grim. Mikhail held Kerry's gaze, willing her to speak. But she turned away, her bottom lip trembling, and the moment was gone.

* * * * *

At five-foot-eight with a wiry, muscular build, Roger Ellery looked exactly like what Kerry thought a CIA officer should look like, square-jawed, cold-eyed and conservative. He didn't waste time with small talk but politely requested they get their stuff together and prepare to depart. Kerry thought she detected an undercurrent of annoyance in his cultured Virginia accent. She didn't know if it was because they hadn't been here when he'd arrived, or if it was because she'd involved him in the situation in the first place.

In the foyer of the inn, Dale gave Kerry a brief hug, and whispered, "Good luck, sweetie. Please keep in touch."

Kerry drew away from her, and looked over at Mikhail a few feet away. His expression was implacable, but his eyes revealed anguish, and something more. Dread. Picking up on his vibrations, Kerry felt alarm skitter through her. Did he know something she didn't?

A moment later, she understood. The six of them left the inn, two of the blank-faced men with Mikhail, and Roger and the fourth man with Kerry. As the two men ushered her toward a helicopter, Kerry, in a flash of panic, realized what was happening. She stopped in her tracks and whirled around.

"No! We want to go together!"

The men on each side of Mikhail—bodyguards or prison guards? —were taking him to one of the helicopters—not the one Roger was directing her to. Mikhail looked over his shoulder at her, his expression bleak, but resigned. He'd known, she realized. From the very beginning, he'd known they'd be separated.

She took a step toward Mikhail, shaking off Roger's warning hand. "No!" she snarled at him. "This isn't part of the deal. He's all alone. He needs me." She moved another step closer to Mikhail.

Roger's hand wrapped around her upper arm in an ironclad hold. "Your part in this is over, Kerry," he said quietly.

Fury washed over her. *How dare he?* He wasn't going to tell her what to do. She struggled to pull away from him, but his hand tightened its grip. "*Let me go, damn you*! I want to go with Mikhail!"

"Impossible," Roger said firmly. "They're taking him somewhere to be debriefed, and you're coming with me."

"Where?"

"To my house in Occoquan. Sharon is anxious to see you."

"But when will I see Mikhail again?"

Roger stared at her, and she was surprised to see something like pity in his brown eyes. "I can't answer that right now."

"But…"

"Kerry, no," Mikhail's soft Russian accent cut in.

She looked at him. He shook his head, his eyes holding hers. "It will be okay. I will see you soon."

Slowly, she nodded. She looked back at Roger. "You can let go of me now," she said. "I'll be good."

As she reached the helicopter, she looked over her shoulder for one more glimpse of Mikhail. He was just about to climb into his copter, but almost as if sensing her gaze, he looked back. Her heart spasmed at the sadness in his eyes, and she knew her own mirrored his. Her throat thickened. She swallowed, but the lump wouldn't budge.

When will I see you again?

Her eyes blurred. Oh, God! Why hadn't she been able to tell him she loved him? Why was it so hard for her to say those words? Mikhail lifted a hand in farewell. Then he turned away and disappeared into the body of the helicopter.

A few moments later, Kerry was strapped into a seat of the other helicopter. It lifted off from the ground and gained altitude, moving south toward Maryland. She stared miserably out the window but saw nothing but gray clouds. No sign of the other copter. Just clouds as heavy with moisture as her heart was with sadness.

She wiped away the tear that rolled down her cheek and pretended not to be aware of Roger Ellery's scrutiny. "You've fallen for him, haven't you? A Russian! Good God, Kerry. Aren't you smarter than that?"

Her chin lifted stubbornly. "He's *Estonian*."

* * * * *

Kerry tried to wait through dinner before bombarding Roger with the question of the day. The same one she'd been asking for three days now. She knew that his wife, Sharon, had gone to a lot of trouble to prepare the perfectly grilled salmon with its delicate lemon-dill sauce accompanied by bite-sized roasted red potatoes and julienne carrots in a brown-sugar glaze.

She was sure the food was delicious—it was obvious Sharon loved to cook—but it might as well have been dry rice cakes for all Kerry tasted it. What was happening to Mikhail? Where had they taken him?

To a safe house, Roger had tersely replied that first day in response to her question. She, on the other hand, had been relegated here to his appropriately upscale Occoquan home, lavishly decorated with contemporary elegance by the multi-talented Sharon, an interior decorator in high demand by the Washington DC area's wealthier clientele.

It was a gorgeous old Victorian house on a hill overlooking the town and the river below, and every room displayed Sharon's warm personality. Kerry glanced around the formal dining room at walls covered in dramatic rose silk and adorned with exquisite art that certainly wasn't purchased at the local Kohl's. The burnished mahogany table at which they were seated rested on a plush rose and black Oriental rug. Above the table hung the most elaborate crystal chandelier Kerry had ever seen that wasn't in a five-star hotel.

Apparently, Sharon and Roger were doing well financially. But then, again, she reminded herself, Roger's dad—her stepfather, if you wanted to be technical—was wealthy, so maybe Roger reaped the benefits of some kind of generous trust fund. After all, that's why Jana had married Erich. She'd taken one look at the British-born, San Diego psychologist, and cash registers started ca-chinging in her little gold digger brain. It didn't take a genius to figure out why she'd left Dad as soon as he'd turned down all those endorsement deals after winning Olympic gold, opting instead to join Greenpeace. Poor naive Dad. He'd really believed Jana would put up with that?

"Kerry, you're not eating," Sharon Ellery said in her soft southern accent, her perfectly shaped brows furrowed. "Don't tell me you don't like salmon?"

Kerry looked across the table at Roger's wife, a petite woman considerably younger than the forty-five year old Roger—about thirty-five, Kerry guessed. Sharon had the good looks of a former sorority girl with shining honey-brown hair and doe-like brown eyes. "It's very good, Sharon. It's just that…I don't have much of an appetite tonight." Kerry shot Roger a dark look. He either didn't notice or pretended not to, shoveling a forkful of tender pink salmon into his mouth.

"Perfectly understandable," Sharon said with a sympathetic smile. "You've had an exciting week, haven't you? And you're quite the celebrity, too. I'm surprised we don't have a contingent of reporters camping out on our front lawn trying to get a statement from you."

"It's just a matter of time," Roger said, shooting Kerry a grim look. "That's why I don't want you to go out."

Kerry bristled. "It sounds like I don't have a choice." She didn't much like being treated like a prisoner. Or being ordered around.

"Just trying to protect you," he said.

"What's a celebrity, Mama?" piped up five-year-old Michelle, her brown eyes bright with curiosity as she clumsily tried to spread butter on a sourdough roll.

Sharon reached over and attempted to take the roll from her daughter. "Let me help, Shelly."

"*No!*" the little girl screeched, dive-bombing the roll out of her mother's reach. "*I can do it!*"

Kerry winced. Her niece's siren-like shriek had gone through her head like a machete blow. *Maybe I'll re-think that having kids thing. Especially if I want to keep healthy eardrums.* It would be a bitch to go through life and not be able to hear Mr. Mister singing "Broken Wings." For some reason, every time she heard that sexy ballad, it immediately brought an image of Mikhail to mind. She smiled dreamily. On second thought… she and Mikhail would make gorgeous kids.

Sharon relinquished the roll with a sigh. "Well, you're making a mess of it. A celebrity is someone in the public eye, honey. Remember, I showed you your Aunt Kerry's picture in the newspaper? That makes her a celebrity. Then again…" Sharon smiled across the table at Kerry. "Being a figure skater, I guess you were already one."

Michelle paused in buttering her roll and looked up at Kerry with renewed interest. "So what did you do to get in the paper?" she asked. "You didn't win a gold medal. I *know* that."

Kerry forced a smile at her niece, trying to think of an appropriate response. *Precocious little brat, wasn't she?* After demolishing half the stick, Michelle finally decided she had enough butter on her roll and crammed the whole mess into her pretty little mouth, then stared at Kerry, chewing thoughtfully. Kerry suddenly had the crazy feeling that *she* was the child, and Michelle the authority figure.

"Honey, that was very rude," Sharon said with an indulgent frown. "Your Aunt Kerry has actually done a very brave thing. She helped a man get out of a horrible country, and now, your daddy is going to find a way for him to stay here in the USA."

Roger swallowed a sip of wine and gave his wife an uneasy look. "Don't tell her that, Sharon. I don't have anything to do with whether Kozlof gets asylum or not. It's not up to me."

Sharon's perfectly plucked brown eyebrows puckered. "But can't you use your influence to help him? I thought—"

"Of course I'll do what I can, but like I said, it's just not up to me."

Kerry looked at him. Did he know more than he was letting on?

He gazed down at his plate, avoiding her eyes. A flutter of disquiet went through her.

"Ready for coffee and dessert?" Sharon pushed back her chair and stood. Moving with elegance and grace, she disappeared into the kitchen.

This was only the second time Kerry had met Roger's wife. The first time had been at their wedding seven years ago. In a misguided attempt to try to establish some kind of relationship with Jana, Kerry had gone back to San Diego for the wedding, but the weekend had been a total waste of time. Jana had been so caught up in the "society wedding of the year" that Kerry might as well have been invisible for all the attention she'd received from her mother. She'd been stupid to even try. Jana would never change. Something would always come before her daughter.

Kerry took a sip of water and frowned at Roger. "So, Roger, when, *exactly*, am I going to get to see Mikhail?"

He put down his wine glass and looked at her. "I don't know, Kerry. If I did, I'd tell you."

He was telling the truth, Kerry realized. And her disquiet turned to fear.

* * * * *

Sean paused in front of the pretty first-class flight attendant and extended his hand, giving her a lazy smile that sent the blood rushing to her 4th of July and apple pie Southern Belle features.

"Grand flight," he said, deliberately intensifying his brogue as he squeezed her hand. American women loved Irish accents. "And, indeed, it was such a pleasure conversing with a beautiful, intelligent woman like yourself."

The girl practically shuddered in delight at his compliment. "Thank you, Mr. O'Flanagan," she said in a syrupy southern drawl.

He figured her undies were soaked by now. The long flight from Salt Lake City would've been unbearable if he hadn't entertained himself by seeing just how quickly he could get the girl hot for him simply by using his eloquent voice. He knew if he'd really poured on the charm, he probably could've boffed her in the lavatory, but he'd had no desire to take things that far. He was a family man at heart, and Elena was his family. No matter how comely the women were, he didn't intend to be unfaithful to his one true love.

But flirting, now, that was a different matter all together.

The flight attendant simpered up at him. "How long are you going to be in Washington, Mr. O'Flanagan?"

He shrugged. "Just a few days at the most. I have some business interests to attend to."

"Well, I have a layover tonight," she said, her china-blue eyes hopeful. "If you like, I could show you around the city?"

For a moment, he visualized rolling around on the sheets with the saucy redhead. A tantalizing idea, but...no.

He put on a regretful face. "Oh, love, that would be grand, but I'm afraid my night is already booked. Otherwise…"

Disappointment flared in her eyes, but apparently she was a quick thinker, because she reached into her pocket and handed him a business card. "Call me sometime. I fly in and out of Seattle all the time."

He smiled. He'd told her he was a businessman based out of Seattle, amused at the way her eyes had lit up when he added that he'd probably be flying this trip off and on for the next few months. "I'll certainly do that. Bye, now."

He stepped off the plane and headed down the corridor leading to the Dulles terminal, whistling a pop song by that John Mayer kid. It was being played to death on American radio stations, and he couldn't get the bloody tune out of his mind. Surprising, really, that he was in such a good mood. Especially after reading **The Irish Times** about a drug bust at Dublin Airport that had ended up with the capture of one of his men. That meant over 60,000 Euros down the drain, for fuck's sake! Ah well, easy come, easy go. For every IRA man who got picked up for drug-running, there were a dozen more to take his place. Anyway, right now, Sean had problems closer to home.

Fagan had screwed up again, but admittedly, this time it hadn't been his fault. Not that Sean was going to assure him of that. Better to let him think he was in trouble because the CIA had outsmarted them all and found Kozlof and the girl first. But Sean had a plan.

It was a gamble, of course, but being a student of human nature, Sean felt like the odds were on his side. Kozlof and the pretty American ice dancer had been on the lam for almost a week, in close quarters, presumably, during those cold winter nights driving across America's heartland. Common sense told him that if you put a good-looking male who didn't appear to have any homosexual tendencies with a luscious young female like Kerry Niles, there was bound to be some sexual sparks ignited. And from what he'd heard about Mikhail Kozlof, he was a man of integrity even if he had something of a reputation as a "ladies' man." Whether he felt just sexual attraction or a genuine caring for a woman, he would have an emotional investment in the woman's future.

So...what if that woman's future was threatened?

Smiling, Sean stepped out of the terminal into the brutal March wind. His timing was perfect because several *Washington Flyer* cabs were waiting for passengers along the curb. He strode to one, opened the back door and slid in.

"The town of Occoquan, please," he said to the driver, his voice cheerful. Then he sat back and relaxed as the cab pulled into the stream of traffic heading away from the airport.

CHAPTER SEVENTEEN

It looked like an ordinary farmhouse tucked into the rolling green hills of the Virginia countryside. Nothing like what Mikhail would've thought of as a "safe house," really. But he sincerely hoped that's what it was. So far, anyway, and he'd been here for four days now, he seemed to be well protected. The 19th Century house perched in the middle of a parcel of land protected on the north by thick woods and on the east by a rocky stream. Security cameras and sensor-armed fences lined the perimeter of the property.

By Mikhail's count, there appeared to be five other people in the house—two guards in military uniforms who took turns keeping watch in the room next to him, a cook he never saw, but who provided perfectly bland meals, an elderly, sullen-faced woman who came in every morning to make his bed, and a man who introduced himself as Mikhail's "handler," Zac Lennart. The latter was a gray-haired, squinty-eyed CIA agent in his mid-fifties with a sizable paunch. A beer-belly, Americans called it. Lennart seemed an unlikely type for a CIA agent, but as soon as he opened his mouth, Mikhail realized why he'd been chosen as his handler. A faint, but unmistakable Ukrainian accent bled through his American drawl. When Mikhail asked him about it, Lennart admitted he'd defected from the USSR as a teenager, but then hurriedly assured him he was an American citizen, and a true blue patriot. He then took Mikhail into the homey study of the farmhouse and proceeded to "debrief" him.

Why are you defecting? Did anyone put you up to it? What do you know that might be of interest to the CIA? Do you have any proof about this cover-up of the Sami massacre?

Mikhail had turned over the disk, and still the questioning went on until the early morning hours. He told everything he knew, numerous times, his head swimming with fatigue by the end of the marathon questioning. But Lennart, even with the age disadvantage, seemed to have limitless resources of energy. He didn't reveal the slightest need for rest as he drank cup after cup of sweet, black coffee, his ice-blue eyes appraising when Mikhail answered yet another question that had been asked before, but simply rephrased. Finally, as dawn brightened the winter sky in the east, Lennart allowed Mikhail to stumble off to bed where he fell into a deep, dreamless sleep for the next twelve hours.

They left him alone on the second day, and he spent it by watching television—mostly news or documentaries. Somehow, without Kerry to laugh and make fun with him, the soaps had lost their luster. His guards—because somehow, that's how he thought of them—refused to bring him a newspaper, but they didn't restrict his TV, so he watched newscasts, like the one he was watching now, of the "developing story" about the Russian ice dancer who'd defected to the United States. He saw clips of himself and Elena skating the original dance, then a black & white publicity shot of him taken over two years ago when he looked rather wide-eyed and innocent. Christ, he hoped he looked more mature now. He felt it, that was for sure. The pretty blond reporter, a Jane Pauley imitation, didn't seem to know all that much, just the usual publicity information distributed to the media. But then Mikhail heard Kerry's name, and his heart contracted as a clip of Kerry and Adam's Olympic performance flashed on the screen.

Oh, God, sweet Kerry.

Just seeing her image again, even on the cold distance of the television screen, sent his pulse slamming. How could it have happened so quickly? A month ago, he'd barely known she existed, and now, when he thought he might never see her again, he felt as if he couldn't breathe. Her publicity shot appeared on the screen, and there it was—that heart-melting smile, the one that sent his knees quaking.

Oh, Kerry, my love. What are you doing right now? Has that stepbrother of yours sent you back to California?

But, no. The screen had changed to a beautiful Victorian house perched on a hill above a charming river town where a group of reporters were gathered with their recording equipment. Mikhail tuned in to the reporter's voice.

"And in the town of Occoquan, Virginia, we have unofficial word that the American skater, Kerry Niles, is holed up in the home of CIA agent, Roger Ellery, although we've been unable to confirm that report. In other news, Arthur Andersen was indicted today in the continuing Enron inquiry…"

With a sigh, Mikhail pushed the button of the remote, and the TV went black. He and Kerry had watched the breaking news about the Enron scandal. Such a tragedy, employees losing their life savings while the big wheels prospered. Where had they been when that story broke? Colorado or Kansas? It all seemed so long ago, yet, less than two weeks had passed. Christ, he wished he could go back in time and recapture those moments of the road trip. One thing was for sure. If he could do it over, he wouldn't fight his attraction to Kerry. No, he would make love to her that first night in the motel during the snowstorm. And then, there would've been several nights of long, slow lovemaking instead of just one.

He grimaced, feeling his penis stir at the thought. Jesus, thinking about making love to Kerry wasn't helping things. He stood and walked over to the window, drawing back the hunter green brocade drapes to peer out. Nothing out there to see except a couple of horses—one black, one chestnut—out for their afternoon exercise. Where the hell was Lennart? Mikhail hadn't seen him for twenty-four hours, not since he'd brought in that younger man dressed in a sober three-piece suit with marine-short hair and remote dark eyes. Introduced as Jess Wallace, the younger man hadn't wasted any time, but asked Mikhail to tell his story once more from beginning to end. And so, again, he'd told the story of his mother's death, of the massacre in the Sami village. They'd taped his statement, (yet again) and departed. And Mikhail hadn't seen Lennart since.

He dropped the curtain and turned away. How long was it going to take before he finally got some word as to what would happen to him? He wanted—*needed*—action. He wanted this to be over. He wanted to go somewhere with Kerry and live quietly, sheltered from this alien world of politics and stealth and hidden danger. He wanted...

Kerry.

He wanted "forever" with Kerry. Why hadn't he asked her to marry him in those last desperate moments before Ellery's men had ripped them apart? Asked her to have faith, and wait for him, no matter what. But then, if he'd done that, and the Americans sent him back to Russia, what then? He couldn't expect Kerry to give up her home, her heritage, and come to live with him in Moscow. That world would be too alien for her. Even now, with the change brought on by western advances, the cultural differences would chip at her indomitable spirit, and he couldn't bear that. No, he'd done the right thing in not asking for any promises. Once this was over, once he knew he was assured of asylum, he would ask her to plan a life with him. Otherwise, there was simply no future for them.

He shook his head, and with a groan, ran his fingers through his rumpled hair. *No!* He had to stop thinking like that. Think positive, he instructed himself. *We're meant to be together. We'll find a way.*

A sound came from outside. He cocked his head, listening. Yes, that was definitely a car coming up the long, tree-shaded driveway. He strode to the window and peered out.

It was a dark sedan with tinted windows. He shook his head. Christ! Did the CIA really think they were fooling anybody with those government-issued cars? The car pulled up in front of the house, and Zac Lennart got out of the driver's seat. Mikhail breathed a sigh of relief. Finally! Perhaps his wait was almost over. The passenger side door opened, and another man emerged from the car. Mikhail didn't recognize him. He was shorter than Lennart, and younger. And in black jeans and a navy sweatshirt, he looked nothing like a CIA agent. He wore no coat, which was odd, since it couldn't be more than thirty-five degrees out there. His dark brown hair was long and shaggy. Even from a distance, Mikhail could see a five o'clock shadow on his narrow jaw.

He wondered who the man could be. Surely not another interrogator? Christ, he was tired of telling his story!

One of the military guards let the men into the house, and a moment later, Zac Lennart appeared on the threshold of the study, the shaggy-haired man just behind him.

Lennart gave Mikhail a tight smile. "How you holding up, Mikhail? Everyone treating you okay?"

Mikhail felt a ripple of irritation at Lennart's false attempt at being fatherly. He'd decided early on that he disliked the man. There was something oily and distasteful under the surface of his solicitous smile and jovial voice. Mikhail didn't trust him, plain and simple. He stared at him now, his jaw set. "Do you want truth...or fairy-tale?"

Lennart looked confused. "Fairy-tale? What do you mean?"

Mikhail gave him a grim smile. "Russian comes to America with information for CIA, wants to defect. CIA accepts deal, and agrees to protect Russian, who then lives happily ever after in America. This, I think, is fairy-tale."

A pained expression crossed Lennart's weather-beaten face. He gave his companion a wary look then said, "Mikhail, this is Quentin Wakeley. He is an agent in the British Special Air Services, the anti-terrorist guerilla force. He wants to have a word with you, but first..." He hesitated, looking uncomfortable. "You don't mind if we sit down, do you?"

Mikhail shrugged, trying to ignore the uneasy feeling thrumming in the pit of his stomach. "It is your house, not mine."

Lennart ignored this, taking a seat on the sofa while Wakeley stood rigidly in front of the fireplace where a cheerful wood fire crackled. Probably trying to thaw out after running around outside without a coat, the dumkoff, Mikhail thought uncharitably.

Lennart peered at Mikhail through wire-rimmed glasses that magnified his squinty blue eyes, giving him a disconcerting owl-like gaze. "I'll put it to you straight, Mikhail," he said, and again, there was just the slightest hint of his Ukrainian accent. "The CIA has decided not to assist you in getting asylum."

His blunt statement hit Mikhail with the force of a brick landing flat on his stomach. For a moment, he couldn't breathe, not even enough to ask why.

But apparently recognizing Mikhail's stricken expression, Lennart went on, "There are several reasons why, but the deciding factor has nothing to do with you, per se. Our country and yours. Things are peaceful now, have been since Gorbachev became buddy-buddy with President Clinton in the early nineties. What would happen to those friendly relations if we decided to give safe harbor to one of Russia's most valuable athletes?" At Mikhail's lack of response, Lennart gave an off-hand shrug. "Surely you understand what an awkward international incident that would be."

Mikhail finally found his voice. "But what about the murder of innocent villagers? The cover-up of it? The drug use by Russian athletes? Does none of that matter?"

Lennart crossed his legs primly and sighed. "I'm afraid my superiors feel that although the deaths of the Sami villagers were unfortunate, it is ancient history. As for what you told us about the illegal drug use of your athletes, well…" Another listless shrug. "We just don't feel that bringing this to the notice of the Olympic Committee would be in our best interest right now."

White-hot anger blazed through Mikhail. "My father died in that Sami village. It is not 'ancient history' to me."

"I'm sorry, Mikhail." Indeed, his apology sounded genuine, but Mikhail didn't believe it for a second. "But like I said, it's the timing that's wrong. Twenty years ago, snagging a defector like you would've been a bright red feather in our cap, but now…" Again, that lethargic shrug. "It's just not the political coup it would've been then."

For a fraction of a second, Mikhail felt like pummeling the dough-faced Ukrainian-American. Oh, sure! *Easy for you to sit there and shrug so complacently. They didn't hand you back to the Russians when you defected, did they, you smug son-of-a-bitch.*

"But don't lose hope, Mikhail," Lennart went on, his eyes darting to Wakeley, still standing woodenly with his back to the fire. "Mr. Wakeley here has a proposition for you." He stifled a yawn and got to his feet. "I'll leave him to explain while I go hunt down Mrs. Stokely and see if she can brew us up some coffee." He ambled out of the room, leaving Mikhail alone with the British SAS agent.

"Why don't you take a seat, Mr. Kozlof, and make yourself comfortable," Wakeley said in a thick Scottish burr. "This might take a while."

Mikhail frowned, but sat down in an easy chair to the right of the sofa. Wakeley moved away from the fireplace and settled down in the other vacant chair, his long, slender hands clasped lightly between his knees. Mikhail studied him. He didn't look like an anti-terrorist guerilla. Well, perhaps, he was just a paper-pusher. He'd probably never come eye-to-eye with a terrorist.

With his sleepy brown eyes and slightly pouting lips, Wakeley bore a slight resemblance to Paul McCartney. In fact, if Mikhail hadn't known better, he would've guessed the man was an aging musician, or perhaps a fashion designer. There was something just the slightest bit effeminate about him.

"I'm told you're acquainted with an Irish-born citizen of Estonia, name of Sean O'Malley, is that correct?"

Mikhail nodded, his curiosity rising. "Yes, he is my skating partner's bodyguard. A black marketer and thug. It would not surprise me to learn he is also a member of Russian Mafia. The man is barbaric."

Wakeley nodded. "Our intelligence knows quite a bit about Mr. O'Malley. You may be right about his affiliation with the Russian Mafia, but that isn't what concerns the British government right now. It's his connection with the Real IRA. Mr. O'Malley left Belfast at the age of seventeen after blowing up a meat market in Newry, killing nine people, including four children. He got off with deportation after informing on the ringleader of the operation, and ended up in Finland where he married a woman who had family connections in Estonia. That's how he started up his pub and black market operation there, and how he came to be involved with Elena Boiko, through her father, Milos. You know, of course, about their affair?"

Mikhail shrugged. "Everyone in Moscow knows. No one cares."

Wakeley smirked. "Well, Liisa Kipelainan apparently cared enough to make a big stink about it. O'Malley's wife. She wasn't about to put up with her husband sleeping around with a Russian goddess like Elena. But funny thing happened after she confronted O'Malley with an ultimatum. Poor woman died in a car accident in Helsinki. Drove it right off a bridge."

Mikhail's heart missed a beat. In his mind, he saw the image of his mother's battered Citroen being hauled out of the Moscow River by a giant crane. Coincidence?

"Of course, they couldn't pin anything on O'Malley. He was too smart for the Finnish authorities. Shortly after Liisa's death, he left Helsinki for good and went to Moscow where he took up residence with Elena and became her bodyguard. But just because he makes his home in Russia doesn't mean he's lost his love for Ireland, and exile hasn't stopped him from entering the country and spearheading IRA operations for the past twenty years. And that didn't stop after the peace initiative. Do you remember that bombing in Omagh in 1998? The Real IRA took credit for it, and we know that O'Malley was one of the key organizers of that mission. We're determined to bring him to justice but it hasn't been easy since he enjoys the protection of the Russian Mafia. We need someone who can get close to him and find out when he'll be back in the UK so we can apprehend him."

Mikhail shifted his leg impatiently. He knew the answer already, but he still had to ask, "And what has this to do with me?"

Wakeley pinned his dark eyes on Mikhail. "We need you to go back to Russia and help us capture Sean O'Malley."

* * * * *

With a strangled groan, Kerry threw the paperback novel across the room. *God! How does crap like this get published?* There should be a law against allowing cover models to pen their own romance novels. Just because they had flowing blond locks and great pecs didn't mean they could write, for God's sake. And right now, she'd give one of her kidneys for a good, *meaty* romance novel. But Sharon's reading material left a lot to be desired. Where were the quality romances? The Mary Jo Putney's, the Teresa Medeiros's, the Cathy Maxwell's? For Chrissake, how could Sharon call herself a romance reader if she didn't have a *single* Nora Roberts on her bookshelf?

Kerry stared at the splayed book on the floor and clenched her teeth in frustration. If something didn't change soon she was going to totally lose it. It was day number five, and still, there was no word from Mikhail, and Roger, *damn it*, wouldn't tell her a thing.

She flopped back on the queen-sized sleigh bed and glared up at the high cream-colored ceiling. This was insane! Roger was keeping her a virtual prisoner here, and for what reason? To protect her from a few reporters camped on the front lawn? *Stupid*! If she wanted to make a statement, why shouldn't she?

With an exasperated sigh, she sat up on the bed and looked over at the clock radio on the bedside table. Three o'clock. Damn! It would be hours before dinner. Not that she was hungry. If anything, Sharon kept her too well fed. Yesterday, it had been sinfully gooey brownies, and this morning, she'd served soft, hot cinnamon rolls so delicate and melt-in-the-mouth delicious that if tasted by the Cinnabon people, it would've made them close up shop and go into real estate. And if Kerry's olfactory system was working up to par, she'd bet that the seductive aroma snaking through the house this very moment was none other than her all-time favorite—Tollhouse Cookies. Dear God, many more days here in the Ellery household, and she'd be mistaken for the Goodyear Blimp.

"*Agggghhhhh*!" Kerry abruptly swung her legs over the bed and stood. She had to get out of this house! Go for a walk, check out all those cute shops lining Mill Street. *Something*! If she had to stay here and watch one more soap opera or another Dr. "This is going to be a changing day in your life" Phil doing his miraculous one-hour mental makeovers, she'd scream her head off.

At the window, she adjusted the Venetian blinds just enough to peer outside. Her bedroom faced the street where a local TV van was parked, as it had been for the past few days. Channel 4 News just wasn't giving up, were they? But many of the other reporters had. In fact, there were only a few of them milling around, borrowing smokes from each other, playing cards and generally trying not to die of boredom.

It was a bright, sunny afternoon, virtually windless, and according to this morning's forecast, not as cold as it had been the day before, with highs reaching close to the mid-forties. Of course, early March was unpredictable in the mid-Atlantic, from what Dale had told her. It might be spring-like one day, and the next, a blizzard would blow in and bury the region in sixteen inches of snow.

Right now, it was gorgeous outside. *Damn Roger and his stupid rules!* Kerry strode to the closet and grabbed her parka. She was going for a walk, and if he didn't like it, too damn bad.

She slipped down the stairs and out the back door, then strode past the in ground swimming pool, covered for the winter. Let Roger try and stop her. By God, he'd regret it. He'd get a taste of the famous Kerry Niles temper, which she'd, of course, inherited from Jana, and God knows that was something that once experienced would never be forgotten nor wished to be experienced again.

She went through the gate and stepped out into a small alley that separated Roger's property from the homes facing away from the river. Turning left, she headed toward Occoquan Road. Five minutes later, she was descending the hill leading to the town and river beyond. Her destination was Mamie Davis Park where a Victorian summerhouse perched on a stretch of winter-brown lawn. She'd noticed it the day Roger drove her through the town on their way from the small airport in Fairfax County. The park had looked so charming and romantic, with the river rolling peacefully behind it.

There were a few people strolling around the town, mostly women lucky enough not to have full-time jobs that could spend their time having lunch and browsing through the many upscale gift shops lining both sides of Mill Street.

Not a reporter in sight, Kerry noted with satisfaction as she stepped through the brick gates of the park and headed for the summerhouse. She took a seat on the bench and contented herself with breathing in the fresh, exhilarating air of freedom. God, she felt like she'd been cooped up in that house for months instead of days. She turned her head and glanced back at the pier built out over the river. A brick-lined path led from the summerhouse to a small bridge connecting the pier to the shore. Kerry got to her feet and leisurely strolled out toward the river. To her right, a never-ending stream of traffic crossed the Rt. 123 Bridge leading into Fairfax County—the only structure that disturbed the tranquility of the charming river town. On the pier, she leaned her arms on the rails and gazed down at the murky water where a couple of mallards swam lazily, oblivious, apparently, to the cold temperature. They were a couple, Kerry thought. Not that she could tell a male duck from a female, but she just had a feeling they were mates. A wave of loneliness swept over her. *Oh, God, Mikhail! I miss you. Where are you?* Why hadn't she heard anything? What if...the thought hit her like a lightning bolt. What if they'd already sent him back to Russia? Pain cut through her, so sharp it took her breath away. *No!* She wouldn't allow herself to think like that.

She straightened and turned briskly toward the summerhouse. There was only one way to get her mind off Mikhail. She'd do what women through the ages had done to keep their minds from dwelling on the male sex. She'd shop.

On the way down the hill, she'd noticed a huge two-storied complex just to the right of a seafood restaurant—crammed with shops of all kinds. Maybe she'd just take her little self over there and check it out. After all, she really should get something for Sharon for being such a great hostess. The cinnamon rolls alone were worth that.

Kerry stepped out of the park and turned left. On her right, a car slowed and came to a stop to let two elderly women cross the street. Kerry's gaze focused on the bumper sticker proudly displayed on the back fender. She grinned.

HONK IF YOU'RE SMARTER THAN QUAYLE.

Good to know she wasn't the only liberal in Northern Virginia. She eyed the woman at the wheel, a blond suburbanite with a shaggy Meg Ryan haircut. In the backseat of the car, Kerry could see an empty car seat and a grinning "Barney" stuck to the inside window. A perfectly normal woman with a perfectly normal life. And probably with a perfectly normal husband and baby waiting at home. Her smile disappeared. God, how she envied that unknown woman. A perfectly normal life sounded really good right now. She could just picture it, living with Mikhail in the country—maybe in Pennsylvania somewhere, picket fence and all. Oh, they'd make beautiful babies. She smiled, imaging what their child would look like. A little girl with Mikhail's blond curls? Or a beautiful little boy with blue eyes and ebony hair like hers?

The elderly women reached the other side of the street, and the car moved on. Kerry had just passed the seafood restaurant, Sea Sea & Company, when another car pulled up next to her. She heard a door open, and glanced over, still thinking about babies.

A handsome man smiled at her. For a split second, Kerry was pleased. She'd never been one to be insulted by male attention.

But then he spoke with a lilting accent, "Good afternoon, love."

A heartbeat of a second passed before her brain shifted into gear and shrieked alarm bells. Irish, she thought. And the thought terrified her. She stiffened, and then turned to run. His smile disappeared. Eyes frosted. He jumped at her.

She opened her mouth to scream, but he reacted like a striking snake, pinning her arms with steel-like bands and covering her mouth with a leather-clad hand. Bucking and thrashing, she tried to bite down on the leather fingers, but he was too strong. He shoved her in the back seat of the car so hard her head slammed against the opposite door, sending a splintering shaft of pain through her skull. Even through the exploding stars, she sensed the Irishman climbing in after her, and the door closing with a thud. The car jolted forward. Kerry moaned, rubbing the rising bump on her forehead.

The Irishman turned to her, hauled her upright and grabbed the lapels of her parka. With one brisk movement, he unsnapped it. Kerry's fuzziness had started to clear. She knew who this creep was—the infamous Sean O'Malley. *Bastard!* Well, whatever he had in mind for her, she'd just as soon pass. Her right hand tightened into a fist. He was tugging at her parka, trying to get the sleeve off her left arm. But when it got caught on her watchband, she punched him as hard as she could in the gut and lunged for the door.

"You little bitch," he hissed, grabbing her by the arms. She struggled and started to scream. He backhanded her, sending her head reeling again.

"The syringe, Boris," he barked.

A moment later, Kerry felt a burning twinge on her upper left arm, and within seconds, she felt her body giving up the fight. She opened her eyes wide, trying to resist the drug, but already, the interior of the car was starting to spin. Groggily, she turned her head to the left, and looked at the blurred image of Sean O'Malley with his mocking smile.

Her teeth clenched. She drew on the last of her swiftly vanishing energy, and spoke in a slow, halting voice, "Fuck…you, you…creep."

And everything went dark.

CHAPTER EIGHTEEN

Mikhail stared at Quentin Wakeley, his brain spinning. Finally, he found his voice. It came out incredulous. "I cannot go back to Russia now. If O'Malley thinks I know anything, he will kill me. And what makes you think I can help you get him, anyway? I am not trained agent."

"We have a plan," Wakeley said evenly. "A cover story that will allow you to go back with minimal risk. In fact, we've already set it in motion."

Mikhail's stomach churned with fury. Who did these people think they were, playing with his life like this? "It sounds to me like I do not have choice in matter."

Wakeley's face looked as if it were carved in stone. "Well, I'm afraid that does seem to be the way it is. But if you help us get Sean O'Malley, you'll be offered political asylum in Britain. You can have the life you've always wanted in the West. Just not in America."

Mikhail stared him down. "You know nothing about what I've always wanted."

"Coffee, boys?" Zac Lennart stepped into the room with a tray holding three coffee mugs, a creamer and a sugar bowl.

Mikhail glared at him. "So, did you know all along that I am to be a spy for the British?"

Lennart set down the tray on the coffee table, his face expressionless. Finally, he looked at Mikhail. "You would have to go back, anyway. At least, here is a way for you to get out again legally."

Mikhail looked back at Wakeley. "Why me? Why not use experienced agent?"

Wakeley shifted uncomfortably and reached for a mug of coffee, avoiding Mikhail's eyes. "We tried that," he said shortly. "He never came back."

Mikhail's stomach plunged. Wakeley took a sip of coffee and finally met his eyes.

"We know from his last communication that O'Malley is engineering a big terrorist operation, one that can set back the peace progress thirty years. Does the name Daniel Sullivan mean anything to you?"

Mikhail shook his head.

"He's one of Dublin's biggest gangsters, involved in gambling, drugs, money laundering, you name it. But what we find really interesting about Mr. Sullivan is his former IRA ties. He spent ten years in a Northern Ireland prison. Just before our contact disappeared, he reported about a meeting between Sullivan and O'Malley indicating they're plotting something big. That's where you come in. We need you to find out what."

Mikhail stood and began to pace, tunneling his fingers through his hair. "How am I to do this? O'Malley man hates me. He is obsessively jealous of Elena, and for some reason, he thinks I am threat to him."

Wakeley gave a thin smile. "Ah, but this is why our plan will work so perfectly. You see, we've nailed down a cover story for you. You are a troubled young man who lost his heart to a beautiful American girl you met in Park City. But now that you are at the point of no return, you are having second thoughts. It's become clear to you that your affair with the American girl is just a fling, and that you really don't belong in America. Your home and your heart are in Russia. You will be welcomed home like the prodigal son."

Mikhail had stood through Wakeley's monologue, watching him with a growing state of disbelief. They had it all worked out. Was he to have no choice in the matter at all?

"Oh, and there's one other thing," Wakeley added. "Something to sweeten the pot. It's a message from your skating partner, Elena Boiko. If you return to her and continue your amateur career as her partner, she'll move your training headquarters to Tallinn, and bring your old coach back." He glanced down at a sheet of paper he'd withdrawn from his briefcase. "Nadya Rostilav. She will be in charge of your training once more."

Mikhail closed his eyes. *Jesus*! Elena was determined to get him back if she was serious about that. She'd hated Nadya. He opened his eyes and stared from Wakeley to Lennart. "So, what you are telling me is that I really have no choice? Is that it?"

The two men stared at him, their expressions inscrutable. Finally, Lennart shifted his leg, and his eyes slid off to a spot behind Mikhail's right shoulder.

"I'm afraid this is the only option we can offer you at this point."

A tense silence fell. Mikhail realized then that all his hopes of remaining in this country with Kerry had just died. His shoulders slumped. *He was going back to Russia.* Slowly he walked back to his chair and sank into it. "So, what do we do now?"

The two men looked at each other. Neither one seemed anxious to answer his question. Finally, Wakeley fixed his eyes on Mikhail and cleared his throat. "You have to do a bit of play-acting. This girl, Kerry Niles. Her stepbrother tells us she's…uh…" He cleared his throat again, and his sallow face flushed a dark red. "…that she's fallen hard for you. That's unfortunate because you're going to have to make it clear to her that it's over."

Mikhail felt as if he'd been sucker-punched in the gut. He tried to find his voice, but couldn't.

Lennart spoke up, "See, Mikhail, the last thing we need is for some lovesick American girl with CIA connections to make a big stink about you being taken back to Russia against your will. She's got to be made to believe this is your choice. Your decision."

Mikhail's lips tightened. "I won't do it. I won't hurt her like that."

Wakeley got to his feet, his jaw rigid. For the first time, Mikhail saw the ruthlessness in his eyes. And suddenly he looked like what he was—a SAS agent.

"You will," he said quietly. "Because if she doesn't believe you're returning without being coerced, and she makes a big deal of it, her life may well be in danger. You don't want that on your conscience, do you?"

Mikhail got to his feet and faced the British agent. "So why not tell her the truth? Tell her this is all a rouse?"

"Because that knowledge would be dangerous for her, as well. If O'Malley suspects she knows something, believe me, her life won't be worth a plugged nickel. Trust us, Mikhail. We know what we're doing. We'll bring her to you tomorrow. If I were you, I'd rehearse my speech tonight. Her life may depend on how convincing you are."

* * * * *

The motel room was dark and somewhat musty like it hadn't been occupied in some time. Only one shabby light on the dresser illuminated the healthy tan of Sean O'Malley's face as he grinned at Kerry from across a small wood-veneered table holding another unlit lamp and two mugs of hot tea. He took a sip from his mug, studying her silently. Her mug of tea was still untouched. She was afraid of what might be in it.

"Why did you drug me?" she asked, her voice still slightly slurred from whatever it was he'd injected into her bloodstream.

"You wouldn't recognize the name," he said. "But never fear, it's perfectly safe. Just something to keep you calm while you listen to my proposition."

"*Elena's* proposition, you mean?" Kerry tried to put as much venom as she could into her voice, but it still came out sounding listless, almost disinterested.

This son-of-a-bitch had kidnapped her right off the quiet main street of Occoquan in broad daylight. She knew she should feel furious, and frightened. But she only felt tired, and somehow, apart from the whole thing.

Drugged, she reminded herself. *You're drugged, idiot.*

Sean smiled. "No, I take full credit for the proposition, but you're right about one thing. Elena wants Mikhail back. And I want Elena to be happy, so I've told her I'll get him back for her. That's where you come in, Miss Niles. I want you to deliver Elena's message to him. It couldn't be simpler."

She shook her head lethargically, trying to clear the cobwebs. "But Roger won't let me see him. I've been trying."

Sean took a sip of tea, and then gazed at her thoughtfully. "Perhaps you haven't been trying hard enough. My suggestion is that you work on your stepbrother a wee bit harder. Turn on the waterworks. Most men can't resist a pretty girl with big, blue, tear-filled eyes. Seeing a woman's weakness makes a macho man like Ellery feel invincible. And of course, we all know that *your* weakness, for example, is that you've lost your heart to Kozlof. Isn't that true?"

Her cheeks warmed. She was beginning to think clearer now. How long had she been here, anyway? She remembered nothing after the pinch of the needle in the car until she woke up here in this musty motel room about a half-hour ago.

"That's none of your business," she said, enunciating as clearly as possible. "Anyway, it doesn't matter what's in that stupid envelope of yours." She glared down at the manila envelope next to the tea tray. "Nothing Elena can say will make Mikhail return to Russia. He's made his decision."

Sean nodded and put his teacup down. "Fair enough. But give it to him, anyway, love. Surely you trust him enough to let him make his own decision, do you not?" When she didn't respond, he went on, "How will you ever know for sure he's doing what he really wants to if you don't give him a chance to change his mind? Oh, and be sure and tell him I didn't harm you during our time together." His engaging grin flashed.

Engaging if you didn't know he was a freakin' psychopath, thought Kerry.

"I wouldn't want him to hold a grudge against me or anything."

* * * * *

Kerry was prepared to follow Sean O'Malley's suggestion and turn on the waterworks to convince Roger to let her in to see Mikhail. Considering how she felt, she didn't think that would be too hard. She'd been on the verge of tears since her arrival here, but her Niles' impassivity combined with her mother's Brennan pride, forced her to keep a stiff upper lip in company. As she descended the stairs for breakfast the next morning, she thought back to those final

273

moments in the car with Mikhail, and it worked. Her throat tightened and tears blurred her eyes.

At the kitchen table, Roger looked up from his newspaper and smiled. "Good morning, Kerry. Help yourself to the coffee. I hope it's not too strong. Sharon had a breakfast meeting with a client, so I made it." He looked at her closer. "You're still upset about being kept from your Russian, aren't you? Well, I have good news for you."

Kerry looked at him, her heart lifting with hope.

He nodded and gave her a smile that was almost warm. "You've been given permission to see him. I'll take you there as soon as you can get ready."

Kerry was already heading for the stairs.

* * * * *

"Lennart just called. He's coming up the driveway with Ms. Niles."

Mikhail looked up and saw Wakeley's grim face in the threshold of the study. His stomach plunged sickeningly like it had just crested the top of a tremendously high roller coaster and was making that first heart-stopping drop. Oh, dear God, how was he going to get through this meeting with Kerry?

Just thinking about lying to her, telling her she'd been nothing but a fling to him, threatened to undo him. How could he say that with any conviction? Surely she'd be able to tell he was lying. She'd see the truth in his eyes, wouldn't she? Because he might be able to make his lips lie, but there was nothing he could do about his eyes.

Yet, he *had* to convince her he didn't care. He'd have to draw on the actor inside him, the same one that could make audiences believe his soul was meshed with Elena's on the ice. He'd have to convince Kerry that their night together had meant nothing to him. Make her hate him. Her life could very well depend upon it.

He got to his feet and began to pace. His body felt ice-cold, yet, his hands were clammy. He couldn't believe they were making him do this. If only there was a way to let Kerry know what he really felt. Something she could find once the heat of anger and betrayal had subsided so she would know that their time together had been sacred to him, despite what he'd told her.

He twisted his silver ring around on his little finger, frowning in concentration. A note wouldn't work. She'd find it too soon, and that would defeat the whole purpose of telling her the lie in the first place. It had to be something else, something that would convince her of his love without putting her at risk. He stared down at his ring.

A car pulled up outside the house, and he strode to the window and peered out. His breath caught in his throat when he saw Kerry get out of Lennart's dark sedan, her ebony hair swirling around her face in the biting March wind.

His heart contracted. He watched her make her way to the front door, moving in that unique gait of the dancer she was. Even in cowboy boots and jeans, she was the epitome of grace.

Mikhail took a deep breath and tried to wipe the eager expression from his face. He couldn't let her know how happy he was to see her again. How, at the mere sight of her, his pulse raced and his blood thrummed through his veins like fine red wine. If he was going to pull this off, he had to appear indifferent. God, it was going to kill him to hurt her.

At the sound of footsteps in the hall outside the study, he stiffened and turned to the door. Kerry stood on the threshold, blue eyes wide with joy, lips parted in expectation.

"Mikhail!" she breathed, taking a step into the room. Then it happened. That smile—the one that made Mikhail weak in the knees—lit up her beautiful, freckled face. "Oh, Mikhail!"

He couldn't move a muscle, couldn't say a word. She practically flew across the room and into his arms, nuzzling her face against the wool of his sweater in a curiously child-like gesture. His heart hammered, and his hands moved of their own accord, flattening on her back and holding her against him. He couldn't stop his hands from moving over the nylon of her parka, pressing her as close as possible.

"Oh, God! I missed you so much." She drew slightly away from him, just enough to peer up at him through wide, blue eyes. Her dimple flickered impishly in her cheek. "What are you waiting for, Estonian boy? Kiss me. I've been suffering from withdrawal this past week."

He knew he shouldn't. Not when he would soon be telling her that their affair had been a mistake. But her full, tremulous lips were so inviting, and God...he might never taste them again.

With his hands cemented to her back, he lowered his head and captured her mouth beneath his. She opened to him immediately, her lips so trusting, so achingly sweet. His head swam. As always, when he kissed her, he was lost. Her warm hands crept under his sweater, pressing against his naked back. He'd been hard the moment she touched him, and now, his cock threatened to take over his brain. He wished it could. He wanted more than anything to lower her onto the sofa, and make slow, sweet love to her for hours.

She broke the kiss just enough to release a ragged sigh and a murmur, "You taste so good…" And then her mouth was hungering for his once more. He felt on the edge of a precipice, just seconds from slipping off. Just another moment, his body demanded. A little more time with her…just one more kiss before he made her hate him.

Somewhere in the back reaches of his brain, he heard the soft clearing of a throat, and the real world intruded. He broke the kiss and looked over Kerry's shoulder to see Wakeley at the door, his brown eyes like granite.

"Can I get you some tea?" he asked, like a polite manservant.

Mikhail released Kerry, trying not to notice her smudged lips and the glitter of desire in her eyes. He put a hand to his head, trying to think. Tea? Maybe not such a good idea. Kerry would probably throw the pot at him in a few minutes.

But he nodded at Wakeley. "Yes. Thank you." Chances were, Kerry would be gone by the time the tea arrived, anyway.

Wakeley disappeared, and Kerry grinned up at him, her dimple teasing. "Tea?" she said. "Uh…there are a lot of things I want to share with you right now, Mikhail, but tea isn't high on the list."

He stared at her, trying to find the words to start a conversation he'd rather die than begin.

Her gaze swept over his face, and her smile disappeared. "You look tired. Haven't you been sleeping?"

"Not much," he admitted, and finally forced himself to move. He took her hands and drew her over to the sofa. "We must talk."

"Oh, that reminds me!" Kerry sat on the edge of the sofa and began to rummage through her bag. Her glossy black hair fell in a silken curtain, hiding her face. "I have something for you. I almost forgot in the excitement of seeing you again." She found what she was looking for, and glanced up, smoothing her hair back, and tucking a strand behind her ear. Mikhail's eyes focused on a small manila envelope in her hands. Instead of handing it over, though, she clutched it to her chest. Her gaze held his, wary, now. "Promise you won't get upset, okay? He didn't hurt me. He just wanted me to get this information to you."

Mikhail stiffened, and a deep chill invaded his body. His hand clamped down on her jeans-clad knee. "Who is he? And what do you mean, he didn't hurt you?"

"Sean O'Malley," she said, watching him closely. "Don't freak out, Mikhail. I was walking along the street in Occoquan, and he pulled up and...uh...invited me to take a ride with him. It was scary at first, especially when he stuck the needle in my arm, but..." Her voice trailed off. "Mikhail, I don't like that murderous look in your eyes. I'm telling you, he was just looking for a way to get a message to you. I'm fine! I don't know what's in here, but he said it's a message from Elena. I told him it didn't matter. Nothing she could say would convince you to go back, but I promised to deliver it, anyway."

"He *drugged* you?" Mikhail almost choked on the words as a blinding fury swept through his body.

"Just to relax me," Kerry said quickly. "He knew I was terrified, and he wanted to talk. It didn't hurt me. Really!"

"Give me envelope," Mikhail said through lips so numb he might've just returned from the dentist's office. His stomach churned with a mixture of fear and rage. Dear Christ, if O'Malley had touched a hair on Kerry's head, he'd beat him to a pulp the next time he saw him.

Kerry surrendered the envelope. Mikhail stood and walked over to the window where the light was better, his fingers tearing at the seal. He pulled the contents out of the envelope, and his heart stopped cold. It felt as if the air supply to his lungs had suddenly been cut off.

He stared at a Polaroid photo of an unconscious Kerry lying on what looked like a bed in a motel room. She was fully clothed in jeans and a sweater, yet, her supine body looked vulnerable, and oddly enough, exposed, somehow—because of the figure sitting next to her—an amiably grinning Sean O'Malley.

A single sheet of paper accompanied the photo, and it wasn't from Elena. It was a neatly printed note written in ink. *We didn't hurt her. This time. Come back to Russia, Mikhail. Elena needs you.*

The note wasn't signed, but it didn't need to be. There was no doubt that this was the handiwork of Sean O'Malley, and yes, Elena, as well.

Mikhail's lips tightened. He should've known Elena wouldn't give up on him without a fight. She was determined to get her gold medal, and she thought he was the only one who could help her do it.

Well, she would get what she wanted. Not the gold medal, but him. He would go back, but only for long enough to get the information the British needed to capture Sean O'Malley. But even if he hadn't already agreed to the Brits' plan, now, with this threat to Kerry, he'd have no choice but to go back. He couldn't risk her life. And O'Malley was ruthless enough to kill her without blinking an eye if it served his purposes.

You're going to pay for this, O'Malley. I promise you that.

"Mikhail?" Kerry asked. "What is it?"

He looked over at her and slipped the photo and note back into the envelope. She lifted a hand and pushed back a strand of hair from her forehead, and Mikhail saw the smoke-colored bruise on her forehead. His stomach spasmed, and for a moment, he couldn't speak because of the rage choking off his air supply. But finally, he managed to suck in a breath. "Just like you said…" He tried to keep his voice even. "A plea from Elena to come home."

He said the word "home" purposely because he'd just realized here was the opening he needed to say the words that would break her heart. He walked toward her.

She grinned and rolled her eyes. "Like *that's* gonna work. *God!* Elena really thinks she's something, doesn't she? You know what her problem is, Mikhail? She eats, drinks and bleeds ice-skating. She has no *life* beyond skating! And that's so pathetic."

"Kerry, listen to me. We must talk." Mikhail fixed his eyes upon hers, forcing himself not to reach out and grab her hands. If he touched her, he wouldn't be able to go through with this. He wouldn't be able to think clearly.

She stared at him, her lips parted. Her eyes still sparkled with animation, the way they always did when she warmed to a subject she felt strongly about. Suddenly she grinned and reached out, clutching his hands. "You heard something, didn't you? They're going to give you political asylum, right?"

Mikhail closed his eyes and took in a deep, shuddering breath. Then, by force of will, he pulled his hands out of Kerry's grip, and placed them on his knees. He looked at her and saw the tiny flare of hurt in her eyes at this rejection of her touch. Anguish choked off his breath, and he swallowed hard, trying to force it away. Oh, God! How was it that he'd never realized before how vulnerable she was? If she couldn't hide her hurt feelings by this slight rebuff, how on earth was he going to be able to tell her he didn't love her? That it had all been nothing but a game to him. How could he do it to her?

Because he must. Maybe later, after the initial heartbreak had healed, she'd realize the truth. Realize that he had to do it to protect her. Right now, he had to be ruthless. He had to make her believe she meant nothing to him.

He stared across the room at a Hunt Country painting of red-coated hunters chasing down a fox, composing his face into what he hoped was a stone-cold mask. When he told her, he didn't want her to see any turmoil in him, no cracks of uncertainty. He had to convince her that this was what he wanted.

"Mikhail?" Her voice sounded small in the cozy study. "What is it? You're giving me the creeps."

He couldn't look at her. Couldn't bear it. "Elena is right," he said slowly. "I will never fit in here. Russia is my home. I cannot give up everything I have known. My country, my career...Nadya. It is too much to ask. I must go home."

He waited for her response, but there was nothing but stunned silence. Finally, Mikhail could bear it no longer, and he turned to look at her. His stomach clenched. Her face had gone sheet-white, her eyes, a stark, midnight blue. He saw her swallow, once, then again, trying, he knew, to find words that wouldn't come. She closed her eyes, and when she opened them, they were swimming with tears.

Jesus Christ! Could a person have a heart attack because of sadness? The way his heart was aching, he felt sure it was about to burst from his chest. Dear, God! Her tears! They cut through him like razor blades. For an insane few seconds, he thought about taking it all back. Admit he was lying. Admit he was forced to play this charade. But sanity returned with a vengeance as he realized that by doing so, he might be signing her death warrant.

He hardened his expression, looking away from her. "Kerry, I am sorry if I led you on. You are very sweet, but...my life is not here. Not with you. It was fantasy...that is all."

She finally found her voice, and it was strident with bitterness. "The least you can do when you fuck me over, Mikhail, is look at me."

His heart dipped, and he forced his eyes to meet hers. They were still filled with tears, but angry now. No, furious. He kept his face rigid, praying it wouldn't show any emotion at all.

"You said you loved me," Kerry went on, her bottom lip trembling. "That was a lie? It was all a lie? That night together at Gettysburg. None of it meant *anything* to you?"

He stared at her grimly. "It was good time. I like you, Kerry. You like me, too. It was that way from beginning. Sexual chemistry. Is that not what they call it? But anything more than that...is not realistic. We are from different worlds. I made mistake, thinking I could live in this country. Now, I know I was wrong. Look...I made bad decision. I was grieving for my mother. Angry at my country for killing my father. I foolishly believed I could avenge them, and that is why I brought you into this. I am most grateful for your help, Kerry, but I should never have involved you."

She jumped up from the sofa and strode to the window. He watched her, his heart in his throat. Rigidly, she stood at the window, staring out at the rolling hills of Virginia just awakening from its winter's sleep. Even from this distance, he could see she was trembling. He released a shaky breath, his eyes falling on her over-sized leather bag on the floor next to his feet. On impulse, he twisted the silver ring off his finger and dropped it into its depths. Maybe someday, she'd find it and know…

She turned around, her eyes spearing him. Two circles of red flared on her pale face, and her eyes sparkled with unshed tears. And something else. Fury? Disgust? No, something different. Something totally unexpected.

Triumph.

"You know what," she said, her voice cutting the air like a steel knife. "*I don't fucking believe you.*"

CHAPTER NINETEEN

Kerry took a step toward Mikhail, her eyes blinded by furious tears. "I just don't believe you. You're lying to me. I don't know why. Maybe it's something you saw in that envelope. O'Malley said something to me about Nadya's safety. He's holding her somewhere, right? Is that what was in the envelope? Does he have a picture of Nadya being held captive?"

She stared at Mikhail, waiting for his response. Who *was* this man gazing at her out of such winter-cold blue eyes? Certainly not the man she'd traveled across the country with a week ago. Not the man she'd curled her body against, breathing in the musky, moss oak scent of him, cherishing the contact of his warm, naked limbs entwined with hers, and feeling the beat of his heart under her cheek. This man was someone completely different; he was the aloof, stone-carved stranger who'd mesmerized her across the crowded tunnel of a Nice arena two years ago. A man she never dreamed she would know, much less share intimacies with. But maybe she *didn't* know him. Maybe this stranger on the sofa was the real Mikhail, and the one she'd fallen in love with had been the imposter.

No! She just couldn't believe that. The imprint of his kiss was still on her lips. She'd felt the eager response of his erection against her belly. That alone, meant nothing, of course. A man could heartily dislike a woman or even be indifferent to her, and still want to fuck her. But the kiss. The kiss couldn't be denied. There had been a tender urgency in it, a yearning, a deep insistency that couldn't be faked. A woman knew when a kiss meant more than physical desire. Mikhail's kiss had told her he wanted her, body and soul.

"You can lie all you want, Mikhail," she said softly. "But I'll never believe it. The way you kissed me a few minutes ago...that was not a lie. Or do you expect me to believe you're that good of an actor?"

Something flickered in the depths of his eyes. Regret? Tenderness? Kerry's heart lifted. Now, he would admit it all. That he was forced to go back to Russia to protect Nadya. That even if he had to go, he'd find a way to come back, to plan a future with her.

She took a step toward him. "Oh, Mikhail, babe, tell me the truth now. If you have to go, I understand. But don't go letting me believe you don't love me."

Mikhail got to his feet and turned away from her. He appeared to be engrossed in a generic-looking Virginia "Hunt Country" framed print on the wall. Similar ones were all over Roger's house in Occoquan, and Kerry was already heartily sick of the motif. "Mikhail?" She moved closer to him.

His shoulders were rigid, his head bowed. She reached out to touch him, but before she could, he turned. She drew in a sharp breath and took a step back. Never in her life had she seen such a cold, unapproachable expression. His eyes, blue as the Pacific, were as chilly as the ocean's depths.

"I do not love you, Kerry," he said slowly. "I am sorry I led you to believe that."

For a long moment, she stared at him. His expression didn't change. A muscle flexed in his set jaw, revealing only the slightest betrayal of emotion. He stood stiffly, his stance as taut as a gymnast readying himself for a jump onto the high beam. Seconds ticked by as Kerry searched his eyes for something—*anything*—that would tell her he was still lying. That he couldn't possibly mean what he'd said. But his eyes were glacier-cold. Unfeeling.

But still, Kerry didn't believe.

"There's nothing you can say, Mikhail, which will convince me this was just a game to you." She shook her head. "I don't know what's going on. Maybe you're trying to protect me. Or maybe it's Nadya who is being threatened, and that's why you're telling me all these lies. But it's not going to work. I don't believe you."

A look of something—desperation?—flickered in his eyes, and again, Kerry's heart lifted with hope. He'd come clean now. Admit it was all ugly lies he'd been forced to tell by Roger and his CIA buddies.

But then Mikhail's eyes frosted over and his jaw tightened. "Do you remember the day you accused me of arranging Cutler's accident?" His voice was arctic, as icy as his gaze.

Kerry's pulse jumped. She tried to speak, but couldn't because of the sudden fear clogging her throat.

"You were right," Mikhail said quietly.

Kerry shook her head.

He nodded, his eyes—a stranger's eyes—holding hers. "I arranged it. It was only way to get you to help me."

"No," Kerry said, her voice almost inaudible. She shook her head again, more vigorously this time. Her stomach churned. "*No!* You wouldn't do that."

"You do not know me, Kerry. You know nothing about who I really am…about what I will do to get what I want. Adam Cutler stood in my way, so I had him removed from equation. It is lucky he survived." He gave a slight shrug. "Either way, he was no longer problem. So, you see, Kerry, I am not the man you thought I was. I am a user. We had good time, you and me. But that is all it was to me. Just good time."

Her heart felt as if it had freeze-dried in her chest. Intellectually, she knew it was still beating, still pumping the blood through her stunned body. It was a miracle, really. The way her heart just kept on working even though it felt like it had been torn out by the roots. *So, there you have it, folks. Screwed again. Metaphorically and physically. Oh, Kerry girl, you sure know how to pick 'em.*

She swallowed hard, and somehow, found her voice despite the huge knot in her throat. "You know something? I thought Joshua was a bastard, but he can't hold a candle to you." She shook her head, and to her frustration, angry tears welled in her eyes. "You *sick* son-of-a-bitch. I'm sorry I ever met you." She turned to the door. "Can you let Mr. Lennart know I'm ready to go? I'll be in the car." Head high and shoulders straight, she walked to the door, amazed, really, that her legs were actually supporting her.

"*Kerry!*"

She stopped and looked back at him. Even now, she couldn't quite quell her belief that Mikhail was play-acting. That this whole conversation had been a staged performance.

But he wasn't looking at her. Instead, he stood with his back to her, staring out the window, his jaw set, shoulders rigid.

"Do not forget your bag," he said, his voice even, controlled.

Kerry contemplated him for a moment.

And they call Elena an iceberg.

"Yeah, right," she said finally, and walked over to the sofa to grab her purse from the floor. In the space of a few seconds, she was at the door again. "You have a nice life, Mikhail," she said, trying for indifference in her tone, and surprising herself when it worked.

She left the room and walked to the front door, then through it, and out onto the front porch. The biting March wind enveloped her, sending her hair flying in all directions, but she didn't even feel it.

Because she was already cold, from the inside out.

* * * * *

Mikhail stood at the window, watching as Kerry slipped into the passenger side of Lennart's car. Her hair, whipped into dishevelment by the wind, obscured her face, so he couldn't tell if she was crying. He made sure he stood to the side of the window so she wouldn't see him if she happened to look up. But he couldn't bear not to watch her in the last few seconds she would be within shouting distance.

It reminded him of his mother, the way he stood here watching Kerry drive away. She used to do the same thing when he'd left after those infrequent visits home to Tallinn. No matter what time of day or night he left, good weather or bad, she would either be at the door, or on the sidewalk, looking after him, a melancholy smile on her weary face, her hand lifted in farewell until he was out of sight. It had always saddened him, seeing her standing there, looking so forlorn. And now, here he was, watching someone he loved go away. It was worse, much worse than being the one leaving.

For all he knew, this would be the last glimpse he'd ever have of Kerry. If something happened to him…or even if he got out of Russia alive, it was entirely possible she would never forgive him for this charade.

Lennart's car began to move around the circular driveway, and then headed off toward the road. Only when the brake lights flared as it reached the intersection did Mikhail's eyes blur with tears.

He pressed his hot forehead against the cold glass of the window, and whispered, "Forgive me, Kerry."

* * * * *

Mikhail stared pensively out the window into a mass of gray clouds as the aircraft descended, making its final approach into Moscow. He felt curiously numb at the knowledge that he would soon be back on his homeland's soil. But then again, he'd availed himself of several glasses of complimentary Smirnoff Private Reserve, sitting here in the luxurious first class cabin the government had so generously reserved for him.

The CIA turnover of the "misguided" Russian ice dancer had been handled deftly and discreetly with an early morning limo ride to the Russian Embassy in Washington DC. There, he'd been politely welcomed back into the open arms of officials sent to bring the prodigal son back home. As they hustled him aboard a nonstop flight out of Dulles London, he'd waited for the other shoe to drop, but to his surprise and growing consternation, he'd been treated with nothing but respect by every countryman he encountered. No animosity, no barely concealed glares of disgust, not even any bawdy attempts at humor about the sexual prowess of American women, for which he was eternally grateful. It would probably, indeed, be bad form to shove a fellow Russian's teeth down his throat, and that was surely what he'd have to do to anyone who made any salacious remarks about Kerry.

Kerry. Christ! He couldn't stop thinking about her. That wounded look on her face. And he had put it there. That's why he'd turned to Mr. Smirnoff for solace during this interminable flight.

But he might as well have been drinking pure water. The vodka hadn't even made him light-headed, much less had it driven out the chaotic voices in his brain. Especially Wakeley's voice from the conversation they'd had the night before he'd been whisked to the Russian Embassy.

"Mikhail, I read in the CIA dossier that you're Catholic."

Mikhail studied the British SAS agent, not at all surprised about the CIA dossier. Why not? They were very thorough. "I was baptized Catholic," he said shortly. "But I do not practice formal religion."

Mikhail didn't feel his spiritual beliefs were any of Wakeley's business, so he didn't bother to add that his choice not to follow a certain dogma didn't mean he didn't believe in a supreme being. But he'd long ago stopped believing that any particular church had a patent on God.

"That's interesting," said Wakeley. "So, why is it you cross yourself before you go on the ice, and after you skate?"

"Habit," Mikhail replied with a shrug. "And perhaps superstition."

"Well, once you get back to Russia, you're going to have a religious re-awakening. Your American adventure has led you back to God, and back to the Catholic Church."

Mikhail stared at him. "Why?"

"Because your contact is going to be a priest. You've heard of the term, 'sleeper,' yes? One of our men was trained years ago to integrate into a society and live a normal life until we need him. His name is Father Augustino at St.

Nicholas the Martyr in Tallinn. I believe that's where you were baptized?"

Mikhail nodded. "Yes, but I do not know him."

He vaguely recalled a young priest who'd helped old Father Thomas celebrate Christmas Mass last year. That had been the last time he'd been in St. Nicholas—the last Christmas holiday he'd spent with his mother.

"I may have seen him," Mikhail added.

"Well, he is your contact when you need to get information to us. He hears confessions on Mondays, Wednesdays and Fridays. When you have something to report to him, you will let him know by taking communion at mass that morning, and then show up for confession that evening. He will be expecting you. Here." He withdrew a key chain from his suit jacket and passed it over to him. "This is a camera. It holds a roll of microfilm. Use it to film anything that might be of interest to us regarding Sean O'Malley. Where he goes, who he meets with, anything that raises the hairs on your neck."

Mikhail took the key chain and peered at it. It looked like a cheap tourist trinket in the shape of an Egyptian scarab. "Very James Bond. How does it work?"

"You can pre-set it for ten seconds. Click this button, and ten seconds later, it takes a picture. Or you can switch the button to manual, like this. You eject the film by hitting this button. Couldn't be simpler. Now, when Father Augustino has a message for you from us, or orders, he will let you know at mass by reading a particular verse from the Bible. Revelation 3:20. 'Listen! I am standing at the door, knocking; if you hear my voice and open the door, I will come in to you and eat with you, and you with me.' That's why it's important for you to attend mass on a regular basis."

Mikhail couldn't hold back a sardonic grin. "I feel like I'm in Hollywood movie. So cloak and dagger."

Wakeley didn't return his smile. "This is dead serious, Mikhail. Do you know why we are using Father Augustino instead of your friend, Vassily Immaakin?"

Mikhail stiffened. Actually, he hadn't thought of that, but now, it did seem odd. A ready-made spy right in Tallinn who hated the Russians, and wanted nothing more than to make them pay for the past would be a perfect recruit.

"No, why?"

Wakeley's face was grim. "Because just after you went on the run with Miss Niles, he was found in his law office, his throat slit from ear to ear."

Horror engulfed Mikhail as he thought of the nondescript lawyer with granite eyes. "O'Malley?" he asked quietly.

Wakeley nodded. "We're quite sure it was his handiwork. There were also signs he'd been tortured. We don't know how much information he might've spilled." His eyes sharpened. "Don't kid yourself, Mikhail. You could be walking into a trap by going back. We'll do everything we can to protect you, but…" He shrugged.

Mikhail tried to keep his face expressionless. "I do not have choice, do I? Not if I want political asylum?"

"Good point. Anyway, back to Father Augustino. He will also be your contact when you are ready to get your coach out of the country. We haven't forgotten our promise to you, you know. When she's ready, let the priest know, and we will make arrangements with our contact in Helsinki to have her picked up."

Well, that was something, Mikhail thought now. Nadya would finally get her wish, and be able to start a new life in the West. And if everything worked out, he, too, would start that new life, too. With Kerry, he hoped. If she ever forgave him.

But what if he'd lied too well, and even after this was all over, she still believed he was involved in the hit-and-run accident that had injured Adam Cutter? What then? He slipped his hand into his parka pocket and heard the crinkle of paper. His heart dipped when he pulled it out and saw what it was. A Ding Dong wrapper. A visceral pain slammed through him. Dear God, would he ever see her again?

There was a slight bump, and Mikhail realized the aircraft had landed. His heart began to race. Home. On Russian soil. As he stood to make his way off the plane, a shiver radiated through him, along with a chilling thought he couldn't quite dismiss.

You're home, Mikhail, and it's possible you'll never leave this place alive.

CHAPTER TWENTY

"Well, what do you think? Is it *me*?" Kerry turned to Dale, a pair of dark-shaded, wrap-around sunglasses, ala Bono, perched on her nose.

Dale laughed and shook her blond head. "Not even close. Try the Madonna ones."

Kerry sighed and took off the sunglasses. "Well, at least they hide the dark shadows under my eyes."

"Hey, you're looking a thousand times better now than you were a couple of weeks ago. I told you you'd get through this."

Kerry put the sunglasses back in their slot, and moved on down the counter, eyeing the costume jewelry that hung gaudily from display stands. She glanced back at Dale. "Thanks for suggesting this. It's fun."

The older woman smiled. "I've never known a woman yet who didn't feel better after some serious shopping. It might not cure a broken heart, but it can serve as a pretty good Band-Aid. Hey, you want to go check out the Coach store?"

"Lead the way."

It had taken Dale two weeks to get Kerry out of her house by dragging her to Reading, home of the oldest outlet center in America. And Kerry had to admit it was doing her good. She finally felt like she'd returned to the land of the living. Or was beginning to, anyway.

After that horrible morning when Mikhail had denied ever loving her, and even worse, had admitted to being behind Adam's accident, she had walked around in a fog for two days, unable to think, much less make a plan. Her life had turned upside down within the space of an hour, and she'd felt like a boat adrift on a stagnant sea.

Sharon, having heard what had happened from Roger, was cloyingly sympathetic, and even Roger had dropped some of his austere reserve and tentatively invited her to stay with them as long as she wanted. But Kerry needed to be left alone in her pain. She briefly considered going back to Lake Arrowhead, but decided the solitude there would probably drive her out of her mind. It would be *too* much "alone." She needed to be with someone who cared about her, but who would give her the space she needed to work things out, to try to decide what to do with her life now that a future with Mikhail wasn't a possibility. She needed...to be mothered.

And just like that, she'd visualized Dale's charming blue and white kitchen, and she'd wanted to be there. With Dale. She was the quiet, calm, sane presence Kerry needed—someone who would give her that space, and yet be ready to listen when it was time to talk.

Maybe that time was now.

The two women ambled through the Coach store, examining handbags and snickering over the outlandish prices.

"I saw a knock-off of this one in Wal-Mart the other day," Dale said, holding a small navy leather knapsack with red trim. "I think it was $16.99."

Kerry tried not to wince at the reference to Wal-Mart. She'd never be able to shop there again without thinking of Mikhail. "And how much is that one? Two hundred?"

"Not quite." Dale grinned. "A real bargain at one-sixty."

Kerry rolled her eyes. "Even if I were filthy rich, I couldn't imagine spending that much for a purse. But this one is cute, I have to admit." She picked up a butter-soft camel-colored duffle. "And it's cheaper. Only...*wow*! It's a steal at one-twenty-five!"

"Get it," Dale urged. "Reward yourself."

Kerry shook her head and put the handbag back on the rack. "No. It's stupid to spend that much for a stinkin' purse. Besides, I'm out of a job, remember? I'm going to have to figure out how to start bringing in some money." She frowned, fingering the soft leather of the purse.

Dale looked at her, her blue eyes sympathetic. "You have plenty of time to think about the future. Kell made sure you're not going to starve."

Kerry turned away from the purses and moved down the aisle. "I know. But I have to do something with my life." She looked back and grinned. "And right now, I want to eat. Let's go find a place for lunch."

Ten minutes later, Kerry took a bite of her Big Mac, then dipped a french fry in honey—something she'd done since she was a kid, much to everyone else's disgust. She slipped it into her mouth.

Dale watched her with a smug smile. "It's good to see your appetite returning."

"Yeah, it must be this fresh spring air," Kerry mumbled, chewing with relish. "If I'm not careful, I'll gain so much weight the ice will break when I step on it. And so much for my job with Ice Capades."

Dale laughed. "All right. Hold on a minute while I get out my violin." She gazed at Kerry, her smile gentling. "You must be feeling better. You're cracking jokes again. The Kerry we know and love is on her way back."

"Thanks to you." Kerry took a sip of her Diet Coke. "I mean it, Dale. If it weren't for you, I don't know who…where I would've gone."

Dale grabbed a french fry and dipped it into a pool of ketchup. "Did you even consider going to your mother?"

Kerry's head snapped up. "Are you serious? Why would I do that?"

Dale shrugged. "Because she's your *mother*?"

"You're more a mother to me than she is," Kerry said shortly. "And so is Catri. Believe me, Dale, if I'd turned up in San Diego, hoping to get consolation from Jana, she would've had to pencil me in between Junior League meetings."

Dale's gaze dropped to a straw wrapper she was twisting and shredding with her manicured fingers. "I didn't get along very well with my mother either. It wasn't until after she'd died that I realized I hadn't tried to meet her halfway."

Kerry felt a pang in her heart as a memory skidded through her mind of the day Jana had first driven her to Lake Arrowhead. There had been a moment in the car when her mother's eyes had softened. When Kerry had felt almost as if Jana was about to place a gentle hand on her knee, give it an affectionate squeeze. A gesture that came natural to most mothers. But it hadn't happened. Of course, Kerry had stopped her, using her smart teenage mouth to make some cutting remark that had immediately frosted over the softness in Jana's eyes. And that hadn't been the first—or last—time Kerry had done that.

"Want some advice, Kerry?" Dale said softly, then went on without waiting for a reply. "Try and forgive your mother for her mistakes. It's the only way you'll be able to heal."

Kerry waded a french fry through the tray of honey. Her appetite had disappeared. "I don't know *how* to forgive her," she said softly.

"It's simple," Dale replied, her gaze direct. "Just give yourself permission to do it."

* * * * *

"Oh, my sweet Mikhail. It is so good to see you."

Mikhail smiled down at Nadya's wizened face, feeling a rush of love at the tender look in her brown eyes. "Likewise." He took the tiny woman in his arms and hugged her tightly. "Have they been treating you well?"

Nadya squeezed him hard then stepped back, her hands clasping his. "What do you think? You see this place? Can you believe an old woman like me, after so many years, is finally living in the lap of luxury?" Her eyes twinkled knowingly. "Elena must have wanted you back quite desperately. Come. Come in. I'll put on the tea."

As Nadya led him into her spacious ground floor apartment, Mikhail gazed around in awe. Yes, Nadya was right. Elena *had* outdone herself. Nadya's new apartment was located in a recently renovated—and quite trendy—section of Tallinn near the harbor. Cobblestone streets winded past shops and restaurants reminiscent of the most upscale European villages. Elena was pulling out all stops in her attempt to keep Mikhail happy. He supposed he should feel flattered—that he was so important to her. But instead, it just made him dislike her more. So far, though, he was managing to hide his feelings. All according to plan.

They'd arrived in Estonia the day before, having spent the first week of his homecoming in Moscow. He hadn't really known what to expect upon his return. Would he be under "house arrest?" Subject to hours of interrogation about his motives for defecting, and his ultimate change of heart? But Elena's political connections had paved the way for a nearly painless reentry into Russian society. There had been a few informal debriefings and some statements to sign, and then nothing to do but pack up his belongings in his old flat and prepare to move to Tallinn to start training.

Now, here he was. Getting ready to start his new life as a spy.

Nadya took him into a sitting room decorated in a fussy Victorian style—fringe-rimmed lampshades, lace doilies on table surfaces and a sofa and chair covered in bright blue and green floral slipcovers. Busy, thought Mikhail. Elena's décor? He didn't remember from his years living with Nadya that she'd had such flowery taste, but then, at that time, she'd lived in a dank little apartment furnished only with the bare essentials. She'd been lucky to have a threadbare rug under her feet.

Nadya, chattering on about the rainy weather the day before and how miserable it had been to stand in line for a pork roast at the butcher because she'd known he was coming and wanted to make him a nice home-cooked meal, bade him to take a seat on one of the horrid slip covered chairs, and bustled into the small kitchen to put on a pot of tea.

Mikhail glanced around the room, and was amazed to see a nineteen-inch color TV in one corner tuned to a frenetic game show whose only objective seemed to be to make a fool of the contestants. It was the first time he'd ever seen a TV in Nadya's home. More of Elena's work?

The tantalizing smell of roasted pork wafted from the kitchen, and Mikhail's stomach responded with a growl. Nadya knew how much he'd always loved her pork roast. During the years he'd grown up in her home, they'd had it infrequently because of the expense and more importantly, the shortages. But apparently, with Elena's patronage, that was no longer a problem. It helped to know the right people.

Full of nervous energy, Mikhail got up from the chair and walked over to a long table in front of a lace-covered window looking out on a quiet cobble stoned street. Framed photographs were artfully displayed on vintage doilies, ones he recognized from his childhood. There was the one of Nadya and her husband, Ivor, at the end of their competition in pairs skating at the 1936 Olympics in Garmisch. He remembered staring at the photo after a hard day of training, and wondering if he'd ever compete in the Olympics. And then, there was the one that had always made him sad. Ivor, handsome in his military uniform just before leaving for the Siberian front in 1943. Sad, because he knew that was the last Nadya had seen her husband alive. They'd had only four years together before he was killed in action.

"The love of my life," Nadya had often told him, tears misting her eyes. "I'll never marry again. No other man could ever live up to my Ivor."

And as far as he knew, there *had* never been another man in Nadya's life. Her skaters became her family. Her career, her lifeline.

She stepped into the sitting room, carrying a tray laden with cups, a porcelain pot of tea, a pitcher of cream and a sugar bowl. Mikhail hurried across the room, took it from her, and placed it down on the coffee table. He was no judge of fine china, but it all looked very genteel, as if Nadya was playing the part of a queen entertaining guests. A sense of disquiet began to churn inside him.

She smiled at him and took a seat on the sofa across from him. "So, my Mikhail, what do you think of my new home? Do you not think Elena has gone a bit overboard?" Before he could respond, her brows lowered, and her eyes sparkled mischievously. "I cannot abide the woman. No matter how sticky sweet she is to me."

Relief swept through him. For a few minutes there, he'd begun to think that Nadya had allowed herself to be swayed by Elena's wealth and power. Now, he felt ashamed of that thought. Nadya was way too smart for that. Of course, she saw right through all these luxuries, and knew it exactly for what it was—a bribe. Not that she had any choice in accepting it.

"She really seems to be taking good care of you," Mikhail said, taking the cup of tea Nadya held out to him. She'd remembered just how he liked it—with lots of cream and sugar.

He took a sip. "Mmmmm…good."

"Sweet enough?" she asked with a smile.

"Perfect. I just wish I had a Ding Dong to go with it."

She gave him a blank look. "What is this Ding Dong?"

"A chocolate cake with lovely white cream inside. From America. It is to die for."

Nadya took a sip of her tea, eyeing him speculatively. "To die for, is it? It was my understanding that you thought everything about America was 'to die for.' I was surprised when the newspapers said you'd had a change of heart."

Mikhail hesitated before answering. His gaze swept the room. He wouldn't put it past Elena to have listening devices hidden in the place.

"I realized I could never leave my homeland," he said slowly. "But yes, at first, I was captivated by everything American."

Her eyes twinkled. "Including a very beautiful American skater?"

His heart twisted, and for a moment, he could barely catch his breath because the pain at the thought of Kerry was so intense. Again, mindful of the possible bugs, he forced a response. "She was just a fling. A silly diversion. I wasn't thinking with my brain, if you know what I mean."

A look of disbelief crossed Nadya's face. Her gaze grew more penetrating. "Mikhail Kozlof, that is very ungentlemanly of you. And not at all attractive, I must say."

Mikhail put a warning finger to his lips, placed his teacup on the coffee table and stood. "I'm sorry, Nadya. That was crude, I suppose, but nonetheless, true." He saw that Nadya was watching him closely, a guarded look on her face. "But the newspapers made a big deal about some huge romance, and it was simply not true. Yes, she beguiled me, and yes, for a few days, I believed I could give up my country to continue the dalliance. But I came to my senses before it was too late."

Nadya didn't speak for a moment, but just silently scanned his face. Then she put down her teacup and stood.

"After dinner, Mikhail," she said slowly. "We will take a nice walk around town. Believe me, you will need to walk off the calories I am going to feed you."

She was true to her word, feeding him a dinner large enough for three men of his size. Besides the succulent pork roast, she'd prepared boiled new potatoes and her specialty—sweet, braided bread, glossy with egg yolk. To satisfy Mikhail's sweet-tooth, she'd baked a beautiful chocolate cake, apologizing ruefully that it didn't have "a lovely cream filling."

After he'd helped her wash the dishes, leaving her small but attractive kitchen sparkling, they'd gone for their walk. For the first few minutes, Nadya linked her arm through Mikhail's and kept up an easy chatter. Then after they'd turned the corner, strolling in the direction of the waterfront, she'd peered up at him with an appraising look.

"So, why is it that you cannot talk freely with me in my home, Mikhail? Is it what I think?"

"That Elena may well be hearing every word we say?" he said. "Yes, that is exactly why. Do not trust her, Nadya."

She snorted. "Like I ever would! What do I look like, some kind of ignoramus?"

Mikhail grinned at her indignant tone. "Not even a little bit." He squeezed her arm. "You look like home to me, Nadya." And she did. She was the only thing left that he cared about in this city. And once he got the information the British wanted, and got Nadya safely out of the country, he never wanted to come back. Not to Tallinn. Someday, after this was all over, he would return to Russia, make his way to the Kola Peninsula to the village where his father had been massacred, and disperse his mother's ashes to fulfill the request she'd written in her will.

He'd brought the urn with him today, asking Nadya to keep it for him. If he should have to leave the country quickly, at least he would know his mother's ashes would be safe with her. When he imagined the moment he would cast them to the winds of the North, he saw Kerry at his side, somehow. He didn't know how he would make that happen, because surely, she hated him with a passion right now. He'd find a way, though. That, he was sure of.

"Okay, Mikhail, we are far enough from my flat now," Nadya said, slowing her steps. "Tell me what is going on."

Across the street, Mikhail saw a small park with benches spaced throughout a grove of birch trees. "Come, let's sit."

They found an unoccupied bench under the canopy of a huge birch. Yesterday's rain had given way to a beautiful spring day, albeit cool, as it always was in late March. Mikhail's gaze swept the sky. He'd never seen it such a crystalline color of blue. A seagull, swooped down, squawking its raucous cry, and snatched up what looked like a discarded bread crust, then darted back seaward with its booty. The chilly breeze carried the salty tang from the Gulf of Finland, a familiar scent from Mikhail's childhood. It brought to mind happier times, moving something deep inside him, but at the same time, giving him a stark feeling of loneliness. It was the sadness of something ending, a chapter closed.

Nadya peered at him, her button-brown eyes speculative. "Mikhail Kozlof, from the time you were a little boy, I always knew when you had something up your sleeve. Now, what is it? What is going on?"

He looked at her. "I cannot go into a lot of detail. It's too dangerous. But I have come back here on a mission for the British. Once I accomplish it, they will give me political asylum." He reached out and took her hand, giving it an anxious squeeze. "That's where you come in. They have also agreed to get you out."

She gazed at him for a long moment, and then slowly, she pulled her hand out of his and cupped the side of his jaw. Her fingers lovingly traced his scar from jaw to cheekbone. "Ah, Mikhail," she said softly. "I love you dearly. You're the son I never had, and I'm so very proud of the man you've grown up to be. Honorable, kind, caring. But my sweet Mikos, what makes you think I want to leave my country? It is all I have ever known. I am no spring chicken. I have no desire to start life over in a new place. This is my home, and I will remain here."

Mikhail shook his head, unable to believe what he was hearing. "You can't be serious, Nadya. Remember the days when the Communists were in power? You were always going on about the West, what a wonderful place it was, how everyone was free to make their own decisions, to build a life without government interference. And now, I'm giving you the chance, and you're telling me you want to stay here?"

She gazed at him sadly. "Mikhail, think about it. I am an old woman. Why would I want to give up my life here to start over in a new place? Here, I have my skaters, a cozy little home. I have my books, my music and my television to watch your competitions in foreign countries. I am happy with my life, my routine. And yes, you are right. I used to prattle on about the West, and what a wonderful place it is. I still believe that. And I wish you well there. Once you get out of here, I hope you will go find your American girl, marry her, and be very happy. This is what you want, yes?"

Mikhail felt his cheeks grow hot. "How did you know?"

She gave him a gentle smile. "Ah, Mikhail, you forget how well I know you. There was something in your eyes when you talked about her. Your lips were saying vulgar words, but your eyes were soft with love." She squeezed his hand affectionately. "Does she know?"

He turned away, fixing his gaze on a squirrel sitting on its hindquarters nibbling an acorn. "That I love her?" He shook his head. "I don't know. I told her I did, but that was before..." He blinked quickly. "Oh, Nadya, I had to lie to her to protect her. And now I'm afraid she'll never forgive that lie."

"My sweet boy, look at me." Cradling his face in her palms, she forced him to meet her eyes. "When this is all over, just go to her and tell her how you feel. If she loves you...and how could she not?...she will forgive you."

Mikhail swallowed hard to dislodge the lump in his throat. He was remembering the stricken look in Kerry's eyes when she'd told him how her mother had deserted her. And then, the stubborn line of her jaw when she'd stated flatly that she could never forgive her for that.

"I hope you're right," he said slowly. "But I think forgiveness is something that is very hard for this woman."

CHAPTER TWENTY-ONE

Elena wanted him. That much was obvious.

But she was still very, very angry with him for costing her the gold medal at the Olympics. Mikhail had broached the subject once shortly after his arrival back in Moscow. It hadn't been easy choking back his revulsion as he'd apologized for his actions, groveled before her, essentially, because he knew his only chance in getting information on Sean O'Malley was through her.

Wearing a remote expression on her elegant face, she'd listened to his explanation that he'd had his head turned by a pretty girl, and allowed his emotions to run rampant over his common sense. He'd begged for her forgiveness, all the time praying his voice rang with sincerity, and his eyes didn't reveal his disgust.

After a frosty moment of silence, she'd given him a cold smile. "It is just a good thing, Mikhail, that my father is no longer alive. I do not think you would've lived long enough to change your mind about returning to Russia. But you know what? I am a forgiving woman. And I know that from now on, you are going to do everything possible to make sure I get my gold medal at the World Championships next year, yes? And we will start with winning the International Grand Prix in Belfast in June. So, my Mikos, prepare to work your beautiful ass off."

And he knew she meant it. For weeks now, they'd been training at their new facility in Tallinn for no less than twelve hours a day. Nadya had brought in a new choreographer to work with them on an updated program, performing to a mix of movements from Vivaldi's "The Four Seasons." The added steps were intricate and technically more difficult than anything they'd done in the past, and Mikhail believed it would take a miracle for them to nail down the routine for the competition in Belfast, but Elena was determined to die trying. And, he thought ruefully, she might just take him with her.

It was just past ten o'clock in the evening, and they'd been at the rink since nine this morning. He was wasted, and wanted nothing more than to go back to his flat and collapse into bed. But he knew it was finally time to act upon Elena's obvious attraction for him. The days were starting to slip by, and so far, he wasn't a step closer to bringing Sean O'Malley to justice.

Mikhail skated to the boards where Elena was taking off her guards. "Hey, wait up, Elena. I want to talk to you."

She glanced up at him. "Yes? What about?"

Her weariness showed in the lavender smudges under her eyes. Mikhail wondered if she was still on the TNG drug, and if so, did it have anything to do with her sallow expression? She was still beautiful, of course, but something didn't look quite right about her.

He purposely came up close to her and placed a hand on her shoulder. Immediately, he felt a tremor go through her. "We've been working way too hard, Elena."

Her mouth tightened. "I told you I wouldn't go easy on you. It's your fault we have to work so hard."

"Yes, I realize that. But Elena, everybody needs some down time." He moved a hand up to her jaw, brushing his fingers over her cheekbone. "I'm worried about you." He allowed his gaze to sweep over her face, lingering on the voluptuous swell of her lips. She reacted to his touch and glance as if she were a candlewick ignited by a match. Her eyes sharpened, then grew soft with desire. Mikhail lowered his voice, "Let's go relax together. Have a few drinks. Listen to some music."

She gazed up at him, her lips parted, barely restrained excitement dancing across her face. "We can go to your flat."

Christ! No subtlety here. He should've known there would be no slow going with Elena Boiko. This would have to be handled very delicately. Sleeping with her was not an option. Making her *think* he'd sleep with her…well, that was different.

"I was thinking perhaps we could go to your friend, Sean's, pub. What's it called? "

She frowned. "Hell's Hole. But why do you want to go there? They play that silly traditional Irish music. All those tin whistles and loud drums."

"I am in the mood for a Guinness," Mikhail said, his voice deliberately seductive. "And…I'm guessing this place has lots of tables in dark, private corners." It wasn't a guess, actually. He'd scoped out Hell's Hole a few days before and saw it provided the exact ambience a man might use to romance a woman—a few compartment-like booths in the depths of the room and tables topped with flickering candles.

One perfectly shaped eyebrow arched, and Elena gave him a cat-like smile. "They are called 'snugs.' But if it's privacy you want, Mikos, I still say we should go to your flat."

Mikhail gritted his teeth then forced himself to give her a heated look. "Elena, I cannot do that because, believe me, I cannot trust myself to be alone with you. And as possessive as O'Malley is about you, I'd be a fool to cross that line."

"Really?" Elena purred, giving him an arch look. "And if you're so worried about Sean, why do you want to go to his pub with me?"

Careful, Mikhail thought. *Elena is not stupid.* Egotistical, yes, and that's what he'd play upon.

He smiled. "Hey, I feel like a pint of Guinness with my skating partner. What's wrong with that? Besides..." He allowed his gaze to sweep over her face and fasten on her lips.

"Besides what?" she said softly, her breath quickening.

"Maybe I just want to study O'Malley. Find out why he fascinates you so."

"Oh, Mikos," she said silkily, her hand brushing against his chest. "He doesn't fascinate me half as much as you do."

And that, Mikhail thought, was exactly what he was counting on.

* * * * *

"Sit down, Daniel, old boy, and let me pour you some fine Irish whiskey." With a friendly hand on his back, Sean guided the bear-like Irishman to a leather chair across from his desk. "Ah, it's so good to see you, man. Almost like old times."

The red-bearded Irishman cast a nervous glance at Beowulf, who sprawled on the rug to the side of Sean's desk, his intelligent brown eyes glued on the visitor. Sean tried not to smirk as he headed for the crystal decanter on the bar. Poor old fucker was scared shitless of the dog. And that quite delighted Sean. It made the man seem more human, knowing he was capable of feeling fear just like anyone else, even if he was a cold-blooded killer. And fuck a duck, Beowulf could smell his fear. Sean forced himself to hold back a snicker. It was amusing to see Daniel Sullivan doing a sphincter-clincher because of a big old teddy-bear dog like Beowulf, who looked much more ferocious than he actually was. But that was a good thing to know, Sean mused. It was always good to know the weaknesses of your enemies—and your friends.

Sean handed Sullivan a Waterford crystal tumbler filled with a generous amount of amber whiskey, and the Irishman downed it in one swallow.

"Now, then." Sean took a seat behind his desk. "To business."

Big Dan, they called him. His friends called him that, at least. His enemies called him Danny Death because he'd left so many dead bodies in his wake during a span of thirty years or so. Most of them had died during Sullivan's twenty-year stint with the IRA—British soldiers, Protestant extremists, innocent bystanders. But in the last ten years, others had ended up dead when they somehow found themselves at cross-purposes with Big Dan. He'd gone into business for himself, and that had made him even more dangerous than he'd been before.

Sean was glad Big Dan still counted him as one of his friends. There had been times when, if not for good fortune, he could've very well ended up a target of Danny Death. But Sean had been very lucky, indeed. Now, if everything went according to plan, Big Dan was going to make him a very rich man.

He looked across the desk and grinned at the older man. "Well? So, how did it go? Did Archangel perform as expected?"

"Indeed, he did," Sullivan said in his thick Belfast accent. His pebble-brown eyes bored into Sean. "That is quite a powerful drug you have there, Sean, lad. Remarkable stuff!

Archangel beat the rest of the field by thirty-two lengths…without breaking a sweat." His thick lips stretched in a pleased grin. But it didn't stay on his face long. "How much do you want for the formula?"

Sean took his time lighting a cigarette. One thing they'd be getting straight right now, he thought. *He* was calling the shots, not Big Dan. He inhaled on his fag and released a stream of smoke, staring lazily at Sullivan's fleshy face.

"Well, now…I want to be fair about it, Daniel. After all, you hunted down the stingers for me. A risky thing to do when you're trying to stay on the right side of the law." He gave an inward snicker. Stupid bugger! Did Sullivan really believe anyone actually thought he'd gone straight after being released from the H-Blocks? Well, perhaps the Brits thought so. People who knew him—the Irish patriots, even those bloodthirsty Protestant devils knew Big Dan Sullivan couldn't walk a straight line if his bloody life depended on it. He was a gangster through and through.

Sullivan's flinty eyes skewered him. "Cut the crap, O'Malley, and tell me your price."

Sean shifted in his chair. "Well, you see, Daniel, there's a wee bit of a problem. I haven't been able to actually get my hands on the formula. Anton Boiko hasn't been as…cooperative as I would've hoped."

Sullivan's expression grew a degree colder. "*Get* him to cooperate."

"I'm working on it. So…why don't we do this? I'll give you a couple of ampoules of TNG, enough for a few more races to tide you over. And I'll do my damndest to get that formula for you."

"Your damndest better be good enough." The Irishman stared at Sean a moment to let it sink in, and then went on, "Let's talk compensation. How much is it going to cost me?"

Sean peered at the lit end of his fag, keeping his expression bland. "Four million."

Sullivan's eyes narrowed. "That's a bloody huge sum."

"But worth it, Daniel. Worth every penny. You'll have your own labs set up, your production teams churning out the miracle drug, and your horses will win every race they enter. Think about it. The Kentucky Derby. The Preakness. Belmont Stakes. All yours."

Sullivan got to his feet. Beowulf's ears pricked and his massive head lifted. "I'll have half of the money wired to your Swiss bank account tomorrow. The other half, you'll get when I have the formula, understand?"

"Quite." Sean stood and thrust out his hand.

Sullivan stared at him a moment longer. "I want that formula before The Kilkenny Cup. June 4th. Don't disappoint me, Sean." He turned and headed for the door. Beowulf growled deep in his throat, but remained in his position on the floor. Sullivan didn't look his way. At the door, the Irishman turned and looked back at Sean. "A wee warning, lad. You have enemies in Ireland. Some have tried to turn me against you. They say you aren't to be trusted. That you put your own aims before the Struggle. You've heard the rumors, I'm sure. Rumors about informing on good Irishmen to save your own neck. I've even heard stories that you may have been responsible for my four years in the H-Blocks. But I don't believe them. You're a good lad, aren't you, Sean? You're a good, loyal friend." For a long, tense moment, they locked gazes. Finally, Sullivan nodded. "Get me that formula, Sean. Slainte." He left the room and closed the door behind him.

Sean sat motionless. Then he swallowed hard.

How had the bloody bastard found out about his statement to the RUC? It had been so long ago. 1985, to be exact. That was when Sullivan went to Long Kesh. Sean had worried for a while after he was released. If he'd known anything, he would've come after him then. But he hadn't, and Sean had assumed nothing had leaked out. But now…

He picked up the phone on his desk and stabbed out a series of numbers.

"Fagan," he growled when a voice answered. "I have a job for you and Boris. Go pick up Anton Boiko, and take him to the warehouse. I want you to get that formula out of him. You understand me? Do what you have to do, but get it."

* * * * *

Over Elena's shoulder, Mikhail saw the door to Sean's office open. A big red-bearded man stepped out and weaved his way through the crowded pub.

"Who is that man?" he asked Elena.

She turned her elegant head and glanced back. Her brow puckered in a frown. "Oh, one of Sean's business associates." She picked up her glass of wine—her second since they'd arrived at Hell's Hole. "Mmmmm…lovely."

Sean took a sip of his Guinness, weighing his words before he spoke. "He doesn't look Russian."

He wasn't, of course. Despite the beard and twenty extra pounds, Mikhail had immediately recognized Daniel Sullivan from the photo in the dossier Wakeley had given him.

Sullivan glanced at his expensive-looking gold wristwatch, and wedged his huge body into a space at the crowded bar. A moment later, the bartender placed a glass of amber liquid and a tumbler of what looked like water in front of him.

"He's not," Elena said, a bored look on her face. "He's from Ireland—one of Sean's potato peasants. You wouldn't believe what a bore he is. Always yammering on about 'the Struggle.' It's nauseating."

Mikhail smiled. "Oh, you know him well?"

Her eyes met his, and her full, beautiful lips gave a seductive pout. "Really, Mikhail, what does it matter where that silly man is from? I thought we came here to talk about…us."

You, you mean, Mikhail thought. He fought to keep his expression bland and reached out to cover her slender hand with his. She started in surprise then relaxed as his thumb methodically brushed over her knuckles.

"You're right," he said softly, gazing into her eyes. "I was just trying to make small talk. You make me feel like a bashful schoolboy, Elena."

"Ah, Mikhail…" Her gaze heated at the contact of his thumb on her skin. "It is my guess that you do nothing like a bashful schoolboy. Let us go to your flat, and you can prove my point."

Christ! How was he going to get out of this? Elena was a piranha, and when she decided she wanted something, she went after it. And she didn't know the meaning of the word "slow."

He opened his mouth to respond, but saw that her gaze had frozen at something over his right shoulder. She uttered an oath and quickly withdrew her hand from his grasp. Mikhail looked around and saw nothing but a mirrored ad for Murphy's stout on the wall behind him. Then in the mirror's reflection, he recognized Sean's athletic body heading toward them, with Beowulf at his heels.

"You must've finished training early, love," Sean said, an easy smile on his face. But his brown eyes were hard as gravel. He looked from Elena to Mikhail. "Is she working you to death, Kozlof?"

Mikhail shrugged, forcing a smile. "The only way I could get her to call it a night was to buy her a drink."

This was the first time he'd come face-to-face with O'Malley since receiving that curiously lurid photo of Kerry in the motel room. It was all he could do to hold himself back from shoving his perfect white teeth down his slimy throat.

Sean's gaze fastened on Elena's wineglass, and his eyes grew colder. "Yes, I see that. And I suppose she didn't mention she's not supposed to drink alcohol?"

Elena sighed. "Just one little glass of wine, Sean. It's not going to hurt me."

Beowulf edged past Sean and placed his muzzle on Mikhail's knee. "How you doing, boy?" Mikhail said, scratching the beast behind his ears. If Beowulf had been a cat, he would've purred with pleasure. The dog panted, his bright eyes fastened adoringly on Mikhail's face as he stroked his black coat.

Sean looked from Elena to Mikhail. "So, tell me, Kozlof, are you two going to bring home that gold medal? Elena tells that this competition in Belfast will set the standards for the coming year. Is that not right, love? That the winners are considered the favorites in the World Championships next March?"

Elena rolled her eyes and took a tiny sip of white wine. "You know this, Sean. I have only told you so ten million times."

Sean placed a hand on Elena's shoulder and squeezed. Mikhail saw the grimace flash across her face, and knew he was hurting her. His immediate instinct was to jump to her defense. As much as he disliked the woman, it went against his grain to see her manhandled by a thug three times her size. But he knew better than to challenge O'Malley. He was as lethal as a great white shark.

Beowulf lost interest in Mikhail and moved a few feet away, settling on his haunches, and giving an audible yawn.

"That, you have, love." Sean said, his voice like raw silk. He turned his granite gaze back to Mikhail. "Kozlof, you won't mind if I steal Elena away for a wee minute, will you? I promise I won't keep her long." As he spoke, he curled his hand around Elena's upper arm and drew her gently to her feet.

Mikhail shrugged and lifted his Guinness to his lips. "No problem."

Elena flashed Mikhail a warning look. "Watch my handbag. I will be back."

Maybe not, Mikhail thought as Sean towed her away toward his office. *If O'Malley had anything to say about it.* The dog got up and padded off behind them.

A movement at the bar caught his eye. The Irishman was heading toward the dark corridor in the back that led to the restrooms. Mikhail slipped his hand into the pocket of his jacket and heard the crinkle of cellophane. The Ding Dong wrapper he couldn't make himself throw away. As always, it brought to mind an image of Kerry, sending a jagged pain through his heart. Focus, he ordered himself. His fingers brushed against the cold brass of the key-chain/camera Quentin Wakeley had given him.

Maybe now was the time to finally use it.

* * * * *

After Sean closed the door to his office, Elena ripped her arm out of his grasp and whirled to face him. "What is wrong with you? You've practically bruised my arm!"

He glowered at her. "What are you up to, Elena? Are you purposely trying to make me jealous? I don't like games like that, you know."

Her chin jutted up. "I don't have the slightest idea what you're talking about. "

He fastened his hands on her upper arms and gave her a slight shake. "I *said*, I don't like games! Why are you bringing Kozlof to my pub? You know I can't stomach the man. It's bad enough I have to watch him put his hands all over you out on the ice, and now, you're practically screwing him in my very own establishment." He gave her another shake. "I won't have it, Elena!"

Her eyes blazed fire. "Let go of me this instant, Sean O'Malley. I won't be treated like one of your…employees." She stared into his eyes for a long moment, and finally, he released her and stepped back. "There is nothing between Mikhail and me. I don't know what you think you saw, but it's only in your imagination. We simply came here for a drink after a long day of training."

He stared at her, his jaw clenched. "Why is it I don't believe you?"

"Because you are a possessive, paranoid control freak," Elena said, anchoring her hand on a curveous hip. She took a languid step closer to him, her gaze scanning his face. Her voice lowered an octave, "Please, Sean, you must stop this nonsense. You are smothering me. I cannot live this way. I must have freedom to make my own choices. You are my lover, not my father, and…" She tapped a fingernail against his chest, her gaze narrowing. "…I will not be treated as your possession."

Sean grabbed her hand and squeezed. She grimaced. "But you *are* my possession," he growled. "Whether you like it or not." His grip tightened on her fingers. She released a soft exclamation of pain. He was unmoved. "I should've had Kozlof killed in America. I brought him back for you so you

318

can have your fucking gold medal. Do you still want it, Elena?"

She tried to tug her hand away, but his grip was like iron. "You're hurting me, Sean." She stared into his eyes, searching for a semblance of human emotion, but couldn't find it. This man standing in front of her was not the Sean of the easy laughter and hot lovemaking; this was the killer Sean, the one who'd personally murdered British soldiers and Protestant enemies without batting an eyelash. He'd rarely revealed this side to her, and now that she was face-to-face with it, it terrified her.

Fear clogged her throat, cutting off her air supply. It was as if an iron band was tightening around her ribcage, and with dawning horror, she knew what it meant. She struggled to pull away from Sean, but his grip tightened. "Sean! Please, let...me...go!" she gasped.

"Answer me, Elena." His brown eyes drilled into hers. "Do you want your gold medal, or shall I arrange an accident for your handsome Mikos?"

She opened her mouth to protest, but the expanding band of iron around her chest grew tighter, cutting off the rich flow of oxygen to her brain. "Please," she gasped. "My inhaler...I need...Sean..." Through the ringing in her ears she heard the agonized wheezing of her lungs as she tried to draw in a breath that wasn't there. Spots danced before her eyes, blurring her vision. But she could still see Sean's cold eyes and the grim smile playing about his lips. Why wasn't he letting her go? Didn't he understand what was happening? She needed her inhaler. Why was he just standing there, mashing her hand in his iron grip, and watching her like this? With horror, she remembered she'd left her purse with Mikhail, and her inhaler was inside it.

Her wheezing was growing worse. Darkness was closing in from around the edges of her vision. But still, she could see Sean's dark, knowing eyes. His expressionless face. No, not expressionless. Not at all. He wore a smug look of satisfaction.

Oh, God! He was watching her die!

Darkness closed in, and then…she was free. She felt as if were floating above the room, and looking down on the very odd scene below. A beautiful, long-limbed blond woman had crumbled to the floor, and a handsome man in black stood staring down at her. Suddenly he moved to a desk and drew open a drawer. Elena looked back at the woman on the floor. Her face was the color of snow, her lips blue. That's me, she realized. *I'm dying. Or perhaps already dead.*

Elena watched as Sean returned to the limp form, and knelt at her side. He placed the mouthpiece of an inhaler between her lips and pressed the mechanism.

Sweet medication bathed her lungs, and suddenly, Elena was back inside her body, grasping the inhaler and sucking its vapor. Sean held her in his arms, rocking her and stroking her hair back away from her temples. Her wild gaze fastened on his face. The smug look of satisfaction was gone. So was the hard, impenetrable expression of the IRA killer. It was her Sean back again. Sean, the lover. His eyes were moist with tears, and dark with something else. Fear?

His lips caressed the clammy skin of her forehead. "Don't cross me, Elena," he murmured, cradling her in his arms. "Don't ever cross me, love. I don't know what I'll do if you cross me."

CHAPTER TWENTY-TWO

Kerry sat at the breakfast bar in Dale's kitchen and squinted through her glasses at The Washington Post in front of her, opened to the sports section. A ceramic mug filled with Dale's special blend of Kona coffee filled the room with a comforting aroma that mingled with a blueberry scent coming from the oven. Kerry had decided that there was no place on earth that smelled more heavenly than Dale Tuomas's kitchen.

She'd been in a good mood this morning—her twenty-ninth birthday—up until a moment ago. Until she saw the front page of the sports section. It wasn't the caffeine in Dale's coffee that had sent her heart racing. It was the black and white photograph of Mikhail and Elena.

Raw pain swept through her, clutching at her vitals and tearing at her soul like the razored teeth of a savage animal. *Oh, Mikhail, where are you now?* She knew she shouldn't read the accompanying article, but she just couldn't stop herself.

"The pull of home is strong, and Kozlof eventually returned voluntarily to his country, and is now once again training with Elena Boiko. Press releases say that his defection was an unfortunate mistake, and he is happy to be back in his country. Because Kozlof missed the World Championships in March, he is working hard with Boiko so they can compete in the prestigious International Grand Prix Festival to be held in Belfast in June."

Kerry suddenly felt light-headed. Mikhail, in Belfast, next month. If she could get there and see him...

What was she thinking?

He's a thug, she reminded herself. An arrogant, ruthless, deceiving bastard. Why did she have to keep reminding herself of that?

"Good morning, Birthday Girl!" Dale stepped into the kitchen, clad in faded jeans and a cotton sweater.

Kerry looked up and returned her smile. "I can't believe you remembered."

"Well, of *course* I did. Don't you remember your twelfth birthday when your dad and I took you to Disneyland? We had a great time that week."

Kerry remembered. It was the last birthday she'd had with her father. Dale looked like she'd been up for hours. Probably had, in fact. All the guestrooms were full, and it was breakfast time on a Sunday morning.

Kerry felt a wave of guilt. She'd intended to get up and help Dale with breakfast this morning, as she had been doing every weekend since her arrival. But the insomnia had been especially bad last night, and she hadn't fallen asleep until almost three in the morning. It had been after eleven when she'd finally awakened. Kerry was just glad Dale had Sarah, an apple-cheeked German woman from nearby Biglerville, coming in on weekends to help.

A buzzer went off, and Dale moved over to the stove and opened the oven door. "Mmmmm...blueberry muffins are ready. You hungry?"

Kerry stared down at the photo of Mikhail and Elena. "Not really," she murmured. A few minutes ago, she'd been famished.

With oven mitts protecting her hands, Dale drew out a large tin of golden-brown muffins, and the delectable aroma intensified in the room. She placed the pan on a wire rack to cool and pulled off the oven mitts.

"Okay." Her gaze settled on Kerry. "Where do you want to go for your birthday lunch? There's a cute little Victorian tea room in downtown Gettysburg we could try."

"Hmmmm...?" Her attention had returned to Mikhail's photo. The perils of falling for a celebrity, she thought. *You never know when his picture will appear and cut your heart to ribbons.*

"What's wrong, Kerry?" From the other side of the breakfast bar, Dale peered down at the newspaper. "Oh."

Kerry drew in a tremulous breath and looked up at Dale. "I just wasn't prepared..."

"I know." The older woman gave Kerry's hand a light pat, and moved toward the doorway. "I have something that might cheer you up. Be right back."

A moment later, Dale returned to the kitchen with a wrapped gift. "Happy Birthday, Kerry! I want you to open this now so you can take it with you today."

Kerry grinned and took the gift. "You are such a doll. But you shouldn't have. Just letting me stay here is more than enough."

"Don't be silly. Birthdays require presents. Go ahead. Open it."

Kerry ripped the paper off, feeling almost like a child again. She loved presents, giving and receiving them, especially that moment of anticipation just before she saw what it was. Holding her breath, she opened the tissue paper and caught a glimpse of soft, camel-colored leather. "Oh,

Dale," she murmured, and looked up into the woman's dancing blue eyes. "You went all the way back to Reading just to get this for me?"

Dale shook her head and grinned. "No. Don't you remember when we were browsing in Jones New York, and I disappeared to go find a ladies' room? I actually went back to Coach and bought it."

Kerry lifted the Coach handbag from its box. "It's just gorgeous. Dale, thank you!" She slid off her stool and gave her a hug. "You're just too good to me."

Dale returned her hug and then released her. Her eyes were misty. "Okay, let me pour you some more coffee, and you've got to have one of these muffins." Her gaze flicked over Kerry ruefully. "We need to fatten you up. You've lost weight since you got here."

"I don't know how," Kerry said. "You feed me enough to sustain an army."

"It's the stress you've been under. Okay, what do you think about a late lunch? About two o'clock?"

"Sounds good." Kerry took a sip of the coffee Dale had refilled for her and then reached over for the sale inserts. She took one last glance at Mikhail's haunting face and covered it with a circular from Sears.

* * * * *

Kerry sat on the edge of the bed in one of Dale's guestrooms, thankfully, not the one she'd shared with Mikhail over two months ago. She hadn't been near that guest suite since she'd come here, in fact, had intentionally avoided even the glass breezeway that led to it. But she hadn't been able to avoid Marty, the cat that had so terrified Mikhail. In fact, Marty had taken quite a liking to Kerry, following her from room to room, meowing for attention. And every time she sat down, within moments, the orange tiger-striped cat would be right there, ready to jump onto her lap and make herself comfortable. Kerry had never been able to resist a cat, and even though this one awakened vivid memories of Mikhail, she couldn't help but fall in love with her.

Right now, Marty lay curled up in the middle of the bed, dozing contentedly, and looking adorably touchable as Kerry took the new Coach handbag from its box and began to transfer the contents of her old purse into it.

"I'm going to get a cat just like you some day, Marty," she cooed. "Cats are better companions than men anyway, aren't they?"

Her fingers brushed against a smooth, circular object at the bottom of her handbag, and her brow furrowed. She drew out the object and stared at it.

Her stomach plunged. The breath left her lungs, and she began to tremble. Marty stared at her, his golden eyes watchful like he sensed the change of energy in the room. Kerry drew in a ragged breath and looked at the ring in her palm—Mikhail's silver pinkie ring—the one his coach had given him years ago. Heart pounding, she held it up to the light streaming in the window, turning it in the bright sunlight to read the inscription.

'To Mikhail, Son of my Heart.'

Kerry took another tremulous breath, her hand cupping the ring. Dear God, how had the ring ended up in her handbag? Staring into space, she brought her clenched fist to her lips, thinking furiously. When had she last seen it on his finger?

It hit her like a lightning bolt. That day in the Virginia farmhouse—the day her world had fallen apart—she vividly remembered him leading her over to the sofa, urging her to sit down. "Let's talk," he'd said. For a moment, he'd held her hands in his, as if reluctant to let her go. He'd been wearing his ring then. She remembered staring at it, wondering why he sounded so serious.

She thought of her instincts that day, her initial refusal to believe Mikhail when he'd told her he didn't love her. She'd been so sure he was lying, perhaps at the demand of others. But then, finally, he'd convinced her. That sober mask had dropped over his face, and he'd stood in front of her like a stranger, insisting in a cold, neutral voice that there had been nothing but sexual attraction between them, and worse, that he had arranged the hit-and-run accident that had almost killed Adam.

And she'd finally believed.

She opened her hand and gazed down at the ring. "He loves me," she whispered. "I wasn't wrong. I knew he was lying." She closed her eyes and swallowed hard to dislodge the growing lump in her throat. "My heart knew."

Marty looked at her and mewed softly. Tears welled in her eyes and began to stream down her cheeks.

A tap came at the door, and Dale called out, "Kerry?"

"Come in." She reached out for a tissue on the bedside stand and wiped her eyes.

The door opened and Dale stuck her head in. Kerry smiled at her, suddenly excited to share her news. But the wary look on the older woman's face gave her pause. "What's wrong?"

"Your mother called a few minutes ago. I guess Sharon Ellery gave her the phone number here." Kerry opened her mouth to speak, but Dale went on hurriedly, "Don't worry. I told her you'd gone out for a walk, but I'd give you her message. She just wanted to wish you a happy birthday." She stepped tentatively into the room and handed Kerry a white slip of paper. "I didn't know if you knew her number or not. So here it is…just in case you want to return her call."

Dale slipped out of the room and closed the door quietly behind her. Kerry stared down at the San Diego exchange. Of course, she had Jana's number in her address book. But it was true she didn't know it by heart.

She opened the hand clutching Mikhail's ring and stared at it through blurred eyes. A miracle had just happened in this room a few minutes ago.

Maybe it was time for another one.

With a trembling hand, she reached out for the phone on the bedside stand, and punched out the phone number on the slip of paper. It rang once, twice…and then she heard her mother's smooth alto. "Hello?"

"Hi, Jana," Kerry said quietly. "It's Kerry."

* * * * *

"Elena, *Elena*! What is *wrong* with you today? You are not concentrating!" Hands on her narrow hips, Nadya glared at the tall blond woman who'd just wrenched away from Mikhail's grasp and was now bent double on the ice, her fingers tunneling through her smooth chignon, sending it in disarrayed strands around her porcelain face. "The competition is in *six* days. We leave on Friday morning. That gives us exactly four days of training left, not counting whatever time we can squeeze out on the ice in Belfast Friday. You have *got* to get this sequence down."

Mikhail gave an imperceptible shake of his head and skated a leisurely circle away from the two women. Nadya was right. If Elena couldn't nail the intricate steps of their free dance soon—like *now*—they would never be ready for the competition on Saturday night. Over and over, she'd tried it, and each time, she'd muffed it, growing clumsier with each attempt.

Elena straightened and whirled to face Nadya, her blue eyes blazing in her pale face. "I know that, you old bat! Can't you see I'm doing my best?"

Mikhail stiffened. How dare she speak to Nadya like that! He opened his mouth to reprimand her, but Nadya spoke first. "That is what I'm afraid of," she said tightly, her mouth grim. "Perhaps we should drop this sequence and go back to the routine you were going to skate in Salt Lake. It is less complicated, and you know it well."

"*No!*" Elena shot back. "I will master this! Mikhail, tell her I can do this. I *will!*"

Her eyes begged him to back her up, but Mikhail wasn't sure she *would* be able to master this sequence. It was fast and complex, requiring split-second timing and meticulous skill. Which she lacked. Sometimes a lack of innate talent could be made up for with time and practice, but in this case, they were quickly running out of time, and practice seemed to be getting them nowhere.

"I think Nadya is right," Mikhail said quietly. "We will have a better chance of winning the gold if we go back to the old routine."

Elena stared at him, her face as white as the jumpsuit she wore, and then she did something totally unexpected. Tears filled her eyes, and choking back a sob, she skated off the ice and clomped her way to a bench. Mikhail and Nadya stared at each other in amazement as she began to unlace her boots. Neither one of them had ever seen Elena cry. Mikhail hadn't believed she was capable of tears or of any emotion that betrayed vulnerability.

"I will talk to her," he said. At Nadya's nod, he turned and skated to the boards.

Elena stopped unlacing her boot, and dropped her head onto her crossed knee, overcome with wrenching sobs.

Mikhail studied her as he stepped off the ice. He'd noticed earlier this morning that she looked paler than usual. Dark shadows etched crescent moons under her eyes as if she'd gotten little or no sleep the night before. He wondered if it was because of the wine she'd had at Hell's Hole. It had only been a couple of glasses, but if she was still injecting herself with that TNG drug, who knew the effect its mix with alcohol could have on her body?

He sat down on the bench beside her and placed a consoling arm around her shuddering body. With a soft moan, she turned toward him, clinging to him like a frightened kitten.

"It's okay," he said, but she only cried harder, her tears wet against his neck. "Elena, it is not so bad. We can go back to the old routine. We can still win."

She shook her head, her voice hitching as she tried to speak. "I...I...know. It is not that. Oh, Mikhail!" And she collapsed into more broken sobs.

He rubbed her back, staring over her shuddering shoulders at Nadya who'd just stepped off the ice and was watching them, a question mark in her dark eyes. Arching a brow, he gave an abrupt shake of his head, and then drew back from Elena, cradling her tear-streaked face in his hands. Nadya shrugged and headed off toward the locker rooms.

"Then what is it?" Mikhail asked quietly. "Tell me."

She blinked, her eyes shimmering, and shook her head. "You won't believe me," she whispered. "No one will believe me."

He felt like giving her an infuriated shake, but forced himself to assume an expression of gentle patience on his face. "Why would I not believe you, Elena? Have you ever lied to me?" She shook her head, staring at him. He smoothed back a blond tendril of hair from her temple, deliberately caressing her skin. "Then tell me. What is wrong?"

She searched his face, her lips parted breathlessly, and spoke in a rush, "I think Sean tried to kill me last night."

Mikhail's blood ran cold. That was the last thing he'd expected her to say. "What do you mean? How?"

She bit her bottom lip and drew away from him, hugging her arms for warmth. "We had a fight in his office." She cast him a slanting look. "About you. He's insanely jealous of you, you know. I think he knows how attracted I am to you." As if a switch had been turned, Elena discarded her little girl distraught routine and once again became the seductive siren. Her eyes flicked over him in leisurely invitation. "How attracted I've always been to you. And he doesn't like it one bit. Anyway, we had words, and he got me upset and I had one of my attacks."

Mikhail stared at her. "That is not so unusual, is it?"

She shook her head. "Not really. But what was unusual was the way he reacted to it. Mikos, he just watched me struggle for air, and didn't try to do a thing to help me until it was almost too late. He was just standing there, watching me die."

"But you didn't die. What happened?"

She shrugged. "He finally got the inhaler he keeps in his desk for me, but I'm telling you, I really believe he was going to let me die. He scares me, Mikos. I'm afraid of what he may do if he finds out how I feel about you." She turned to him, her eyes wide with alarm.

Mikhail couldn't tell if it was feigned or genuine. It didn't matter. He saw the opportunity before him, and decided to take it. He allowed his gaze to sweep heatedly over her face. "And how *do* you feel about me?"

The tip of her tongue snaked out of her mouth, moistening her full bottom lip. It was a ploy designed to drive a man insane, but Mikhail only felt disgust. He hoped he could hide it as he smiled down at her.

"Let me show you," she whispered. "Tonight. Let me come to your flat and make love to you, Mikos."

He brushed his thumb over her luscious bottom lip, feeling her tremble beneath his touch. "You know that's impossible," he said. "Do you want Sean to kill me?"

"No." Her eyes became as cold as marbles. She grabbed his hand and squeezed. "But you can kill *him*, and then there will be nothing to stop us from being together."

CHAPTER TWENTY-THREE

Mikhail stared at Elena. "You're joking, right?" She gazed back out of guileless blue eyes. "You're not seriously suggesting that I off your boyfriend?"

She sighed. "Oh, I don't suppose you have it in you, do you? But I'll tell you this, Mikhail. As long as Sean is alive, there is no chance we can be together. He is crazy jealous, and he watches me like a hawk. Dear God, he gets worse every day. If it weren't for his stupid pub and black market business, he'd be here right now, hovering over me, watching my every move." She brushed a strand of hair away from her face with frustrated impatience. "No wonder he is driving me to find a way to get rid of him."

Mikhail weighed his words before saying, "Perhaps killing him isn't the answer." He watched her expression. "Maybe we could find another way to get rid of him."

Her eyes narrowed. "Such as?"

Again, he chose his words carefully. "I would think since you have been with him so long, you'd know all kinds of interesting things about him. Information that other parties would be happy to get their hands on. Information that could put him away for a long time." He stopped, allowing the suggestion to sink in. This could be a trap, his mind shrieked. Maybe O'Malley had put her up to this. But he didn't think so. Elena was not a good actress.

She stared at the smooth expanse of ice on the rink. Mikhail watched her, not daring to add another word. It would be dangerous to push her. And if he was wrong, and this *was* a trap, well, he'd blown it already, hadn't he?

Elena turned her head, and gave him a long, assessing look. "That's an interesting idea," she said finally. "I'll give it some thought." Straightening, she looked around, once again all business. "Where is Nadya? Taking a break, I suppose. Does she not realize how little time we have left to perfect this routine?" She bent down and began to re-tie her bootlace. "Go get her, Mikhail. We have work to do."

* * * * *

Sean brought his Mercedes to a stop in the alley between two warehouses he owned in the industrial area of Tallinn. He jumped out and walked briskly to a side door of the long gray building on the left. The May night was cold and damp, more so, this close to the harbor. Would spring never arrive? Even though they were already in the "white nights" season, calendar-wise, the glimmer of the midnight sun appeared to be the only sign of spring so far. It had been a bitter winter with blinding blizzards and dangerous ice storms. And to Sean's mind, spring seemed to be reluctant to make its appearance. Brazil was looking better every day, but after Reilly's panicked phone call, it seemed farther away than ever.

Dark clouds scudded across the eastern sky, shadow dancing with the orange glow of the sun just above the horizon. From the nearby dock to the west, the tide lapped rhythmically against wood pilings. The air was thick with the stench of brine and decaying fish from the herring plant up shore, worse tonight than usual, it seemed. Or maybe that was just his foul state of mind.

Sean unlocked the door and slipped inside the dimly lit warehouse. His jaw set grimly, he took a flight of metal stairs two at a time, and stepped inside a small office lit by one overhead florescent light. He didn't speak immediately, but allowed his gaze to sweep over the room's occupants—three men, two of which stared back with wary eyes and guilt-ridden faces. The third man didn't look at him at all, but just stared glassily through him with one good eye. Sean's gaze came to rest on him.

Anton Boiko, like all the other Boiko men, had been a handsome man the day before. The resemblance between him and his niece, Elena, was remarkable. They both had that blond, blue-eyed Aryan look that had so captivated Hitler and his followers.

But sometime between morning and now, Anton Boiko had lost his looks. His face was unrecognizable because of the dried blood and purple bruises. His left eye bulged out grotesquely, a swollen mess of destroyed pulp. His lips were inflated three times their normal size and caked with fresh blood.

Sean walked across the room to a small table at Boiko's side and stared down at the bloody jaws of a pair of pliers and a herring tin containing several molars with roots attached. Also bloody.

"Christ!" Sean muttered, then impaled Fagan Reilly and Boris Shlusvaka with his stone gaze. "You weren't supposed to bloody kill him! Which one of you imbeciles is responsible for this?" Like he couldn't guess. He looked at Reilly who shifted his weight and glanced uneasily away.

Boris cleared his throat. "I don't know what happened, boss. He just stopped breathing. I wasn't using any extraordinary measures. Just the usual tactics."

"Yeah, boss," Reilly interjected. "I figure the poor old bastard had a weak heart. Know what I mean? Just couldn't take the stress. Heart attack, I told Boris. Not our fault he keeled over and died." He shook his unkempt head. "I even thought about giving him mouth-to-mouth, but after what Boris did to him…" He glanced over at the corpse and gave a visible shudder.

Sean felt like shuddering himself. He wouldn't wish Fagan Reilly's rotten, fetid breath on his worst enemy. The bumbling Irishman had fallen silent, and now both he and Boris were staring at Sean as if they were condemned prisoners on a pirate ship about to walk the plank. He gritted his teeth. He could cheerfully slice their throats at the moment.

"Please tell me," he said softly, his gaze raking from one to the other. "That you got the formula out of him before he died."

The Russian and the Irishman stared back silently, Boris slightly shame-faced, and Reilly clearly terrified.

Sean's heart sank. This was not good. In fact, it most definitely sucked. But he'd been in tight spots before, and had always managed to get out of them. This time would be no different.

He took a deep, calming breath and glared at Boris. "Go to Boiko's lab and get me his computer files, and all the paperwork you can find. If that formula isn't there, then we'll simply have to create one. And you…" His gaze skewered Reilly. "Get rid of the fucking body."

* * * * *

Every time Mikhail stepped into the sanctuary of St. Nicholas the Martyr and inhaled the exotic scent of sandalwood incense, he felt as if he were taking a step back into his childhood. Unlike other parts of the USSR, most of the Catholic churches in Estonia had defiantly continued to serve mass despite the disapproval of the Communist government, and his mother had dutifully brought him to church every Saturday or Sunday while he lived at home. Stepping into St. Nicholas now brought her face to mind, and it was moments like this that he missed her so much it nearly brought him to his knees.

He paused at the font and dipped his fingers into the holy water. Genuflecting, he turned and headed down the middle aisle toward the altar. Father Augustino was expecting him. He'd met the priest a couple of times before, and they'd exchanged polite conversation, but this was the first time he'd had any information to pass along to him. As Wakeley had instructed, he'd gone to mass that morning and taken communion—the signal to the priest that he needed to make a "confession" that evening.

The priest was waiting near the confessional. The bluish light from flickering votives played across his rotund face. His eyes—the gentlest brown eyes Mikhail had ever seen—were watchful and intelligent. How long had this unlikely looking spy been in the employ of the Brits, Mikhail wondered? He felt reassured by the priest's outward calm. For the first time since his return, Mikhail felt as if he wasn't alone in his mission, and it was a good feeling.

The priest bowed his head. "Good evening, my son. Do you wish to make confession?"

Mikhail nodded, and Father Augustino opened the door to the confessional. Inside, Mikhail drew his mother's rosary beads from his pocket, along with a small plastic bag containing the chip of microfilm from the scarab key chain camera. He waited until he saw through the screen that the priest had settled into his seat.

"Bless me, Father, for I have sinned..." He crossed himself, and began to rattle off whatever came into his mind. "I lost my temper with Elena again today." As he spoke, he tucked the plastic bag with the microfilm into the grated screen. Seconds later, it was gone. Soon, Mikhail hoped, it would be on its way to London. It wasn't much. Just confirmation that O'Malley had met with Daniel Sullivan, but it was a hell of a lot more than he'd had before. Which was nothing.

He finished his confession, and the priest gave him ten Our Fathers and ten Hail Marys, then blessed him. After a moment's silence, his melodic voice floated through the screen.

"Whenever you need to talk, my son, I will be here."

"Thank you, Father." Mikhail stood and left the confessional, feeling as if a heavy weight was finally beginning to lift off his shoulders.

* * * * *

Elena was awakened by the thump of the dresser drawer closing. Not once, but several times. Then she heard the squeak of the closet door. She turned on her side and half-opened her eyes. Sean's side of the bed was empty. That was unusual. With the late nights he kept at Hell's Hole, he didn't usually get back to her *dacha* on the outskirts of Tallinn until two in the morning. Once he fell into bed, he didn't stir again until noon at the earliest.

She reached for the alarm clock on the bedside table and saw by the illuminated hands that it was four in the morning. With a soft groan, she turned off the alarm and flopped back onto the bed, her arm covering her eyes. What the hell was Sean doing, and why did he have to make so much noise doing it?

She'd had trouble falling asleep the night before, thanks to that interesting little conversation with Mikhail. It kept going through her mind hours afterwards. Of course, she hadn't been serious when she'd suggested that he kill Sean, although come to think of it, that option *was* growing in attractiveness. When, exactly, had she come to the conclusion that she'd be better off without Sean than with him? Probably about the time Mikhail had started looking at her as a desirable woman. It had taken him long enough. In fact, Mikhail was the only man she'd ever gone after that hadn't succumbed to her overtures within…what?…minutes? But now, it all made sense. Sean intimidated Mikhail. And why wouldn't he? Everyone knew Sean wasn't a man to cross.

That was something she'd do well to remember. The thought hit her like the sharp edge of a knife. If Sean had any idea she was even *thinking* about betraying him…

But he wouldn't find out. Not until it was too late to do anything about it.

She almost felt sorry for him. Such a silly dream he had. Taking her off to his South American hideaway, and fathering her children. Like she was some kind of baby-making machine or something. Did he really think she'd ruin her perfect shape by spitting out his little Irish brats? Not a chance in the world. She'd never understood that whole "maternal thing." Why on earth would a woman voluntarily give up her figure, her sleep and her sanity in exchange for wiping snot from runny noses and changing shitty diapers? It defied logic.

The closet door creaked again. Then came the clatter of wire hangers as they, apparently, tumbled to the hardwood floor.

"Son of a bitch," Sean muttered.

Elena bolted to a sitting position. "*What the hell are you doing?*"

Sean turned toward her, grimacing. "Sorry, love. I was trying to be quiet."

"Well, you were doing a bloody bad job of it," Elena snapped. Her fingers kneaded her temples where the telltale onslaught of a headache threatened. "What are you doing up this early?"

With a soft meow, a white Persian cat jumped onto the bed and made her stealthy way up Elena's legs. Snowball parked herself on Elena's belly and closed her eyes. Sean reached down to grab the clump of hangers that had fallen and clumsily placed them back on the rod. Then he grabbed a shirt and turned to the foot of the bed where a suitcase rested.

Elena stroked Snowball's silky fur, her eyes on Sean's suitcase. The cat purred contentedly. "You're going somewhere?"

He nodded, rolling the shirt and tucking it into the suitcase. "I have to go to Belfast early. Business."

"But I thought we were going together tomorrow."

He was back at the closet, pulling out a pair of trousers. "Something has come up, so my plans have changed."

Elena watched him. "Oh. Does it have anything to do with that little operation you're planning on Sunday?"

He froze, and then turned to look at her. Even in the dim light from the bathroom, she saw that his eyes were cold. She had to force herself not to the draw the covers up around her chin in a childish urge to protect herself. Instead, she gazed at him defiantly, her hands still clutching Snowball's soft warmth.

"Didn't I tell you not to ask me questions about that?"

She managed an off-hand shrug. "Well, maybe you shouldn't have told me anything in the first place."

"Don't make me regret it, Elena."

Her heart skipped a beat. Was he threatening her? The cat must've sensed her tension. With a peeved yowl, she leaped off Elena's tummy and scampered out of the room.

"You know I had too much to drink that night," Sean continued. "And I told you the next day to forget what I said. It's dangerous for you to know my plans. If my enemies got hold of you…"

Elena watched his expression change, and her heartbeat steadied. He was simply worried about her. Worried that someone might harm her in order to get information about him. She thought about what Mikhail had said the day before. Something about information that would put Sean away for a long time.

"Oh, sweetie…" She beckoned Sean over. "Come here."

Sean tossed his trousers across the suitcase and came to her. He sat on the edge of the bed and cupped her face in her hands. "I don't know what I'd do if I lost you, love. Do you know how precious you are to me?"

She nodded, gazing into his eyes. "I think so."

"Good." With the edge of his thumbs, he traced her eyebrows, and then lifting her chin, took her mouth in a hungry kiss.

Elena kissed him back, her thoughts spinning. If she told Mikhail what she knew, would it be enough? How would he know who to get the information to? And would he be able to get it to the right people in time to stop the carnage on Sunday?

Sean drew away from her, his fingers threading through her hair. "God, I wish I had time to make love to you. But I have a flight to catch. I'll give you a call after you check in at the Royale Viscount tomorrow afternoon. Keep the bed warm for me, love."

He gave her another hard kiss and then went back to his packing.

* * * * *

Vivaldi's *allegro* from the Spring movement of *The Four Seasons* blared from the PA system. Mikhail held Elena in his arms as they moved across the ice in perfect synchronization, their skates flashing, turning, always moving in precision. She twirled, gave him a brilliant smile, and with one smooth movement, placed a skate blade onto his thigh. He lifted her, revolving once, twice, then placed her back on the ice with delicate ease.

Yes! They'd finally managed to get through this sequence without a screw-up. Now, if only they could do the same with the hauntingly beautiful movement of "Winter." That was the toughest part of their free dance, the staccato steps meant to be reminiscent of icicles hanging from a snowbound cottage, followed by the technically difficult footwork that mimicked the soaring violins in the "allegro non molto." True, it wasn't as difficult as the routine they'd planned. After the incident where Elena had burst into frustrated tears, she'd finally relented and gone back to their Olympic free dance routine. Thank God! She'd been way too ambitious in thinking they could nail down the new moves for Belfast.

Just as the "summer" movement began, the music cut off, and from the boards, Nadya clapped her hands and motioned them over. "Very good," she called out. "You've got it. Now, Elena, for the "summer" movement I want you to try this." She skated out on the ice to demonstrate.

"I'll be right back," Mikhail said, stepping off the ice and heading for his sports bag to get his bottled water.

The doors leading from the lobby flew open and two uniformed policeman came toward him. Mikhail straightened and watched their approach.

"We were told we could find Elena Boiko here," said the older man, his eyes fastened on the slender blonde on the ice. "Is that her?"

"Yes. I'll get her." What was this all about, he wondered. "Hey, Elena! Couple of men here wants to talk to you."

Elena turned and stared. Then like the graceful prima donna she was, she casually skated over to the boards, and arced to a stop, spraying ice. "Yes? What is it?"

"I'm afraid we have bad news," the older policeman said while the younger one gazed at Elena, an unconcealed look of adoration on his face. Mikhail supposed it was the first time he'd seen the beautiful Elena Boiko outside of TV.

"A body was pulled out of the harbor this morning. Personal items washed up onshore were in the name of your uncle, Anton Boiko. I'm afraid we need you to come to the morgue to identify his body."

The blood drained from Elena's face. "*Oh, my God!*" She grabbed at Mikhail's arm, her nails biting into his skin.

His thoughts were spinning. He knew without a doubt that this had something to do with O'Malley. But what?

"What happened to him?" Elena demanded when she finally found her voice again.

Mikhail heard a noise behind him, and turned to see Nadya staring at them with wide eyes. "What is wrong?"

"He appears to have been beaten to death," the policeman said slowly. "We won't know for sure until the body is autopsied. Please, can you come with us, now?"

Elena's eyes widened in panic. "No! I cannot do this. Please, I just can't."

"You're the next of kin," the policeman said patiently.

Elena whirled toward Mikhail, her hand clawing at his arm. "Mikhail, you will go with me, yes? I cannot do this alone."

"Of course, Elena." He turned to Nadya. "You might as well go home. I don't believe she'll be up to training any more today."

Nadya's dark eyes swept from him to Elena. "Perhaps we should think about not going to Belfast?"

"Absolutely not!" Elena shot back, eyes blazing. "Even if it is my uncle in that morgue, and I do pray it isn't, he would not want me to put my career on hold for him. Tomorrow, we go to Belfast, no matter what." She turned to the policeman. "We will change into our shoes and be with you shortly."

* * * * *

Kerry felt as if she were going to fall asleep standing up. God, it was taking forever to get through customs. The only other times she'd been to the UK, it had been with the U.S. Figure Skating team, and their officials had handled all the paperwork. Today she was on her own.

She hadn't slept a wink during the transatlantic flight to Heathrow, despite the blankets the flight attendants had handed out, and the muted lights. She'd been way too excited, knowing she'd be seeing Mikhail soon. Well…soon was probably too optimistic of a word. Her flight to Belfast wouldn't leave for several hours, assuming, of course, she *made* it on the flight. Customs was taking so long, she was starting to worry she wouldn't make it to Belfast in time for the competition tonight.

She glanced at her wristwatch…almost seven in the morning. All she could think about, even to the exclusion of Mikhail, was how much she wanted to get to Belfast and check into her hotel room so she could take a nice hot bath and fall into bed for several hours of uninterrupted sleep.

The woman ahead of her moved forward a few more feet, and Kerry wearily followed her. Only two passengers stood between her and the customs agent.

She gritted her teeth and tried to keep her eyes open.

* * * * *

Sean sat at the Lufthansa Airlines gate where his flight to Belfast was about to board in another half-hour, his eyes on a pretty, but slightly disheveled-looking American woman sitting a few rows across from him. Small world, it was. And what lovely luck that they would be sharing the same flight.

He'd recognized her right away, despite the fact that whatever make-up she might've had on at one time had evaporated, leaving her pale-skinned and freckled, and her black hair looked as if it hadn't seen a brush in twelve hours or so. Despite all that, though, she was a looker. He'd thought so during that little kidnapping adventure, even fantasizing momentarily about what it would be like to have a wee taste of Kozlof's leftovers. But he'd discarded the idea without really considering it. He didn't like mixing business with pleasure, and he rarely did. But the few times he had were because of the drink.

Like when he'd told Elena about the operation planned for this weekend. He'd done that under the influence of too much Guinness, and he'd sorely regretted it the next day. But after gently questioning Elena to find out just how much he'd revealed about the plan, he'd been reassured that it hadn't been much. All he had to do then was to steer her in a different direction, and that, he'd done. No way did Elena know the details of the plan for Sunday.

Everything was on target. Everything was working out splendidly, and even Anton Boiko's inopportune death hadn't turned out to be more than an inconvenience. Boris and Fagan had found the TNG formula in Boiko's lab, and Sean had had it delivered to Big Dan in plenty of time before his race in Kilkenny. By now, Sean's Swiss bank account would have inflated another four million dollars, and soon, he and Elena would be lying on the beach in Rio, soaking in the brilliant sun. Of course, it was going to take some doing to convince her to give up her quest for World Championship gold, but he had no doubt he'd do it. When she found out how much money he had stashed away, a gold medal would mean nothing to her.

He smiled, his gaze resting on Kerry Niles. She was slumped in her seat, eyes closed, her chin propped in the palm of her hand. Poor girl. Exhausted, apparently. Interesting, though, how she was here at this time. It was because of Kozlof, of course. What was it with Kozlof and women? They swarmed over him like bees on a honeycomb.

His brow furrowed. How could he use Kerry's appearance in Belfast to his advantage? Despite his confidence in Elena's eventual surrender to his desires, he couldn't deny that her feelings were changing toward him. It wasn't something he could put his finger on. Just a sixth sense. He didn't like the way she looked at Kozlof. Like she was a tigress stalking her prey. Sean had been watching Kozlof, too, trying to determine whether he was romantically interested in Elena. So far, he'd seen nothing that made him think so. But maybe Kozlof was being especially careful.

The newspapers in America had played up the romance angle of Kozlof's defection. Supposedly, the heat between him and the American skater had been intense. And now, here she was on her way to Belfast just a day before Kozlof was to arrive. What would happen when they saw each other? A slow grin spread across his face. Better yet, what would happen if Elena were to find out, in a most dramatic way, that Kozlof was much more interested in the American girl than he was in her?

* * * * *

"I could *kill* the bastard!" Elena snarled, pacing around the small living room of Mikhail's flat. She turned, resting her hands on her slim hips, and glared at Mikhail. "He did it, Mikhail. He killed my uncle. My only living relative. And do you know why? I'll tell you why. Because he is a ruthless *bastard*!"

Mikhail handed her a tumbler of vodka he'd just poured. "Drink. Then we'll talk."

Elena downed the vodka like a pro then sat down on the sofa. She watched Mikhail settle into a chair across from her. "If I tell you everything I know about Sean, can you protect me? He will kill me if he finds out I've betrayed him. I have no doubt about that. He says he loves me, and I believe him, but that won't stop him from taking his revenge against me if he knows I told you this."

"I will do whatever I can to protect you, Elena," Mikhail said. "But if you give me enough to put him away, he won't be a threat to anyone. Now, what makes you think he's responsible for the murder of your uncle?"

"I don't think. I *know*." Elena ran a finger over the rim of her tumbler, her eyes fixed upon Mikhail's face. "Years ago, my father hired my uncle to come up with a new drug that would enhance stamina and strength. It was designed for my brother, an Olympic speed skater. They call it TNG."

Mikhail felt his pulse flutter, thinking of his father and the other Sami villagers who died because of TNG.

"There were a lot of bugs to work out of the early formulas. Apparently, there were some unfortunate deaths when they tested it on humans."

Mikhail tried to keep his expression bland, not allowing his disgust to show.

"As you know, my father was high in the ranks of the KGB. He saw the potential for using this formula in the war against Afghanistan, and he put my uncle to work to convert the TNG into a gas that could be used in chemical warfare. Uncle Anton was a good man, and he did not want to have anything to do with this, but he could never stand up to his older brother. And so, the formula was perfected. But before Uncle Anton turned it over, my father died of a heart attack. And Uncle Anton took this as a sign that the formula should be destroyed for the good of mankind."

Mikhail kept his eyes on Elena. Funny how she didn't mention that a new TNG formula had been created, and how it had been helping her skating for years. "So, what has O'Malley got to do with all this?"

Elena got up and moved over to the liquor cabinet. "I need another drink." She splashed a couple of fingers of vodka into her tumbler and turned to face him. "Sean has always been obsessed with this TNG formula, ever since my father told him about it one night at Hell's Hole. I think he made arrangements then to buy the formula for his own use. But of course, Father died before Sean could get it, and Uncle Anton made it clear he wasn't going to cooperate. He told Sean the formula had been destroyed, and couldn't be recreated. Sean didn't believe him. And rightly so. My uncle, like all the Boikos, has…" she paused, a shadow crossing her face, "…*had*…a huge ego. He wouldn't destroy his brainchild. But he would keep it from people he felt were dangerous. Unlike my father, Uncle Anton never liked Sean, never trusted him." She took a sip of her vodka. "Sean made a deal with this Irish gangster to sell him the TNG formula for some stinger missiles, and a great deal of money.

And he went to work on my uncle, trying to get it. That's why my uncle is dead. They tortured him to get the formula, and then they killed him."

"Do you think they were successful? Did they get the formula?"

Elena's brow furrowed. "I don't know. Uncle Anton was very stubborn, and he was a brave man. But who knows what happened? He may have given Sean what he wanted."

Silence fell. Elena took another sip of vodka. Mikhail stood and began to pace, his forefinger rubbing at his scar. He stopped and turned to her. "What are the stingers for? Anything in particular that would be of interest to…say…the British?"

Elena swallowed the last of her drink and said, "Possibly. Do you think they would be interested in knowing what his plans are for Sunday?"

"I think they might. Tell me what you know."

Elena smiled like a cat getting ready to feast on a captured bird. "Sean is planning to assassinate Tony Blair on Sunday when he speaks at the Queen's Golden Jubilee celebration in Belfast."

CHAPTER TWENTY-FOUR

Kerry stepped out of the driving rain into the elaborate foyer of the upscale Royale Viscount hotel on Great Victoria Street. She closed her umbrella and ran her fingers through her damp hair to get it into some kind of order. Lot of good the umbrella did.

She glanced around for the reception desk and saw it to the right. Taking a deep breath, she headed for it, hoping they wouldn't throw her out on the street because of her bedraggled state. Twenty-three hours without sleep didn't make for the best impression.

Thank God, there was no line at reception.

"Hi," she said in response to the good-looking clerk's smile and courteous greeting. He wore a tiny gold nametag that said "Neil Morrissey." "I have a reservation under Kerry Niles." She held her breath, praying nothing had gone wrong with the reservation. If she couldn't fall into bed within the next ten minutes, she was going to faint. Forget the bath, even. Her priorities had changed. Bed, first, then bath.

The clerk's fingers flew across the keyboard. "Ah, yes, we have you in Room 628, Miss Niles," he replied in an effeminate Irish accent. "Just sign here, and I'll have a steward take your luggage to your room."

Kerry signed, and then looked up at the clerk. "Can you tell me if Mikhail Kozlof has checked in yet? I understand the Russian figure skating team will be staying here for the International Grand Prix Competition."

Thanks to Catri, who still kept in touch with a Russian skating official, Kerry had been able to find out where their athletes were staying. Fortunately, the hotel hadn't been full, and she'd been able to make her own reservation.

The hotel representative again tapped on the keyboard. "He hasn't checked in yet, Miss Niles. We're expecting the Russian team tomorrow afternoon. Shall I leave a message for him?"

Kerry rubbed her forehead wearily. She couldn't think. Would it be best to leave a note for Mikhail, or simply try and track him down at the arena during practice tomorrow? Her fingers toyed with his ring on its sterling chain. What if she left a note, and it got into the wrong hands? For all she knew, anything left for a Russian skater might be handed over to their officials. That's why she didn't dare leave the ring.

An idea hit her. *Of course!* "Yes, I have something I want you to give him. Just a minute." She placed her carry-on bag on the counter, and rummaged through it, then pulled out a rectangular white box. The hotel clerk watched with curiosity as she slipped her thumb under the tab and opened it to reveal twelve foil-wrapped cylinders—Hostess Ding Dongs.

"Do you have a pen I can borrow? Something that will show up on foil?"

"Will this do?" The clerk handed over a waterproof medium-point marker.

"Perfect!" Kerry scribbled "Room 628" on the bottom of a foil-wrapped cake. "If you're the one that gives it to him, can you make sure he looks at the bottom? And please, if you can, give it to him discreetly. Not in front of a bunch of people if there's any way possible."

"I'll do my best." Neil smiled and snapped his fingers at a passing steward. "Have a good stay with us, Miss Niles."

"Thanks."

Kerry turned and followed the steward to the elevators, already fantasizing about what it was going to feel like to crawl under crisp, clean sheets and fall asleep to the music of the rain pelting against Belfast streets.

* * * * *

Interesting, Sean thought, watching the elevator doors close on Kerry Niles and the steward. He'd been standing close enough to hear the gist of her conversation with the hotel clerk. And he'd caught a glimpse of a silver-foiled object she'd scribbled on and then left for Kozlof. He hadn't the foggiest idea what it was, but it would obviously mean something to the Russian. And if he were a betting man, Sean would bet that it was her room number she'd jotted down on the object.

Very, very interesting, indeed.

His cell phone rang. He pulled it out of his jacket pocket and walked away from the reception desk. "Yeah?"

"It's me, boss." Reilly's raspy voice broke through intermittent static. "Can you hear me?"

"Just barely. What is it?"

"You…right…good thing…bug planted…Elena…plotting against you…Kozlof."

Sean frowned. "You're breaking up bad, Reilly. Did you say you've got something on Elena?"

"Aye, boss. On tape…I…" His voice disappeared into the static.

"Reilly? You still there?" Jesus Christ, these fucking cell phones were bloody useless.

"Yeah, boss," came his faint response. "Want me...send it?"

"Yeah, send me the tape. Overnight, got it? I want it in my hands first thing tomorrow. You hear me, Reilly?"

"Yeh. Got it, boss."

"And Reilly? Get rid of the priest. I don't want to take any chance on having this mission fucked up. You got me?"

"Yeah, I got you, boss. See you..."And his voice disappeared into oblivion.

Sean turned off the cell phone, his jaw tight. His good mood of a moment before was gone. He'd only caught bits and pieces, but it was enough to raise the hairs on the back of his neck. Elena and Kozlof plotting against him. He'd been right to plant the bug in Elena's purse before leaving her *dacha.* Good thing he'd trusted his instincts. But *Christ!* He didn't want to believe she would betray him. Maybe it wasn't as bad as it sounded. Maybe Reilly had interpreted it wrong. God knows he wasn't the brightest candle on the birthday cake. Well, tomorrow would tell the story. As soon as Sean got the tape in his hands, he'd know how to handle it.

He just wished he didn't love her. That would make things so much simpler if she was just another expendable woman to him. He thought of Liisa. It had been easy enough to get rid of her, but with Elena, it would be different. Da was right. It didn't pay to get emotionally involved with anyone when you were wedded to a cause. And when, exactly, had a quiet life with Elena become more important than the cause?

Back to the matter at hand. Kerry Niles. Sean decided to give Sinead Farren a call. The comely Real IRA operative was not only an expert locksmith, but she looked damn good in a maid's uniform. And she was conveniently located right here in Belfast.

He'd clearly heard the room number the clerk had given Kerry Niles. 628. It would be easy enough for Sinead to get access to the room. Sean was going to give Elena a little test. And dear God, he prayed she would pass it.

Because her life just might depend on it.

* * * * *

Mikhail hurried down the cobblestone street toward St. Nicholas the Martyr, bowing his head against the torrent of rain mixed with sleet falling from slate-gray skies. He hoped the wintry weather wouldn't delay their flight tomorrow morning. He was more anxious than ever to get out of the country, especially now that he had the information that would buy him asylum.

He'd barely been able to conceal his excitement at Elena's startling revelation about Sean's plan to assassinate Tony Blair. It had taken every ounce of his self-restraint to remain calm, almost disinterested, as she told him what she knew. It wasn't much, but more than enough information to give to the Brits. He knew when, where and how. Surely that would be enough for them to capture O'Malley before he could carry out his plan.

Even though the "white nights" had started in mid-April, the sun was virtually invisible on this bleak wintry-like evening, and the streetlights had come on, glistening golden on the wet cobblestones. Mikhail glanced at his watch and quickened his step. He wanted to catch Father Augustino before he left for the night. Of course, he hadn't taken communion at mass that morning, so the priest would have no reason to expect him. The information had to go out to England tonight. He wanted Wakeley and his men to be ready to take him under their protection as soon as he arrived in Belfast.

Through the sleet, Mikhail saw the graceful spires of the Catholic Church up ahead and breathed a sigh of relief. He strode faster, already imagining its aromatic warmth beckoning him in from the cold. This will probably be the last time I ever step foot in here, he thought as he pulled open the ornately carved door.

He shrugged out of his raincoat and hung it on a coat rack in the vestibule, then pulled off his gloves and tucked them into the pockets. Slipping a hand into his trousers, he felt for his mother's rosary beads. It probably wouldn't hurt to say a prayer before he left. That this would soon be over, and he'd be free to find Kerry again and try to explain why he'd lied to her.

Mikhail stepped into the sanctuary and looked around, unsurprised to find the pews empty. After all, it was the dinner hour. Most everyone was home by the fire on this wintry-like night. Mikhail just hoped Father Augustino hadn't gone home as well. He had no idea where to find him if he wasn't here.

Votives flickered near the confessionals. Mikhail walked toward them. He was pretty sure that Father Augustino's office was somewhere in that vicinity. If he was here, that's probably where he'd be.

Mikhail stopped and lit a votive for his mother's soul, and dug in his pocket for a coin. He murmured a silent prayer, crossed himself, and then turned to look for the corridor from which he'd seen the priest emerge a few days before. There it was, almost hidden behind a pillar. Mikhail stepped into it, peering down the long, gloomy length of the corridor. A dim light spilled out from one opened door.

Mikhail cleared his throat and called out, "Father Augustino, are you here?"

There was no response, no rustling of paper, no noise of any kind coming from the room. Mikhail frowned. Someone had to be here. Unlike many churches, St. Nicholas the Martyr was kept locked when the priests had gone, a tradition that had begun several years ago when unruly drunken youths had vandalized several churches in the city.

Mikhail headed toward the open door. Maybe the priest had taken a bathroom break. He would go into his office and wait for him. Sooner or later, the priest would show up to turn off the lights and lock up.

The room was empty. Mikhail scanned the priest's desk and saw a full mug of coffee sitting next to a legal pad that had been written on in blue ink. The handwriting was precise and neat, filling three-quarters of the page. The next day's sermon, Mikhail guessed. He reached out and touched the coffee mug. Still slightly warm. Wherever the priest was, he hadn't been gone long. Mikhail sat down on a chair across from the desk and waited.

Five minutes passed, and there was still no sign of Father Augustino. Mikhail frowned. Where the hell was he? When ten minutes had passed, Mikhail stood and stepped back into the hallway. The bathroom had to be behind one of these doors. What if the priest had fallen sick or something? It only took Mikhail a moment to find the restroom, and another two seconds to realize it was empty. His stomach began to churn.

By the time he reached the sanctuary, alarm bells were clanging in his brain. He stopped, staring at the confessional. That would explain why the priest had left his coffee soon after pouring it, and his half-written sermon on his desk. Someone had come in seeking to make confession. But that didn't make sense, either. If Father Augustino was hearing confession, why had Mikhail heard no voices? No sounds at all when he'd come into the sanctuary?

It was then that he saw what he'd missed before, and his heart began to drum. He moved toward the confessional, his eyes locked on the dark pool of liquid seeping from under the door. In the glimmering candlelight, it looked like the dark, rich syrup Mother used to serve on her Sunday morning flat cakes. But Mikhail knew it was nothing as innocuous as that.

"Father?" He opened the door of the confessional, and his heart lodged in his throat.

Father Augustino sprawled against the wall of the confessional, the left side of his head blown away. Blood and brain matter splattered the wall, creating a gory mosaic of horror. The priest's eyes were closed, as if he'd been praying or deep in thought at the time of his death. His hands still clutched his rosary beads. They were splashed in blood. The entry wound on the right side of his temple was small, but the bullet had mushroomed inside his brain, blowing out a huge portion of his skull as it exited.

Mikhail fought back the bile that rose in his throat, his eyes fixing on the screen that separated the priest from his confessor. That's where the shot had come from, he guessed. Someone had stuck the nuzzle of a semi-automatic weapon through the grate and shot the priest at point-blank range. Mostly likely, he'd used a silencer.

A professional job. One that had the earmarks of Sean O'Malley. He hadn't been the one to do the actual killing, but it had been done on his orders. Which meant…Sean was on to him somehow. How much did he know about Mikhail's mission? And how on earth was Mikhail going to be able to get word to Wakeley now that his contact was dead?

Mikhail whirled around and headed for the vestibule. He had to get out of here in case the assassin was still around. If O'Malley knew about Father Augustino, then he knew about him, as well. And that meant they'd be looking for him.

He grabbed his raincoat and drew it on, then slipped out the door of the church, casting a wary glance up and down the street. No one around. He breathed a little easier and stepped out into the wintry mix.

Where to? He couldn't go back to his apartment. Sean's men might be waiting for him there. And he wouldn't risk putting Nadya's life in danger, so that was out. He needed to find a safe place to spend the night. If he could just make it through the night, and catch the flight to Belfast tomorrow, he would find a way to get a message to Wakeley.

There was only one place to go, and that, in itself, could be dangerous. But there was no other choice.

He would have to spend the night with Elena.

* * * * *

Elena was curled up on the sofa, wearing the pink georgette pajamas Sean had bought her in Paris a few weeks ago when he'd stopped there on one of his frequent business trips. Snowball was curled up beside her, happily nibbling on the remains of a dish of Beluga caviar Elena had nibbled at before realizing she didn't want it. She was way too nervous to eat. It was doubtful she'd be able to eat at all until after the competition ended on Saturday night.

Saturday night. She could hardly wait. It would be her night to shine, her night to finally capture that gold medal that had eluded her for so many years. Okay, so it wasn't an Olympic medal. That was a bitter pill to swallow. It would be another four years before she could make that dream come true.

Still, the International Grand Prix was nothing to sneeze at. It was third in importance in the figure skating world, ranking just after the Olympics and World Championships. To win gold in Belfast meant she would be the queen of the ice-dancing world for a year at least.

She yawned, and tried to concentrate on the movie she'd put into the VCR, "3 Men and a Baby," a clever American remake of a French film. Amusing enough, she supposed, but she found herself identifying with the mother who left the baby behind with the three men, wondering why on earth the bachelors would fight to keep the squalling brat in the end. That really defied logic. Oh, well, that was Hollywood.

Snowball finished the last of the caviar and looked up at Elena out of her unusual eyes—one blue, one amber—and meowed plaintively. She stroked the cat's soft fur and smiled. "Sorry, *meelaya*, that's all there is. Are you going to be a good girl with Auntie Ekaterina? Mummy is going on a trip tomorrow."

Funny, how the only way she could see herself as a "mummy" was with her cat.

So far, she'd managed to keep that little secret from Sean, but it hadn't been easy. Especially during those times he went on, ad nauseum, about hearing the pitter-patter of little feet. It had taken every bit of her self-control to keep a halfway interested look on her face. Poor Sean. He was a hopeless romantic in a killer's body. This time, though, he'd gone too far. This time he'd killed a Boiko, and that, he was going to pay for by spending the rest of his life in a British prison cell. Or she would die putting him there.

The movie had ended. Elena pushed Snowball aside so she could get up, and the cat protested with an indignant yowl. "Oh, you're so spoiled," she admonished her with an indulgent smile. "Come on. Time for bed. Mummy has to be at the airport early tomorrow."

She turned off the TV and scooped the plump cat up in her arms. It was definitely going to be a sleeping pill night. The injection of TNG the sports doctor had given her this morning still zipped through her system. It always made her feel wired as if she'd been hooked up to an IV of pure espresso. Just another of the annoying little side effects of Uncle Anton's miracle drug. The others were a nuisance, too—the jaundiced skin, the lack of appetite, the weight loss and the one that worried Sean the most—the worsening of her asthma. But that was a small price to pay for success. Nothing would induce her to give up TNG. Not after she saw how much more strength and energy she had while under its influence.

Cuddling Snowball, Elena turned out the light and headed for the bedroom, but the ringing doorbell stopped her in her tracks. She glared down at Snowball and slowly turned around. "If that's Fagan Reilly coming by to check up on me," she muttered, "I swear, I may have to strangle him."

It would be just like Sean to have that stinky-breathed paddy spy on her while he was gone. But when she opened the door, much to her delight, she saw it wasn't Reilly who stood there. It was Mikhail.

He was swaying on his feet and bleary-eyed, which surprised her, because she'd never thought of Mikhail as much of a drinker, except for the occasional Guinness. But it was obvious that's what he'd been doing, and she supposed she should be angry with him. After all, they were leaving for Northern Ireland tomorrow. But it was hard to be mad when he was standing in her doorway looking so deliciously disheveled. He apparently hadn't shaved since morning, and his chiseled jaw was stubbled with soft blond hair—a sleepy, sexy look she couldn't resist. Even his reddened eyes and the jagged scar that sliced across his cheekbone didn't detract from his virile beauty. In fact, the scar made him all the more desirable, Elena thought.

"I need a place…to stay tonight," he said, his words slurring.

Elena smiled and drew him inside. Maybe the little sleeping pill wouldn't be necessary after all.

Good sex would work just as well.

CHAPTER TWENTY-FIVE

"Damn it, Mikhail." With a grunt of disgust, Elena tore her mouth away from his and lifted herself to a sitting position astride his reclining body. She glared at him. "How much have you had to drink, anyway?"

Mikhail slackened his jaw and gazed back out of half-closed eyes. "Jus' a coupla...drinks."

He wished he could fake a drool. That would really turn her off. But even without it, he thought he was doing okay.

Elena had practically attacked him after he stepped into her *dacha*. Within moments, she'd had him flat on his back on the sofa, and was on top of him, her mouth devouring his, her lower half grinding at his groin, much to his horror and revulsion. But he hadn't tried to stop her. Instead, he'd summoned a vision of Kerry in his mind, not so that he could imagine it was her he was kissing, but to remind himself that it wasn't. That way, there was no chance in hell he would get an erection. The thought of sleeping with Elena was just about as exciting as sleeping with a big, hairy tarantula.

But he'd known that was what Elena would expect to happen if he spent the night with her. That's why he'd stopped off at a bar on his way over and had three drinks—two of which he'd actually consumed for courage. The third he'd spilled on his sweater to give Elena the impression that he'd been drinking all evening. Then he'd gone into the restroom and applied two drops of the Visine eye drops he'd bought earlier at a chemist's, and immediately his eyes had begun itching and streaming. Years ago he'd discovered he was allergic to the stuff, and tonight that knowledge had come in handy. The itching and tearing only lasted about thirty minutes, but the redness lingered for hours. And if being drunk and impotent wasn't enough to discourage Elena, Mikhail had a back-up plan.

She stared at him morosely for a moment, and then slithered backward on his thighs, her hands going unerringly for his zipper. She gave him a lazy smile, a sultry look in her eyes. "I know a surefire way to get you in the mood."

Alarm jolted through him as she began to unzip his jeans. Time for the back-up plan. He hadn't touched a woman sexually—or had one touch him—since Kerry, and he damn well wasn't going to change that tonight.

He grabbed Elena by the arms and swung her off him. "I'm gonna be sick," he moaned, scrambling up from the sofa and covering his mouth with a hand. "Where's the bathroom?"

"Down the hall!" Elena pointed the way, a sour look of disgust on her face. "And hurry! I just had the carpets cleaned."

Inside the bathroom, Mikhail took the small bottle of syrup of Ipecac out of his pocket, took a deep breath and tipped it into his mouth. An extreme measure, he knew, but then, he was dealing with Elena. He had to make sure to squash any remaining plans she might have for romance, and he couldn't think of a better way to do it.

Within minutes, his stomach began churning, and his mouth filled with saliva. An unwelcome heat blasted through his body as bile rose in his throat. Seconds later, he dropped to his knees and clung to the toilet, spewing Finlandia-laced vomit into the bowl. Christ, he thought, still retching moments later, surely there couldn't be anything left inside him to throw up. But even feeling this bad, he couldn't deny the sense of satisfaction he also felt, thinking of Elena hearing the horrible sounds coming from the bathroom.

Finally, when there really was nothing left to throw up, he managed to get to his feet and stumble over to the sink. Shivering now instead of sweating, he rinsed out his mouth and stared dully into the mirror at his gray face and reddened eyes. Jesus, if Elena still wanted him now, she was a real sicko. He looked like a walking corpse.

Poor choice of words. The thought had summoned the image of poor Father Augustino, his brains splattered on the wall of the confessional. Another shiver raked his body. Had anyone found the priest yet?

"Mikhail, how are you doing?" Elena's seductive alto came from out in the hall.

Mikhail grimaced and opened the door. "Like I died and went straight to hell."

Elena stared at him, frustration glimmering in her eyes. She released an exasperated burst of air. "Mikhail, what were you thinking? Getting sloshed the night before we leave! We could've had such a fun night, you asshole."

Mikhail swayed on his feet, and it wasn't entirely an act. "I need to lie down."

Elena rolled her eyes and turned to lead the way back into the living room. "I'll get some sheets and blankets. You can sleep on the sofa."

Mikhail grinned, and followed her.

* * * * *

In the bathroom of her hotel room, Kerry applied lipstick and did a final check of her hair before turning out the light.

She grabbed her purse and was just about to open the door to go down to the restaurant when someone knocked.

"Housekeeping," said a cheerful feminine voice with an Irish lilt.

Kerry opened the door. "Wow! You get started early, don't you?"

A pretty woman with shoulder-length dark brown hair gave her a bright smile. "Yes, indeed, ma'am," she said, her brown eyes sparkling with good humor. "But I can come back later if it's an inconvenient time for you."

"Oh, no," Kerry said. "I'm just on my way down to breakfast. The room is all yours."

The maid's smile widened. "Thank you, miss. You have a grand day, now."

"Thank you. You, too." Smiling, Kerry headed for the elevators.

She loved Ireland. The people were always so friendly.

* * * * *

Sinead Farren watched the attractive raven-haired American step into the elevator, and then she slipped into the woman's room and closed the door.

She didn't know why Sean had ordered her to bug the room and set up video equipment, or why he wanted her to do the same thing in Room 937. But she wasn't paid to know why, only to follow his orders. And that's what she was going to do.

Just before she left the room, she opened the closet door and placed one final bug inside the lining of a light denim jacket that hung on the rack. Then she slipped out of the room and headed for the elevator to take her up to the ninth floor.

* * * * *

Mikhail took a seat in one of the comfortable chairs located in the vast lobby of the Royale Viscount while one of the skating federation officials checked the team into the hotel. After last night's staged binge that had resulted in very real nausea, and the long, uncomfortable flight from Moscow, all he wanted to do was crawl between the sheets and get some much-needed sleep. But Elena had already made it clear she intended to get some practice time in at the arena this afternoon, so that just wasn't going to happen.

She was barely speaking to him because of last night, and that was fine with him. At least he wouldn't have to worry about her showing up at his room tonight. Then again, with O'Malley somewhere in the vicinity, he doubted he'd have to worry about that.

Right now, his biggest problem was trying to figure out a way to get a message to Quentin Wakeley in London. In less than forty-eight hours, Sean O'Malley would be making an attempt on Tony Blair's life. The prime minister was scheduled to speak at eleven on Sunday at the Waterfront Hall for the Queen's Golden Jubilee celebration. According to Elena, that's when Sean would act. It was imperative that Mikhail get a message through to Wakeley to warn him of the planned assassination. But how? He couldn't use the phone in his room. Because of his attempt to defect during the Olympics, O'Malley's spies would be especially watchful of him. Most likely, his phone would be tapped. Also, his movements would be watched by the federation. After what happened in America, how could they possibly trust him not to try to defect again? But there had to be a way for him to get a message to Wakeley. Maybe Nadya could help him?

He glanced at the sprightly little woman. She was chatting with her good friend, Natasha Kosco, the coach of one of

Russia's rising stars, Irina Morenko. Sensing his glance, Nadya looked over and smiled, giving him a wave.

He returned her smile, but his heart fell. Christ, he didn't want to involve her. It was just too dangerous.

"Mikhail." One of the skating officials, a redheaded woman named Katya Nikovinoska, appeared in front of him, a grin on her freckled face. "You have a fan at the reception desk." She glanced over at a handsome young man who grinned at him and waved. Katya's green eyes danced. "I think he thinks you might be..." Her voice lowered. "...a bit light on your feet." She snickered.

"Oh, good Christ," Mikhail muttered, heat rushing to his face. "Did you tell him I'm not?"

"No. Tell him yourself." Katya's grin widened. "He wants to meet you. Go on over and do some PR for your country."

Despite Katya's teasing tone and the sparkle of good humor in her eyes, Mikhail knew he was being given an order. He suppressed a sigh and got to his feet.

The hotel clerk's smile widened as he approached. "Are you really Mikhail Kozlof?"

Mikhail nodded, smiling. "Yes, I am. How are you doing?"

"Just fine. It's really good to meet you. I'm a big fan." The clerk kept his eyes on Mikhail's face. "Can I get your autograph?" Reaching under the counter, he brought out a piece of paper, and something else. A silver-foiled cylinder.

Mikhail stared at it, wondering why it looked so familiar.

"Sign this." The clerk moved the paper and a pen toward him, and then lowered his voice. "This is for you. A young woman left it for you yesterday, and asked me to give it to you as discreetly as possible."

Mikhail's gaze met the clerk's. He looked down at the foil-wrapped disk again, and his heart bumped. He'd just realized what it was. A Hostess Ding Dong.

Trying to keep his expression natural, Mikhail signed his name on the sheet of paper, then grabbed the wrapped cake and slipped it into the pocket of his coat.

The clerk raised his voice, grinning from ear-to-ear. "Oh, this is so cool! I can't wait to tell my boyfriend I met you. He's going to be so jealous."

Mikhail's thoughts were spinning, but he managed to mutter something intelligent, and then turned away from the reception desk. Everyone in the Russian contingent was staring at him, wide grins on their faces, some of them not even bothering to hide their laughter.

Mikhail grinned back at them, flushing. Not because of embarrassment, though. Because his blood was singing as it traveled through his arteries. *Kerry. Oh, my God. Kerry.*

Was she here? *Could* she be here? Oh, Christ. It was too much to hope for. But who else would've left a Ding Dong for him? He could barely wait to get to his room so he could look at the wrapped cake. Could she have somehow put a note with it?

The Russians applauded as he joined them, and for a few minutes, Mikhail took some good-natured ribbing from the others. He grinned and joked back. "Well, what can I say? When you got it, you got it."

It seemed to take forever before the rooms were all sorted out, but finally, Mikhail got his assignment. Room 937. And of course, Elena was on the same floor. As the elevator rose, she glared at him in the small space, and Mikhail knew she hadn't forgiven him for last night.

Cool, he thought. She'd get over it by tomorrow…that is, if she wanted to perform well in the competition. Nothing could screw up a performance quicker than anger between the skating partners.

Anyway, maybe he wouldn't even have to compete tomorrow night. If Kerry was here…*oh, please, God, let it be true*…maybe he could use her to get a message to Wakeley, and with any luck, the Brits would have him picked up before tomorrow night's free dance competition.

Mikhail inserted the key into the lock of his room, and stepped inside, placing his suitcase on the floor. He closed the door behind him and double-locked it then reached into his pocket and drew out the Ding Dong.

He turned it over and saw what was written in a black marker. His heart began to drum.

"Rm. 628."

* * * * *

The phone was ringing when Kerry stepped into her room. She'd been shopping at Castlecourt Centre, figuring that Mikhail probably wouldn't arrive until afternoon. After breakfast, she'd been so vibed from the coffee, she'd known she wouldn't be able to go back to her room. The only alternative was to shop. Big sacrifice. She'd found a dangerous red silk dress in a little boutique, and if all went the way she hoped, she'd be wearing it for Mikhail. Maybe tonight.

Her heart beat faster as she dropped the packages on the bed and reached for the ringing phone.

It stopped in mid-ring.

Damn! She picked it up anyway, and of course, got nothing but the dial tone. Had it been Mikhail? Trembling, she dialed the reception desk.

"Front desk. This is Neil. How can I help you?"

Relief flooded through her at the sound of his friendly Belfast voice. "Hi, Neil. This is Kerry Niles in Room 628. Can you tell me if Mikhail Kozlof has checked in yet?"

"Yes, Miss Niles. He just went up to his room no more than fifteen minutes ago. And I gave him your message."

Kerry caught her breath. *It had been him*! "What's his room number? Can you transfer me?"

"Of course. He's in Room 937. Hold on, please."

Kerry's hand tightened on the phone as it began to ring in Mikhail's room.

* * * * *

The knock came again at the door, followed by Elena's irritated voice. "For God's sake, Mikhail. We don't have all day. Let's go."

Damn it to hell. Mikhail put down the phone in mid-ring. She wasn't there, anyway. If it *had* been Kerry who'd left the Ding Dong. But then, who else? Who else could possibly know those Hostess cakes meant anything to him?

"Mikhail? Are you coming?"

"Yes!" he barked, grabbing his skate bag from the bed.

He'd try again when he got back to the room.

* * * * *

Kerry waited fifteen minutes, and then tried Mikhail's room again. If that had been him who called, why hadn't he answered? Maybe he'd gone into the shower. It was possible, wasn't it? That he'd called just before jumping into the shower? Or maybe he'd run out to get ice.

She hadn't left a message the first time. What she wanted to say couldn't be boiled down to a sound bite. No, that wasn't exactly true. She couldn't leave a message because she wasn't sure what to say. And she wasn't going to this time either.

"No message," she said to the operator who picked up after the sixth ring.

What if she left a message, and then never heard from him? The waiting would kill her. If he was going to reject her, better that he do it face-to-face than prolong the agony.

But he's not going to do that, she told herself. He loves me. She touched the silver ring hanging around her neck. And he *had* called. She was sure it had been him. Later, she'd try again.

The phone rang, and her heart jumped. "Hello?"

"Miss Niles, it's Neil at the front desk. I hope you won't think this is presumptuous of me, but did you catch up with Mr. Kozlof?"

"No, actually. We seem to have missed each other."

"Well, he left with the other Soviet skaters shortly after I talked to you. They had their gym bags with them, so if you know where they're training, you might be able to find him there."

"Thank you." Kerry's heart began to race. "Uh...why...?"

"Because I'm a hopeless romantic," he said, a smile in his voice. "And I figure a girl that leaves a chocolate message to a lad must be in love."

Kerry smiled, her eyes burning. "Thank you. Thank you so much."

* * * * *

Kerry stepped into the Belfast Ice Arena and headed toward the double doors separating the lobby from the rink.

"Excuse me, Ma'am," called out a young woman at the ticket window. "We're closed for a private event today."

Kerry thought quickly, and pulled out her USFSA ID. "I'm with the American skaters," she said, not feeling a bit of shame for telling the little white lie. After all, technically, she still *was* a member of the United States Figure Skating Association. She'd never officially given up her membership.

The woman smiled. "Oh, I thought you looked familiar. Go on in, then. The practice sessions are closed to the public, and I've been instructed to guard the place with my life."

Kerry smiled. "And you're doing a wonderful job."She walked through the double doors, thinking how glad she was she'd had the foresight to bring her ID.

Four couples were training on the ice, two ice dancers and two pairs. Vivaldi's "The Four Seasons" blared from the PA system, and one couple—the only one Kerry saw—performed to the music. They wore sashes of bright red, and Kerry knew that meant their music was playing for their run-through, but even if she hadn't known that, it would've been obvious by the elements they performed to every strain of the violins. Mikhail looked like an elegant lion with his golden mane flying as he moved over the ice. Perfection in motion.

Oh, Mikhail...

He'd let his hair grow longer. She'd forgotten how beautiful he was—the way he floated over the ice so effortlessly as if he had wings on his skates. His gaze held Elena's, and Kerry clearly saw the love of the sport etched on his face. His simple black practice costume gave his body a clean, elegant line and emphasized the strength of his powerful thighs as he moved through each element with precision and confidence. And as always, when Kerry saw Elena and Mikhail skate together, she couldn't help but think what a striking pair they made. Of course, Elena was as gorgeous as ever, despite her somewhat sallow complexion, and she looked right at home in Mikhail's arms. Kerry caught her breath at the look on his face! So intense, so passionate.

An overwhelming doubt swept over her. What if she were wrong? What if he'd left the ring as a...token of their time together? A sentimental goodbye gift. Had she read too much into it? Had she come halfway across the world only to make a fool of herself?

Mikhail lifted Elena to his shoulders where she went into a swiftly changing series of complicated positions. Setting her gently back on the ice, the couple went into a spin, Mikhail's hand clasping her outstretched leg, and then breaking apart, they segued into a challenging bit of precise footwork. Apparently, this segment had been giving them problems because having completed it successfully, Elena gave Mikhail a brilliant smile. He winked at her, and Kerry felt as if an icy hand had reached inside her rib cage and clutched her heart.

The gesture seemed so flirtatious. No. More than that, it seemed intimate, an expression of tenderness, maybe love. Was something going on between them? Had Elena finally managed to make Mikhail her lover?

The couple circled the ice, rounding the corner where Kerry stood. Mikhail turned Elena in his arms, facing Kerry. He looked up, and her pulse jumped, but his gaze moved on past her. At first, she didn't think he'd recognized her, but then seconds later, his head whipped around, and his eyes focused on her for a brief moment before the next movement in their routine turned him away. Was it her imagination or had his face paled? Kerry's heart raced. He *had* recognized her. She knew it. What would happen now?

She slid her hands into the pockets of her denim jacket, hugging herself for warmth in the frigid air of the rink. Her gaze followed Mikhail as the couple glided over the ice. He turned to face Kerry again, and this time, his eyes held hers, tumultuous and wary at the same time. He turned away, and it was Elena who faced her, but she was totally caught up in her performance, oblivious to onlookers.

As the music ended, Mikhail and Elena performed their final element, finishing the free dance with Mikhail on his knees, his head pressed to her belly. Her back was arched, her arms outstretched, eyes closed in the throes of passion.

Kerry's throat tightened. Their sexual tension was palpable. How could it be faked?

Elena broke away from Mikhail and spoke in rapid Russian. Kerry caught the gist of it. Something about the Choctaw during the "summer" movement. But Kerry didn't think Mikhail was listening. He'd gotten to his feet and was looking at Kerry, his eyes unreadable. She sensed he was trying to send her a message, but had no idea what it meant.

"*Mikhail!*" Elena said sharply when she realized he wasn't paying attention.

Mikhail dragged his gaze from Kerry, but not quickly enough. Elena started to look over in her direction, but Mikhail grabbed her arm. "One more time," he said in Russian.

She shrugged, and allowed him to lead her to the center of the ice. The music began again, and they started their routine from the beginning. This time, Mikhail didn't look at Kerry once.

There were two possibilities, Kerry thought. Either he didn't want Elena to know she was here, which totally made sense. Or else, she'd been horribly wrong in coming here...because he didn't want to see her.

She turned slowly and headed for the double doors. Well, it was done. He knew she was here.

The next step would have to be his.

* * * * *

Mikhail looked over Elena's shoulder and saw Kerry disappearing through the double doors. His heart was slamming in his chest. *Had* been since he'd looked up and saw her standing there, an expression of yearning on her face. His first thought had been "Oh, my God! She *is* here!" and then his second had ripped through him. *She still loves me.*

The realization had warmed him, thrilled him, filled him with joy, but then, on its heels had come another, a horrifying thought. What kind of danger would Kerry be stepping into because of him? He remembered how O'Malley had kidnapped her in Virginia, and the threat he'd made against her to encourage him to return to Russia. Kerry would never be safe as long as O'Malley was free. Until Mikhail was safely in the protection of the British, he couldn't risk involving her. How could he even have contemplated for a moment getting her involved? And that meant he had to stay away from her.

When he'd called her room shortly after receiving her message, he hadn't thought things through, hadn't thought about the possibility of danger to her. His only thought had been how much he wanted to hear her voice. But when he'd realized Elena was about to catch a glimpse of her, it had hit home. For all he knew, Kerry could be walking into a trap. And that's when he knew what he had to do.

He had to stay away from her. It was the only way to protect her.

* * * * *

Sean paced the small living room of the safe house on Falls Road where he'd been staying during his last few visits to the city. Declan Byrne, a high-ranking volunteer in the Belfast brigade of the Real IRA, had provided the house. It was in a run down Catholic neighborhood used to the comings and goings of hard-eyed strangers. No one asked questions, even when their appearance coincided with a devastating bombing or a shooting. Sean, though, wasn't a stranger to Falls Road. He'd grown up here, and from the age of eight had roved the streets with other Catholic lads bedeviling British troops by throwing homemade petrol bombs whenever the opportunity presented itself. He'd killed his first man here—a skinny British private with peach fuzz still on his adolescent face. In his dreams sometimes, Sean still saw the boy's startled brown eyes as the bullet ripped through his heart. Much to his surprise, Sean hadn't felt exhilaration at the killing of his enemy, as he'd thought he would. In fact, he'd felt bloody sick to his stomach. But after that, killing had become easier.

He turned his thoughts to Sunday and his rendezvous with Prime Minister Blair. It had been a long time since he'd carried out an operation himself, but this one was special. This was his last one and it was only appropriate that he'd be personally involved.

Too bad the target was Tony Blair, not Margaret Thatcher. Sean quite liked good old Tony. For a Brit, he wasn't half-bad. Maggie, though, was a different story. That bloody old bat had been responsible for the deaths and imprisonment of many a good IRA lad, and for that, Sean would dearly love to blow her to smithereens. Ah, but life wasn't a wee bit fair, was it? Not when that evil witch got to live out her life in luxury, while the likeable Tony Blair would be made to pay for her sins, simply because he carried the title of PM.

Ah, well, that wasn't Sean's problem. If all went well, by Sunday night, he and Elena would be on an airliner, heading for South America, and by this time next week, they'd be living the good life.

He frowned. Well, that remained to be seen. After what he'd heard on the tape Reilly had sent by overnight post, he was in a quandary about what to do about Elena. For sure, she'd betrayed him by telling Kozlof about his deal with Sullivan and the plan for Tony Blair. Good thing she didn't know the actual plan. In fact, he'd purposely misled her, anticipating this very situation. He'd never trusted Elena. Loved her, yes, but hadn't trusted her. She'd sell a kidney to the highest bidder if she thought it was the right price. But there was the rub. He loved her.

Any other man would've ordered her death sentence by now. And that had been his first inclination as he'd listened to the tape, his fury growing with every word. But later, when he'd had a chance to let it all sink in, he'd reminded himself that Elena had been justified in her anger about her uncle's murder. Sean had known she thought of him as a surrogate father, and had also known she wouldn't take his death well. So, in the heat of passion, she'd blurted out everything to Kozlof, and was plotting against him. Sean had a feeling, though, she was already regretting her rashness. They'd been partners for years, and she knew a good part of her success was due to him. After all, hadn't he been the one to convince Anton Boiko to start up the TNG program again so that Elena could achieve her dream? Surely, she hadn't forgotten that.

If so, he'd have to remind her.

He'd decided to give her another chance. But first, he'd give her a little test, one she'd have to pass to prove she *deserved* another chance. Listening again to the tape, he'd noted there hadn't been any romantic overtures from either Elena or Kozlof. Maybe his imagination was running wild about Elena's interest in him. He hoped so. He really did. Because he could forgive Elena's anger about the murder of her uncle. That was perfectly understandable. But what he couldn't—*wouldn't*—forgive was if she betrayed him because she wanted another man. Elena belonged to him, and no one else.

He looked at his watch. Damn! Where the fuck was Reilly? He should've called by now. He dug his cell phone out of his jacket pocket and dialed a number. After two rings, Reilly picked up.

"Hey, boss." Reilly sounded as if he were munching on something. No surprise that he'd ordered from room service on Sean's Euro. "What's up?"

In the background, Sean heard the raucous sounds of one of the British sit-coms Reilly was apparently addicted to. His lips tightened. "That's what I want to know from you. Has Kozlof and the American girl met?"

"No, boss. Just a minute." There was a pause, and Sean heard something that sounded like Reilly had taken a gulp of something. Better be water, he thought, not Guinness. "I've been listening all afternoon. She tried his room a couple of times, but he'd already gone to the arena. Some queer down at the reception desk told her where he'd gone, and a few minutes later, she left."

"Did Sinead get a bug planted on her?"

"Sure thing. I heard everything, clear as a bell. She went to the arena and stayed for about ten minutes. Only person she spoke to was some female when she first walked in. I could hear music, so I suppose she was watching the skaters. But she didn't speak to anybody else."

Sean thought for a moment. "He must've seen her. You know damn well *she* saw *him*."

Reilly took another bite of whatever it was he was eating in his hotel room. He didn't bother to try to subdue his noisy smacking. "Don't know, boss. I guess so."

"He won't contact her," Sean said, still thinking. "He's afraid of bringing her into this. He won't want to risk her safety." He peered out the window that overlooked the quiet street. A light rain was beginning to fall. Rio seemed a million miles away. "Okay, Reilly. Here's what we're going to do…"

CHAPTER TWENTY-SIX

She couldn't take it anymore.

Kerry turned off the television and jumped up from the bed. This was insane! Waiting around for the phone to ring.

The compulsory dance competition had ended over two hours ago with Elena and Mikhail in the lead. Kerry had used her ID to secure a decent seat where she'd watched them skate, and every time Mikhail's movements brought him facing in her direction, the hairs on her arms had stood at attention. But if he'd seen her, he hadn't given any indication. She'd been sure, though, that he'd call her room once he got back to the hotel.

But she'd heard nothing. It didn't take a brain surgeon to figure what that meant. She was a complete dork for reading something into the appearance of Mikhail's ring in her purse.

And like the idiot she was, she'd been pacing around her hotel room, waiting for him to call. As if she were a high school wallflower hoping to hear from the star quarterback. She hadn't even gone down to the hotel restaurant for dinner before the competition, instead, she'd ordered a meal from room service. The perfectly prepared pan-seared salmon and roasted potatoes had been totally wasted on her, though, because she'd barely eaten a bite. She was too nervous, too focused on the telephone to eat.

It was almost eleven now, and it had dawned on her—finally!—that hey, maybe she'd gotten it all wrong. Maybe she'd come all the way to Northern Ireland for nothing. Mikhail wasn't interested, and he wasn't going to call.

Her mouth tightened as she reached for her denim jacket in the closet. *So, screw you, Mikhail Kozlof.* She was young and attractive, and she was here in one of Europe's most interesting cities—especially when one was young and attractive—and she wasn't about to waste another moment. She'd heard about a club over on High Street that was supposed to be really popular with the singles crowd. U2 had played one of their first gigs there, and rumor had it that Bono still stopped in whenever he was in town.

That'll teach Mikhail, Kerry thought, zipping up her jacket with more force than necessary. *I'll go to the club, meet Bono, and make him fall madly in love with me. And I'll invite Mikhail to our wedding.* Only one problem with that. Bono was already married. Well then, she'd find someone else. Wasn't that sexy rock star, Devin O'Keefe, from Belfast, or had he defected to Dublin like most of them did?

She opened the door, and was just about to close it behind her when the phone rang. She stood still. It rang again. She closed her eyes and shook her head. *Don't do this. Don't get your hopes up again. It just sucks when they're dashed.*

But despite the admonishing voice in her head, she found herself turning around and heading to the bedside table. *You're a glutton for punishment, aren't you?* It rang a third time, and she picked it up, her pulse hammering. "Hello?"

"Miss Niles, this is Neil Morrissey at the reception desk."

Kerry slumped in disappointment, and slowly sank to the bed. "Hi, Neil," she said weakly. "What's up?"

"I have a message for you from Mikhail Kozlof."

Her heart tripped into overdrive. "You do? Wha…" she stammered. "What is it?"

"He wants you to meet him in his room. Number 937."

For a moment, Kerry couldn't find enough strength to speak. "When?" she finally asked.

"Right now. As soon as you can get there."

Elation swept through her. But with it, something else. Confusion. Her brow furrowed. "Thank you, Neil." Her hand trembled as she disconnected.

It wasn't until she'd hung up that she wondered why Mikhail hadn't called her himself. But then, after his previous attempt to defect, he was probably being watched closer than ever. If they knew she was here, they'd want to make sure she didn't get anywhere near him.

She laughed out loud. "Just try and stop me."

She sat on the bed a moment, trying to compose herself. *Oh, Mikhail, I'm so sorry I doubted you. Again.* Why was it she found it so easy to believe she was being rejected? Was she doomed to suffer abandonment issues for the rest of her life? God in Heaven! Dr. Joyce Brothers would have a field day with her psyche.

Kerry stepped into the bathroom to check out her appearance. When she'd been about to leave on a mission to pick up carousing rock stars for a one-night-stand and possible marriage, she hadn't really cared what she looked like. She'd figured she could pull her weight in a pub without primping. Now, though, knowing she would be seeing Mikhail, she ran a brush through her hair and applied new lip-gloss in a glistening rose tint. She even contemplated changing into that daring little red dress she'd bought at the boutique this morning, but then decided she just didn't want to take the time to do it. Besides, if Mikhail felt the way she did, he wouldn't care if she were dressed in silk or in denim.

After one final check in the mirror, she turned off the bathroom light, grabbed her purse, and on impulse, the opened box of Ding Dongs, and stepped out of the room. At the elevator, she pushed the "up" button and waited, her heart in her throat, her breathing erratic.

The elevator dinged, and the doors opened. Kerry stepped in and pushed the button for the ninth floor.

* * * * *

Mikhail lay on his bed, his head propped on two flimsy hotel pillows. The television was on, but he wasn't really watching it, just channel-surfing. It was just after eleven, and he knew he should try to get some sleep because they had an early morning practice scheduled—one last time on the ice before the first of the two dances tomorrow—but his mind wouldn't rest. His thoughts kept spinning in circles. How could he get a message to Wakeley? Would that gay guy down at reception help? But if so, how would he make contact with him without alerting O'Malley or his spies? They were watching him closely. He knew it. In fact, he was surprised they hadn't set up a fucking guard outside his door.

And Kerry. *Oh, my God, Kerry!* It was killing him to think she was just three floors down from him. So very close. All he had to do was get in the elevator and take it down to the sixth floor, walk down the hall and stop in front of Room 628. Knock and wait. She would open the door. Her incredible blue eyes would widen, and then that smile—her heart meltingly sweet smile—would light up her pretty freckled face...

Good Christ! He groaned and sat up on the bed, cradling his head in his hands. He had to stop doing this to himself. No way was he going to risk her life by making contact with her. Not until O'Malley was safely in custody. Only then would it be safe to see her. He just prayed she'd stick around long enough. If only there was a way to get a message to her. To tell her to trust him, to wait, to believe in his love. But how? How to get that message to her?

A knock came at the door, and Mikhail stiffened, his fingers pressing against his temples. If that was Elena, trying to worm her way into his bed, he truly didn't know if he could stand it. She'd been in a horrible mood all day, snapping at Nadya and giving him the cold shoulder because she was, evidently, still pissed at his alcoholic binge that last night in Tallinn. It would be just like her to treat him like a slug she'd found under a rock during the day, and then expect him to make love to her that night. He really just didn't think he could fake any kind of warmth— or even civility—to her right now.

He thought about ignoring the knock. Maybe she'd think he was asleep and go away. But the knock came again, more timidly this time. He straightened, his eyes on the door. That wasn't Elena. His heart began to hammer.

No. She wouldn't. Would she?

He scrambled off the bed and flung himself at the door. Peering through the peephole, he caught his breath. *Oh, dear God.*

Kerry was standing in the corridor, chewing her bottom lip and staring off down the hall in anxiety. Mikhail closed his eyes and stood still. Be strong, he told himself. *Pretend you're not here and she'll go away.*

There was silence from the hallway. *Had* she gone away? He was torn between praying she had, and desperately hoping she was still there. He looked through the peephole again and his heart jolted. She was turning away, her shoulders slumped.

And Mikhail's fingers acted independently of his mind.

He tore open the door. "*Kerry!*" His voice came out hoarse with longing.

She turned, her eyes wide, an expression of hope mingled with fear on her lovely freckled face.

Without thinking, Mikhail reached out and pulled her into the room. The door closed behind her. He fumbled at the double-bolt, his heart pounding. The lock made an audible click.

He turned and stared at her. She gazed back, her face pale, eyes still wearing that haunted, uncertain expression. His gaze swept over her. She was dressed in faded denim jeans, a yellow cable-knit sweater that zipped up the front and an unzipped denim jacket. And, of course, her usual cowboy boots. He couldn't imagine Kerry without her cowboy boots. Her hair was loose, spilling around her shoulders like an inky river. His fingers itched to lace through the ebony strands, to cup her small head and expose her elegant throat to his mouth.

He tightened his hands into fists and tried to compose his turbulent thoughts into words. There was so much he wanted to say.

Why did you come? Dear God, it's not safe for you here. You shouldn't have come, but oh, God, it's good to see you. I need to touch you. Hold you just for a moment.

Instead, he said nothing. Just stared at her, his heart racing, his eyes mesmerized by her ripe, sweet mouth. Her musky rose fragrance wafted over him, making him light-headed with longing.

It was Kerry who finally spoke, "Did you get my Ding Dong?"

God, he'd missed that darling American accent. He swallowed hard and managed to nod.

"I brought more," she said.

For the first time, he noticed the rectangular white box in her hands. He smiled, and to his horror, felt his throat tighten with emotion. It was such a small gesture, but it meant so much.

Kerry met his gaze, her eyes glistening with unshed tears. "I got your ring," she whispered, fingering the silver ring that hung from a chain around her slender neck. "I thought…I hoped…" Her voice trailed away uncertainly.

It was his undoing. With a soft groan of anguish, he grabbed the Ding Dong box, and tossed it on the bed. Then he wrenched her to him, his mouth claiming hers. Her fingers laced into his hair as she gave herself up to his kiss, her lips parting to allow in his exploring tongue.

Mikhail's head began to spin, but one thought pierced through the deepening fog of desire.

He was at home now. Finally at home.

* * * * *

Kerry broke for air long enough to drag in a breath, and her lungs filled with Mikhail's familiar oak moss scent of "Cool Water," the cologne he'd bought at Wal-Mart. Oh, dear God in heaven, how could a man smell so good?

His hands slid under her hair to cup her skull, tilting her head back before claiming her mouth again for another long, intoxicating kiss. He broke it finally, but his lips continued to nibble at hers as if he were starving for her taste.

"It has been so long," he whispered in between kisses. "Too, too long."

"I kn…" His mouth smothered her attempt at agreement.

His lean, hard body pressed against hers, and elation swept through her at the pulse of his rigid sex against her belly. Her hands, which had been gripping his waist, stole under his Denver Bronco sweatshirt to slide upward, drawing in his body heat, moving over the crisp hairs of his chest. She dragged her mouth away from his, and with a soft gasp, whispered, "Take it off, Mikhail. I need…"

He released her and stepping back, tugged the sweatshirt over his head. Kerry's gaze centered on his chest, moving over the light carpet of blond hair that narrowed to a vee below his sweatpants. He gazed back, eyes glittering. Kerry could barely breathe. They moved at the same moment into each other's arms. A soft sigh of pleasure escaped her lips as she brushed kisses over his chest, occasionally pausing to tug gently at his nipples. He groaned, and his hands cupped her behind, molding her tight against him. She could feel his heart racing beneath her mouth. For a moment, she paused, and laid her head over his sternum, just listening to the thunder of his heart. He stood still, and one hand moved up to her head, cradling it against him.

"We should not do this," he said quietly.

Kerry closed her eyes, lost in the beat of his heart.

"You have put yourself in danger by coming here," Mikhail went on, his voice low and urgent. "I may not be able to protect you."

Kerry opened her eyes, turned her head and stretched up to plant a kiss in the hollow of his throat. "I'm where I want to be," she said softly. "I'd rather be in danger with you than be without you."

Mikhail drew away just far enough so he could peer into her eyes. His fingers brushed her jaw-line. They were trembling. He gazed at her, his thumb moving over her lower lip in a tender caress. "I love you," he said, his eyes holding hers. "And if something happens to you because of me, I would never be able to forgive myself."

"That's why you left me in Virginia?" she said. "Because you were afraid for me, isn't it? That's why you lied about being responsible for Adam's accident."

He nodded. "It was the only thing I could say to convince you I did not love you. And it worked, did it not?"

"For a while. But once I found your ring, I knew it had been a lie." She reached up and took his face between her hands. Her fingers traced the line of his scar. "But you know what? My heart always knew it was a lie. It's just that sometimes...I don't listen to my heart. Instead, I listen to those negative voices inside my brain that tell me I'm not worthy of being loved. Especially by someone like you."

"*Oh, God, Kerry!*" Mikhail wrenched her to him, his hand cradling her head against his chest. "Don't you know how very lovable you are? I think I fell in love with you that very first moment I collided with you in the tunnel in Nice. Do you remember that?"

Kerry smiled. "I remember every moment I've been in the same room with you. Every single moment." She tilted her head back and gave him an impish grin. "So, are you going to make love to me, Estonian boy, or just stand here keeping me all hot and bothered the rest of the night?"

His white teeth flashed. His eyes seemed to grow even bluer, and more turbulent than before. "That sounds quite like an order, *American* girl."

She arched an eyebrow. "Then what are you waiting for? Get *to* it."

Eyes dancing, he tugged her jacket from her shoulders and tossed it to the floor. His fingers moved to the zipper of her sweater and began to inch it down. Her breathing quickened. Mikhail parted the sweater, his gaze sweeping over the white seamless cups of her bra. He reached out and traced a finger along the upper trim, just barely brushing her skin. She trembled under his touch.

"I love your breasts," he whispered. "They are perfect size for my hands." And he flattened his palms against them, fingers outstretched to caress her bare flesh. His eyes held hers.

"I know," she said raggedly, swaying on her feet. "You've told me that before."

Her body ached for him. She felt like a tender fruit, ripe and ready to fall from the tree. Still palming her breasts, he leaned forward and took her mouth in another slow, drugging kiss. Finally, he broke the contact and moved away slightly. Her gaze roved over his body, and her breath quickened as she took in the hard bulge beneath his gray sweatpants. She couldn't wait to feel him inside her.

"It has been almost three months," he said. "There has been no one since you. Since Pennsylvania."

Kerry felt a rush of shame for her previous suspicions about Mikhail and Elena. Her insecurity was to blame, but that didn't make her feel any less ashamed of herself for doubting him.

"Me, too," Kerry said.

His eyes softened. "I want to give you pleasure," he said slowly. "But once I am inside you, I do not think I will satisfy…"

Kerry shook her head. "You always satisfy, Mikhail."

"But still…" His eyes blazed with an inner fire. "I must make certain."

He stepped closer, and his hands moved to the zipper of her jeans. She held her breath as he unzipped them, and then lowering himself to his knees, he tugged the faded denim down over her hips. They pooled around her boots. She stood before him, wearing only her purple satin and lace bikini panties and her unzipped sweater over her bra, her hands tangled in his silken blond hair, eyes closed, barely breathing. He kissed her belly—soft, succulent kisses that traveled in a vee-shape around her navel. She shivered, and the heavy, velvet warmth between her legs intensified. His hand cupped her left buttock, stroking the satin in slow, tantalizing circles.

She gasped when his fingers hooked into the side strings of her bikini, and slowly slid the satin material down over her thighs. "Oh, God, Miki!" she murmured, eyes closed. "You're driving me out of my mind."

The fire was blazing now. She needed his touch, craved it, would die if she didn't get it soon. Her panties fell to her boots, and she tugged them off, tossing them somewhere to the side. She pressed her pelvis toward Mikhail, silently inviting his mouth, his fingers. She was moist and aching. Swollen and vulnerable.

"Please," she whispered.

He didn't keep her waiting. She felt his moist breath on her sex, a soft sigh of reverence, and then his warm, supple fingers slid into her, caressing, taking, and giving all at the same time. She cried out in awe, her nails digging into his scalp. And then, still with his fingers imbedded in her folds, the other hand clasped upon her right buttock, his mouth lowered to her.

"Oh, dear God!" she cried out as he brought her to a hard, quick climax.

She was still shuddering when he scooped her up into his arms and deposited her on the bed. His chest moved with his erratic breathing as he tugged at her cowboy boots, dropping them to the carpeted floor, each one making a dull thud on the carpet. He stepped back, his eyes holding hers, and quickly, stripped out of his sweatpants. Her eyes widened at the magnificence of his erection. She'd forgotten how...healthy!...he was.

He stood beside the bed for a moment, and allowed her to look her fill. His eyes danced mischievously. "I will now do as you ordered, American girl," he said in precise English. "I will make love to you, but like I said, I do not think I will last long."

"*Now*," Kerry said through clenched teeth. Even though she was still trembling from the climax he'd brought her to, the inferno inside her was already building again. "Do it now, Miki."

The bed shifted as his hot, lean body covered hers, chest-to-chest, thigh-to-thigh, sex-to-sex. His mouth settled on hers, and she tasted her own essence on them. Her legs parted, and his hard cock nudged against her opening, sending fireworks dancing behind her eyes. In one smooth, sure movement, he plunged into her, and Kerry cried out, her nails digging into his back.

"Oh, yes, Mikhail. *Yes!*" She arched her back, surrendering to him, allowing him to take all of her, every sinew, every beat of her heart. She closed her eyes and gave herself up to him. "Don't ever go away again," she whispered, her teeth clenched against his salty throat. "Not ever. Promise me."

Mikhail groaned with each exquisite plunge into her. "Promise," he gasped. "I promise."

And then, there was no more talk. Only motion and beauty and love.

* * * * *

Sean sat in his darkened living room and watched the live feed from Kozlof's hotel room on the telly. Damn! That Sinead was good. Setting up that hidden video equipment had been a bloody brilliant idea! It was like going to the local porn theater and watching a double feature in the dark.

Still, porn might be too crass of a word for what was going on between Kozlof and the comely American skater. The Russian was in love. That was one thing Sean hadn't really believed until now. It was enough to almost bring a tear to the eye.

Almost.

One thing was for sure. Elena was going to shit a bloody brick when she saw this little videotape in the morning. Little did she know, though, that her reaction to Kozlof's bedroom entertainment with the American would seal her fate, one way or the other.

And not just her's, Sean thought, a grim smile on his lips as he watched Kozlof and his girlfriend cuddling after making love. Elena would be sealing the fate for all three of them.

As well as his own.

CHAPTER TWENTY-SEVEN

"I'm starving." Kerry scooted up in bed, not bothering to cover her nudity. For some odd reason, it was way too hot in the room. She eyed the light sheen of sweat on Mikhail's bare chest, and had to restrain herself from attacking him again. God! He was beautiful, from the top of his golden head to his long, sexy toes.

He lay on his side, watching her, his elbow propped on the bed, chin resting in his hand. His eyes twinkled. "I happen to know someone brought in delicious Ding Dongs."

Kerry grinned. "Cool! What happened to them?"

He shrugged. "Who knows? That same someone probably crushed them."

"Me?" Kerry reached out and ruffled her fingers through his disheveled hair, then scooted out of bed to search for the box of Hostess cakes. "I would never be so careless as to crush perfectly good chocolate."

He watched her, a wry grin on his lips. "Not when in your right mind, anyway. But I do not think you were concerned with chocolate at moment in question."

"You *think*?" Kerry spotted the box upside down on the floor a few feet from the bed. "Ah, here it is!" One of them must've tossed it there during their sexual frenzy, but she'd be damned if she could remember doing it. She grabbed the box, and several foil-wrapped cakes rolled out onto the floor. Kerry scooped one up and tossed it to Mikhail. "Here you go."

He caught it with his left hand. Kerry scrambled back into the bed with the box of the Ding Dongs. Mikhail slid up to rest his back against the headboard, and began to unwrap his cake.

He took a bite and closed his eyes in ecstasy. Kerry grinned. "Good?" Her fingers tore at the foil of her Ding Dong.

"Mmmmm…exquisite." He swallowed and opened his eyes. His tongue flicked out to capture a bit of cream smeared on his bottom lip.

Kerry felt the temperature in the room rise another degree.

"I missed these," Mikhail said. His gaze moved lazily over her. "Almost as much as I missed you."

"I missed you more." Kerry looked up from her snack cake. "I'd give up chocolate for you." She'd meant it to come out teasingly, but somehow, to her own ears, at least, it didn't sound that way at all.

Mikhail's eyes met hers. The amused light disappeared as a pregnant silence fell between them. Kerry's cheeks heated, and suddenly she felt shy. *Unbelievable!* The last time she'd felt shy with a member of the opposite sex, she'd been twelve. And this particular male had just spent the last twenty minutes exploring every crevice of her body with his tongue.

"Well, I wouldn't *want* to give up chocolate," she said with a slight smile, trying to lighten the moment. "But I would."

Mikhail stared at her, his expression still serious. "Why?" he asked quietly.

Kerry's heart dipped. Her gaze shifted away from the intensity of his. She gave a slight shrug. "Because you're so sexy?"

"No." He reached out and took her chin in his hand, forcing her to look at him. "Why?" he asked again, softer and more insistent this time. His thumb traced leisurely over her bottom lip.

Kerry looked into his deep blue eyes, and the words whispered through her mind, but as much as she wanted to say them, something held her back, just as it had in the car in Pennsylvania. It was silly. She knew that. But in the past, every man she'd loved—her father, Vladimir, even Joshua—had left her. "I love you" had been the last words she'd uttered to her father before he'd been swallowed up by the deadly avalanche. Those words, too, had been on her lips when she said goodbye to Vladimir on his deathbed. Joshua, of course, had dropped her shortly after she'd admitted her love for him. Maybe she was superstitious, but what if she said those three little words to Mikhail, and then something happened to him? He would leave, or be taken away...

But would *saying* it out loud really make a difference? Mikhail stared at her, his expression compelling. It was as if he were willing her to say the words that had dwelled in her heart for months.

She took a deep, quavering breath. "I love you," she whispered.

He smiled, and his hand slid up her face, brushing a strand of hair away from her temple. "I know." He leaned forward and kissed her mouth. His lips tasted of chocolate.

Kerry sighed into his kiss, her free hand, the one not holding the Ding Dong, curled around his neck possessively. For a long, delicious moment, they nibbled at each other's lips as Kerry's blood turned to warm syrup. But when his hand captured her right breast, sending electric impulses shooting through her lower belly, and igniting a furnace between her legs, she broke the kiss and playfully pushed him away.

"Hey! No fair. You had your Ding Dong, and I didn't get mine yet." She gave him a mock glare. "I didn't eat dinner because of you, you know."

"Why is that my fault?"

She laughed at his indignant expression. It was hard to look indignant while naked and eating a Ding Dong. She took a big bite of her cake and gave a mock swoon, "Oh, yes. *Yum*! Did I really say I'd give up chocolate for you?"

He popped the rest of his cake into his mouth. "Answer me. Why is it my fault you did not eat dinner?"

"Because I was waiting for you to call, you jerk. Do you have any idea how close I came to giving up on you?" She stared at the cream in the center of the cake, thinking that really, Mikhail had the right idea a moment ago. She could always eat later.

"I do not understand…" Mikhail began.

Kerry grinned and stuck her index and middle fingers into the cream center, scooping out as much filling as she could get. Then she gave Mikhail a saucy look. "The cream is my favorite part anyway." She reached down between them and wrapped her hand around his semi-soft member, smearing it with the cream filling.

His eyes widened in surprise. "You are such a naughty girl."

Kerry laughed as his penis began to swell in her hand. "You have no idea how naughty I can be." She popped the remaining piece of chocolate into her mouth, continuing to massage the cream filling over his hard shaft. Swallowing, she turned to him with a devilish grin and pushed him onto his back. Kerry rolled over on top of his hard, lean body, and then slithered downward. He groaned with pleasure when she took his artificially sweetened flesh into her mouth.

And she knew what she'd said was true. She *would* give up chocolate for Mikhail.

* * * * *

"Thank you," Kerry murmured later, running her hand over his hair-roughened chest. She lay with her head anchored against his shoulder, her eyes closed.

"For what?" he asked. His fingers played with a strand of her hair.

"I called my mother on my birthday," Kerry whispered. "We had a good conversation. I told her I realized I'd been walking around with a huge chip on my shoulder for years, and I'd like the chance to develop a relationship with her. If it hadn't been for you—and Dale—I don't know if I would've had the courage to do that."

"And what did she say?"

She smiled up at him, her face shining with something like amazement. "She said that's what she wanted, too. And then she started to cry. It was the last thing I expected."

"I am happy for you, Keroshka." He kissed the tip of her freckled nose.

"I know things won't change between us overnight, but at least now I'm willing to try."

He drew her closer, anchoring his chin on the top of her head. The fresh, citrus scent of her hair surrounded him. "Love makes us more forgiving, yes?"

She nodded. "I guess so. It's nice not to be angry any more."

Outside the window, a lark lit onto the sill and began to chirp.

Kerry sighed, stretching out her legs. "I should go back to my room." Mikhail snuggled her closer. "No. I want you to stay right here. Forever," he added firmly.

Kerry laughed softly, nuzzling her nose into the hollow of his throat. The caress sent a pleasant shiver through him. "We can't stay like this forever, silly. You have a competition to go to this afternoon."

"Christ," Mikhail snorted, his fingers playing with her silky hair. "After spending night with you, I will be lucky if I have strength to lace up my skates."

Kerry's hand stroked his bicep with a butterfly touch. It felt so good, holding her in his arms like this, so warm and…right. He wished there was a way she could stay right here. But the room was brightening with the first glow of dawn. Still holding her, Mikhail stretched one arm above his head and groaned. "What time is it, anyway?"

Kerry peered over at the radio alarm clock on the bedside table. "Almost five. What time are you supposed to meet Elena for practice?"

The thought of Elena was like a dark shadow blocking out the light. Mikhail frowned. "Seven o'clock," he said, his voice heavy with sarcasm. "She wanted to sleep in today."

Kerry laughed. "Slothful pig! Imagine lying in bed so late! It's disgusting."

Mikhail grinned. "My thoughts exactly." He sighed. "I guess you *should* go. Who knows? She may actually get up at any moment and decide to move the practice up. It would be just like her. And I don't want her to find you here."

"Why?" Kerry's hand moved teasingly over his chest. "You don't think she'd be happy for us?"

"Hah! As happy as disturbed nest of vipers."

Kerry chuckled.

A brief silence fell. Mikhail knew they were both trying to find the energy—and the will power—to part. It had to be done, but Mikhail wanted to hold onto this time with her as long as possible. Here, in his arms, he could protect her. Once she was gone, he couldn't guarantee her safety. Their future was so uncertain. Last night had been incredible, and even if he were to die today, he would be grateful for the hours they'd had together. But it wouldn't be enough. A lifetime with Kerry wouldn't be enough.

"When this is all over," he said slowly. "Once we're safely in England…will you marry me?"

He heard her catch her breath, and drew away just enough to gaze down at the pale oval of her face in the early morning light. Her eyes were luminous. She lifted her hand and lovingly traced the angles of his jaw. A tremulous smile played about her lips.

"Yes, Mikhail," she whispered. "I'll marry you."

Relief swept through him, and for the first time, he felt—he *knew*—they would get through this. Kerry had come back into his life, and this time, he would never let her go. Cupping her face in his hands, he kissed her. Her mouth clung to his for a long, sweet moment, and then, trembling, she drew away.

"There's just one thing," she said.

Mikhail's pulse jumped at her solemn expression. "What?"

"I've always wanted a cat."

A brief silence fell between them, and her lips curved in a mischievous grin.

Mikhail kissed the tip of her delectable nose. "You shall have your cat. If you would sacrifice chocolate for me, I suppose I'd be a cad if I could not learn to tolerate a cat if your heart is set on one."

"You'd do that for me? Even if you're scared of it?"

"I'm not scared of a little cat!" Mikhail scoffed, feeling his skin crawl at the thought of one of those whiskered devils. "It *will* be little one, yes? A kitten?" When she didn't respond, he added doubtfully, "Even kittens look sweet but turn vicious in heartbeat."

Kerry snuggled closer. He felt her smile against his chest. "Give me a year," she murmured. "And I'll have you loving cats just like I do."

"I will do better than that," he said, stroking her head. "I will give you lifetime."

"Deal."

Mikhail sighed with happiness. He was just about to remind her it was time to go back to her room, but before he could speak, Kerry looked up at him. "Mikhail, I want to help you contact Wakeley."

In between their love-making, he'd told her the whole story of what had happened from the time they'd parted in Virginia, giving her the details of O'Malley's plan to assassinate Tony Blair, and explaining his problem of how to get a message to the British SAS agents. It had been a cleansing of sorts to tell her everything, but even as he'd done so, he'd wondered if it was a smart thing to do. But time was running out, and he was still no closer to finding a way to contact Wakeley. Kerry might be the only alternative.

"Did you hear me, Mikhail?" Kerry asked.

"Yes. I am thinking about it. "

"What's to think about? You can't do it. I *can*."

He shook his head. "I do not like it. You should not be involved."

"I *am* involved. It's my future that's at stake, too. Please, Mikhail, give me his number. I'll go right now. I'll call from a phone booth I saw in Castlecourt yesterday. Then I'll come straight back to my room and stay there until we can meet." When he didn't speak, Kerry squeezed his arm. "It's the only way, Mikhail. Give me the number."

Still, Mikhail hesitated. Yes, it was an answer, but why did his gut tell him it was the wrong one? Unfortunately, it was the only one he had.

"No one knows I'm here, right?" Kerry whispered. At his nod, she went on, "Well, then, I'm the only logical choice. Now, let's assume your contact in London has some instructions for you. Should I just give the message to Neil? You know, that good-looking guy down at the desk? He's a real romantic, you know."

"How do you know he is working today?"

"Because he told me he has to work all weekend, and his boyfriend is mad because he wanted to go to the country."

"Sounds like high maintenance boyfriend," Mikhail said wryly. "Okay, let me think." He rubbed a hand over his eyes. "Wakeley will, I hope, give you time and place for us to rendezvous. We will meet and go together."

Kerry stared at him. "You want me to come with you?"

"Of course," Mikhail said firmly. "We will not be separated again."

At the door, he kissed her, and she clung to him for a long moment. When they finally parted, her eyes were shining. "It's going to work out, Mikhail. I know it."

He nodded. "Just be careful."

"Don't worry." She curled her hand around his neck and drew his head down for another kiss. "I love you, Mikhail." A soft waterfall of laughter fell from her lips. "It's so easy to say now. *I love you*!"

"And I, you." He smiled and gave her a gentle nudge. "Go. Before I change mind and drag you back to bed."

A dimple flickered at the corner of her mouth. "I'm going!"

Mikhail watched her as she glanced up and down the hall to make sure it was clear and then stepped out. "Wait!" he said suddenly.

She turned and looked back at him.

"I just remembered," Mikhail said. "Earlier you said something about waiting for me to call. That you were close to giving up on me. What made you change your mind and come to my room?"

Her brows furrowed. She released a soft grunt of exasperation. "Your message, silly. To come to your room. If it had come any later, I would've committed bigamy with Bono."

The elevator dinged from down the hallway, and Kerry waggled her fingers at him. "Later."

Mikhail watched her move down the hall in her coltish stride. He was still reeling from her words. As their meaning sank in, he felt as if a slow-moving glacier had invaded his internal organs.

He had left no message for Kerry. *So, who had?*

* * * * *

Kerry stepped into a narrow, cobbled lane leading to a labyrinth of shops. She'd remembered seeing one of those charming red phone kiosks here the other day when she'd been shopping.

It was still early, and only a few of the shops had opened. The cobble-stoned lanes were practically empty of strollers, except for the few people going in and out of a nearby coffee shop. There was no one at all in the maze of shops where Kerry had seen the public phone the other day.

Mikhail had given her concise instructions.

She'd taken the service elevator down to the hotel kitchens and left by the delivery entrance, watching for anyone who might be following her. She'd seen no one. After she contacted Wakeley, she would leave any instructions with Neil, and then go to her room and stay there until it was time to meet Mikhail for the rendezvous with Wakeley.

God knew when that would be. Kerry just hoped she'd get hold of him. She stepped inside the red kiosk and deposited three coins, having no idea how much a long-distance call to England would be. Luckily, the change pocket of her wallet was filled with Euros. She punched out the number Mikhail had written on a slip of hotel stationery and chewed on her bottom lip as she waited for the connection.

It rang twice before it was picked up. "Wakeley," said a terse British voice.

"My name is Kerry Niles," she said quickly. "I'm calling for Mikhail Kozlof about Operation Tango."

"Go ahead."

Kerry wilted with relief. Wakeley's voice was strong, reassuring. For the first time since Mikhail had told her the gravity of his situation, she felt as if they were no longer in this alone. Still, Wakeley and his men were across the water in England, she reminded herself. Who knew how long it would take them to arrange a pick-up for Mikhail?

"He has the information you want, but it's imperative you pick him up tonight in Belfast. Lives are at stake, and tomorrow will be too late."

Mikhail had been insistent that she not reveal on the phone Sean O'Malley's plan to assassinate Tony Blair. Obviously, he didn't quite trust the British to get him out, so he was holding onto the information for insurance. Kerry knew how that went against his grain, but she understood his reluctance to trust them. After all, they'd been behind the lies he'd told her back in Virginia.

There was a brief hesitation on the other side of the line. Then Wakeley said, "Can you give me about ten minutes to arrange a pick-up? Do you have a number where I can call you back?"

Kerry read off the phone number of the pay phone.

"Stay by the phone," he instructed, then disconnected.

Kerry stepped out of the phone kiosk and began to pace up and down in front of it. A gale of laughter sounded from around the corner, and a young couple came into view, arms entwined, eyes fixed upon each other's faces. Lovers, Kerry thought. Maybe even honeymooners. They were in a world of their own.

Kerry glanced down at her wristwatch. How much time had passed? Only three minutes? Jesus!

Last night with Mikhail had flown by. She still couldn't quite believe they were back together. Oh, what a night it had been. Her entire body still tingled from his gentle touch—and his *not* so gentle touch. She grinned. For a man who didn't like cats, Mikhail sure was a tiger in bed. And she couldn't wait to be with him again.

The phone rang, and her heart thumped. She grabbed it before it could ring again. "Yes? This is Kerry."

"Okay, here's what I want you to tell Mikhail. The pick-up has been arranged for tonight at ten o'clock at the northwest section of the Botanical Gardens near the duck pond. Got it?"

"Yes," Kerry said. "He'll be there."

CAROLE BELLACERA

CHAPTER TWENTY-EIGHT

It took Elena a few minutes to open the door to Sean's knock. And when she finally did, he saw she was not a happy camper. She stood at the door dressed in a slinky nylon halter-top and low-waist drawstring pajama bottoms. Her blond hair was tangled about her shoulders in a way that Sean usually associated with a good romp in the hay. If it weren't for the fact that he knew Mikhail Kozlof had just kissed his light o' love goodbye and sent her back to her room after a night of what looked like very good sex, indeed, Sean might've been suspicious. But Elena's bed-head had nothing to do with getting the love tunnel cleaned. The dark smudges under her eyes told the true story. She hadn't slept well last night, maybe not at all—another side effect of TNG. The drug worked so efficiently it was almost as if she were main-lining straight caffeine, and the effect seemed to be cumulative. With every year she'd been on Anton Boiko's miracle drug, her insomnia had grown worse.

Well, one way or another, she would stop taking it.

Elena stared at him dully, and there wasn't even a gleam of welcome in her cloudy blue eyes. "Good God, Sean. What are you doing here at this hour? I was just about to get into the shower."

Sean gave her a slow grin. "Well, under ordinary circumstances, I'd have to say my timing was impeccable, but not this morning. I thought we might watch a wee bit of telly."

"Have you lost your mind?" Elena looked at him like his head had just swiveled on his neck and he was about to spew out a stream of pea soup. "It's six o'clock in the morning!"

"And I'm in the mood for a little soft porn." Sean chuckled and pushed past her, heading for the TV and VCR.

Elena followed him. "I don't think you get it, Sean. I'm meeting Mikhail at the arena in an hour. We are training this morning!"

Sean squatted in front of the VCR and inserted the videotape. "Well, I wouldn't count on Kozlof having much energy this morning, love. He had a…shall we say…*strenuous* night."

Sean switched the channel to 3, and hit the power button of the VCR. An image appeared on the screen of a couple in the middle of a passionate kiss. Sean grinned. How long would it take for Elena to realize who it was?

"What is this?" she asked in exasperation. "Sean, I really don't have time for this nonsense."

"Look closely, my love," he said. "And you may recognize the stars of this little skin flick."

He sat down on the foot of the bed, his eyes on the TV. On the screen, Mikhail and Kerry were still kissing hungrily as if they couldn't get enough of each other. Suddenly they broke apart, and Kerry tugged at Mikhail's sweatshirt. "Take it off, Mikhail!"

Sean heard Elena gasp. He turned to look at her, a grim smile on his lips.

"That's Mikhail and that American bitch!" she snarled.

"See? I told you you'd recognize the stars."

Two dots of color appeared on Elena's high cheekbones. It was the healthiest he'd seen her skin look in months. Bare-chested now, Mikhail held Kerry against him, cradling her head.

"Why are you showing me this disgusting footage now? It's ancient history."

Sean realized Elena thought she was watching footage from Mikhail's flight with Kerry across America. He savored the moment, surprised that he was enjoying it so much. He had to remind himself that Elena might very well be signing her own death certificate, depending upon her reaction to this video tape.

"Not anymore," he said quietly. Elena's eyes were fixed upon the television screen where Mikhail's hands were busy unzipping Kerry's yellow sweater. "Not unless you consider, oh, nine hours ago, ancient history."

"What?" Elena looked at him in astonishment. "What are you talking about?"

Sean watched her closely. "This was videotaped from Kozlof's room last night." The blood drained from Elena's face, leaving it a sallow shade of white. Sean felt his own blood begin to chill. "This tape holds the next five hours of everything that goes on in his room. It's quite interesting. Enlightening, too."

Indeed, it had been *more* than enlightening. Between the love-making, which was entertaining in itself—in fact, he'd picked up a couple of pointers from Kozlof's bag of sexual tricks—Sean had confirmed what he'd been suspecting for months—that the Brits had promised Kozlof asylum if he helped bring Sean to justice. And Kozlof's pillow talk with Kerry Niles had also alerted him to the fact that Mikhail hadn't been able to get a message to his SAS contact in London about the planned assassination of Tony Blair. Not that Kozlof knew the truth, anyway. He only knew the version that Elena had relayed to him.

Sean looked at the woman he loved and saw her chest rising and falling with her heightened breathing. If he could take her pulse right now, it would probably be in the stratosphere. She was staring at the TV, her face frozen in shock as Mikhail eased Kerry's jeans over her trim hips, revealing a lacy pair of purple bikini panties.

"She has nice taste in undies, does she not?" Sean said. "I think Kozlof is impressed."

But apparently, he wasn't impressed enough to keep them on. Elena watched in horror as Mikhail hooked his fingers in the side strings of Kerry's bikini and slid them down her firm thighs. When he moved his hand between them and sank to the floor in front of her, Elena's lips curled back from her teeth, and her angry hiss almost drowned out the moans and heavy breathing coming from the lovers on the TV.

"*Turn it off!*" The venom in her voice cut through Sean like a knife. "*Right now! I don't want to see any more!*"

Sean hit the "mute" button, shutting of the increasingly loud sounds of the couple's lovemaking, but kept the VCR on. "Why, Elena? Are you not happy for your skating partner? It looks like he has found true love."

Elena blanched as Kozlof began to perform oral sex on his girlfriend. "Did you hear me? *Turn it off, damn you!*"

"I don't think so, Elena. In fact..." Sean hit the "rewind" button, and the tape began to run backward. It was almost comical seeing Kozlof rapidly pulling Kerry's undies back up, and rezipping her jeans and sweater. "I think you missed some really interesting dialogue." Sean stopped the tape back at the place where Kozlof nestled the American woman against his chest.

On the screen, Kozlof drew away from Kerry and traced his thumb over her bottom lip. "I love you," he said in

English. "And if something happens to you because of me, I would never be able to forgive myself."

"*Aggggghhhhhh!*" Maddened with rage, Elena grabbed a vase of flowers from the nearby writing desk and threw it at the TV set. It missed, shattering against the wall, and raining down on the TV. "*Bastard!* That's not true!" Elena shrilled. "He's lying. It's *me* he loves! Not that freckle-faced little Chatty Cathy! I don't know what his game is, but he's *lying* to her!" Elena glared at the TV, her body stiff, fists clenched.

Sean watched her, feeling a mix of satisfaction, sorrow and resignation. So. Now he knew. It hadn't been his imagination at all. He pointed the remote at the TV and hit the power button. The screen went dark.

"How long?" he asked quietly.

She turned and gave him a level gaze. Her breasts still rose and fell with her rapid breathing. "How long what?"

"How long have you been in love with him?" His voice remained calm, matter-of-fact.

Her face went a shade paler. Her blue eyes stared back at him, startled. "In love with him?" She shook her head in denial, but it was too late. Way too late. "I am not in love with him. Did I say that? I said *he* is in love with me. He *has* been for years."

Sean put the remote aside and stood. Elena shrank back as he approached her. He knew she was terrified. As she should be. "So. If you are not in love with him, Elena, why such an emotional reaction to that video tape? Why is it you cannot bear watching Kozlof make love to another woman?"

"Because I don't like being lied to," Elena snapped. "You can understand that, can't you? It's a betrayal."

"A betrayal." Sean nodded. "Ah. Yes, I believe I understand now. It's not a good feeling, is it now? To trust someone, and then find later, they have betrayed that trust. I know exactly what that feels like." His gaze skewered her. He watched the fear intensify on her face as she realized her mistake. She backed up as he moved closer, until finally, there was nowhere else to go.

He stopped inches from her. She gazed up at him, her bottom lip trembling, smoky blue eyes glinting with fear. "Speaking of betrayal, I've discovered that your skating partner is working with the British to bring me in. You wouldn't know anything about that, would you, love?"

Elena shook her head, her face bloodless. "I don't know what you're talking about, Sean."

He smiled. "Really? Let me ask you something, Elena." His hands cupped her face gently. He could feel her trembling. Despite her height and the strength of her TNG-enhanced body, he knew he could snap her neck as easily as he could a dry twig, thanks to the training he'd received growing up on the streets of Belfast. As he looked down into her eyes, he knew she knew it, too, and was terrified that he'd do it.

But no. He couldn't do it. He loved her. And after all, he'd promised her that gold medal.

His thumbs traced lovingly over her eyebrows, and he saw relief settle over her face. He smiled down at her. "Are you really going to come with me to Rio?" he asked. "Are you going to be the mother of my children?"

Elena nodded eagerly, her hands sliding up his chest. All traces of fear were gone now. "Of course, darling. As soon as I get my Olympic gold medal in four years. Then we'll go anywhere in the world that you want, and I'll give you lots of babies."

"What if I don't want to wait four years?"

Her smile faltered. "Don't tease me, Sean. You know how much that Olympic medal means to me."

His hands slid down her neck to her shoulders and tightened. He kept the smile on his face, but he knew she saw the ice in his gaze. "I sense that time is running out for us," he said softly. "We may not *have* four years. If something should go wrong…if…say, Kozlof manages to turn me over to the Brits, what will you do? Will you play the broken-hearted prisoner's woman? Or will you go on with your life as if I never existed?"

"Oh, don't be melodramatic," she said with a sigh. "You're too slick to be brought down by someone like Mikhail Kozlof. You Irishmen are *so* glass half-empty."

Sean held her gaze. "As long as I have you, darling, my glass is always half-full. I *do* have you, don't I, now?"

"Of course." To her credit, she managed to look him in the eye, but Sean wasn't fooled. Elena was lying through her perfectly aligned pearly-whites. He saw the falsehood in the arch of her brows, the wary look in her eyes. In her very stance.

His heart dropped. For a long moment, he just looked at her, his hands still resting on her shoulders. His grip had loosened but Elena knew better than to move away. Instinct, Sean decided. She wasn't exactly sure what was going on here, but knew it was in her best interest to carry on with her charade of loving him.

She'd never loved him, he realized. He'd been nothing but a tool to her, one she'd manipulated to get what she wanted—like when she'd begged him to bring Kozlof back to Russia when it would've been simpler just to have him killed. Yes, he'd served her well, especially when it came to stud service. Always there, always ready, always wanting her.

And always loving her. Even now, gazing into her deceitful eyes, he still loved her.

I killed my wife for you, Elena, you bitch.

Liisa had been plain and boring, but good-hearted. A good Catholic girl who would never have divorced him, even after they'd found out she could never have children. From the very beginning, Elena had known his desire for children was his weakness. That desire to carry on the O'Malley name had driven him to get rid of a barren wife, one that he no longer loved, but by no means had hated. In fact, right up until the end, they'd been good friends.

Dead, now for three years, and buried in a graveyard outside Helsinki. Dead because of Elena Boiko.

"I'm sorry I lost my temper, Sean," she said now, back-pedaling furiously. "It's just that…Mikhail is so stupid. Screwing that girl the night before a competition. Has he no common sense? Does he not realize that he needs all his energy for our performance tonight?"

Sean shrugged and moved away from her. "Well, true love will win out. And after all, Kerry Niles is a comely girl," he added, gauging her reaction. "It would take a strong man to resist a woman like that."

A flicker of anger flashed across her face, but was immediately disguised with an ironic smile. "Men! Always thinking with your cocks instead of your brains." She turned away with a snort of disgust. "I must get in the shower."

"I'll hang around and drive you to the arena," Sean said. He waited until she reached the bathroom door before adding, "Shall I give Kozlof a call and see if he wants a lift, as well?"

Elena gave him a glare over her shoulder. "*Fuck* him!"

The bathroom door slammed behind her. Sean gave a grim smile. "Too late," he muttered. "He's already fucked." *In more ways than one.*

Scanning the hotel room, he saw Elena's skate bag on a bench next to the dresser. He went to it and rummaged in the side pocket until he found two brand new asthma inhalers, their seals unbroken. He pocketed them, then drew out the two inhalers in his other pocket, and slipped them into the bag.

The shower went on in the bathroom. Sean stared at the door a moment. Then he shrugged out of his jacket and tossed it on the bed. His hands went to the zipper of his trousers.

A moment later, he stepped naked into a humid cloud of steam. Through the glass shower door, he could just make out the tantalizing sight of Elena soaping her delectable body. His penis, already rigid, throbbed in response. Sean grinned as he reached out to open the shower door.

It would be the last time he ever made love to Elena. And it was going to be good.

* * * * *

The original dance competition was over by three, and the free dance segment didn't start until seven. That gave Mikhail four hours to sit in his hotel room and wonder how he was going to make it through to ten o'clock tonight.

Just before he'd left with the Russian team for the arena at noon, he'd stopped by the reception desk on the pretense of asking for more clean towels, and Neil had relayed Kerry's message.

Pick up tonight at ten o'clock at the duck pond in the Botanical Gardens. She'd meet him at the kitchen exit at nine-thirty, and they'd go to the gardens together.

His relief at hearing Kerry's message had been overwhelming, but still, he worried about the intervening time. Not to mention how close he'd be cutting it at the arena. The competition itself would probably take two hours, and then, if they should win—and they probably would because they were first in the standings right now—there would be the medal ceremony to get through. Would there be enough time to get from the arena to the hotel by nine-thirty? If not, would Wakeley wait? Surely, he would.

The elevator door opened, and Mikhail hung back to let Elena step in first. Her lips tightened, and she stepped into the elevator, avoiding his eyes. He followed her and punched the button for the ninth floor.

What kind of bug had crawled up her ass, he wondered. She'd been a worse witch than usual today, barely speaking to him, and when she had, she'd snarled like a hellcat. During their original dance performance, he'd felt the animosity radiating off her like heat from a furnace. And for the first time in their career together, he'd sensed her skin crawling at his very touch. That couldn't be good for their performance, he thought. Yet, somehow, her revulsion hadn't revealed itself to the judges, and they'd remained in first place.

The elevator doors opened, and she stepped out, moving purposely towards her room.

"Have a good rest," Mikhail called after her, inserting the key into the lock of his room.

"*Fuck you!*" she screamed, and went into her room and slammed the door.

Stunned, Mikhail stared at her door. "Crazy bitch," he muttered, then his lips quirked in a sardonic grin. *Don't worry, Elena. Just a few more hours, and you'll never have to see me again.*

If all went well.

413

He stepped into his room, went to the bed and sat down, reaching for the phone in the same motion. Just one more phone call. He had to make sure Kerry was okay.

The phone rang in her room, and Mikhail held his breath. Three rings. His heart started to pound. Four rings. Fear clotted his throat. Five rings. And suddenly, in mid-ring, it was picked up.

"Hello?"

He went limp at Kerry's voice. *Thank God*!

"Sorry," he said slowly. "Wrong number." He waited, unable to hang up just yet. He could hear her breathing.

"Oh," she said finally. "No problem." And she hung up.

Mikhail replaced the receiver in its cradle. "Stay safe, Kerry," he whispered. "Just a few more hours."

* * * * *

Kerry had her bag packed and ready to go. She was leaving with Mikhail come hell or high water, and if Wakeley didn't like it, well...he could just go screw himself. Nothing was going to separate her from Mikhail again.

She just had to get through the next two hours.

Stifling a yawn, she reached for the can of Diet Coke on the bedside table, took a sip and looked back at the TV. The Academy Award winning movie, "A Beautiful Mind," was half over, but Kerry still hadn't figured out why, exactly, it had won Best Picture. Either she had incredibly bad taste, or the whole voting academy had been on drugs to choose such a lame movie. But then, there was a third possibility. She was so distracted by real life that she probably hadn't given it the attention it deserved.

Her thoughts flew to the arena, only a few streets away. Mikhail and Elena wouldn't have skated yet. Being in first position, they'd be in the last group to compete. What was he doing right now? She imagined him sitting in the locker room, perhaps watching the monitor on the wall showing the competition. Was he thinking of her? Wondering if they would make it out safely tonight?

She smiled, remembering the three "wrong numbers" he'd made since she'd locked herself in her room after returning from Castlecourt. It had been a long, boring day, the hours broken up only by room service for lunch and dinner—and those phone calls. She'd known he'd just needed to hear her voice, reassuring himself she was okay. That last time, she'd been on the toilet. Good old Murphy at work. Without even taking time to flush, she'd drawn up her jeans and ran for the phone, terrified he'd hang up before she got there. Just hearing his voice saying "wrong number" had been the drug she needed to hold onto her sanity. He couldn't say more, but she knew what he was telling her. "Hold on. Just a while longer."

She looked at her watch. Seven-forty. Less than two hours now.

A knock at the door startled her. She scrambled off the bed.

"Maid service," a lyrical feminine voice called out through the door. "I've fresh towels for you, ma'am."

Kerry peered through the peephole and saw the pretty dark-haired maid who'd cleaned her room the day before holding a pile of fluffy, white towels. She opened the door and stepped back to let the young woman in. "I was wondering how come I didn't get any clean ones this morning." She'd used the last one after her shower this morning. "You can just put them in the bathroom."

"Sorry, Ma'am." The Irishwoman gave her a bright smile. "A problem with the hotel laundry. A bloody nuisance, it is." She took the towels into the bathroom.

Kerry wondered if she should tip her. She was never sure about these things. Better safe than sorry, she thought, and headed over to the dresser where she'd stowed the Coach handbag Dale had given her. She dug her wallet out of it, and fished a coin from the change pocket. The maid stood a few feet away, obviously waiting for a tip, so, she'd guessed right.

Kerry turned and held out the coin. Then froze. The pretty brunette was no longer smiling—and in her dainty hands, she held an automatic pistol.

"Get your wrap and come with me," she said quietly, her Irish accent just as charming as it had been before. "And don't try anything, Miss Niles, because I fucking guarantee I'll blow your pretty head off."

CHAPTER TWENTY-NINE

Elena twirled in Mikhail's arms, floating lightly over the ice like a butterfly at play. It was their last element before they reached the middle of the rink and struck their final pose, he on his knees, his hands locked on her thighs, his head pressed against her belly as she arched her back, her arms flung upward and outward. They held the pose for three, maybe four seconds, and then the applause of the crowd exploded throughout the arena. Mikhail released her, and stood. Holding his hand, Elena moved slightly away from him and curtsied to the crowd.

Enthusiastic fans stood at the boards, flinging flowers onto the ice. They'd surely just witnessed one of the best performances in the history of ice dancing, Elena thought, beaming. She rose from her deep curtsy, and kissed her fingertips, releasing her love to all those beautiful, passionate people on their feet, cheering and clapping and letting her know how very much they appreciated her performance in the final competition.

Four minutes ago, Elena had stepped onto the ice with Mikhail, and the two of them had taken the crowd's collective breath away. Every step, every movement, every lean and every lift had been perfectly timed. They'd covered the entire surface of the ice, their bodies moving to—living and breathing—the violins of Vivaldi, *becoming* the music.

It had been a dream come true.

And now, it was over. There was nothing left to do but soak in the crowd's adoration and wait for the scores. Which would, she knew, be all five-eights and five-nines, if there was any justice in the world.

When she turned to wave and curtsy to the other side of the rink, Elena caught Mikhail's eye, and her smile froze. *Bastard!* He'd used her to get information about Sean's activities, and then betrayed her with that American slut. But he was going to pay for it. Sean would see to that. She didn't know what he planned to do, but one thing was for sure. Mikhail Kozlof was the last person she'd want to be right now. Sean was ruthless when someone had double-crossed him. And one didn't have to double-cross him to feel the brunt of that ruthlessness.

There had been a moment this morning when she'd thought she'd find out first-hand about his cruelty. Something in his eyes had chilled her blood. He'd looked as if he'd wanted to kill her with his bare hands. And she knew Sean was no stranger to murder. Oh, he rarely got his own hands dirty, but if he was angry enough, she had no doubt that he would.

The list of his victims—the ones she knew about, anyway—was unnerving. There was Ivan, of course, her first dance partner. And then Liisa, his cow-faced Finnish wife. She'd done nothing except be unable to get pregnant. It had happened just days after Elena had told Sean she wanted to have his babies. A lie, of course. It had been the only way she knew to get him to break his ties with the holier than thou Liisa. But Elena hadn't expected Sean would go so far as to kill her. That had been the first time she'd realized the extent of his brutality. He was not a man to be trifled with. Look at how he'd arranged the car accident that had killed

Mikhail's mother after she'd been caught snooping around. And poor Uncle Anton! He hadn't cooperated with Sean, and had ended up at the bottom of the Jagala River.

For a few moments there this morning, she'd been very much afraid her name would be added to Sean's list of victims. But thank God, she'd managed to avoid that bullet. She knew that because when he'd joined her in the shower, he'd shown her exactly how much she meant to him. He'd had tears in his eyes when he'd climaxed.

Such an enigmatic man, her Sean. A pussycat in the bedroom and a snarling lion in his business dealings. *One you'd be a fool to cross.*

Elena smiled, thinking of the man at her side, waving at the enthusiastic crowd. Did Mikhail have any idea that he probably had only hours to live? Whatever Sean had planned for Mikhail and that freckle-faced little bitch of his wouldn't be pleasant. And Elena could care less now that she'd seen that disgusting skin flick Sean had recorded the night before. Just thinking about it sent her blood boiling.

He's all yours, Sean. I won't protect his devious ass anymore.

Especially now that her elusive gold medal was in reach. She didn't need Mikhail anymore. Not after today. Once she had the International Grand Prix gold medal, she could skate with Mikhail Gorbachev, and still walk away with the gold. It was all about reputation. Next year, she'd wear World Championship gold, and in four years, in Turin, *Olympic* gold would finally be hers. All of her dreams were coming true.

The crowd still roared as Elena broke away from Mikhail and began to circle the ice to retrieve the flower bouquets, some held by adoring fans who hoped for a hug and a kiss from their favorite skater. Elena personally abhorred the disgusting pawing from total strangers, but it was all part of the game, and she'd learned to live with it. A little girl with cascading strawberry blond curls grinned up at her as she extended a bouquet of red and white carnations. Elena's smile stiffened at the dusting of freckles over her pert nose. It reminded her of that bitch, Kerry Niles. Pretending she hadn't noticed the gift of flowers, Elena reached out and took a single-stemmed rose from a young man standing behind the girl, rewarding him with a brush of her lips against his jaw. A crestfallen look crossed the little girl's face, but Elena turned away and skated to a stuffed black bear that had been tossed onto the ice. It would look darling on her bed with the rest of her collection.

She bent over and grabbed the bear, but as she straightened, she felt the first tightening of her bronchial tubes. A soft, almost imperceptible whistling came from her lungs as she inhaled.

No! Not now! Not when I'm so close to seeing my dream unfold.

She placed a hand over her racing heart, and forced herself to take in a deep, cleansing breath. And this time, there was only the slightest of wheezes. *Good. Just relax.* She filled her lungs again, drinking in the sweet, cool oxygen. *Okay. It's going to be okay.*

Mikhail was already at the boards, heading for "Kiss and Cry." Nestling flowers and the stuffed bear to her chest, Elena skated after him, her gaze searching the VIP area for Sean. He always carried extra inhalers just in case of an attack. And of course, Nadya, who was glowing at them from "Kiss and Cry," would also have inhalers in her bag. So, if the worst should happen, they'd be ready for it. There he was! God, he looked good in that beautiful Aryan sweater and English tweed jacket. She flashed him a radiant smile and waved her bouquet. He responded with a grin, the creases around his mouth deepening in a way that always made her heart beat faster. What a handsome man he was!

For the first time in months, Elena found herself anticipating a quiet celebration with him—in bed, of course. Sean was always dependable when it came to lovemaking. Why on earth she'd been so infatuated with Mikhail Kozlof when she had Sean O'Malley wrapped around her little finger she'd never understand. Anyway, that was over. From now on, she was going to concentrate on Sean. Maybe even give him the gift of a child...after she'd won that Olympic gold medal, of course.

"Beautiful skating, Elena," Nadya said as Elena stepped past her into "Kiss and Cry." "Both of you. I am so proud."

No thanks to you, old woman. Elena took a seat next to Mikhail and fixed her gaze on the scoreboard. *Look at her!* Nadya was beaming as if *she* were the one who'd just skated the performance of her life, when in truth, she was nothing but an over-the-hill has-been who hadn't performed on the ice since being widowed by her war hero husband hundreds of years ago. And even then, at her prime, she hadn't been that good.

No, Elena had earned this medal on her own. Well, Mikhail had helped, of course. But men were replaceable. She was the star!

The technical marks flashed on the scoreboard, and the crowd roared. Elena caught her breath. One 5.7, one 5.9, and the rest 5.8s. Her stomach began to churn. *Fucking American judge!* Naturally, *she* would be the one to give them the low score. The scores disappeared and were replaced by the artistic impression marks. The crowd cheered. All 5.9s. Yes!

Nadya threw her arms around Elena, shrieking with joy. "You did it! Look at those ordinals."

Every judge except for the American had placed them first. On her left, Mikhail slipped an arm around Elena and gave her a hug.

"Looks like you finally got your medal," he said into her ear.

His familiar aftershave with its notes of lavender and jasmine washed over her, and for a brief moment, she leaned into him, overcome by the familiar attraction she'd always felt for him. But then she remembered the image of him and the American in bed together. Frowning, Elena drew away from him and forced herself to sit stiffly, her chin high in the air, her eyes refusing to meet his.

"It is happening just the way I always knew it would," she said curtly.

Fifteen minutes later, as she stood with Mikhail on the podium awaiting their medals, the impact of it all hit her again. This *was* just how she'd dreamed it would be. Except in her dream, she'd been gazing at the five intertwined Olympic circles. But that would come. It was only a matter of time.

The World Figure Skating official had already placed the silver and bronze medals around the necks of the second and third-place finishers, and now moved toward Elena and Mikhail. She looked down at the gold medals on the silver tray, and her heart rate accelerated. Oh, they were so beautiful with the embossed leaves encircling the lone figure skater in a layback position. The other side would have the logo of the International Grand Prix and be etched with the date and place, leaving a space for their names and competition category to be added after the presentation.

The skating official, a tubby little man with a shiny bald head and glittering dark eyes took one of the medals from the tray, and Elena obligingly bent her head. He slipped it around her neck and handed her a bouquet of flowers, then congratulated her with a handshake. He turned to Mikhail, and she gazed down in awe at the medal in her hand. Finally. *Finally*!

After Mikhail received his medal, the skating official moved away, and the Russian national anthem began to play. Elena watched her country's flag rise toward the ceiling of the vast arena, and to her surprise, she felt her throat tighten and her eyes blur with tears.

Oh, Papa. I wish you could be here to see this.

She'd tried so hard to make him proud of her, but had always fallen short. Before Yuri died, Papa had been obsessed with him and his speed-skating career. And when the asthma attack had ended his young life, Elena, through her grief, had thought that now, finally, her father would give her the love and attention she'd always craved. But even then, he'd barely noticed her, preferring to take solace in his work with the KGB. She'd known then that she had to do something dramatic to gain his admiration. And what could be more dramatic than winning a gold medal for Mother Russia?

Elena swallowed hard, trying to rid herself of the growing lump in her throat, but the reflexive action only seemed to make things worse. The muscles in her throat tensed, and her eyes began to burn. Tears spilled over her lids and began to stream down her face. She opened her mouth to draw in a breath, and was startled to hear a low whistling coming from her lungs. That was when she realized that the tightening she felt was not only in her throat but also in her bronchial tubes. Air! *There was no air!* She gasped, trying to draw in a breath, but a horrible wheezing rattle erupted from her lungs. Instead of sweet, life-giving oxygen, she felt as if she were inhaling a cloud of nails.

"Mick...*hail!*" She clutched at his arm as the edges of her vision began to fade. Flashing lights danced before her eyes.

She felt herself falling, and somewhere in the distance, she heard the gasps of horror coming from the audience. And then she felt the impenetrable cold of the ice surface seeping into her outstretched body. She opened her mouth, trying to draw in oxygen like a landed fish—oxygen that simply wasn't there. And all the time, she could hear the tortured sound of her breathing. No, not her breathing. Her *attempt* at breathing.

Inhaler! I need my inhaler!

She clutched at her chest, as if her fingernails could somehow reach inside and claw out her constricted bronchial tubes. Instead, she felt the cold metal of the gold medallion resting against her red-sequined skating dress. A moment before, it had meant everything to her. It had meant a new beginning, a lifetime of honor and esteem. It had meant she'd finally achieved a goal that would've made her father proud. But now, this gold medal would be nothing more than a piece of jewelry she'd wear to her grave.

Because she knew she was going to die. Right here, right now.

"Elena, here."

She opened her eyes and stared up at Nadya. Poor, wizened-faced Nadya. And the old woman had an inhaler in her hand. Of course! How could she have forgotten the inhalers Nadya carried?

"Breathe in, honey."

Elena's lips closed greedily around the inhaler's mouthpiece. She sucked desperately. But something was wrong with the inhaler. There was no fine-misted spray of sweet medication. There was simply…nothing. Elena pushed the inhaler away and tried to draw in another tortured breath. She was conscious of Mikhail at her side, holding her hand and telling her to hold on.

Alarm flickered in Nadya's eyes as she realized the inhaler wasn't working. The woman tossed it aside and rummaged in her bag for another one. Elena clutched at it like a starving baby reaching for its bottle, fastening her mouth around it. She tried again to inhale the life-giving medication. Nothing. The container was dry. Empty. *Jesus Christ in Heaven, what is going on?* With what little strength she had left, she threw the inhaler aside.

"*Shad...*" She tried to say his name. *Where is Sean?* He was always prepared.

The agonized sound of her ragged attempt to breathe was loud in the stunned silence. Her vision began to darken. She felt as if what little oxygen she had left in her body was being slowly squeezed out as if a giant anaconda had coiled itself around her.

And then, there he was. Sean. On his knees next to her. She reached out and grasped his hand. With her last piteous gasps of breath, she met his eyes, begging him to save her. To come to her rescue as he had so many times in the past. Sean, her hero.

But why was he doing nothing? Just staring at her, his expression stone-like. And then, she realized what was happening. Sean was watching her die. Why, Sean, *why?*

Suddenly there was a movement at her side, and a man in a white coat settled down next to her. The Russian team doctor. He drew out a syringe from his bag, and her heart lifted with hope. An injection had saved her last time. How could she have thought for a moment that Sean would let her die? He loved her!

Just before he injected the needle, the doctor looked up at Sean. Elena's gaze darted to Sean's face, and then to the doctor's. Cold claws of fear scraped at her bowels as she realized the "doctor" was Boris Shlusvaka, one of Sean's hired thugs. The needle pierced her arm, and the injected fluid burned into the muscle. But it wouldn't help. She knew that now.

She looked up at Sean, wishing she could speak. Wishing she could ask him *why*?

He gazed down at her, his brown eyes sad and resigned. He brushed a gentle hand over her forehead, then leaned down to her, his lips caressing against her ear. "I helped you get your medal, Elena," he whispered. To the crowd it would look like he was comforting her. "I did it because I love you." He drew away and took her gold medal in his hand. "I just wish you could've loved me, as well."

And in that moment, she understood why. Panic and terror welled inside her.

Sean was not going to be her hero this time.

* * * * *

Shaken, Mikhail left the ice rink. It was nine-sixteen. He had fourteen minutes to get back to the hotel and meet Kerry. Back on the ice, a medical team was still working on Elena, but it didn't look like they were going to bring her back. Her heart had stopped ten minutes ago, and despite several attempts to shock it back to life, the rescue squad's portable monitor displayed a flat-line. Mikhail could hardly believe it. He'd known Elena wasn't in the best of health, and had always figured the TNG couldn't be doing her asthma any good, but he'd never dreamed it would kill her.

But he'd used the chaos surrounding her collapse to make his getaway. With any luck, he and Kerry would be on their way to England within the hour. *Please God, let that happen*. His only regret was that he wouldn't be here to see Sean O'Malley get what he deserved.

Mikhail stepped into the tunnel leading to the dressing rooms. He passed a couple of skaters who gave him sympathetic looks and murmured their dismay at what had happened to Elena. Mikhail nodded and moved on. He'd left his Nikes in the dressing room. It would only take a few moments to change, but he was already resenting every second that would delay his rendezvous with Kerry.

"And where might you be off to, Kozlof?"

The pleasant-sounding Irish voice came from just behind him. Mikhail whipped around, and his heart plunged. A relaxed and smiling Sean O'Malley stood just a few feet away. He didn't look at all like a man who'd just watched his lover die in his arms.

He'd wanted her to die, Mikhail realized. And on the heels of that thought, another one followed. The ineffective inhalers Nadya had taken from Elena's bag. Ineffective or empty? And why had there not been any back-up inhalers in the bag?

Sean stared at Mikhail, still wearing his engaging smile, but his brown eyes were like granite. Mikhail considered trying to make a run for it, but he knew the attempt would be pointless since he was still wearing his skates. He had to think of something else. But what?

"Is Elena...?" he began.

"Dead?" Sean cut in, and nodded. "Quite. It looks like Nadya has fallen down on her job to make sure she had plenty of working inhalers in her bag. I guess we'll have to fire her for that."

"You sick bastard," Mikhail growled. "You killed her, didn't you?"

Sean's grin disappeared. "I loved her. You know what it's like to be in love, don't you, Kozlof? You know how it messes with your brain and turns your world upside down. You know what it's like to hold your woman in your arms and make plans for the future with her, do you not? Plans for marriage and children and...*cats*."

At first, Mikhail wasn't sure he'd heard the man right. But in the following silence, Sean watched him. The mocking grin had returned to his face.

"Oh, yeh, Kozlof. I know all about your little pillow talk with your light o' love, Kerry Niles. She loves cats. They scare you shitless. But you're willing to put up with one for the love of your lady. How very noble you are."

Mikhail's heart had begun to thud at Sean's words. How had he known that? How *could* he know?

"Ah, yes. Love is a many-splendored thing. Don't we all know it? But here is one wee thing I'm guessing, Mikhail Kozlof. You don't have the slightest idea what it is like to *lose* the woman you love, like I just did. But..." His face brightened as he drew a lethal-looking automatic pistol from inside his tweed jacket. Mikhail felt his limbs go weak. "You will. Before the sun rises, you will know *exactly* what that feels like." He gestured the gun toward the locker room door. "Get your ass in there, and get out of those skates. We're going for a wee ride, and I don't want the carpet marred in my friend's van."

Sean pushed him into the locker room and stood by the door as Mikhail warily took a seat on the bench and began to unlace a skate. He gauged the distance between him and Sean. Too far. He'd be dead before he got halfway to him. His fingers brushed across the blade of his skate. He remembered the slice of the blade into his cheekbone years ago, the burning gush of blood between his fingers. If only O'Malley would come closer. He could try and use his skate as a weapon.

With his free hand, O'Malley had dug a two-way radio out of his jacket. "Bring her in," he said shortly.

Mikhail's heart skipped a beat, and a muscle in his jaw began to twitch. No. Kerry was waiting for him back at the hotel. O'Malley didn't even know she was here, right? But then...how had he known about their conversation about the cat? His heart began to thud.

The locker room door opened, and Kerry stepped in, followed closely by an attractive dark-haired woman in a maid's uniform. She had one arm wrapped around Kerry's collarbone, and in the other, she held the gun's nuzzle pressed to Kerry's temple.

Mikhail's mouth went dry.

CHAPTER THIRTY

Mikhail lurched to his feet, but Sean's steely command froze him. "Sit back down, Kozlof, or your girlfriend will die, right here, right now."

He sank back to the bench, his eyes on Kerry. "Let her go, O'Malley," he said between clenched teeth. "She has nothing to do with this."

Sean didn't bother to reply. He just laughed. A short, harsh bray that told Mikhail just how ridiculous his plea was.

Kerry's face was pale, her eyes frightened. Terror clawed through Mikhail. *Why* had she come to Belfast? It would've been better if she'd never found the ring. If she still believed the lies he'd told her.

"What are you waiting for, Kozlof?" Sean said brusquely. "Get those fucking skates off and get into your shoes. I've got a schedule to meet."

"What are you going to do to us?" Kerry demanded. A spark of anger flared in her eyes. She was rewarded with a nudge of the gun against her temple.

"You'll find out soon enough," the maid said in a thick, Belfast accent. Her grip on Kerry seemed to tighten.

Mikhail tugged off a skate and let it drop to the floor, then began to work on the other one. If he could just figure out a way to overpower O'Malley and the woman...

But he couldn't risk it. Not with Kerry here. Not with that gun pressed against her head. He wished he'd followed his impulse of a few moments ago to use his skate as a knife blade and disarm O'Malley. Now, it was too late. The other skate dropped to the floor with a clunk. Mikhail reached for his Nikes, his mind working, trying to find a way out.

Where was O'Malley taking them? Obviously, he'd gone mad. Had the murder of Elena pushed him over the edge? What had he said a few minutes ago? *You don't have the slightest idea what it is like to lose the woman you love.*

Oh, dear God. His fingers trembled as he tied the laces of his shoe. Surely he wasn't planning to kill Kerry in front of him? That couldn't happen. O'Malley would have to kill *him* first.

He fastened his eyes on Kerry, and spoke in Russian, "I will not let him hurt you, my love."

Sean laughed and replied in Russian, "Do you think I cannot understand your language, you stupid man? After living with Elena for so long?"

Mikhail tied his other sneaker, then glared across the room at O'Malley. "I know you're fluent in Russian. I meant for you to hear. And I mean it, I will not let you hurt her."

"Is that a fact?" The smile was still on Sean's face but his eyes had taken on a glacial chill. "Well, it appears to me that you may not be in the best position to make demands."

"You've got *me*, O'Malley," Mikhail said quietly. "Let her go. She has done nothing to you."

Kerry shook her head violently. "*No, Mikhail!* I won't leave you."

The Irish woman glanced at O'Malley, and Mikhail felt a glimmer of hope. She was listening, at least.

"She's an innocent in this," Mikhail went on, his voice roughened with emotion. "You've wanted me for a long time. Now you've got me. You will gain nothing by killing us both."

Sean's grin widened. "Except satisfaction."

That's when Mikhail lost it. "*You fucking maniac!* Wasn't it enough for you to kill my mother? What kind of monster are you, anyway?"

Sean shrugged. "It was nothing personal against your dear old ma, Kozlof. Purely business. She got too close to exposing a little matter the Boiko family preferred to keep quiet."

"The massacre of the Sami people in Kalevalo? *My* people, did you know that, O'Malley? Did you know my real father was one of the villagers who died?"

A flicker of surprise crossed Sean's face. "No, that I didn't know. But it makes no difference. Your mam should've left well enough alone." His lips twisted in a sardonic grin. "Actually, you're lucky you've lived as long as you have. You would've died in Park City if not for that incompetent, bloody idiot I employ."

"You son-of-a-bitch," Kerry burst out. "I should've known it was *you* behind Adam's accident."

Sean looked at her and gave a shrug. "Nothing personal. Like I said, Reilly is a moron. Come on, let's go." He gestured Mikhail to his feet.

He got up slowly, his brain spinning. He knew he was clutching at straws, but it was worth a shot. "The SAS knows all about everything, O'Malley," he said. "I was able to get a message through to them. They've already got you under surveillance. They know about your plans for Tony Blair at Waterfront Center tomorrow. They'll be waiting for you. If you kill us, you'll spend the rest of your life in a British prison cell. Is that what you want?"

Uncertainty flickered through O'Malley's eyes, and Mikhail felt hope rise inside him. If he could just bluff his way out of this…

Sean shook his head, and an easy grin flashed across his face. "The information Elena gave you is wrong, Kozlof." His smiled widened. "Did you really think I was so stupid that I'd give her the details of my plan to kill the good PM?" He gave a harsh laugh. "I'm not planning to take him out during his speech tomorrow. No, indeed. My plan is much more dramatic than that. You know about the stingers? Of course you do. Well, tomorrow morning, the PM will be landing in Belfast by helicopter. Well, I should say he's *scheduled* to land. Unfortunately, as his copter descends over Dundrum Bay, a most devastating mishap will occur. There won't be anything left of Mr. Blair or his traveling companions. My only regret is that I'm not the one to fire the stinger."

Despair ripped through Mikhail. He had underestimated O'Malley.

Sean's cold eyes moved to the Irishwoman. "Come on, Sinead, let's go. Reilly is waiting for us."

Mikhail's eyes met Kerry's. He tried to communicate reassurance to her, but it was hard. When he wasn't at all sure they'd get out of this alive. But surely he'd find a moment—a few seconds was all he needed to catch O'Malley off guard.

The Irish maid pushed Kerry toward the door, and O'Malley ordered Mikhail to follow them. They stepped into the dimly lit tunnel and headed toward the exit. The tunnel was curiously empty. Mikhail supposed Elena's collapse had kept the shocked athletes glued to the scene and the crowd in their seats. It seemed like hours had passed since the medal ceremony; yet, it had only been about fifteen minutes.

Mikhail followed Kerry and her captor out the fire door leading into what looked like a delivery area. No alarm sounded. Apparently, O'Malley had thought of everything. The cool Irish night enveloped him, carrying the hint of rain and wildflowers in its breeze.

A perfectly lovely place to die, Mikhail thought morbidly.

O'Malley seemed to pick up on his thoughts. "Ah, the fresh air of my homeland." Even in the darkness, Mikhail could hear the smile in his voice. "There are worse places to die, wouldn't you say, Kozlof? Like drowning in the Moscow River…your car filling up with water, and no way out."

Hot rage engulfed Mikhail, and he didn't think, just reacted. He rammed his elbow back violently, catching O'Malley in the gut. The sudden movement caught the Irishman by surprise but it wasn't enough. Just as Mikhail drove the heel of his hand against O'Malley's teeth, the Irishman slammed the butt of the gun into his forehead. Mikhail dropped to the asphalt, blinding pain slamming through his head. Stars exploded behind his eyes as Kerry's screams reverberated through his ears. For a moment, his vision disappeared. Then, slowly, it returned, and he saw O'Malley staring down at him, blood dribbling from his bottom lip. The sight of it gave him a grim sense of satisfaction.

"That was really stupid, Kozlof," O'Malley said through clenched teeth. "Get up on your feet, asshole, and get moving."

His head still ringing, Mikhail managed to get up. He felt Sean's gun poke into his back, and he began to move toward a white paneled van idling a few yards away, lights off. Keeping his gun pointed at Mikhail, O'Malley pounded his free fist on the side panel. Nearby, the Irish girl, Sinead, kept her gun trained on Kerry. When there was no response to his knock on the van door, O'Malley frowned. "Open up the fucking door, Reilly."

Mikhail's eyes moved back to Sinead. Should he lunge at her and try to get the gun while O'Malley was preoccupied with getting them into the van?

"Watch them," O'Malley growled at the Irish girl, and sidled up to the driver's side window. "Reilly, you stupid fuck, open the bloody..." His voice trailed away. "*Jesus Christ!*" His head whipped toward Sinead. "*Fuck!* They're both dead!"

Even in the darkness, Mikhail could see the pallid look on O'Malley's face as his eyes scanned the area around them. "Let's get out of here." He opened the driver door and pulled out Reilly's limp body. As it tumbled to the asphalt, Mikhail caught a glimpse of a small-blackened bullet hole in his right temple. He heard Kerry gasp, and his own stomach roiled. On the passenger side of the van, another man was slumped forward in his seat, his face streaked with blood—the Russian thug who'd suffered a case of bruised balls via Kerry, Mikhail guessed.

Sean wrenched at the side door of the van, and it rumbled open. Just then Mikhail heard a whispering thump from behind him, and O'Malley flinched. His gun went flying. A red bloom appeared on his right shoulder. His hand went to the bullet wound, eyes widening in surprise.

"A wee moment of your time, Sean-boy," a voice with a thick Belfast accent came from somewhere behind them. Three men stepped out of the shadows, each of them armed with automatic weapons. The man in the middle, big and bear-like with red hair and a beard was clearly the leader. He looked at no one but Sean, and in contrast to his voice, his face was anything but jovial. "I had a wee bit of a bad luck at the race track today, Sean, lad."

Holding his wound with a blood-soaked hand, Sean managed a weak smile. "Your horse didn't win, Big Dan? Aw, but nothing is guaranteed in life, is it, now?"

Big Dan stared icily at Sean. "Oh, he *won*, alright. No other racehorse in the field could touch him. It's what happened *after* he crossed the finish line that concerns me. He dropped dead, Sean. My best racehorse is dead because of your bloody TNG."

Sean's eyes darted to Sinead as blood welled between his fingers. "What are you standing there for, you stupid woman? Kill him."

But Sinead didn't move.

The big Irishman smiled at her. "Good work, lass. You'll find a nice bonus in your paycheck the end of the week."

Sinead grinned back at him. "Always a pleasure to do business with you, Danny."

For a brief moment, Sean looked confused, then a sick realization crossed his face. "You bitch," he said finally. "You double-crossing *bitch*." Then, amazingly, he grinned at her. "Good on ya, Sinead. You've never looked sexier to me."

Nonplussed, Sinead shifted uncomfortably. Mikhail looked at Kerry, who still stood in her grip. The woman's gun was just inches away from Kerry's temple. She was pale, but appeared to be calm. In shock, Mikhail guessed. He didn't know what was going to happen. But with O'Malley wounded, his henchmen dead, and this girl apparently working against him, he felt more hopeful than he had moments before. But then again, if they'd become involved in some kind of Irish gang war, he and Kerry could well end up just as dead.

Danny took a step closer to Sean, his eyes glacier-cold. "I know all about how you informed on me, Sean. Because of you, I spent four years in a British prison cell. I wanted to kill you when I got out. I planned to, I did. But you know, our fathers worked side-by-side in the IRA. The best of friends. Because of that I decided to give you another chance. You were young and scared when the Brits were interrogating you. And I have no doubt they used some of their bloody torture tactics on you. And you caved. It happens." He shrugged. "Who knows? I might've done the same thing. So, I was willing to forgive and forget. And how do you repay me? By selling me a toxic formula and murdering a three million dollar racehorse. Now, is that a friendly thing to do?"

Sean shook his head. "It was a mistake, Danny. We found the wrong formula, that's all. Boiko died before he could give it to us, so we had to search his lab...we thought we had the right one." Blood soaked the sleeve of Sean's tweed jacket, black and oily-looking in the darkness. Clutching his wound, he stood swaying in front of the big Irishman.

He was losing blood quickly, Mikhail thought. Wouldn't be standing for long.

"Have a heart, Big Dan," Sean said shakily, summoning a weak grin. "We go back a long ways, and you know I wouldn't have betrayed you if I'd had any other choice. But you were right about the Brits. The torture tactics...the white noise, the cigarette burns. I still have scars on my crotch from their bloody fags. I was only nineteen. I was scared. And then they threatened to kill my mum. So, I told them everything about the bombing in Newry."

Danny stared at him for a long, grim moment, and then his pistol lowered. Mikhail could see the relief in Sean's eyes.

"One problem with that, Sean," Sullivan said slowly. "You see...I don't have a heart."

Pfssst. That odd, whispering sound Mikhail had heard before cut through the silence. O'Malley let out a painful howl as his right kneecap exploded in a spray of flesh, bone and muscle. He dropped to the ground, writhing in agony. Danny stepped over to him and stared down.

"I didn't know for sure you were the one to betray me until just now." He pointed his gun at Sean's left kneecap and squeezed the trigger.

O'Malley screamed as it shattered. Kerry flinched and turned away. Mikhail fought back the bile rising in his throat. The Irishwoman stared impassively as if she saw this kind of atrocity every day.

Danny turned away disdainfully and gave a curt nod to his two partners. "Kill him."

The men aimed their automatic weapons at Sean's still writhing body on the pavement.

Mikhail closed his eyes. In the distance, he heard the thump of helicopter blades, but just for a couple of seconds. The sound was drowned out by the angry beelike buzz of automatic weapon fire equipped with silencers.

The firing stopped. Mikhail opened his eyes and saw Danny exchange a look with Sinead. "Take care of the witnesses."

Mikhail's stomach turned over. His eyes met the Irishwoman's. He saw hesitation, indecision. Beside her, Kerry stood rigidly. The moon slid out behind a cloud, and he saw how pale her face was. Yet, she held her head high, her chin lifted defiantly. Mikhail felt a rush of tenderness sweep through him, and he wanted more than anything in the world to hold her one more time. His brave, spirited Kerry.

The helicopter blades grew louder. Sinead glanced up at the sky, then looked at Danny.

"I'm sorry, Danny, but I can't do that." She released Kerry and with both hands, aimed her weapon at Danny and his men. "Drop your weapons, lads. It's all over."

A searchlight from the helicopter beamed down onto the parking lot, bathing Danny and his men in its glow. White-faced, Kerry ran to Mikhail. He clutched her to him. The Irishman looked at Sinead, and amazement combined with something like admiration crossed his fleshy face.

"Well, son of a fucking bitch," he muttered. "Who is it you're working for, lass?"

Sinead kept her weapon trained on the three men. She nodded up at the helicopter. "Them. You're under arrest by order of Her Majesty's Special Air Services."

Mikhail held Kerry tightly, and as she tried to look toward Sean's body, he stopped her. He'd already caught a glimpse of the grisly sight of the Irishman's head, half blown away, the wall behind him splattered with blood and brains. Mikhail's stomach heaved, and he looked away, grateful that Kerry's face was pressed against his chest.

She stirred in his arms. He looked down and saw her gazing up at him. "Is it over?" she asked.

He smiled at her, and then bent his head to kiss her forehead. "Yes," he said. "That's Wakeley climbing out of the helicopter."

She grimaced, then spoke in a choked voice, "Let me go!"

Mikhail frowned. "Why?"

"*Now!*" She pushed against his chest in an effort to get free, her face a peculiar shade of gray. He did so, and she stumbled away from him. Her hands on her knees, she bent over and began to retch into a lilac bush.

Mikhail turned away, waiting patiently for her to finish.

EPILOGUE

Seven Months Later
Lapland, The Kola Peninsula

The wind howled around the small clapboard house on the tundra, and it shuddered slightly in its wake, creaking and groaning as if in agony. Kerry looked up from across the table where she was finishing a bowl of thick reindeer soup. She grinned at Mikhail as he chewed a chunk of crusty bread.

"You think we're going to make like Dorothy and end up in Oz?" she asked.

He stared back, an incomprehensive look on his handsome face. Kerry shook her head and bit into a piece of bread. In many ways, she and Mikhail were still cultures apart. There was so much she had to teach him. She made a mental note to visit the video store and pick up a copy of "The Wizard of Oz" when they got back to England.

She rephrased the question. "Do you think this house is going to hold up against the wind?"

Mikhail shrugged. "Uncle Vaino says he built this place thirteen years ago. I imagine it has withstood many bad winters."

"Well, that's good to know."

Across the plain, simply furnished room, a fire blazed in the hearth, popping and crackling as the logs burned. Kerry took a sip of strong, black coffee, admiring the twinkle of the diamond on her left hand in the soft light of an oil lamp on the table. The stone wasn't huge, but it was beautiful, especially now that it was partnered with a delicate gold wedding band.

Hard to believe seven months had passed since that foggy summer night in Belfast when they'd almost died at the hands of Sean O'Malley. Wakeley's helicopter had flown them to London where the two of them were sequestered in a townhouse in Aylesbury. With the information Mikhail had given them about O'Malley's operation, the British government had canceled Tony Blair's trip to Northern Ireland, and early that morning, the SAS had arrested the would-be assassin whose white truck containing the stinger missiles had been spotted from the air near the coast. The Irishman, a known IRA triggerman, had been apprehended without incident. A week later, Mikhail's request for political asylum had been approved.

Kerry looked from her ring to her husband, and felt her heart lift with joy. Her husband. She could still hardly believe it, even though they'd been married almost four months. Dale, Catri, Adam, Brandi and even Jana and Kerry's stepfather, Erich, had flown over to England for the wedding. In a quiet moment during the reception, Jana had hugged Kerry and with tears in her soft brown eyes, had wished her a long and happy marriage. Kerry had impulsively invited her to spend a few weeks in England with her next summer, and she'd accepted, much to Kerry's surprise and delight.

In August before their September wedding, Kerry had returned to the States for Brandi and Adam's wedding. Apparently, their romance had blossomed into genuine love during Adam's recovery from the accident. In another year, they planned to start training together on the ice. Kerry was thrilled for them—especially Adam. Finally, he'd have a partner whose passion for him would bleed through her pores.

Kerry stayed a week in her townhome in Lake Arrowhead, exchanging daily telephone calls with a lonely Mikhail while packing up all the items she wanted to keep. She'd sold the rest, and then put the furnished house on the market. It had sold within days. She'd said a tearful goodbye to Catri and Brandi, accepted an affectionate hug from Adam who could barely keep his eyes off his new wife, even as he told Kerry how much they were going to miss her.

And without a second thought, she'd flown home to Mikhail. Home. It wasn't a place at all. It was a very special someone, and her someone would become a British citizen. Now, here they were back in Russia. Quentin Wakeley had arranged for Mikhail and Kerry to travel to Russia on a special visa so he could disperse his mother's ashes in the land she'd loved so dearly. Nadya had traveled up from Estonia to the Sami village to deliver the urn, and had graciously been offered a bed in Vaino's house.

They'd been here almost a week, and the visa expired in less than forty-eight hours. Still, Laila Kozlof's ashes rested in the urn. Mikhail had wanted to release them to the arctic wind during a night when the northern lights displayed their glory in the heavens. His mother had so loved watching the aurora, and it would be a fitting final goodbye to her if he could disperse them during their display. But so far, every night had been overcast, and time was running out.

Kerry looked over at the door that led outside. "What's taking your uncle and Nadya so long? Does it take a half-hour to feed the reindeer?"

Mikhail's meeting with his uncle had been emotional. Vaino was a small man with weathered brown skin, sandy hair and dancing blue eyes—eyes that looked exactly like Mikhail's, Kerry thought. His smile, too, reminded her of Mikhail. How much did he look like his late brother, Mikhail's father? She knew Mikhail had wondered that, too. Vaino spoke fluent Finnish, as well as some Russian and his native Sami language. On their first evening together, he had told stories about growing up with Mikhail's father, and Mikhail had listened, hungry for any information about the mysterious Sami tribesman he'd never known. It had been difficult for Kerry to hold back tears at the yearning look on Mikhail's face. She could almost read his mind. *If only...*

Mikhail looked across the table and grinned. "I have feeling that feeding reindeer is not only thing Nadya and my uncle are doing."

Kerry stopped chewing and stared. "You mean...?"

Mikhail nodded sagely. "Have you not noticed how Uncle Vaino looks at her?"

"And you think she...?"

He smiled. "I think she has finally found a man who can take the place of her beloved Ivor."

Kerry laughed in delight. "I love it! It's like a fairy-tale! Your uncle *is* really handsome. I can see where you got your looks from."

"Thank you," Mikhail said. "It is in genes. Have you ever seen Nadya laugh so much since she met Uncle Vaino? I think that is good sign for true love."

"Well, you make *me* laugh, and not to sound arrogant or anything, but I'm pretty good at cracking you up, too."

Mikhail kept a straight face, but one eyebrow arched. "*Especially* when you sing."

"Hey!" Kerry flung a chunk of bread at him. "I'm a *good* singer. You're just jealous."

A soft mew interrupted their bantering.

Kerry looked over and saw a huge black and white cat pad into the room. Without hesitation, it pounced up onto Mikhail's lap, and purring, made itself comfortable. Mikhail took a sip of coffee, and Kerry noted his hand didn't tremble a bit. Still, he wasn't stroking the cat. But that would come in time. Back in their small house in the village of Chatham, their shorthaired orange-striped tabby, Ruby, would be missing them, even though Gloria, their teenaged neighbor, promised to stop in twice a day to feed and pamper her. Just yesterday, Mikhail had mentioned Ruby, wondering how she was doing. It wouldn't be long before Kerry had him cuddling her like a baby.

The front door opened, and a burst of wind swept into the house. The cat yowled in protest and jumped off Mikhail's lap, hi-tailing it back into another, warmer, room. Nadya stepped inside, her cheeks reddened, a thick fur hat pulled down low over her head. Just as Mikhail had noted, she was laughing. Behind her, wearing a plush coat made of reindeer skin and a matching hat, followed Mikhail's uncle. His eyes danced in merriment. He stamped snow from his reindeer-trimmed boots and pulled off his gloves, rubbing his hands furiously.

His gaze shot to Mikhail. "Your mother's spirit is among us, Mikhail," he said with a grin so similar to Mikhail's that even if Kerry hadn't known they were related, she would've guessed it. "It is happening."

Mikhail sat up in his chair, a light flaring in his eyes. "The aurora?"

Vaino nodded. "Nadya and I were just watching the show. It is brilliant, Mikhail. The night you have been waiting for."

Mikhail scrambled up. "Why did you not come get me? What if they have stopped?"

Nadya and Vaino exchanged an amused glance. "Did I not tell you he is impossibly impatient?" she asked archly.

Mikhail's uncle shrugged. "Just like his father. I'll bet he is stubborn, as well." He grinned at Mikhail. "Do not fret, my nephew. The lights will dance for hours."

"I'm sorry," Mikhail apologized, grabbing his heavy, sheepskin-lined coat. "It's just I am excited. Come on, Kerry. I will get the urn."

Kerry was already on her feet, reaching for her coat. A moment later, they were both wrapped up from head to toe, with only their eyes exposed. Mikhail held the urn in his left hand. He reached for Kerry's hand with his right.

They stepped out into the black polar night. Kerry had never been so far north before, and had been prepared to find it depressing with the constant darkness of winter. But she'd quickly changed her mind on the first afternoon she'd experienced the magic of the twilight hours when the world was painted in vivid colors of blue and violet. Maybe it was because she was here with Mikhail, but she found it unbelievably romantic.

She squeezed Mikhail's hand as the arctic wind bit through her, but as soon as she saw the incredible light show in the northern sky, she forgot all about the cold.

"Oh, my God, Mikhail!" She raised her voice over the howling wind. "It's magnificent!"

Green bled into purple, then blue, then wild, exotic pink—shimmering, rolling, dancing in the sky. Kerry looked up and saw Mikhail's face, his eyes shining in awe. A thick, woolen scarf covered his mouth, but she knew he was smiling. She knew also he was filled with joy just as she was.

They walked out onto the tundra, and Mikhail stopped, withdrawing his hand from hers. He opened the cap of the urn, took a deep breath and flung the contents to the wind.

Almost as if by magic, the wind dropped, and a curious silence filled the night around them.

"Goodbye, Mother," Mikhail said softly. "Be at peace." He turned to Kerry, his eyes soft. "She brought you to me. And for that, I will always be grateful."

Kerry smiled up at him through sudden tears. "I wish I'd known her."

His eyes, also misty with tears, met hers. "She would've adored you, Keroshka."

He reached out and unwrapped the length of scarf around the lower half of her face. He tugged his own scarf down, and a moment later, his mouth covered hers. His lips were cold, but his tongue was warm, and Kerry sighed into it, knowing that as long as she lived, she'd always remember this blissful moment in Mikhail's arms.

Finally, he broke the kiss. She gazed at him, her gloved fingers tracing the scar on his cheekbone. Standing on tiptoe, she brushed her mouth over his for another brief kiss. Afterwards, Mikhail rewrapped her scarf over the lower half of her face. Then he grabbed her hand, and turning, led her back to the small clapboard house, surrounded by the luminous dancing of the northern lights.

The End

CAROLE BELLACERA

*C*arole Bellacera's work has appeared in magazines such as Woman's World, The Star, Endless Vacation and The Washington Post. She is the author of four acclaimed novels published by Tor/Forge Books. Carole's first novel, "Border Crossings," a hardcover published by Forge Books in May of 1999, was a 2000 RITA Award nominee for Best Romantic Suspense and Best First Book, and a nominee for the 2000 Virginia Literary Award in Fiction.

Other Books by Carole
- Border Crossings – Forge Books, May 1999
- Spotlight – Forge Books, April 2000
- East of the Sun, West of the Moon – Forge Books, July 2001
- Understudy – Forge Books, June 2003
- Chocolate on a Stick – Baycrest Books, Sept 2005

Upcoming:
- Lily of the Springs

Available at Amazon.com, Amazon Kindle, Smashwords.com and other retailers.